THE MOMENT OF TRUTH

Borgo Press Books by BRIAN STABLEFORD

THE MOMENT OF TRUTH

A Novel of the Future

by

Brian Stableford

THE BORGO PRESS

An Imprint of Wildside Press LLC

MMIX

CONTENTS

CHAPTER ONE

The First Day: Early Afternoon

Hugo Victory watched his potential client, Mrs. Allison, as she studied the image on the computer-screen with the utmost care. The face on the screen looked twenty years younger than the one she was wearing and had slightly better bone-structure, but the real challenge Victory had met in constructing it was to restore the original distinctiveness of the face.

On the occasion of their first meeting, three days before, Victory had easily deduced that Mrs. Allison had first had cosmetic surgery some twelve or fourteen years earlier. Although the work had been expertly done, it had been carried out with the crude tools available at the time, and in tightening up the features it had caused a quasi-generic rigidity whose consequence was noticeable lack of expressiveness. Although the face he was proposing to build could not demonstrate the range of its expressiveness in a still picture, it did display its individuality.

Mrs. Allison was impressed, but not overly so. "That's very clever software," she observed, "and you're quite an artist—but I suspect that it's rather flattering."

"Not at all," Victory assured her. "My machinery can restore all the flexibility of authentic youth to the skin and the underlying tissues. It can restore *beauty*, in every sense of the word, not by approximating some kind of average, but in the true sense of perfecting the particularity—the paradoxical uniqueness—of a beautiful face."

"Paradoxical uniqueness?" Mrs. Allison queried, arching an eyebrow with a slight effort that Victory's exceedingly sensitive eye had no difficulty in detecting.

"The great mystery of human beauty," Victory told her, "is that it's not a matter of closeness of conformity to some kind of archetype. Human faces can be perfect in countless different ways. I believe that it results from the way a new-born baby's brain is programmed to recognize the face of its mother; it has to be able to recognize a face as a face, but it also has to be able to recognize a particular face as *the* face: the face that will mean more than any other, the face that it will love. Our adult sentiments are still based in those kinds of instincts, so we still retain the same ambiguity. We need to be able to recognize the face we love both as a category specimen and as something uniquely special. Because of that dual necessity, there is a generic idea of beauty, but also an individual ideal.

"Until now, plastic surgery has only been able to aim, more-or-less vaguely, at the generic idea of beauty. Now, and in the new era to come, we shall be able to aim, with consummate precision, at the individual ideal. What you see on the screen only has the same quality as a photograph; the living, expressive face will be more beautiful still. I can not only take twenty years off your apparent age—I can give you the flawless beauty that authentic youth was never able to deliver, thanks to the vicissitudes of nature."

A lesser woman might have said something along the lines of "Can you really do that?" but Mrs. Allison was old school. She had booked her appointment as "Mrs. Gregory K. Allison," as if she had no forenames of her own, and she had confided none to Victory—not, he assumed, because she wanted to boast that she was married to a self-made billionaire, but simply because that was the proper way to represent herself. Her own family's means might well have been exceedingly mediocre—she still had faint traces of an Eastern European accent, and was old enough to have spent her childhood under Communism—but she had evidently adapted to being the second wife of a seriously rich man with the greatest of ease. She knew perfectly well what modern technology had made available to her—albeit, for the moment, at a phenomenally high price. She knew, too, that the price might not fall as steeply as the prices of newly developed technologies had fallen in the past, or even at all. The economic effects of the ecocatastrophe were sending the prices of everyday necessities relentlessly higher, and if the Global Environmental Model could be trusted, there would soon be many luxuries that were not attainable at any price at all, even by the likes of Gregory K. Allison.

If Mrs. Allison could hang on to good health for another forty years, Victory thought—and there was no earthly reason why she shouldn't, unless the methane trapped beneath the seabed suffered such a catastrophic release that all the oxygen in the atmosphere were to be consumed by apocalyptic fire—it might become possible to secure her rejuvenation indefinitely, or at least for another hundred years. She had been born at a propitious moment in history, provided that civilization did not collapse entirely. The likelihood was, though, that for people as rich as Gregory K. Allison and his wife—or even as modestly wealthy as Hugo Victory hoped to be—the burgeoning ecocatastrophe was something that would happen to other people. Such as they were no longer dependent on nature's bounty.

"How do you change the shape of the bones?" Mrs. Allison wanted to know. "I can understand how the itsy-bitsy robot-controlled scalpels do their work, more or less, but I don't see how you can alter the underlying skeleton."

"Bone is living tissue," Victory said. "Broken bones knit quite rapidly, and routine growth continues discreetly after we have grown to our full stature. Changes in the dimensions of functioning bones are rarely desirable, but they aren't difficult to induce now that we understand the fundamental mechanisms. The changes I'm proposing to make in your facial bones are delicate, so the computer will have to be very cleverly programmed, but the upside is that the transfiguration will be accomplished in a couple of days rather than the weeks required for the modification of limb-bones."

"Clever computer programs go wrong more often than simple ones," Mrs. Allison observed. "I'm not sure I like the idea of being entirely at the mercy of computer-driven robot scalpels."

"You won't be. The purpose of the machine and its programming is to facilitate my work, not to replace me. I remain in full control, but the machine's sensors allow me to see what I'm doing in much greater detail, and the robotic components allow my fingers to manipulate instruments much smaller in dimension and finer in effect than any I could actually hold. In the first phase of the operation there'll be hardly any cutting—access to the bones is very discreet, involving the controlled movement of tiny devices through blood and lymph vessels, and in the margins between cell membranes; the intervention is mostly a matter of stimulating stem cells and activating lysosomes. The second phase is slightly more dramatic—the second operation will take five hours rather than two, and the healing process will take a full week—but cell-destruction will be highly selective and executed with the utmost care."

"Unless something goes wrong," the woman persisted.

"It's delicate and difficult work," Victory admitted, "but my tools are adequate to the task. It's true that the technology is new; there are only seven machines like the one to which I have access in the world at present. Three are in Europe, three in the USA and one in China. Everything has gone smoothly so far, but I can't give you an absolute guarantee that unexpected problems won't materialise at some stage. I understand that some people would prefer to wait, and let others take the risks of innovation. If we can avoid the worst effects of the ecocatastrophe there might be sixty machines in operation in twenty years time, and the treatment might be much more widely accessible as well as having a proven track record."

Mrs. Allison was smart enough to understand the psychology behind that ploy. "What woman fearful of losing her looks would want to wait for years, Dr. Victory? And what rich woman would want to wait until a new treatment became *more widely accessible*? Don't play games with me. All I want is to cut through the sales talk to a reliable picture of what you can do for me, and an accurate risk assessment."

Victory smiled and nodded his head. "There are always slight risks in this kind of treatment," he conceded. "We don't yet know exactly what the machine can do, and what its limitations are. At some stage, one or other of its users will overreach its capabilities, or make a mistake—that's inevitable. On the other hand, the plan mapped out here is a moderate one, well within the machine's compass, and well within mine. My assistant could do it with ease—almost all of the artistry is in the software, and I can assure you that its translation into a surgical operation will be even better than its translation into the image you see on the screen. I've already worked a hundred metamorphoses far more complicated than this one, and the other surgeons and trainees using machines of this type must have done a thousand. If and when something does go wrong, it's far more likely to happen to one of the less practiced operators, or in the course of a more adventurous operation."

Mrs. Allison met his eyes squarely. "In the course of your charity work, perhaps? That would qualify as *adventurous*, I suppose." The sarcasm inherent in the statement was softened by the delicacy of her tone.

Victory had explained to Mrs. Allison when he first saw her that he would have great difficulty fitting her into his schedule, at present, because he was reaching the critical phase of the series of operations he was carrying out on Amahl Sahman. She must have known, in any case, before she booked her first appointment, that the final phase of the boy's treatment was about to begin; even in the absence of the sterling work done by the hospital's press officer during the last few months, the papers and the TV news would have kept careful track of it.

"The *pro bono* work I do is considered by some to be more of a luxury than the work I do at full price," Victory said, lightly. "To the children themselves, of course, it's a matter of life and death—but when they come from North Africa, or South America, or Azerbaijan, some onlookers are likely to think that saving their lives is a pointless exercise, given the likely effects of the ecocatastrophe on regions like those. As you imply, though, it's as much experimentation as charity, allowing me to test the full potential of the techniques that I use on paying clients. I don't mind admitting that it's also a matter of personal conscience. I have so many clients eager to pay me a fortune for youth and beauty—even people with far less potential for perfection than you retain—that it seems only fair to use a portion of their money to deliver helpless children from the hell of malformation."

"The hell of malformation," Mrs. Allison echoed. "A neat turn of phrase. As opposed to the heaven of perfect form, I suppose?"

"The heaven of perfect *forms*," Victory corrected her, politely. "There are, as I said, many kinds of beauty. It would be a dull world if we were forced by our inherited prejudices to aspire to exactly the same face, so we ought to be very glad that our ideals support and encourage such variety. You want to be perfectly beautiful, of course, but you also want to be *yourself*, to possess the beauty that is uniquely yours. In your case, Mrs. Allison, it would be a privilege to bring that beauty out. Although we all have our potential, we are by no means equal, and your potential is, I think, quite marvelous.

"Now, that is mere flattery," she told him, feigning modesty, "And if I were as marvelous as you imply, I wouldn't need better bone-structure. I'm willing to indulge you in that, though, provided that you don't attempt anything drastic. Drastic changes always leave too large a margin for error—although I'm delighted that your work with Amahl has been error-free. The radiation damage must have made your work even harder than usual."

"It wasn't a problem," Victory said. "Fortunately, his refugee camp was outside the immediate contamination footprint of the nuke. He was checked over very thoroughly by the Red Crescent, to make sure that he was in good enough health to withstand the rigours of the treatment and to obtain the full benefit of the repairs."

"And it's been a triumph, for you and for the machine."

"There's a little way to go yet. The reformulation of the bones of his face is complete, but I'll be doing the final moulding on the day after tomorrow—an operation of the same sort as the first phase of your treatment, though somewhat more complicated. After that, it will be necessary to move very rapidly; the final phase will also be roughly parallel to the second phase of your own treatment, but far more complicated. That sequence of operations will be the most arduous one I've ever attempted. It will be challenging in the extreme, but I hope and expect to complete it successfully, with the aid of my team."

"Of course. When do you expect to carry out the final operation?"

"If everything goes well on Wednesday, I ought to be able to complete the final phase on the following Monday. The timetable has to be fluid, though, in case of complications. There's a lot of supplementary work to be done in between; the program for the final operation can't be finalised until the results of the bone-reformulation come in. As you can imagine, the dimensions of the metamorphosis are far greater than the modifications I'm proposing to make to your skull—perhaps a hundred times greater."

"But you *can* fit me in, can't you, Dr. Victory?" she said. It was not so much a request as a command.

"If all goes well on Wednesday," he said, "I can add you to Thursday's list; at present I've left the afternoon free in case Amahl needs a supplementary intervention. That would mean that the optimum time to do your second operation would be Sunday. Fortunately, my assistant is scheduled to use the machine that afternoon, and the work she's doing can easily be postponed. The only potential difficulty would be the aftercare; if the worst did happen, and you and Amahl both needed supplementary interventions...well, time isn't elastic."

"I have every confidence in your ability to do everything you need to do, Dr. Victory," Mrs. Allison said, "Within the limitations imposed by the clock. I have every confidence in your discretion, too. I think you'll have enough publicity over the next two weeks, without the press taking an interest in any arrangement that you and I might make, don't you?"

"No one will hear about it from anyone on my team, Mrs. Allison," Victory promised, "and the hospital press office is very efficient in controlling the flow of information. As you say, the fact that so much media attention will be focused on Amahl should make it easy for us to direct attention away from our other patients. In that respect, your timing is perfect."

"I do hope that's way it plays out, Dr. Victory," she said, meaning that it had better be, if he hoped to keep his own public profile in perfect condition.

"Does that mean that you want to go ahead with the treatment, Mrs. Allison?" Victory asked, formally.

"I wouldn't still be here if I didn't, Dr. Victory," she retorted. Victory saw her face change slightly then, as she switched back into polite mode. "You have the reputation of being the best there is in Europe or the States, and that's why I came to you."

"Thank you," Victory said. "I'm glad you did." He was perfectly sincere—as, he assumed, was she.

"One thing that still puzzles me is why the machine is located at the university hospital. Wouldn't it be more conveniently housed in a private clinic? You are in private practice, after all."

"It's not my machine," Victory said, wondering why she was making that particular point now that everything was settled. "I'm just one of the favoured few who are privileged to use it.

The machine's lodged at King's because it's a research tool as well as an operating instrument. My role is partly that of teacher—my trainee, Majeke Hemlet, is contracted to the NHS—and we surgeons aren't by any means the only ones involved in the technology's continuing development. I've had to become an expert software engineer myself, but only within the narrow confines of my own programs—the engineers working on the fundamental software are making refinements week by week, and so are the people who actually manufacture the nanoscalpels and the lasers. It makes good sense to use a teaching hospital as a focal point of the collective endeavour."

"I see," Mrs. Allison said. She pointed at the screen. "Can you print a copy for that for me? I'd like my husband to take a look at it."

"Certainly." Victory only had to press a key; the laser printer was already set up. The machine sucked in a sheet of treated paper, and began to whirr softly.

"It's very grey outside," Mrs. Allison observed, casting an anxious eye at the sky above Harley Street. Victory's wasn't the topmost office in the suite—Rachel Rosenfeld's psychiatric practice was directly overhead—but it was far enough from street level to have a view of the sky.

"Yes it is," he agreed, "but there's a tangible south-westerly breeze. The air quality index is reasonable."

"The air quality index hasn't been reasonable since I was as young as that picture implies," she said, dryly. "Mercifully, I don't have to go outside."

Victory's building had an enclosed elevator down to the sub-basement garage, where Mrs. Allison's air-conditioned Porsche was parked, alongside Victory's imitation antique Bentley, Dr. Rosenfeld's stubbornly functional Lexus and the acupuncture clinic's twin Saabs. Mrs. Allison would be able to go all the way back to Gregory K. Allison's custom-built mansion near Chalfont St. Peter without breathing a single millilitre of unfiltered air. In theory, clients of the various clinics were supposed to leave their vehicles elsewhere, but Mrs. Allison was by no means the only exception that Victory had made. Even Dr. Rosenfeld, whose clients were mostly from a different social stratum, often gave them the security code that let their vehicles into the building's garage, and Victory never made any complaint.

Victory removed the glossy A4 sheet from the printer, and handed it to her. She looked down at it intently, making sure that no flaws had crept in during the transfer of the image. None had.

"I'll confirm the appointments with Claire," Victory said. "She'll give you all the information you need in advance of your admission." He opened the door for her so that she could precede him into the reception area.

Victory had closed his schedule to further consultations until the end of the month, but Mrs. Allison had had to be accommodated, even at short notice, because her husband was simply too important for her to be fobbed off. The surgeon had found out that morning that Claire had added yet another client to his appointment-book at even shorter notice, assuring him that it was someone he would want—and perhaps need—to see; as he guided Mrs. Allison to Claire's desk, he observed that the other client was already waiting in the reception area.

The newcomer was a man, but there was little more about him that could be determined by a casual glance. He had the hood of his overcoat up, concealing every part of his head that wasn't screened by the large lenses of his dark glasses and a capacious filter-mask. Some such discretion wasn't unusual—even female clients inquiring about surgery that was purely cosmetic often preferred to hide their faces—but this particular individual seemed to be taking the tendency to extremes. As if the hood, mask and shades weren't enough, he had balanced a big black briefcase on his knees like a defensive wall. He might have been more relaxed, Victory thought, if the last interior designer to refurbish the building—some years before Victory had moved in—had not thought it a good idea to place a glass wall between the reception area and the stairwell, so that would-be patients could see where they were going. The corollary of that decision was, of course, that any patients on their way up to or down from the uppermost floor could also look in.

Mrs. Allison looked the waiting man up and down before going to Claire's desk, but he continued to stare steadfastly ahead, refusing to glance in her direction.

"If you'll just give me a minute or two to tidy up, Mr. Gwynplaine," Victory said to the seated man, with the utmost politeness, "Claire will show you in when I'm ready."

The hooded figure nodded.

Victory repeated the dates he had suggested to Mrs. Allison to his secretary. He had discussed the matter with her in advance, so Claire already knew what to expect; she made an ostentatious note, and took up the information-pack that was waiting on her desk, ready to go through it item by item. As befitted a plastic surgeon's secretary, Claire was an exceptionally good-looking woman, but Victory couldn't help noticing the slight looseness of the skin on her neck, the slight darkening of the mole beneath her left eye and a deepening frown-line on her forehead. Soon, he thought, it would be necessary to suggest that it was time for her to correct nature's little errors.

When the formalities were complete Victory shook hands with the billionaire's wife, and then went back into his consulting-room.

He took another long look at the image on his computer screen, then replaced it with an image of Mrs. Allison's face as it actually was. He keyed in a further instruction that replaced it yet again. The new transformation stripped the overlying tissues away to reveal the muscles beneath and their attachments to the bones of the skull. This depiction was replaced in its turn by a modified image of the same sort, carefully displaying in diagrammatic form the work he would have to do in sculpting the bones and reshaping the muscles.

The software Victory used to display his plans and intentions had started out as a standard commercial package, intended as much for advertisement purposes as to assist him in planning his procedures, but he and his IT consultants had modified it considerably in order to take aboard the innovations made possible by the new machine and the idiosyncratic artistry of his own technique. As he had told Mrs. Allison, he had perforce become an expert in the subtle manipulation of the exceedingly complex package of programs, gradually obtaining a sense of their aesthetic logic. He felt comfortable with them now, not merely in the sense that he could massage the instructions they issued to his nanoware, but in the fuller sense that they seemed like extensions of his own unique artistry.

Victory was completely confident of his entitlement to be considered an artist, and a great one—as brilliant in his own way as any other great enhancer of the beauty of the female face. He thought of himself as the Dante Gabriel Rossetti of his century, privileged to work in flesh itself rather than merely in oils. Now that he no longer had to hold his probes and scalpels in his own clumsy fingers, being able instead to control blades that were almost invisible to the naked eye, he knew that the distinctive style of his work was becoming more and more apparent with every operation he did. No one else in England, he believed, could give the same quality of life and beauty to a female face— or, for that matter, a male one.

Victory decanted copies of the files on to the data carrier that doubled as a fob on his key ring, so that he could work on them at the flat and the farmhouse if necessary, and sent a further copy over the privileged link to his terminal at the hospital. Then he buzzed Claire to signal that she could show Mr. Gwynplaine into the consulting room.

CHAPTER TWO

The First Day: Afternoon

When Claire had closed the door again, Mr. Gwynplaine reached out to accept Hugo Victory's proffered handshake. The plastic surgeon felt an unexpected tremor of unease as their hands met, almost as if something beyond the beck and call of consciousness wanted to recoil, as it might from a snake or a spider. Victory was amazed by his own reaction, having trained himself to be perfectly impassive in confrontation with all human deformity. He took control of himself firmly. "Won't you take off your coat now, Mr. Gwynplaine?" he said. "The filter-mask too—you certainly won't need it in here, however bad the air might be in the street."

Gwynplaine set his briefcase down. He took off the filter-mask and put it in is overcoat pocket before pushing back his hood and unbuttoning his coat. Wordlessly, he handed the garment to Victory so that the surgeon could hang it up. He was still sporting his dark glasses, but the extent of his trouble was now perfectly evident. He took up his briefcase again before he sat down.

Victory understood immediately why Claire had taken it for granted that he would be interested to see this particular client. If ever there was a person in need of plastic surgery, it was surely the man who was positioning himself with the utmost care in the very chair that the lovely Mrs Allison had occupied only minutes before—and if there was one man in the world who could give Mr. Gwynplaine exactly what he needed, Victory thought, it was Dr. Hugo Victory, the Dante Gabriel Rossetti of the flesh, ever-ready to ply his wares in Goblin Market.

"I have to warn you that I shall not be able to treat you immediately, Mr Gwynplaine," Victory said, smoothly. "I'm a very busy man, and I'm approaching the critical phase of a very complicated series of operations just now. I can see, though, that your scars have been untreated for some considerable time, so I dare say that you won't mind waiting for another month or two."

16

"I read about the Palestinian boy in the newspapers," Gwynplaine said, in a voice that was eerily distorted by his inability to make full use of his lips, although long practice had evidently enabled him to find a way of pronouncing every syllable in a comprehensible manner. "I've been following the case with great interest. That's why I'm here."

Victory studied the other man's facial musculature very carefully while he was speaking, trying to judge the exact extent of his inability to form a meaningful expression. It seemed that the damage inflicted on Gwynplaine's face—obviously by fire—had paralysed many of the muscles, while twisting others into permanent contraction, leaving the man incapable of any kind of smile and forcing upon him a curious mocking sneer that he could not possibly intend. Gwynplaine might not be quite as old as he looked, but Victory judged that he must be at least thirty, and that the hideous scars must have been in place since late childhood. Victory had never seen anyone so badly burned by a house fire—not, at any rate, anyone who had survived the experience—so he assumed that Gwynplaine must have been caught up in one of the early twenty-first century's many violent conflicts, perhaps as a boy soldier but more likely as an innocent bystander—an exceptionally ugly case of "collateral damage" caused by "smart bombing." The man's speech defect made it impossible to judge his accent, but there seemed to be a strong probability that he wasn't English. The backs of his hands had been burned as badly as his face, but what little unscarred skin could be seen suggested that his skin-tone was not unlike Amahl Sahman's, so he might easily have come from the Middle East, or even Indonesia.

The surgeon readied himself to take a closer look. "I wonder why you've left it so long before seeking treatment, Mr. Gwynplaine," he said, hoping to tease out more information. "Perhaps the medical facilities available to you as a child were very limited?"

"I'm afraid you've mistaken the reason for my visit, Dr. Victory," Gwynplaine said. "When I say that I'm here because of Amahl Sahman, I don't mean that the publicity give to your treatment of him prompted me to seek your help for myself. I mean that I'm here in connection with his case. I believe that I might be able to help you with it."

Startled, Victory glanced down at the note Claire had made when she had accepted the appointment. There was nothing there about Amahl Sahman—but Victory observed that Gwynplaine had come to Harley Street in person rather than making the appointment by telephone, and he realised that Claire must have jumped to the seemingly-obvious conclusion. The mere sight of the man's face had convinced her that it wasn't necessary to follow the usual procedure of asking him the reason for his request for an appointment.

As if reading his thoughts, the slightly monstrous voice added: "Please don't hold your secretary responsible. I fear that I encouraged her to make the assumption that I was a potential patient rather than stating my real business. I was afraid that she might turn me away." As he spoke, the fire-scarred man lifted the briefcase that he had brought with him and snapped the catch.

Victory sat down in his own chair, more amazed than annoyed. Claire had strict instructions to inquire the exact nature of clients' business—instructions intended to exclude journalists and salesmen—but the mistake was perfectly understandable. Gwynplaine was obviously not a salesman or a journalist—but what was he, then? The ancient briefcase was something a fossilized academic might have carried defiantly through a long career of eccentricity, but Gwynplaine's calm assertion that he might be able to help Victory with Amahl Sahman's case was not the kind of statement an academic might make—not, at any rate, at this late stage in the treatment. The most likely conclusion seemed to be that Mr. Gwynplaine was some kind of crank.

Victory made as if to stand up, to signify his displeasure at the deceptive intrusion, but changed his mind and settled himself again. The other and more intriguing possibility, he thought, was that Gwynplaine really did want—and desperately need—his services as a plastic surgeon, but was reluctant to say so, or knew that he could not possibly afford the relevant fees, and had therefore devised an absurdly roundabout strategy for making Victory's acquaintance. If so, the matter might need delicate handling—not least because Gwynplaine's injuries presented as much of a challenge, in their own way, as Amahl Sahman's. They might provide an equal, though quite distinct, test of the new machine's capabilities and his own artistry.

The object that Gwynplaine produced from the capacious bag was a book. Its sturdy but strictly utilitarian leather binding bore no title. Victory guessed, on the basis of the worn and perished condition of the leather, that it might be eighteenth century, or even seventeenth. Gwynplaine laid the book on the desk, and pushed it towards Victory.

Victory looked down at it curiously, but did not open it immediately. He was thinking hard, trying to figure out the best way to overcome the psychological barriers that the disfigured man had erected about himself and cut through to the probable heart of the matter. "I'm not a book collector, Mr. Gwynplaine," he said, gently. "I have a liking for Pre-Raphaelite and Symbolist paintings, but it doesn't stretch as far as illustrations. In any case, I don't pursue my hobbies during working hours."

"This is about Amahl Sahman," Gwynplaine reminded him. "I'm not trying to sell you the book—but I think you'll be very interested to look at it."

Victory frowned, more in puzzlement than displeasure, but he opened the volume. He was surprised to discover that it was a manuscript rather than the product of a printing press. Its pages seemed to be made of parchment rather than mere paper. Victory required a few seconds fully to absorb the realisation that the introductory page on which his eyes fell was impossible to decipher, not because the handwriting was eccentric but because the words were inscribed in a language he had never seen before.

"What is this?" he asked, wonderingly.

"It's a record of the secrets of the comprachicos," Gwynplaine said, as if the term ought to be instantly recognizable. "It seems to be complete—which is to say that it includes the last secret of all: the purpose for which the organization was founded, long before it became notorious for its other activities."

"I have no idea what you're talking about," Victory told his mysterious visitor. He was about to add something along the lines of: *How can this incomprehensible scribble possibly have anything to do with my work?* when he turned another page. His protest died on his lips, unvoiced.

Although the script remained utterly inscrutable, this page bore an illustrative diagram, and it was immediately obvious what the subject of the book might have to do with his work.

Victory had seen a great many anatomical texts in his time, but he had never seen an account of the musculature of the human face as finely detailed as the one he was looking at. It was easily the equal of Albrecht Dürer's anatomical studies, although it was more intricate, and seemed indicative of an uncanny appreciation of the inner architecture of the human face. It seemed to Victory that the author of the diagram addressed him as one artistic genius of plastic surgery to another, even though the message appeared to emanate from an era in which plastic surgery had been unknown. His interest increased by a sudden order of magnitude, although the surge of excitement was quickly damped down by the suspicion that his inferences must have been mistaken. The book could not really be old; it must, in fact, be very modern indeed.

"I hope you will permit me to explain," Gwynplaine said, mildly.

Victory turned to another illustration. This one had been carefully modified, in a manner that was uncannily—impossibly, it seemed—similar to the transition between the images he had displayed on his computer only a few minutes earlier. A layman might have seen nothing but a confusion of arbitrary lines scrawled on the underlying image of the facial musculature, but

19

Hugo Victory saw a set of ingenious instructions for surgical intervention.

If this were genuine, Victory thought, *it would rewrite the history of plastic surgery. Even if it's fake, it's work of astonishing quality. If the text lives up to the promise of the illustrations, it might help to rewrite the textbooks. Even if it was manufactured this year, it must have been complied by someone exceptionally knowledgeable—and with a rather original turn of mind, unless I'm completely mistaking the import of these admittedly unreadable instructions.*

He continued to scan the pages avidly, trying with all his might to make sense of the plans set out therein but not quite succeeding.

"Please go on, Mr Gwynplaine," the surgeon murmured, his eyes transfixed by one illustration after another. "Tell me what you came here to say. But start, if you will, by telling me who the comprachicos are, or were. I'm afraid I've never heard of them."

"Really?" Gwynplaine queried. "They were forgotten for a long time, but interest in their ideas has revived considerably in recent years. I'm surprised that you haven't run across any mention of them, given that you're a plastic surgeon."

"I'm a very busy man," Victory told him. "My attention has been very closely focused on my work these last few years, especially while the new machine has been in development. Exploitation of the opportunities offered by computer-directed nanoscalpels has required virtual obsession. The newspapers often make the machine sound like a miracle-worker in its own right, but we're still some years away from developing an AI that will allow it to work without a human partner. Although the work is done at a cellular level, there's still an important aesthetic component to the guidance of the nanoware, and no one's yet succeeded in gifting an AI with unambiguous self-awareness, let alone a sense of beauty. The former will doubtless come, but the latter...well, let's just say that I don't expect my particular expertise to be matched by a software package for a very long time to come."

"I apologize," Gwynplaine said, his strange voice taking on an oddly musical quality in spite of its slight impediment. "I should have realised that your work places exceptional demands on you. The miracles you've worked must indeed have required enormous concentration and Herculean labour. Comprachicos means *child-buyers*; it was the name give to an organization that some historians regard as a religious sect or cult, others as a strange tribe. Both descriptions appear to have some truth in them. Even in their decadence, in the eighteenth century, the comprachicos took pride in being tradesmen rather than thieves, pious rather than godless, and members of a brotherhood whose ties were based in blood relationships as well as secret oaths. They had always been wanderers, and were often confused at that time with gypsies, but they were a very different breed; they arrived in Western Europe much earlier than the Roma. Even nineteenth-century historians took care to point out that, while the Roma were pagans, the comprachicos were devout Catholics, and might have been Christian even before their westward migration."

The man with the fire-scarred face paused to remove his dark glasses. His eyes were uninjured, and unexpectedly blue, although the lids were scorched black. Victory met his gaze, but felt another thrill of repulsion, so irrepressible as to seem instinctive. He cursed himself for his weakness.

"The nineteenth-century accounts of their history identify the comprachicos' last protector in England as James II," Gwynplaine went on, "and state that they were never heard of again after fleeing the country when William of Orange took the throne. Until recently, historians thought their story had ended then, but it seems that it had merely reached a pause. The comprachicos' retreat into obscurity is perfectly understandable; the Pope, presumably under pressure from a Pauline Cabal within the College of Cardinals, excommunicated the entire organization. That was one reason why the Protestant William was secretly supported by Rome against his Catholic rival, and such succour as those members of the organization who fled from England could receive in France was limited and covert. The entire society retreated to Spain, and even then found it politic to vanish into the Basque country of the southern Pyrenees. They have remained invisible to history ever since—but they had been invisible before, and the wonder may be that they were ever glimpsed at all."

"I was under the impression that the entire College of Cardinals consisted of followers of St. Paul," Victory observed. Having met Gwynplaine's eyes once, he was now looking down at the book again, turning pages one by one with increasing rapidity. He stared raptly at one image after another, breaking off each time only because he was desperately eager to see more. The diagrams were all brilliant, but they were not stylistically identical. It appeared that more than one anatomist had been involved in the compilation of this remarkable anthology. Some of the instructions—if he were correct in his growing confidence that he had an intuitive understanding of their implications—were equally remarkable.

"There have always been factions even in the Vatican," Gwynplaine said, equably, "but the secret societies within the Church are no more significant than those without, and only

21

slightly more influential. The suggestions of heresy helped to ensure, however, that almost everything written about the comprachicos has been written by their enemies, intended to demonize them. They were attacked as mutilators of the children they bought, charged with using their techniques to produce dwarfs and hunchbacks, acrobats and contortionists, freaks and horrors. It is true that they could and did produce monsters—but even in the Age of Reason and the Age of Enlightenment, the demand for such produce came from the courts of Europe, including the papal court. Europe's aristocracy delighted in the antics of clowns and clever fools. The comprachicos sold wares of those kinds to Popes, Kings, Tsars, and Sultans. The clowns that caper in our circuses even to this day use make-up to produce simulacra of the faces that the comprachicos once teased out of raw flesh."

Victory sucked his lip, realising that he had not mistaken the strangeness of the instructions imposed on the anatomical diagrams. They were not, for the most part, suggesting ways in which plastic surgeons could make faces look younger, repair injuries, or compensate for the kind of genetic disaster that had afflicted Amahl Sahman. Many, though not all, were suggesting ways in which faces might be tormented into hideous caricatures.

The surgeon looked again at Gwynplaine's face, momentarily. It was perfectly obvious that the flesh had been badly burned, but there was no way of knowing whether his features had been surgically modified before the fire. Was it possible, Victory wondered, that Gwynplaine had *allowed* himself to be burned, in order to obliterate the traces of a previous mutilation?

"Yes, Dr. Victory," Gwynplaine went on, speaking more effortfully now, "the comprachicos often used their plastic arts— arts that men like you are rediscovering rather than inventing— for purposes that you or I might consider perverse, but that was not their primary aim. That was not the reason for which the company first came to the western extremes of Europe, in the days when the Goths still ruled Iberia and Gaul and the Church's hold on Christendom was very precarious."

Although Victory was still quite certain that he had never heard of the comprachicos, he recalled hearing the contention that families of beggars in ancient times had sometimes crippled and mutilated their children in order to make them more piteous. He had heard, too, that the acrobats of Imperial Rome had trained the joints of their children so that they could be dislocated and relocated at will, preparing them for life as extraordinary gymnasts. For this reason, he was not inclined to dismiss Gwynplaine's story entirely. His eyes were still fascinated by the book; his fingers were still turning the parchment pages reverentially. The anatomical diagrams and the fanciful surgical

schemes superimposed upon them seemed marvelous and astonishing.

"What *was* the reason for the organization's existence?" the
surgeon asked.

"To reproduce the face of Adam."

That startled Victory into looking up. "What?"

Gwynplaine seemed quite impassive, but that was hardly
surprising. "Adam, you will doubtless recall, was supposed to
have been made in God's image. The comprachicos believed that
the face Adam wore before the Fall was a replica of the Divine
Countenance itself, as were the faces of the angels. When Adam
ate from the tree of knowledge of good and evil, however, his
features became contorted—and when God expelled him from
Eden, that contortion became permanent, ensuring that Eve and
his children would never see the image of God again.

"The comprachicos believed that, if only they could find a
means of undoing that contortion, thus unmasking the ultimate
beauty of which humans were once capable, they would give
their fellows the opportunity to know the appearance of God.
That sight, they believed, would provide the most powerful possible incentive to seek salvation, and would prepare the way for
Christ's return and the commencement of his Millennial reign.
Without such preparation, they feared, men would stray so far
from the path of righteousness that God would despair of them,
and leave them to make their own future and their own fate indefinitely."

"So they really were a cult?" Victory said. "Crazy like flying
saucer cultists rather than evil like money-grubbing brainwash-
ers, I presume?"

"They were devout Christians," Gwynplaine said. "Unorthodox, to be sure—but they were not condemned as heretics by
the Roman Church until the eighteenth century. There are factions both within and without the Church that have similar beliefs, and others that have rival beliefs you might consider
equally odd."

"But you don't—consider them odd, I mean."

"I know that the face of Adam was a reflection of the face of
God."

"Speaking metaphorically, of course."

"Speaking literally, Dr. Victory."

"But there never was an Adam or an Eden," Victory said,
now attempting to meet the oddly plaintive eyes of his frightful
visitor with a frank and assertive stare. He suspected that there
was not a man in England who could win a staring-match against
such opposition, if Gwynplaine chose to assert himself.

"You're mistaken, Dr. Victory," Gwynplaine stated, bluntly.
"May I suggest that we're wasting time? My purpose in speaking

of Adam was to help you to understand why the comprachicos studied as they studied, acted as they acted, and left behind the record that you find so fascinating. It doesn't matter whether you believe in a literal Eden or not. What does matter is the illustration of the book, and its relevance to the task you have in hand."

Victory knew that he ought to let the matter drop and return to the question of what Gwynplaine actually wanted from him, but he couldn't resist putting in one more blow for the cause of science against superstition, and hopeful sanity against blind fundamentalism. "We know the history of our species," he stated, as he dropped his gaze to the book again. "*Genesis* is a myth, not a historical record."

Even as he spoke, however, Victory felt a bizarre flicker of doubt, of a kind that he had never felt before. He had never been a religious man, and had not stepped into a church since the day of his ill-fated wedding, but he had been brought up in a Christian country, and had not been untouched by its myths. There was a fraction of a second when he felt his scientific attitude shimmer and slip—but then he pulled himself together, and reasserted his sanity.

The important thing, he said to himself, silently, *is that this book is not a myth. Whether or not it's genuinely old, it's a record of rational speculations—and perhaps actual experiments—of which the accepted history of medicine has no inkling. The myths don't matter, but the reality does. At the end of the day, it might still be his own face that he has in mind, his own inner Adam he wants to recall—but whatever he thinks he wants, or says he wants, this book is something that I ought to study, when I have the time.*

CHAPTER THREE

The First Day: Late Afternoon

While Victory considered his position, Gwynplaine took up his explanation again, apparently accepting Victory's judgment that further argument was necessary. "The comprachicos had a different opinion as to the history of our species," he said. "They knew, of course, that there were other men on Earth besides Adam when the Fall occurred—how else would Cain have found them in the east of Eden?—but they trusted the word of scripture that Adam alone had been created in God's image. It seemed logical to them, in consequence, that Adam's face must be the face of all the angels: the ultimate in imaginable beauty. It seemed plausible to them that the replication of such a countenance might be enough in itself to bring back the Age of Miracles—and a worthy design, even if its realization fell short of that apocalyptic ambition."

"But it's utter nonsense," Victory said. He did not try to muster as much conviction in his tone as he would have thought reasonable on another occasion. He knew that he had to humour the man—but he was uncomfortably aware that there was something about Gwynplaine's peculiar voice that was strangely corrosive of scepticism.

Gwynplaine leaned forward and placed the palms of his hands flat upon the open pages of the book that he had laid on Victory' desk, preventing the surgeon from turning the next page. "All the secrets of the comprachicos are recorded in here," he said, flatly, "including the last—the secret of reproducing the face of Adam."

"If they knew how to achieve that," Victory objected, "why didn't they do it? If they could perform such an operation, why didn't they succeed in bringing about their renaissance of faith, the day of judgment, and the salvation of humankind?"

"According to the book, the crucial operation was a success," Gwynplaine told him, "but the child died before his flesh could heal. The surgeon who performed the operation died too, not long afterwards. The project was carried out here in London, not two miles east of Harley Street, and the surgeon in question was as eminent in his day as you are in yours—but the timing was disastrous; the year was 1665. The plague took them both. There was no one else in England with the requisite skill to make a second attempt, so a summons was sent to Spain—but by the time the call was answered, London had been destroyed by the great fire. The record of the operation was thought to have been lost.

"When William came to power and the remaining comprachicos fled to the continent, they no longer had the book. Their subsequent experiments failed—but the book had not burned in the fire, as they presumed. It was saved, secreted by a thief who did not know its nature because he could not read the language in which it was written. It was lost for more than three centuries, but it was recently rediscovered by someone who understood what it was, even though he could not read it. You will not find a dozen scholars in Europe now who *can* read it, and perhaps only one in England other than myself. In fifty years time, there might be none at all, even if the ecocatastrophe proves less destructive than everyone fears. Alas, the ability to read the text is quite useless without the skill, the art and the instruments necessary to carry out the instructions. I have many skills, Dr. Victory, but not that one."

"So you came to me."

"Yes. What I need is a collaborator with the skill and art necessary to carry out the instructions that require an expert hand and surgical instruments. It is conceivable that I might do better to take it to California or Paris, and that is what I shall do if you will not agree to help me—but I came to you first, partly because I was also told that you have the most skilful and artful hand, and better equipment than the comprachicos ever thought possible, and partly because you have a such a golden opportunity ready to hand."

"You want me to follow instructions set out in this book, to give Amahl Sahman the face of Adam? You can't be serious, Mr. Gwynplaine."

"I'm perfectly serious, Dr. Victory. All the preliminary work has been done, if the reports in the press can be trusted. In two days time, you will begin the final manipulation of the facial bones, which you have knitted together with the utmost care. They are still malleable, and their various connections with the muscles will have to be remade in any case. Everything that the comprachicos' prescription requires to be done, Amahl Sahman requires to be done. Nothing the book asks of you will injure or inconvenience your patient in any way. Quite the reverse: if you can give him the face of Adam, you will enhance his future prospects immeasurably. He will be famous for a while in any case, but you have it in your power to increase the magnitude of that celebrity—and your own—dramatically."

"I don't believe...." Victory trailed off. That was the wrong way to handle the discussion, he felt sure, but he was also uncertain as to where the limits of his unbelief lay, or how relevant they were. He could not believe, and could not imagine how he might be persuaded otherwise, that he or anyone else was capable of moulding a face of authentically miraculous quality—not even one that could launch a thousand ships, let alone precipitate Christ's return to Earth and the day of judgment. Nor could he believe, until he could be persuaded otherwise, that some obscure cult of butchers—no matter how much esoteric knowledge of anatomy they had accumulated over the centuries—could possibly have designed a face more aesthetically pleasing than any his software has so far been required to imagine or construct.

On the other hand, if he were to be persuaded of the latter fact....

Victory shook his head. *In any case*, he thought, *how can any apocalyptic miracle be necessary, in a world where millions are fighting half a hundred wars, each of which makes Troy seem a mere skirmish...a world in which the accelerating ecocatastrophe has already judged humankind as profligate, gluttonous, idolatrous and suicidal*? He looked at his visitor again.

Gwynplaine's blue eyes had hardened now, seeming every bit as intimidating as Victory had suspected that they might. "You agreed long ago to reconstruct the boy's face," the fire-scarred man pointed out. "You undertook to manipulate the ruin of his features into a face that is not merely recognizably human but handsome. No one has given you a photograph to copy; no one has put any constraint on your judgment as to what is practicable or desirable. You have undoubtedly programmed a sketch of some kind into your computers, to guide your hand as it operates the nanoblades, but it still requires final modification to exactitude. Your secretary told me, when I persuaded her to give me an appointment today, that you could not see me tomorrow, because you will be making exactly that kind of modification in advance of the operation you expect to carry out on Wednesday. In the aftermath of that operation, you will have to modify the programs again, to take account of the boy's continuing progress. There is no reason at all, practical or ethical, why you should not incorporate the comprachicos' designs into your scheme."

"There are a dozen reasons...," Victory began.

"There is none," Gwynplaine contradicted him. "If, when I show you the designs for the face of Adam, you can find some terrible error, or a manipulation that is impossible of achievement, then there will be a reason. If the design has no evident flaw, and no error of specification, there is no reason why you

27

should not attempt to construct that face rather than the one at which you are presently aiming. Indeed, there is one very good reason why you should. I am offering you a better design than you could ever improvise yourself."

"I doubt that," Victory said.

"So you should," Gwynplaine assured him, "until you have proof, which the book will provide. When it does, you will have no further cause for hesitation. You do not believe that the mere sight of a surgically remodelled face could bring about any miraculous result, Dr. Victory, so you have nothing to fear in that respect—but even if you did, could you believe that any such miracle would be a bad thing? You only have to pick up a newspaper or look out of your window to realise that the end of the world into which you were born has already begun, and that its decline cannot be halted in the absence of a miracle. What do you have to lose, Dr. Victory?"

Victory was struck yet again by the absurd suspicion that Gwynplaine was reading his thoughts—and not merely reading them, but turning them back upon himself, using their strength against him. It was the disturbance caused by that suspicion rather than any mere reflex that made him voice the retort that rose so readily to his lips, although he would not have done so had he not been so discomfited by the situation. "What do I have to gain?" he countered.

As soon as the words were out of his mouth, Victory knew that they were foolish—that they put him in a very bad light, and opened the door to a negotiation of the wrong kind.

Gwynplaine could not smile, but he shifted his bodily position slightly, as though he were relaxing from a forced rigidity. He did not move his hands, though. They still lay upon the book, which was open in the middle; the final pages, and many others, were still undisclosed.

"Apart from far greater celebrity and professional respect than you have already, Dr. Victory," the fire-scarred man said, placidly, "you might gain a great deal. If our project were to succeed, even if it were only to demonstrate that the face described in the book had no particular power at all, I would be prepared to give you the book, for which I would no longer have any need. Even as a mere antique, it is so valuable that there are dozens of men who would gladly stoop to theft to acquire it. There are probably hundreds who might resort to violence to acquire the secrets they believe it to contain. To a plastic surgeon, it would be uniquely valuable as a record of more than a thousand years of research and experiment."

"You make it sound like a direly dangerous thing to possess," Victory said, uneasily—although the uneasiness arose from his awareness that he had been wrong-footed, not the prospect of receiving such a gift, even if the gift turned out to be a fake.

"If that worries you, Dr. Victory," Gwynplaine said, "You could easily photocopy the pages and deposit the original in the British Museum—or sell it at auction, if you prefer."

Victory knew that if the book were his, he would not do any such thing. He had other possessions that people might be avid to steal, and defences against the possibility, which he would be more than ready to strengthen as and when the need arose.

"Have you ever been advised that you might be wise to seek the services of a psychotherapist?" Victory inquired, more by way of delay than insult. "My colleague upstairs has an excellent reputation, I believe." He knew that the last vestiges of his intention to humour Gwynplaine and win his confidence had now been devastated, but he had been drawn out of his argumentative depth.

"Dr. Rosenfeld's reputation is doubtless well-deserved," Gwynplaine countered, "but I have no more need of her services than you have. Accepting my commission will not endanger you in that respect. It is not necessary that you believe what the comprachicos believed, or what any of their rivals may have believed, in order to undertake this project—and it is probably best to approach it with a far more open mind. You need no more motive than curiosity—but you *are* curious, are you not?"

"If you wanted me to operate on *you* according to instructions penned by some seventeenth-century barber," Victory said, "I might be prepared to consider taking the risk—but I can't operate on a hapless child without grossly violating the principle of informed consent."

"Nonsense," said Gwynplaine, firmly. "The consent obtained for what you have already done came from the Red Crescent, the foreign office and the sponsors who will take responsibility for him when his treatment is complete, not from the child himself. Amahl understands nothing; he consents meekly to everything because he has no other choice and no other hope."

"That doesn't absolve me from my duty to observe the principle," Victory said. "I don't actually know who the boy's legal guardian is, but the hospital administration will be able to tell me. Not that it matters—how could I possibly suggest to the boy's guardian that I try to give him a face I found in some ancient manual of surgery produced by a bunch of lunatics?"

"As it happens," Gwynplaine countered, "I do know who the boy's legal guardian is, and I have every reason to think that he would be only too eager to give you permission—or, indeed, to order you to do what I am asking of you. The reason I came to you, however, was to persuade *you* that this course of action is both practicable and moral. I will tell you, when the time is right, who the person is who is legally entitled to give you the permission you require—but that person does not know, as yet, that I have the book, and I have my own reasons for wanting to keep that information secret until the last possible moment. In the meantime, what I am asking from you is to give me your expert judgment on the viability of the comprachicos' plan. If you judge, having given it your most careful consideration, that it is impossible, or that the face it would produce is in some way defective, then we need not trouble anyone else. If, on the other hand, you *were* to be persuaded that the sequence of operations is not merely practicable, but would produce a face of exceptional beauty, then we shall be in a position to go to the boy's guardian to obtain his consent. All I am asking, for the moment, is that you explore the possibility, without any further commitment. Are you willing to do that?"

Victory said nothing for a full minute, while he wondered what to say. Eventually, he said: "Very well, then—let me see this so-called last secret."

Gwynplaine gave no sign of thinking that he had won the argument. He simply turned the pages *en masse*, displaying one less than a dozen leaves from the end—presumably the first diagram in the final sequence. He withdrew his hands so that Victory could study it.

After three minutes, Victory turned to the next page. Three minutes later he turned to the next. Then he began skipping—but while two or three still remained, Gwynplaine leaned forward to place his hands on the book again, preventing him from turning the final pages.

"Can you see any fatal error?" the scared man asked.

"Not yet," Victory admitted, "but I'd have to see a full translation of the captions. Even then, I couldn't tell simply by looking. I'd have to input the instructions into my computer programs, bit by bit, and run a whole series of virtual tests. I'd have to be able to display the modified musculature, and the intended face itself."

Gwynplaine immediately moved his hands to close the book. Victory regretted not having left his own hand in place on the page, so that he might protest the action—but had he done so, the delicate parchment page might have torn, and that was the last thing he wanted.

"I'll bring you a complete translation of the instructions tomorrow morning," Gwynplaine said. "You will have plenty of time to analyse the instructions fully, and satisfy yourself that following them can do no harm. I shall make sturdier copies, so that you will be able to examine them more carefully. You will be able to feed the data into your computer model page by page, as you wish. If you discover that anything is amiss, at any stage in the process, you may call a halt and revert to some other design. You can agree to this without committing yourself to anything further; if you do, I am more than willing to work on it all day tomorrow, and as many days thereafter as are necessary."

Victory was still hesitant; he felt that Gwynplaine had snared him even though he had not committed himself to anything.

"If you say no now, Dr. Victory," Gwynplaine went on, as if reading his mind yet again, "you will never see me or the book again. I shall make my offer to someone else." It was obvious that the scarred man did not believe that Victory would say no at this stage, although he surely had to be aware that it would take something like a miracle to persuade the surgeon to put into practice anything that he might learn from the book's tantalizing pages.

Victory was unable to meet Gwynplaine's eyes, even for a moment, and he was acutely conscious of his own exceedingly unprofessional frown. "Who the hell are you, Mr. Gwynplaine?" he asked, roughly.

"Gwynplaine is as good a name as any," the man with the unreadable face told him, teasingly. "I have none more authentic."

"What language is the book written in?"

"It's an eastern European script," Gwynplaine said. "The comprachicos continued to use it after their migration precisely because it was unknown to any scholar in the west. I could teach you the basics of it, once our work is complete, if you would like to decipher the rest of the text yourself—or I could tell you the name of a man who can translate it for you, and would be very glad of the opportunity."

"How did you come by it? If there are so many people who'd go to extreme lengths to possess it, how did you end up with it? Could anyone challenge your entitlement to give it to me, if we did make a deal?"

"Others might challenge my entitlement," Gwynplaine admitted, "but they would never be able to demonstrate their own entitlement to claim it. Possession, in this case, is the whole of the law. If it makes you feel better, though, I can assure you that I did not steal the book; nor did I commit any other crime in obtaining it"

Victory was still outwardly hesitant, but he knew that Gwynplaine must be fully aware that he was putting on a show, for appearances' sake, even if his visitor's apparent mind-reading ability was pure guesswork. The surgeon felt that he was on the threshold of the most momentous opportunity of his life. He had seen enough of the book to know that he ought to make the minutest possible examination of it, in order to explore the possibilities outlined in it. He needed to possess it, if he possibly could, whether it was what Gwynplaine claimed or not.

For the first time in his life, although he was no stranger to temptation, Hugo Victory was faced with an irresistible lure.

"I have to look in on Amahl in the morning," the surgeon said, finally. "It's not just courtesy—I need to check that everything's okay. I was planning to come back here to start work on the computer at ten-thirty or eleven. I don't know how hard it will be to make further modifications to my plans, but I can't stay up all night. I have to operate first thing on Wednesday, and I'll need to be in perfect shape."

"That's fine, Dr. Victory" Gwynplaine said. "I'll be waiting for you, with the translation. I'm very grateful to you for seeing me and hearing me out." He moved with surprising dexterity as he removed the book from the desk and deposited it carefully within the voluminous briefcase.

Victory felt a pang of regret as he watched the volume disappear, but reminded himself that no matter how revealing or useful the illustrations might be in their own right, they would be far more so with the accompanying instructions translated into English. The plastic surgeon sat back in his chair and watched passively as Gwynplaine donned his dark glasses, then got up and fetched his coat from the peg.

The scarred man replaced his filter-mask and pulled his hood over his head. Ten years ago, Victory thought, a man so costumed would have seemed conspicuous on any street in London; today, he could walk up Harley Street without attracting a second glance, even on a day when the air quality was reportedly good and no polluted rain was falling. Ten years before, the eco-catastrophe had been something people talked about as if it were a distant prospect, except perhaps in Africa and the Far East; now, largely thanks to the predictions of the Global Environmental Model—whose sophistication increased with every year that passed—it had become a powerful generator of fervent paranoia, and no one expected to remain unscathed by its effects, even in a nation whose food technology was progressing by leaps and bounds. Nowadays, people's hearts were lifted not merely by the increasingly rare sound of birdsong, but by the hum of house-flies and drone of wasps; everyone knew how delicate the supposed balance of nature had become, and no one any longer believed that the loss of entire biological families was irrelevant to human existence. Filter-masks were not so much utilitarian instruments as badges of concern, ostentatious emblems of GEM-licensed anxiety.

"Until tomorrow, Dr. Victory," Gwynplaine said, holding out his hand to be shaken.

Victory refrained from reminding his visitor that he had not committed himself to anything at all. It was true, in a literal sense—but he had a curious sensation of having already set his conscience aside in order to make a bargain that might somehow turn out to be Faustian in nature.

CHAPTER FOUR

The First Day: Evening

A few minutes after Gwynplaine had gone. Victory went out to tell Claire that she could go home. He didn't rebuke her for her error in not making certain exactly what the fire-scarred man wanted of him, but she seemed slightly anxious about it.

"Mr. Gwynplaine didn't ask for a further appointment," she said.

"He's coming in tomorrow morning," Victory told her. "We'll probably be working together for most of the day, once I get back from the hospital." The secretary seemed so surprised that he added: "It's okay. I've already completed the plans for all three of Thursday's ops, including Mrs. Allison's, and the work on Amahl's program only requires some fine tuning. I'll be staying in London all week, and I don't have any social engagements at all; there'll be time to do all that needs to be done."

"Yes, doctor," she said, although the ghostly frown line on her forehead deepened even further as he confessed that he had no social engagements, giving the impression that she worried about his excessive dedication to his work.

"I'm fine," he assured her. "I'll make sure I eat properly, even if I have to brave the hazards of the hospital canteen."

When Claire had put on her coat and departed, Victory went back into his consulting-room, and reactivated the computer. He opened one of Amahl Sahman's files, and reviewed the preliminary program he had made for Wednesday's surgery.

Because the boy's facial bones had only just been knitted, after a series of operations to bring them into position, the plan was sketchy and indistinct. Victory still had to pick up the latest X-rays from the hospital, and to feed in various other recent data, before he could begin to make it firmer and sharper. To have a definite model from which to work—even a model as peculiar as the one in Gwynplaine's book—would actually make the following day's work a little easier, if he could be convinced that it could not possibly do any harm. Further down the line, when he had to finalise the schematics for the following Monday's operation, he would have to be far more careful about any commitment he might be tempted to make, but that prospect still seemed fairly distant. In that respect, Gwynplaine had timed his appearance and his bizarre request to perfection.

Perhaps, Victory thought, the timing was just a little *too* perfect—but if Gwynplaine had been following the reportage of Amahl's case in the broadsheets carefully, he would have had plenty of opportunity to gauge his moment. The surgeon was already beginning to regret wasting so much time on peripheral matters, instead of pressing Gwynplaine on such concrete matters as the name of Amahl Sahman's guardian, but he supposed that he would be able to find that out without too much difficulty...and the story that Gwynplaine had told was certainly intriguing, however preposterous it might be.

After closing Amahl's files, Victory summoned his favourite search engine, and fed in the word *comprachicos*. He was momentarily surprised by the number of hits it registered, but when he began to look at the sites that headed the list his astonishment soon turned to annoyance. He had to scroll down a very long way before he reached anything that looked remotely respectable.

By the time Victory finally shut the computer down, the sky over Harley Street was pitch dark and street-lamps were shining brightly. The sky had taken on the peculiar jaundiced hue produced by a combination of light-pollution and the ever-present cocktail of organic pollutants that never forsook the city unless blown away by a gale or sluiced out of the sky by a deluge. He turned his keys in the mechanical locks of both the consulting-room and the outer office, even though both doors also had pass-code-protected locks. He was still deep in thought as he walked along the carpeted corridor to the elevator—and was astonished to find, when it stopped and the doors slid open, that it wasn't empty.

"Working late again, Dr. Rosenfeld?" Victory said to the occupant, in a spirit of light banter. "Is there an epidemic of mental illness brewing?"

Dr. Rosenfeld was some twenty years older than Victory, but she had worn relatively well for someone who appeared to have conscientious objections to cosmetic surgery. She was a tall, rather large-boned woman who must have been athletic in her youth. Her abundant grey hair suited her profession, and gave her a certain imperious style. Victory would have taken some pleasure in trying to find the unique beauty within her angular features without actually remoulding her jaw, but it was difficult to judge what potential there might be while the flesh was confused by so many blemishes and unwarranted facial hair, not to mention the burgeoning wattle and the asymmetrical nasal cartilage. "Everybody's insane these days, Dr. Victory," the psychotherapist replied, in the same cheerfully sardonic spirit, as she moved aside to give him more room in the confined space. "Even if it weren't for the side-effects of all the aerosol residues, dioxins and PCBs, anxiety and depression would be running rampant. My humble clients often work by day, so they need evening appointments. I'm surprised to find you still here, though. I thought plastic surgeons had more control over their hours. You're not turning into a workaholic, I hope?"

"I've always had obsessive-compulsive tendencies," Victory said, punching the button marked GARAGE for a second time when the doors seemed reluctant to close. "I wouldn't be without them. They're the wellspring of all my achievements. Most of my night shifts are spent at the hospital, though. I was doing some research this evening, relevant to a couple of new patients."

"The Palestinian boy?" she queried. "The newspapers are still reporting that one almost daily. You've done the hard work now, I suppose?"

"Not entirely," Victory said, as the elevator finally began its slow descent. "We're in sight of the winning-post, but the next week is going to be hectic. I'll be spending as much time at the computer as I will in the theatre, and it's easier to do that kind of work here than at the hospital. If I'm on site, people tend to assume I'm on call." He glanced at his wristwatch. "It's later than I thought, though," he observed. "I had some other things to look up—you know how the time slips away when you're on line."

"I certainly do," the psychotherapist agreed. "I have to keep track of the opposition, and the Turings your colleagues at Kings are developing as counsellors are surprisingly good."

"Non-directive interrogation has always been easy for AIs," Victory observed. "If the ability to talk the hind leg off a donkey were all it took to facilitate the spontaneous generation of self-awareness, cyberspace would be even more crowded than Stamford Bridge on a derby day. Mind you, I'd rather it was some online doctor that set out to conquer the virtual world than some Alexander cooked up by the U.S. military or—God help us—the French civil service."

"Not to mention some Las Vegas gambling machine or some ultra-complex shoot-'em-up game," Dr. Rosenfeld added, readily entering into the playful spirit of the enterprise. "On the other hand, I'm not so sure I'd want any of your software to grow a mind of its own—that kind of interest in mere beings of flesh and blood might lead to some nasty experiments."

"No chance of that, I'm glad to say," Victory assured her. He hesitated for a moment, but there didn't seem to be any issues of client confidentiality at stake, so he gave way yet again to temptation. "Tell me, Dr. Rosenfeld, did you ever hear of a cult called the comprachicos?"

Victory had asked the question because Gwynplaine had seemed slightly surprised that he hadn't heard the term, and because he'd been surprised and confused himself by what had turned up when he'd fed the word into the search engine. That confusion had only been further increased by what had turned up when he'd refined the search by adding in such terms as "lost book" and "anatomical drawing." He was interested to know what a person of Dr. Rosenfeld's education and interests might have heard about the subject. When he saw her tense up, however, he realised that he had accidentally hit on something.

The psychotherapist hesitated far longer over her reply than Victory had hesitated over the question, so he knew that, in her case, the issues of client confidentiality must be serious. The elevator bumped on to the bottom of its shaft before she had finished thinking about it. The doors slid open smoothly, but Rachel Rosenfeld didn't step out immediately. Instead, she put her hand on the left-hand door in order to prevent it sliding to meet its partner. "Yes I have, as it happens," she said. "What prompted you to research them tonight?"

"That's a real AI counsellor's answer," Victory observed, without moving out of the elevator. "Zero informational content, smoothly turning the inquiry back on the questioner. What prompted me to research them tonight was that I heard the name for the first time this afternoon. I never did much history at school—I specialised in science from thirteen on, and I've been narrowly focused on medicine since I turned eighteen. I never dreamed that a cult of amateur plastic surgeons had started up in the Dark Ages and practiced right through to the Great Fire of London. It's an amazing story, if any of it's true. Did you know that there are people on line offering rewards of ten thousand pounds for information leading to the recovery of any documents relating to their methods and procedures?"

"Yes, I did," she answered. She moved out of the elevator, finally consenting to go on ahead of him. As they moved towards their parked cars, though, she turned her head to face him and said: "I hardly think that information would be of any practical use to you, Dr. Victory, given the advanced methods and procedures at *your* disposal."

"No practical use, perhaps," Victory said, following meekly behind her, "but one can't be practical all the time. The historical interest of any such documents would be immense—but I have the feeling that it isn't historical interest that moves the people offering the rewards. Have you looked at any of the conspiracy theory links? There are people out there who think that the comprachicos were involved in mysterious ways with the origins of the Templars, the Cathars, the Jesuits, Opus Dei, and a dozen other groups whose names I'd never heard before."

"It's difficult to take that sort of thing seriously," Dr. Rosenfeld observed, as she clicked the remote control to unlock her Lexus.

"You're really trying hard to be no help at all, aren't you, Dr. Rosenfeld?" Victory said, keeping his tone amiable even though he was intrigued. "Presumably you have a patient whose crazy secrets you're anxious not to divulge—but if you've scoured the web yourself, you must have found out all kinds of things that aren't confidential, and you must have formed general opinions. Why not throw me a bone, hey?"

"An interesting metaphor, for a plastic surgeon," the psychotherapist observed, pausing before getting into her car—but the effort of maintaining such a rigid professional pose was too much, and she relaxed into a smile. "I don't usually endorse such terminology, but crazy is about the size of it, in this case. The comprachicos seem to be fashionable nowadays, presumably because people have had more than enough of last century's occult fads and are scraping the bottom of the barrel in their search for new ones. They'll become bored with the comprachicos, the Visionary Martyrs and the Sons of Job soon enough, just as they became bored with the Templars, the Rosicrucians and the Bavarian Illuminati. The more secret societies get talked about, the less effective their glamour becomes. Whatever reality there might once have been within the myth of the comprachicos is now obscured by dense layers of newly-minted fantasy. In a couple of years, you'll probably find books full of their so-called secrets offered for sale on e-Bay, and very nicely forged too. After that, interest will move on. It's a waste of time, Dr. Victory, and you have better things to do. Not just the Palestinian boy; even your ladies who lunch are a worthier cause than phantoms of that kind."

She opened the door of the Lexus then, but she waited politely before getting in, in case he had anything further to say.

Victory was well aware that the psychotherapist still hadn't let slip a single item of hard information, so he decided to cut to the chase. "So what's your view?" he asked. "Were they just making freaks for service as court jesters and circus exhibits, or were they really trying to reproduce the face of Adam?" He had found enough references to the controversy on the web to feel that he wasn't letting out anything that Gwynplaine had told him in confidence.

Dr. Rosenfeld seemed slightly uncomfortable about being put on that particular spot, but she didn't duck the question. "I think they were just making horrible faces," she said. "I don't believe they had the knowledge or the skill to do anything more than that. Compared with your peers, Dr. Victory, they were non-starters. No sane person in search of self-improvement would ever have gone to them in 1600 for a face lift, or even a boob job. If they were around in the days of the Renaissance alchemists, it's understandable that one or two of them might have got delusions of grandeur, and it's always the guys with the delusions of grandeur who write things down—but if any of them did start trying to reproduce the face of Adam, they got no further than the hopeful imbeciles looking for the philosopher's stone, the elixir of youth, the secret of invisibility and a working perpetual motion machine. All they can ever have made, if they did exist, was a mess. Can I go home now, Dr. Victory?"

"I'm sorry to keep you, Dr. Rosenfeld," Victory said, not having made the slightest move even to unlock the pastiche Bentley. "I got carried away by a new fascination. You're right, of course—even if a few crazy medieval cultists did manage to convince themselves that their destiny was to replicate the face of Adam, they couldn't actually have got past square one, could they? Not even as far as Michelangelo did while painting the ceiling of the Sistine Chapel. May I wish you pleasant dreams, or is there no such thing in your line of work?"

"You may," she said. "And I hope you get the fullest possible benefit from your own beauty sleep." She closed the door to make sure that she had had the last word, and started the engine of the Lexus.

Victory stood to one side while she drove away, then went over to the Bentley, wondering what kind of patient Dr. Rosenfeld might have that could tie up something like the comprachicos in knots of confidentiality. Someone paranoid, presumably, who took it all too seriously: someone who thought that the ecocatastrophe was the result of an evil scheme hatched by the world's elite and their extraterrestrial buddies, as a means of killing off the poor and underprivileged.

He started the Bentley, and made his own exit from the garage.

He didn't have far to go; when he worked late he didn't bother to drive all the way to Oxfordshire to what he liked to call his "farmhouse," although the only livestock raised there now were Mrs. Benedict's bantams. He had a flat in Westbourne Park, whose amenities were a trifle constrained but would be advertised nevertheless as a "highly desirable residence" if ever he decided to sell it. Given that there was no one except Mrs. Benedict to go home to nowadays—she had kept the cottage following her husband's death, in order to continue serving as his housekeeper—and also given that she was always more than glad not to have to cook for him when he stayed "in town," there was little to tempt him out on to the M40 in mid-week. He rarely entertained at the farmhouse any more, the flat being infinitely more convenient for the majority of his occasional assignations.

In fact, the frequency of his adulterous liaisons had declined steeply since his divorce three years before, although the number of opportunities remained much the same. Consenting to seduction by his married patients no longer seemed the sport it once had, now that there were no ties on his side—and the obsessive-compulsive tendencies he had mentioned to Rachel Rosenfeld really had got a secure grip on him. He was definitely a workaholic, whose Don Juan days were behind him.

Victory wondered briefly, as he turned left out of Baker Street on to Marylebone Road, whether he might make an exception for the rejuvenated Mrs. Allison, if the occasion arose, but he decided that there was no point even thinking about it. She seemed to be far too "old school" even to consider anything as tacky as screwing her cosmetic surgeon in gratitude for making her wrinkles vanish and hoisting her cheekbones by a millimetre or so. He started wondering, instead, whether Rachel Rosenfeld might have been flirting with him just a little, as she teased him with the non-disclosure of anything interesting she might know about the comprachicos. She too was recently divorced—and not, he suspected, for the first time.

The surgeon turned on the radio, although he had only a few minutes to listen, and tuned into a news channel. There was nothing about Amahl Sahman—even the broadsheets had relegated it to page ten for the time being—but the droning voices discussing the possible significance of the GEM's analyses of the latest sea water analyses, insect counts and soil laterization statistics were strangely reassuring in the wake of his bizarre day. If it hadn't been for Gwynplaine, he thought, he could have taken a real pride and satisfaction in adding Mrs. Gregory K. Allison to his client list, but now he had seen that damnable book, the prospect of enhancing that list with all Mrs. Allison's envious friends seemed trivial and unimportant.

The traffic was as heavy as ever, in spite of the latest hike in fuel prices; it seemed that motorists in the capital still took the inexorable escalation in their stride, prepared to pay whatever it cost to maintain their habits and their lifestyles—and no one any longer seemed concerned about saving for a future that might turn into Hell at a moment's notice. While the entire human race was living beyond its means, so the popular thinking went, why should any individual behave differently? There were no serious delays, though, and Victory had always considered the Bentley pastiche a car worth driving slowly; the days when Green Warriors used to throw stones at it seemed to be long gone.

When the vehicle was safely stowed away in another subterranean hidey-hole the surgeon climbed up to the flat, every step seeming to increase his tiredness. He ordered a meal from a local restaurant, and printed out an evening newspaper to while away the time as he awaited its delivery. There was nothing about his Herculean labours in the paper either, although there were plenty more alarmist statistics.

By the time Victory had eaten, it was almost time for bed—which virtually ensured that his dreams would not be pleasant—but he wound down as best he could by watching a sketch show on TV and finishing the bottle of wine that had been delivered with his meal. He never touched his computer terminal, and even contrived to avoid much more thought about the day's remarkable events.

He was undressed and about to climb into bed when the phone rang. When he saw NUMBER WITHHELD on the display he snatched back his hand to let the answering machine take the call, but he hovered nearby to listen, just in case it was something other than a nuisance call.

After the beep, a male voice immediately began speaking, with not the least hint of hesitation or uncertainty.

"I fear that you'll never see the book again, Dr. Victory," the voice said. "Gwynplaine will make you work from photocopies. You might want to make copies of your own, no matter what warnings he gives you. There are people who'll pay handsomely for copies of the copies, and the time might come when you'll be glad of that opportunity. If and when Gwynplaine tells you who he really is, you really ought to try to believe him. You probably won't be able to, but if you don't try, you won't stand any chance at all of figuring out what's happening."

As the voice drew to an apparent close, Victory snatched up the phone, scared that the messenger might simply ring off.

"Who are you?" he demanded, bluntly. "What do you want?"

The voice laughed. "You wouldn't believe me if I told you," it said. "Think of me as a friend who calls you up occasionally just to keep you up to date on how things seem to be going, and to tip you off if things seem to be getting hot. For now, you can call me Asmodeus."

The name rang a faint bell, but Victory couldn't place it; it seemed potentially more expressive, as pseudonyms went, than Gwynplaine, and he thought that it might be revealing once he had looked it up. "Fine," Victory said, "but who are you really? I'll do my best to try to believe you."

The voice laughed again. "We'll have to learn to trust one another first. I'm a fair dealer, though; I'm always prepared to give away information for free, as a gesture of goodwill. There are more people on to Gwynplaine than he suspects, and news of that sort tends to travel fast. You'll have other calls, I'm sure.

You're not in any mortal danger, so far as I can tell, but there are some strange people mixed up in this, and a few of them have melodramatic tendencies. These are paranoid times, Dr. Victory, and people sometimes get scared of the silliest things. Be grateful that you and I are sane."

"And Gwynplaine? Is he sane?"

"I wouldn't go as far as to declare him sane, even though he and I are old friends. He's sincere, though, and he's definitely on the side of the angels, in spite of what others might think. Sleep well, Dr. Victory. You have a busy day tomorrow."

This time, Victory had no chance to get in a reply or a further question. As soon as the sentence was finished, the man who called himself Asmodeus rang off.

"Well," Victory murmured, "I'm grateful that I'm sane, but I'm far from sure about you." He wondered whether Asmodeus might be Rachel Rosenfeld's patient, but it seemed unlikely that she would have rushed off to tell a client that the man whose office was downstairs from hers had buttonholed her in the underground garage to ask about the subject of his delusions. What he had said to the psychotherapist wasn't protected by any formal principle of confidentiality, but everything he knew about Dr. Rosenfeld, gleaned from brief conversations *en passant*, suggested that she was a thoroughly professional person, with a professional person's habits of discretion. It was surely more likely that Gwynplaine was under observation—that rumour of his appointment with Victory had somehow been spread, or that he had actually been followed to Harley Street from wherever he was lodging.

There was a pile of books on the bedside cabinet, one of which was a dictionary that Victory used when doing cryptic crosswords. He picked it up on the off chance, even though he presumed that Asmodeus must be a proper name, and looked for the word.

Proper name or not, there it was. *Asmodeus: the demon of anger and lust in Jewish demonology, sometimes ranked as king of the demons, with Lilith as his queen; also known as "the devil on two sticks" by virtue of his depiction as a cripple on crutches in a satirical novel by Alain-René le Sage.*

"Now what," Victory said to himself, aloud, "could a lame demon of lust possibly want with a plastic surgeon?"

He chuckled as he closed the dictionary again, and got into bed.

CHAPTER FIVE

The Second Day: Morning

As Victory drove to the hospital the next morning he kept his mind focused entirely on Amahl Sahman—not only the difficult work that he still had to do, but also the heroic work he had successfully completed.

He remembered the day that the boy had been flown into Heathrow from Amman. Once all the diplomatic formalities were out of the way and Victory finally got Amahl to himself, he had been able to obtain a far better idea of the magnitude of his task than had been provided by photographs and awkwardly-translated medical notes. At that point, he had almost regretted accepting the challenge: to look at Amahl's face in the flesh was daunting in the extreme. It was almost impossible to believe that any human agency could correct such a natural catastrophe.

Although Amahl's condition was extremely rare, in a purely statistical sense, it had become almost commonplace in the annals of modern plastic surgery, by virtue of providing a kind of ultimate challenge that every surgeon worth his salt had to be enthusiastic to tackle. Most of the surgeons who got the chance, however, were able to tackle the syndrome at a much earlier developmental stage, working with patients who were only three or four years old. Amahl was ten.

Shorn of the jargon, what had happened to poor Amahl was that the bones in the front of his skull, which should have conjoined and neatly fused together during embryonic development, had failed to do so, sprawling messily within his flesh. As he had grown older, the sprawl had become increasingly exaggerated, and the flesh they were supposed to support had been subjected to ever-greater stresses. The effect on his features had been worse than horrid—far worse, Victory now thought, than anything the legendary comprachicos would ever have been able to contrive in their quest for the ultimate in human grotesquery.

Amahl's mouth and tongue had been functional, in the elementary sense that he could swallow liquids and some solids, and make noises that were sometimes intelligible. His nose had been functional too, in that he had a sense of smell, and his vision had been reasonably good, in spite of the abnormally wide spacing of his eyes. The distortion of those features, however, had gone far beyond the merely unesthetic. Amahl had had great difficulty chewing because his disparate jaws offered little leverage, and his lips had been permanently twisted. His distorted palates had been prone to ulcers. His over-exposed nasal membranes and sinuses had produced mucus continuously, as if afflicted by an eternal allergic reaction to life itself. The fissures in the upper part of his skull, though not wide, had rendered his brain very vulnerable to penetration. He had been very lucky to survive so long, and would not have had long to live if left untreated, even if he had continued to avoid all the accidents that might finish him off instantly.

Ten years before, or even three, the task facing a plastic surgeon in Victory's position would have been merely to improvise a structure of bone and flesh that was capable of sustaining the child's life into adulthood, and to produce a face that was sufficiently well-ordered to be recognizably human. The best result possible would have been extreme ugliness. Victory's peers had already done better, albeit with more promising raw material, and Victory had intended to do better still. With the equipment at his disposal, he had been confident all along that he could do far more than merely manoeuvre the bones into a rough approximation of the plan incarnate in human cytoplasm; he could aspire to reproducing that plan exactly, and perhaps better than nature had ever been capable of achieving. Nor had he had to be satisfied with the prospect of making a patchwork out of the irremediably distorted cytoarchitecture of the facial flesh. That too he had legitimately hoped to restore to the state that nature would have dictated, had its scheme not gone awry—and in that respect too, he still had every chance of aiming beyond mere normality to produce a handsome face, charming as well as flawless.

There was a sense in which Amahl, now that the position of his facial bones had been adjusted, offered far more promising clay for moulding than any of Victory's incipiently elderly patients in search of renewal. The child's flesh was still innately capable of further growth and shaping; it could cooperate with the work that Victory wanted and intended to do, adding its own energies to his. He would be working with the grain of time, not against it. He could not only save the boy's life, and make him fit for any human company; he was free to exceed that brief if he cared to, and attempt something exceptional: to produce a face that was not merely beautiful in its present appearance but had the capacity to grow more beautiful still as Amahl matured to adulthood.

Victory had operated on many other children, including some whose amendments had to be categorized as cosmetic rather than remedial, but he had always done so in a spirit of minimal intervention. He had done what he had been paid to do, or had offered to do for free, as economically as possible. He had tried to bear future probabilities and possibilities in mind, but always in a precautionary spirit. He had never felt free to indulge himself fully in *speculative* endeavour. Amahl's case had offered, and still offered, that kind of scope—not merely because of the extreme predicament of the patient, but because Victory believed that he was entirely ready to make the attempt.

The fact that Gwynplaine had shown up in his office, Victory told himself, was really an irrelevance. Whatever plan he decided to follow—and he could not believe for a moment that he would be unable to devise one himself that would be considerably better than anything in Gwynplaine's book—he would have to be prepared to venture further than he ever had before. He would have to be eager to invent and to improvise, to make his bid to improve on nature.

There were no reporters waiting for him at the hospital, although the trust's public relations officer, Christina Legrange, came to intercept him before he stepped into Amahl's room. She was a tall woman of about forty; Victory longed to reshape and restock her eyebrows, and trim the excess fat from her cheeks. "I know you're busy, Hugo," she said, "but if you could let me have a progress report so I can put it in today's noon press release, I'd be very grateful. We need all the good publicity we can get, at present."

"I'll phone you when I'm through, Chris," Victory promised her, "but I have to get back to Harley Street as soon as I can, to work on the software. It's going to be a long day. By the way, do you know who Amahl's legal guardian is?"

"Not offhand," the press officer replied. "I can probably look it up. All the consent forms were signed and sealed long ago—you have a virtual *carte blanche*. There isn't a problem, is there?"

"No, I was just curious," Victory told her, blandly. "I was wondering what would happen to him afterwards—he won't be going back to the refugee camp, will he?"

"No, there's no possibility of that. He doesn't have any family there now. I think he'll be staying in this country, at least for a while. If he goes back to the Middle East eventually, he'll be fixed up with proper schooling and a decent place to live."

"Thanks," Victory said. "I'll get the report to you well before noon."

Amahl seemed to be glad to see him. The child had always been remarkably patient and docile, but in the beginning it had been mere passivity; nowadays, there was a glint in his eye that was definitely hopeful, even though the boy had not yet seen a picture of the face that would be his when it was all over.

Victory had been forced to admire the way the boy had stood up to the stress of repeated surgery. Children far less afflicted than Amahl tended to learn the arts of meek endurance very quickly, but they also tended to lose their ingrained habit as repeated anaesthesia confused their brains. Amahl had never had any substantial education, and would probably have been classified way below the "special needs" category had anyone bothered to test his cognitive abilities, but his very innocence afforded him a measure of protection against disorientation and anxiety.

The boy still could not understand a word of English, but Victory talked to him anyway while he made his examination, making the most of his tone of voice. "It's not going to be easy," he told the boy. "The last few months must have seemed like years, but the longest days of all will be the ones making up the next fortnight. If all goes well, you'll only need to go into the theatre once more after tomorrow, but it'll be the longest and most difficult session of all, and if anything goes awry you'll be straight back in. You'll hardly have time to recover from the disorientating effects of the first dose of anaesthetic before you're being prepped again. We'll keep the pain under control, of course, but that will only make you feel more out of it. You've been in an alien place since day one, though, and you've coped very well. You can do this. I don't know many who could, but I know that you can—and it *will* end. Or, rather, it won't. The cutting and shaping will end, but your life will begin—really begin. All it requires is patience, and your real life will be under way at last. The nightmare part will be over."

Amahl was looking up at him, still unable to focus on Victory's face in spite of the fact that the distance between his eyes had been considerably reduced, but attentive nevertheless. The boy's ears, had they been seen in isolation, would have seemed very ordinary, and his hearing had never been significantly impaired.

Victory's assistant, Majeke Hemlet, came hurrying into the room then, as if expecting a severe dressing-down for being late—but Victory only nodded in acknowledgement of her appearance. She was only twenty-six, barely past her basic keyhole training, but Victory had favoured her over more experienced candidates because he felt that her lack of ingrained habits and preconceptions would be an asset as she learned to use the machine. Thus far, she had only worked with the simplest programs, but she was ready and very eager to try more ambitious projects, and her interest in Amahl's case was appropriately intense.

"I was just explaining to Amahl that he won't be aware of the situation getting better for a little while yet," Victory said, as Majeke handed over the data she had brought. Before looking at it he looked down at his patient again, and continued talking directly to the boy: "It will get better, though. You've already come a long way, and now the goal is in sight. I'll finish the job—depend on that. Nothing will ever be able to drag you back to where you were, not even death itself. When you die—which won't be for a long time—you'll die knowing that you lived, knowing that you could look the world in the face. You're going to make it, and when you finally emerge from the drugged haze, you're going to be profoundly glad that you did. You're going to be so proud, so pleased, so much a winner that you'll likely feel better than anyone else in the world has ever had the opportunity to feel. No one else has ever been where you've been and emerged to take an honoured place in human society; you'll be the first."

The uncomprehending child attempted some kind of reply, or at least a gesture of vague assent. The sound that emerged from his carefully remodelled lips did not seem at all plaintive, but strangely matter-of-fact.

"Quite so," Victory said, continuing to talk while he scanned the notes. "A little more practice, and you'll be able to pronounce every syllable in your language and mine. I can't quite promise you the face of an angel, but you'll be an Adam of sorts nevertheless. The world will be your Eden, even if you do eventually have to go back to some miserable strip of desert way too close for comfort to the pollution footprint of the Temple nuke, to live on UN handouts."

When he paused, Majeke took up where he left off. "That's unlikely, by the way," she said. "You're already famous, Amahl. The interim reports don't generate headlines any more, but when Dr. Victory is done, the headlines will be even bigger than the ones you got when your plane first landed. When you're finally ready to leave the hospital, the paparazzi will be flocking around like greedy seagulls. You and Dr. Victory will probably be on all the chat shows, so it would be a really good move to learn a few words of English for your remade tongue to pronounce, if you can. You'll have a speech therapist, of course, but there won't be much time for you to make headway before the media exposure starts—you'd best make the most of what you have."

Amahl spoke again, seemingly content to generate sound without making overmuch effort to shape its into syllables—but Victory could detect a clear difference between the sounds he was making now and those he had been making a few weeks before.

"That's right," said Victory. "It *would* be better if Majeke could do the chat shows with you. She's so much more photogenic than me, and it's all natural, although she'll need some work on those incipient cheek-pouches before she's much older, and her lips could do with being a trifle fuller." He took the boy's hand in his in order to shake it. "We'll show them, you and I, what a good team can accomplish. Majeke and I will leave you to the nurses now. They have some tests to do, but there shouldn't be anything worse than mild discomfort. We'll get down to serious work tomorrow, and then we'll go flat out until we reach the finishing line."

"What's wrong with my lips?" Majeke demanded, as they left the room and made their ay to the team meeting. "They're absolutely fine the way they are."

"Of course they are," Victory agreed. "But I had to say something to make the kid feel better about himself, didn't I?"

"You could have mentioned the worry lines around your own eyes, and those suspicious bags. Are you getting enough sleep?"

"Bags under the eyes aren't caused by lack of sleep," Victory told her. "That's an old wives' tale. Not that I have any."

"I'm on call Saturday night," Majeke said. "I could do a little slice-and-shut then, with an old-fashioned scalpel. Or I could squeeze you into my Sunday list, if you insist on the machine."

"Ah," Victory aid, "I'm afraid I'll have to steal your Sunday slot. Something's come up."

"Something urgent or something rich?"

"Wealth gives birth to urgency," Victory riposted.

"It sure does," his assistant replied. "That's why the ecosphere is rushing to destruction." By this time they had reached the room where the team meeting was to be held; had the anaesthetist and the nurses not been waiting there, Majeke might well have made a stronger protest, but in the event she contented herself with adding: "I will need to make the time up as soon as possible, Dr. Victory. I need the practice if I'm to keep making progress."

"Of course you do," Victory said. "I'll try to make it up to you by passing on one or two of my operations. I'll need to reduce my own burden if I'm to maintain the concentration that Amahl's case requires."

"Thanks," Majeke said. "I will be assisting on Sunday, I presume?"

"Of course. It's not a difficult operation, but it is an important one. I need you there."

When the meeting eventually closed, having settled all outstanding business, Victory went back to his office to finish up his own paperwork. He remembered to phone through his report to

Christina Legrange before he went back to the Bentley. "Have the Allisons been in touch with you, Chris?" he asked, when he had assured her that Amahl's case was on track and given her the relevant details.

"Yes they have," she said. "Very clever of her to slip in and out while the media will be looking the other way—but Gregory K. knows all about that, of course. We'll doubtless get our share of the glory eventually, when she begins to show off her new face. Good luck tomorrow, Hugo."

"Luck," Victory assured her, "has nothing to do with it. Did you manage to find out who Amahl's official guardian is, by the way?"

"No—the files are all marked CONFIDENTIAL and sealed. I'm afraid you'll have to go all the way up to the chief exec's office to get clearance to open them. It's probably just a formality, but you know how these things are."

"Sure," he said. "No problem."

It was already ten-forty when he steered the Bentley out of the hospital car park, but he would have been in Harley Street before eleven if there hadn't been a standstill caused by an accident in Newman Street. The usual silent assembly of gawpers had accumulated, looking doubly sinister because nine out of ten of the fascinated watchers were staring through tinted spectacles mounted atop bulky filter-masks. Victory wondered, as the car waited to pass through, whether the new fashion might really be a response to the density of modern CC-TV cameras, bidding to recover the long-lost anonymity of faces in crowds. He eventually arrived at his consulting room at twenty past.

Gwynplaine was sitting patiently in the reception area, dressed exactly as he had been on the previous day, holding his briefcase on his knees in exactly the same defensive posture as before.

"Sorry to keep you waiting, Mr. Gwynplaine," Victory said, before consulting Claire about incoming messages. Gwynplaine continued to wait patiently until Victory was able to say: "Come on through."

"How did things go at the hospital?" Gwynplaine enquired, as he divested himself of his coat and filter-mask. Once he was seated he took off his spectacles as well.

"As well as can be expected," Victory replied. "Have you brought the book?"

"I thought it best to leave it in a safe place," Gwynplaine told him. "I've brought the photocopies of the relevant pages, as I promised, with translations of the accompanying texts. They'll be entirely adequate for our purposes." He began pulling sheets of paper out of his briefcase and laying them separately on the desk.

The color photocopies seemed sharp and bright, and the translated annotations were neatly inscribed, but Victory soon found reason to protest. "They're not all here," he said. "The sequence is incomplete."

Gwynplaine looked at him steadily. "There's far more here than you need for the initial operation," he said. "There's also enough to bring the program for the fleshwork to the brink of completion. If all goes well, I'll give you the last two pages when the time comes."

"I'm the surgeon—and the programmer," Victory objected. "I think I ought to be the one who decides when it's necessary for me to have the data."

"I have to take certain precautions," Gwynplaine said, his face as expressionless as ever and his tortured voice as plaintive.

"Don't you trust me?" Victory complained.

"I have far more trust in you than you can possibly have in me," Gwynplaine replied, equably, "but that's not the issue. There are good reasons for not bringing your computer programs to their final state until it's necessary to do so."

"What reasons?"

All Gwynplaine said in reply to that was: "We'll have to proceed very carefully when the time comes. By then, hopefully, we'll both have learned to trust one another a little better. We'll need to."

"It won't be easy," Victory said. "Trust comes with knowledge and understanding. At present, I have no idea what your real name is, or where you live, or what your ultimate objectives are."

"I want to recreate the face of Adam," the fire-scarred man told him, flatly. "I have no home, and it really doesn't matter where I'm staying. As for my real name...as I told you before, I never underwent any formal ceremony, and thus have no given name. Gwynplaine is as true a name as any I've ever used. Thus far, the only one of us who has entrusted the other with any information of value is me."

"And I suppose," Victory said, not knowing how injudicious it might be, "that if you were to tell me who you really are, I wouldn't believe you."

Gwynplaine did not seem particularly surprised by this observation, but he did lower his eyes in what might have been a gesture of disappointment. "Someone else knows that I have come here," he inferred. "You've been contacted. May I ask by whom?"

"I don't know," Victory said. "He used a pseudonym too."

"Was it Asmodeus?"

Victory hadn't wanted to give so much away so soon, but he felt sure that Gwynplaine would be able to read his reflexive reaction to the name. "That's what he called himself," he agreed, only a little reluctantly.

"He's an interested party," Gwynplaine said. "He'll keep watch as best he can, but he certainly won't spread the news around. I don't mind your talking to him in the least; you may tell him whatever you wish. Be careful, though. There are other interested parties, some of whom might not be so friendly."

"Are you suggesting that someone might be willing to kill me in order to stop me doing what you want?"

"I doubt it, but it's not impossible. People have tried to kill *me* before now—but then, there are people who might be willing to kill me simply to acquire the book for themselves. None of the parties who have long taken an interest in the book or the project will think it justified to use violence to stop you—indeed, the greater number of them would prefer that you complete your part of it—but a lunatic fringe has sprung up recently, of individuals whose notions of the project and its likely consequences are seriously deluded. Were one of them to discover your involvement, I couldn't entirely guarantee your safety. I can assure you, though, that neither I nor Asmodeus means you any harm, and that either one of us would do what he could to protect you if we became aware of any imminent danger."

"You're not being very specific," Victory said, bluntly. "Everybody from whom I've sought information seems extremely reluctant to give me any straight answers."

"Everyone?" Gwynplaine repeated, sharply. "Do you mean that you have discussed it with someone other than Asmodeus?"

"I did some background research on the web," Victory told him. "I also consulted one of my colleagues. I was interested to know what the word *comprachicos* might signify to the average educated person."

"Ah," Gwynplaine said. "And what did Dr. Rosenfeld have to say?"

Victory nodded his head, unsurprised by the accuracy of Gwynplaine's guess. "You mentioned her name yesterday," he said. "I thought at the time that you'd simply read it on the plaque outside the front door on your way in—but then she clammed up tight as soon as I mentioned the word, and it seemed like a little too much of a coincidence. Do you know her patient, then? I mean the one whose confidence she couldn't violate by talking about comprachicos. It wouldn't be your friend Asmodeus, by any chance?"

"No," Gwynplaine replied. "Asmodeus has no need to seek help from a psychotherapist. It won't be any inconvenience to us that someone with an interest in the comprachicos should have chosen to consult a neighbour of yours, and I dare say that it's a coincidence—unless, of course, people have been set to watch this building in anticipation of the possibility that I might contact you. I should have anticipated that, I suppose, but I couldn't have done anything about it if I had."

"You think that someone might have registered as a patient with Dr. Rosenfeld simply to get access to the building?"

"It's not impossible. I should warn you, Dr. Victory, not to believe everything you might hear said about me. As I've already told you, some of the people interested in my ambitions are seriously deluded about the nature of my project."

"Whereas I have the advantage of knowing nothing at all about it."

"On the contrary, Dr. Victory. You know everything except that which you could not, at present, believe. You might enable me to recreate the face of Adam, with the aid of a three-hundred-year-old book. Given that you think that I'm mad merely for believing that, what more could I possibly add that would not increase the margin of my apparent insanity? What matters for the present, Dr. Victory, is what is described in these images and instructions, and what *you* believe the result of following the instructions might be. I can't imagine that it will take long to convince you that you can do no possible harm if you do as I ask. The manipulations you will be asked to carry out will not in any way threaten the well-being of Amahl Sahman."

"Can you guarantee that the crazies who might want to kill me to prevent my replicating the face of Adam won't direct their murderous intentions towards him?" Victory asked.

Gwynplaine thought about that for a moment, then said: "Again, I doubt it, although it's not inconceivable. On the other hand, I doubt that you can guarantee that the child will not be endangered by the operations themselves, whether or not you take my proposals aboard. It's my sincere belief that if you follow my plan, you will actually reduce that risk, to a greater extent than the slight additional risk of assassination by a madman. We must study the diagrams now, so that you may be convinced of that fact. I'm surprised, quite frankly, that you have hesitated so long. I would not have thought that a man like you would be so eager to waste time, when there is so much of such great interest spread out before your eyes."

Victory accepted the rebuke, and consented to scrutinize the images that Gwynplaine had arranged on the desktop.

CHAPTER SIX

The Second Day: Afternoon and Evening

Almost as soon as he began to inspect the documents with minute care, Victory was absorbed into his study, captivated once again. It was not only the amazing skill of the anatomical representations that captured him, but the daring of what they proposed. This time, he could read the captions and the notes, and he soon realised that they were at least as astonishing as the diagrams themselves.

It required only a few minutes for Victory to assure himself that, if he were to undertake the series of modifications indicated in the first diagram, the patient thus treated would be well on the way to acquiring a face that would be at least as expressive as any he had ever designed before. A few minutes further inspection allowed him to insert himself, imaginatively, into the sequence of operations sufficiently to grasp something of its aesthetic logic. Had the sequence been more orthodox, he might have been able to conjure up an approximate image of the face itself, but the sequence of amendments was not orthodox, by the standards of modern plastic surgery, and he could not lay imaginary skin upon the remodelled muscles with any confidence. He was certain that the face would not be ugly or plain, but the exact quality of its beauty lay frustratingly out of his grasp. Its general conformity was easy enough to perceive, but its individuality was not.

Victory felt a conviction growing in him that the face described by the comprachicos' specifications would indeed be subtly unlike any other, and that it would be powerful in some indefinable way, but he could not see it in his mind's eye—and while he could not visualise the face, he was unwilling to trust his feeling.

The surgeon knew that the admission he had drawn from Gwynplaine that what they were proposing to do *might* endanger his patient, if only indirectly, had given him an excuse to back out immediately, if he cared to use it—but he knew that he would not. Gwynplaine had won again; the preliminary phase of their bargain remained sealed, even if the possibility of future hesitation had been carefully conserved. Victory could see no reason why he should not use the earliest phases of the sequence as a basis for the following day's operation; whether this was the face of a hypothetical Adam or not, its basic conformation was perfectly sound. There was no obvious reason why the final reshaping of Amahl's facial bones could not comply with this pattern.

When Victory began to compare the implications of the photocopies with the provisional figures he had already established in his program for Wednesday's surgery, he soon discovered that there was a closer correspondence between the two than he had expected, or seemed plausible as a matter of pure chance. As Gwynplaine had suggested, the provisional plan he had made, in response to Amahl's apparent needs, only required its own innate logic to be expanded to fall into closer step with the comprachicos' schema. He could not see any way to improve on the specifications contained in the photocopies, although he had to admit that, if he had not seen the photocopies, he might not have been able to attain the apparent optimum they suggested.

He looked up at Gwynplaine, but Gwynplaine already seemed to know what he was going to say.

"The world has been waiting for this for more than three hundred and fifty years," said the man with the disfigured face, "and perhaps for more than three and a half thousand. However little you believe of what I've told you, you do know that this might be an epoch-making project, don't you?"

"It might," Victory conceded. "But there's a long way to go before I can be sure of that."

When the surgeon had talked to her in the garage, Rachel Rosenfeld has expressed the belief that the comprachicos were macabre butchers, some few of whom might have entertained vague and hopeless delusions of grandeur. The more he studied Gwynplaine's photocopies, however, the more convinced Victory became that it was not so. However they had gained their knowledge, there was no doubting that the comprachico surgeons—or whoever had taken it upon himself to fake their work—had an extraordinarily sophisticated understanding of the complex musculature of the face. The people who had made these illustrations had been intimately interested in improvement as well as disfigurement, and they were true artists, perhaps equal in stature to Victory himself.

Surgery, Victory knew, had been the most effective component of the medical arsenal for centuries before the advent of Pasteur's germ theory and the organic chemistry that had paved the way for the discovery and synthesis of the powerful armaments of the modern pharmacopeia. Even before the domestication of effective anaesthetics, surgeons had saved many lives that would otherwise have been lost—but they had done so by such crude methods as amputation and the Caesarean section. The surgeons of the official historical record had come by their anatomical knowledge belatedly, and what they had learned from their dissections had accumulated very gradually. Victory had never imagined it possible that there might be esoteric surgeons who knew far more, maintaining the secrecy of their wisdom and their practices—but if the originals of these photocopied diagrams really did date from the seventeenth century, they put the most fanciful tales of the secret wisdom of medieval herbalists and magicians firmly in the shade.

"This is an extremely ambitious series of interventions," he told Gwynplaine, eventually. "The early phases would be simple, given that I can reshape the facial bones, but if I were to follow the sequence through it would eventually require me to sever and relocate the anchorages of eight different muscles. There can be no guarantee that the nerves will function properly when the reconnections heal, even assuming that they all heal."

"But you've performed similar operations before," Gwynplaine said.

"Not on such a scale. It's true, I suppose, that Amahl would be the ideal patient on which to attempt such a radical series, given the unsatisfactory nature of many of his existing anchorages and insertions, but I hadn't planned on attempting to be quite as ambitious."

"The final modification of the bone-structure will make the work easier," Gwynplaine said, keeping his voice as neutral as possible, given its innate awkwardness.

"The writer of these instructions obviously assumed that the underlying bone-structure would have to be a fortunate natural occurrence, discovered after assiduous searching. Given that I can actually create the contours, that part of the job will be straightforward—and you're right, it will facilitate the later stages sketched out here. Even so, there are some moves that I wouldn't have thought of attempting. I've always tried to work without disturbing the attachments, by sculpting the muscles themselves."

"You will be able to reduce that kind of endeavour considerably if you use this approach," Gwynplaine said. "That is why I believe that you will actually decrease the risk inherent in the long period of anaesthetization the boy will have to endure."

"The instructions aren't *completely* clear," Victory complained. "Even if we can work out exactly what's meant, it will require a lot of work to refine my computer programs in order to take aboard these kinds of restructuring. Tomorrow's task I can handle easily enough; if I were to attempt a reconfiguration of

Monday's sequence along these lines I might test my computer skills to destruction. My programs aren't just for drawing up plans and creating an anticipatory display; they play a leading role in the active control of the nanoscalpels. I don't know if I can test this sequence rigorously enough to trust it, even if I can make the necessary modifications to the software."

"Let's take things one step at a time, Dr. Victory," Gwynplaine said. "Are you willing to keep further options open by accommodating the preliminary modifications into Wednesday's operation?"

Victory hesitated for more than a minute, but eventually said: "I don't see what harm it can do. Up to that point, at least, it's a sound plan, not too different from the one I'd have designed if I'd never seen these diagrams."

"Good. Let's proceed on that basis."

"I won't be able to go much further, even in terms of a purely hypothetical model, without seeing the final pages."

"There's a good deal that can be done in advance—but I promise you that I'll show you the final pages in good time to make the final modifications, before the last phase of the treatment begins—Sunday afternoon, at the latest."

"There'll be no time on Sunday; I'm operating on that day. I'll need the full sequence on Friday if I'm to have any real chance of producing a computer simulation of the operative sequence."

Gwynplaine seemed to be considering the matter, but when he spoke, it was to say: "You must be operating on the woman who came out of your office yesterday, before I came in. You mentioned my name in her hearing, but not *vice versa*. Was it Mrs. Allison, by any chance?"

"That's none of your business," Victory told him.

"But she is the person you're operating on this Sunday? You weren't scheduled to use the machine when I first checked."

"Again," Victory said, "that's not your concern. How, exactly, did you manage to check out the rota for the machine?"

"I have a few computer skills of my own," Gwynplaine muttered. "If I had realised that Mrs. Allison might get in the way of our business...I'll get the final pages to you on Saturday. That will be time enough; the final modifications are very subtle and they won't require any radical reprogramming. The only departures from your normal procedures are right in front of you, as you've already observed. This is the way the job requires to be done, Dr. Victory. I don't ask you to trust me, but I do ask you to trust yourself. As you begin to accommodate these instructions into your plan, you'll gain in confidence. You'll see the logic of what we're doing—and the artistry."

Victory experienced a sudden flash of inspiration. "You don't want me to preview the result," he guessed. "You don't want me to be able to produce an image of the face of Adam on the computer before I begin to produce it in the flesh. I'm afraid it's necessary—I can't proceed without it."

"Of course you can," Gwynplaine countered. "It might well be necessary that you should. To see a reflection of the Divine Countenance in a human being is one thing; to see it on a computer screen might be something else entirely. I have no way of knowing what effect it would have on you, but I'd rather not take the chance."

"I thought you believed that it would ignite religious faith in me, and make me avid for the Kingdom of God," Victory said. "I think you should let me worry about the effect it might have if I see the preview."

"I'm sorry, Dr. Victory," Gwynplaine said, patiently, "but I can't let you worry about yourself when you have no idea what's at stake. I'll tell you everything I can, but until you've fully appreciated the miraculous artistry of what you'll be doing, you won't be able to believe me—and perhaps not even then. I have your best interests at heart, Dr. Victory—please humour me in this."

Victory no longer had any desire to humour Gwynplaine, but he knew that the other choice was already unacceptable. The sequence of operations described by the photocopies was too intriguing to be left untranslated into his own language. The plan was highly original, but he could already see the merits of Gwynplaine's argument about grasping the logic and artistry as he became more accustomed to its underlying train of thought.

There seemed to be no reason why the process couldn't work. He had modified muscle insertions before, though not in such a wholesale fashion. There had occasionally been healing problems, and sometimes consequent problems in the action of the relocated muscles, but those problems had mostly been a reflection of the advanced age of the patients. In a boy of Amahl's age, the techniques ought to work...but there was no way to be sure of the collective effect of the set of modifications, unless Victory were permitted to model the result in the virtual space of his computer. Until he obtained the final details he needed to set up that model, he would be working in the dark.

"You're asking a great deal, Mr. Gwynplaine," he said, weakly.

"I'm offering a great deal," Gwynplaine retorted. "Not just the book itself but the sum of what it contains: the accumulated knowledge and developed philosophy of the comprachicos."

"And what you get out of it is a reproduction of the face of Adam: a face whose mere existence the comprachicos allegedly thought capable of bringing about a renewal of faith sufficient to precipitate the last judgment. If that were true, my newly acquired knowledge wouldn't be of much practical value, would it?"

"Whatever effect the boy's face might have could not be instantaneous," Gwynplaine pointed out, mildly. "He would probably need to grow to maturity before it could have its full and final effect—an effect that would have to compete with the unfolding ecocatastrophe."

Victory looked down at the photocopied images again. "The programs would have to be modified in the light of Amahl's progress in any case," he mused. "Given that the bones still have to undergo the final phase of their preliminary remoulding...." He paused, and then began again: "If a seventeenth-century surgeon really did set out to follow this plan with nothing but his own hand to guide blades as large and blunt as the scalpels of that era, he must have had astonishing faith in the steadiness of his hand and the eyes of a true artist. I doubt that even a native speaker of the original language could have found the instructions entirely clear."

"You only have to step into the National Gallery to witness the fact that there were men in the past with steadier hands and keener eyes than anyone alive today," Gwynplaine said. "But your technology will compensate for the deterioration of the species, as it does in every other compartment of modern life. As to the lack of final clarity in the instructions, I'm prepared to trust your instincts. If you'll only study the procedures with due care, and incorporate them into your computer programs with due diligence, I'm certain that their logic will become increasingly clear to you—and their creativity too. There's as much art in this business as science, as you know full well."

There was no point in further procrastination, so Victory said: "I'll get started on the reprogramming right away. We need to get on with it, if I'm to have the initial programs ready for tomorrow."

"I'm ready," Gwynplaine said.

"There won't be much for you to do. You'll have to be patient—but I might need you, so you can't go just yet."

"That's all right," Gwynplaine said. "I'd like to stay, while I can. I'll take a look at some of your books, if I may."

Victory nodded. "Be my guest," he said—and since the die was irredeemably cast, he set to work.

They sent out for lunch, and dinner too. Claire brought both meals in on trays, neatly set out with stainless steel cutlery and crystal glasses. She gave no outward sign of thinking that there was anything unusual in Gwynplaine's continued presence, although her curiosity must have been working in overdrive.

"Mrs. Allison called to check the details of her admission," the secretary said, before leaving the room after delivering the second meal. "I've warned her that we can't guarantee the schedule absolutely. There were three more enquiries, but I told them all that we won't be scheduling any more consultations for four weeks. Two of them said they'd be more than happy to wait, so I booked them in for the first week in April."

"Thanks," Victory said, automatically. "You can go home now—you've put in enough overtime recently, and I'm very grateful."

"Yes, doctor," the secretary said, meekly. "Shall I see you tomorrow?"

"Probably not. I'll go straight to the hospital in the morning, and I'll probably go straight home when I finish there. All being well, I'll be able to call in first thing on Thursday before I clock in at King's."

"Right," Claire said. She turned to face the unmasked Gwynplaine before she went, and said: "Goodnight, Mr. Gwynplaine."

"If anyone should ask about me in the next few days," Gwynplaine said, mildly, "It might be better not to give them any specific information."

Claire looked at Victory, who nodded.

"No problem," she said.

When the secretary had gone, Victory looked at Gwynplaine inquisitively. "So it was Mrs. Allison I saw in your waiting room," Gwynplaine said, thoughtfully.

"What does the name mean to you?" Victory asked, sharply.

"It might be just a coincidence," Gwynplaine said, "but probably not. As I told you before, there are people who might have set sentries to keep an eye on you."

"Don't be ridiculous. Mrs. Allison is far too wealthy to serve as anyone's hireling. The fact that she had the appointment before yours is pure coincidence. How did you guess her name?"

"Perhaps I'd seen her before," Gwynplaine said. "Her picture, at least."

"I dare say that you had," Victory said, "but that's not why you put her name forward. What has Mrs. Allison got to do with your business?"

Gwynplaine hesitated, and then shrugged his shoulders. "Gregory K. Allison is Amahl Sahman's guardian," he said. "He arranged for the boy to come here, so that you might operate on him, and undertook to take care of him thereafter. If he knew all along that I would come to see you...well, this might be a more complicated business than I assumed. It changes nothing, though. Gregory Allison won't interfere. He'll probably summon you to see him, but he won't interfere."

"Are you saying that Gregory K. Allison has booked his wife in for surgery in between Amahl's operations so that he can keep a closer watch on what I'm doing?"

"Quite possibly. It doesn't matter. His people won't try to stop you. His involvement might get others excited, but it might also make them think twice before doing anything silly. Will Mrs. Allison be placed in a room near Amahl's?"

"Probably next door, given the hospital admin's notion of VIP treatment. Why?"

"It will enable her bodyguard to keep an eye on him too. That's a good thing, although I don't believe for an instant that the boy is in any danger. I doubt that Allison does, either—but he's an exceedingly careful man, by all accounts. Shouldn't we get back to work?"

Victory shook his head, to clear it rather than to signal negativity. He wondered what account Gregory K. Allison might give him of Gwynplaine, if the billionaire really did summon him for a chat in advance of the operations on his wife and his ward. He decided that he might as well get back to the point, though. "You're not intending to take these photocopies with you when you leave tonight, are you?" he asked. "That would be very inconvenient—especially if you were unable to return here when you intend to do so."

Gwynplaine shook his own head slowly, again more in confusion than denial. "You're right," he said, with a slight sigh that might have signified reluctance or regret. "You'll need access to them whether I'm here or not, so they'd better stay here—provided that that you have a safe place to keep them in."

"Perhaps I should make back-ups," Victory said.

The scarred man thought about that for a moment before saying: "It's up to you, but I really wouldn't advise it." His tone seemed carefully neutral even by his unexpressive standards. "You'll also have to make sure that the defences protecting your computer data are in good order. Given that our association doesn't seem to be a secret, your systems here and at the hospital might come under the scrutiny of some ingenious prying eyes."

"My safe is a good one," Victory said, "and my computer security is supposed to be the best. I try not to email hospital-related documents, even at the best of times—I keep data in transit about my person, if it's at all possible."

"Good," Gwynplaine said. "Could you direct me to the bathroom, please?"

Victory looked his temporary collaborator briefly in the eyes, but could not meet the other's gaze for long. He told his visitor where the lavatory was, and told him the codes that would enable him to return through the outer and inner doors of his consulting rooms.

When Gwynplaine had left the room Victory breathed a slight reflexive sigh of relief. Then he returned to work on the translation of the instructions contained in the photocopies into computer code.

Compared to the surrounding circumstances, the labour of translation now seemed perfectly straightforward and delicately elegant. The surgeon's sense of connection with the innate artistry of the comprachicos' plan increased again, and it seemed to him that he was being assisted to remember something that he had always known but never grasped—as if the face of Adam, and the face of God, had always been locked in some secret cavity within his soul, patiently awaiting rediscovery.

Victory was now certain in his own mind of two things, however: firstly, that he was absolutely determined to see a computer image of the face of Adam before he gave the slightest consideration to the possibility of moulding it in anyone's flesh; and secondly, that he did not trust Mr. Gwynplaine any further than he could throw a feather into a gale-force headwind.

CHAPTER SEVEN

The Third Day: Morning, Afternoon, and Evening

In the next three hours Victory had to call upon Gwynplaine three times to check the implications of the captions, but on each occasion the scarred man confirmed that Victory was correct in his estimations.

"That's good," Gwynplaine said, when they finally called it a day. "You've obviously mastered the fundamental logic of the operational sequence. You'll be able to work without me, if it's necessary." He watched with seeming approval as Victory put the photocopies in his safe and switched off his computer, then added: "Everything will go well tomorrow; I'm sure of it. Everything will go well from now until the end. We can do this, you and I."

"Perhaps," Victory agreed. "But who are you, really?

"I'm not who the others think I am," Gwynplaine replied. "Asmodeus knows more of the truth than anyone else, but even he can't know everything. The rest are fools or liars. Please accept me for what I am, Dr. Victory. Whatever I was before I was disfigured, and whatever I was made into thereafter, I'm my own man now. I'm just Gwynplaine—nothing more and nothing less, no matter what anyone else might think." By the time this statement was complete, the dark glasses, hood and filter-mask were all in place. He certainly didn't look like any ordinary man.

"You can use the elevator any time you like," Victory said, as he paused to double-lock the outer office. "The code to activate the side-door beside the car entrance is 62397. You might have a better chance of evading surveillance that way."

"Thank you, Dr. Victory," Gwynplaine said. "I'll do that."

They parted in the garage. Victory waited in his car until Gwynplaine had gone out before starting the imitation Bentley's engine. No sooner had it begun to purr, though, than his mobile phone rang. When he saw NUMBER WITHHELD on the display he muttered a curse, but he switched the engine off again and waited. As soon as the voice became audible on the answer-phone he gave it his full attention.

"If you're tempted to go back up to your office and make a second set of copies before you leave, Dr. Victory," Asmodeus said, "please don't take them with you back to your flat. I'm not the only one who knows about your arrangement, alas, and we're living in desperate times. Your office safe is probably secure, for the time being, if only because the others will be forming queues to keep watch on it—and the people who want the experiment to go through far outnumber those who'd like to prevent it, for the moment. The flat might be too tempting, and so might you, while you're in transit. If you decide to place a second set of copies at a second location, choose it very carefully—and try to make sure you're not followed there."

Victory picked up the phone. "I don't like the way this game is being played," he said. "I know you conspiracy buffs get off on all the cloak-and-dagger stuff, dropping mysterious hints by the score and never letting slip a single item of real information, but I'm a simple soul. If you want anything from me, now or ever, you'll have to give me something in return. Gwynplaine has given me something solid, so I'm prepared to play along with him for the time being, but what do you have to offer, Mr. Asmodeus? How's life as king of the demons, by the way? Is Lilith well?"

"Lilith and I have been divorced for some time," Asmodeus replied, in a tone whose amusement seemed genuine, "and I've abdicated as the demon king. I'm no longer the demon of anger, either—but lust might be a different matter, and envy too. As for solidity...that's actually what's at stake here, in a manner of speaking. I'm willing to make a gesture of good faith, if that's what you want. I won't tell you who Gwynplaine is—that's up to him—but I will tell you the name of the only other man in England who can understand the script in which the book is written, if you wish. Will that be enough to buy me the right to keep up to date with your progress?"

"I don't know," Victory said. "Will he be able to tell me anything interesting, about Gwynplaine or the book?"

"About Gwynplaine, no. About the book, yes. I think you'll be interested in what he knows—he's a much more reliable source, in regard to the legends of the comprachicos and other interested parties, than any you'll find by trawling the net."

"He wouldn't be Dr. Rosenfeld's patient, by any chance?"

"No, he wouldn't. He's perfectly sane—as solid as you could wish. What's more, he's right here in London, easily accessible by road or tube. I can even text you his home number."

"Go ahead," Victory said.

"He's Huw Williams, of University College. He's an expert in the history of Eastern European cultures, from the Bulgars and the Armenians to the Kazaks and the Ingush. Don't photocopy the pictures for him just yet, though. Start by making handwritten copies of some of the notes and instructions that Gwynplaine's translated for you. I doubt that he'll be able to correct Gwynplaine's translations, but he'll certainly be intrigued by the fact that you're asking. I don't know exactly how much he really knows, but at least he'll be coming at the problem from a direction that you can understand and endorse. How much you tell him about your involvement is, of course, up to you."

As soon as the sentence was finished, Asmodedus rang off. He didn't seem to believe in hellos and goodbyes. A few seconds later, however, the phone beeped and the promised number was texted through.

It only took Victory a few seconds to figure out that Asmodeus hadn't really given him very much, and perhaps nothing at all. If Huw Williams of University College was London's foremost expert on obscure Eastern European languages, anyone he cared to ask at King's, or any other location on the academic grapevine, would probably have pointed him in that direction—if he had thought to ask. Even so, it was a nudge in a direction that did, indeed, seem to Victory to be one that he could understand and trust.

He turned the radio on and drove home very carefully, keeping a lookout all the way for any vehicle that might be trailing him. He saw nothing, and heard nothing of real interest on the news, although the results of the latest clathrate survey, integrated only that morning into the Global Environmental Model, had sparked the usual apocalyptic mutterings. To make matters worse, the results of latest post-licensing surveys of the latest batch of DNA vaccines seemed to indicate that the possibility of mutational side-effects might not be as low as the original field trials had suggested.

As soon as he got home Victory switched on his domestic terminal and went to the UCL website. There really was a Huw Williams on the staff, with a publicly-accessible profile that had a photograph, a list of the courses on which he taught, and a selective list of publications, all of which did indeed seem to be related to the cultural history of Eastern Europe. The only contact information given there was an internal email address.

Victory rang the number that Asmodeus had texted him.

"Huw Williams," said the voice at the far end, after picking up on the fifth ring. The Welsh accent wasn't very strong, more suggestive of Swansea than Gwynedd.

"Is that Huw Williams of University College—the expert on Eastern Europe?"

"Yes. Who's calling, please?"

"This is Hugo Victory. I'm a plastic surgeon, currently doing most of my work at King's. You might have seen my name mentioned in the newspapers."

"You're the one who's been operating on the Palestinian boy."

"That's right. I'm sorry to trouble you, but in the course of some research I'm doing I've run across some exotic script, which appears to be in an obscure Eastern European language. I wonder if I might fax you a few samples when I finish work tomorrow evening, in the hope that you might be able to confirm that for me. If you could translate them, I'd be very grateful, but if not...."

Victor left the sentence dangling.

"I'll be happy to take a look," Williams said. "You can send the fax to this number, with the usual supplementary code. I'll take a look as soon as it's convenient. I've got your number here on my display; I'll store it so that I can phone you back when I've got an answer."

"Thanks very much," Victory said. "I'll look forward to hearing from you."

After hanging up the phone he went back to his terminal. He decanted copies of the specifications for Mrs. Allison's first operation from his key ring, and summoned up the image in which he intended to remake her. He studied it carefully, trying to see it not as his own goal but as the goal at which the surgeon who had operated on her twelve or fourteen years before might have been aiming. Was there some kinship, he wondered, between that endeavour and the one that Gwynplaine wanted him to carry out? Was it possible that Mrs. Gregory K. Allison had also been the subject of an experiment based on techniques developed by the comprachicos?

There was something in the face that moved him—not merely its beauty, but something further. When he had first built the program, he had taken full credit for the superlative work himself, but now he was not so sure. There was something in the as-yet-uncreated face that struck a chord within him, creating a resonance that he had never felt before.

All in the mind, he muttered, as he closed the file and shut down the computer. *There comes a point when obsession with one's work carries one beyond the bounds of reason—I must be closer to it than I thought.*

He had not transferred the results of the evening's labours to his key ring fob, so he could not decant those into the machine at the flat; even before receiving Asmodeus' warning, he had decided that discretion might be necessary on that account. He would be able to summon the program from his terminal at the hospital via a secure link that had been specially installed between King's and Harley Street.

He wound down by watching an American sitcom on TV, laughing along as if he too could see the signs telling the studio audience how to react. When he finally went to sleep, his dreams did not disturb him, and he forgot them all as soon as he awoke.

He listened to the news while he got ready for work, and was not unhappy to learn that the latest generation of anti-obesity pills had turned out to increase the risk of stomach and bowel cancer in seven out of eight mouse models. "If God had meant us to control our weight with pills," he told the radio, "he would never have invented liposuction. No biochemical method will ever be able to match the delicate refinements of nanoware surgery." He was fully aware, of course, that his so-called nanoscalpels were not nanotechnology in any literal sense, hardly qualifying as "micro-" in terms of their actual dimensions, but the modern fashion was to regard anything miniaturized as a step on the way to authentic nanotechnology, just as the fashion was to regard any significant advance in IT as a step on the way to authentic Artificial Intelligence; he was confident that the next generation of computer-assisted surgical instruments would further increase the secure lead his own profession currently held over its pharmaceutical rivals.

As he drove along Praed Street a filter-masked adolescent threw a stone at the Bentley, but vanished into the crowd of commuters emerging from Paddington Station before Victory could figure out whether it was a renascent Green Warrior or merely an envious vandal. The surface of the bonnet recovered from the dent within minutes and the smart paint had recovered its gloss by the time he turned into the hospital car park.

Victory lost no time in starting work. He had the operating machinery ready to go by eight forty-five. At nine, Amahl Sahman was wheeled into the theatre, followed by Majeke Hemlet, Senior Anaesthetist James Deakin, and two specialist nurses. Victory inserted his hands into the operating-gloves and focused his attention on the screen before him. He threw himself into his performance with total concentration, and spared no thought for anything beyond the reach of his computerized instruments for the next five hours.

The surgeon was quite unaware of the passing of the time, and his assistants knew better than to talk among themselves. Some of his colleagues joked with their nurses and anaesthetists, others listened to music as they worked, but Victory liked silence—not funereal silence, because he was not a dealer in death, but the reverential silence that must have been typical of churches in the days when people either believed in miracles or had no other source of hope for the improvement of their conditions.

Victory was not so foolish as to think himself godlike, but he did think of himself as a man who had hope in his gift, not merely for the kind of person who had no more chance of entry to heaven than a camel had of passing through a needle's eye, but also for the kind of person that Amahl Sahman was: a person to whom cruel fate had done its absolute worst. As he completed the skeletal work, Victory felt that he was not merely repairing injuries inflicted by the slings and arrows of outrageous fortune but restoring something more primal, moulding the clay of calcium into the archetypal skull of which all others were slightly flawed copies. He felt, as he added a delicate human touch to the mechanical work of his robotic servitors, that he had now attuned himself to a perfect sympathy with the force that had shaped human being, whether that force were to be conceived as an intelligent designer or the inexorable mathematical logic of natural selection. Indeed, he felt more than mere sympathy—he felt that he understood the aesthetics of skull-design even better than that experimental force could have contrived, by virtue of having a lifetime's experience of such metamorphoses under his belt. That he was standing on the shoulders of giants he did not doubt, but he had no doubt either that he had seen a little further than any other man, and perhaps a good further than the mildly myopic giants themselves.

It was good work, the best he had ever done—but he expected that of himself every time he met a new challenge, and he felt certain that he would do better when Monday came.

When he finished the day's work, Victory felt quite exhausted. He had been seated the entire time, and his hands had done all their work in virtual space, but he had exerted such tight and minute control over the muscles of his arms and fingers that they ached. His exhaustion was as much mental as physical, but the residual hormonal cocktail flowing through his system coupled his tiredness with a curious sense of exaltation.

He ate a late lunch with his team in the hospital restaurant, chatting happily to them now that the job was done. Then he returned to his instruments, reactivating the secure link connecting his hospital terminal to the one in his consulting room so that he could recover further results of the previous evening's labours. It was, however, Mrs. Allison's plan that he carefully integrated into the mechanisms controlling the robots that assisted his manipulation of his tiny tools. He set the unfinished plan that he *might* use in the course of Amahl's final sequence of operations carefully aside.

Victory remained at his hospital station for a further five hours, not quite as lost to the stream of ordinary time as he had

been during surgery but very nearly so. He was eventually interrupted by Majeke Hemlet, who had come to deliver a report on
Amahl's progress.

"He's fine," the trainee surgeon said. "Awake and as cheer-
ful as can be expected, given the residual wooziness of the anal-
gesia. We'll have to check the bone-development again on Sunday morning, but if nothing unexpected turns up he'll be ready
for phase two on Monday. I see you've added an extra patient to
tomorrow's schedule as well as hijacking my Sunday slot."

"Is that a problem?" Victory asked.

"No, of course not. I assume that I'll be just as superfluous
to the requirements of that procedure as I am to all the rest."

"You're not superfluous," Victory assured her. "If anything
were to go wrong, you'd be the one who'd have to take urgent
action—I couldn't do anything in a hurry, with my hands stuck
in the gloves manipulating the nanoscalpels."

"Nothing does go wrong," Majeke said, trying to modulate
her voice so that it didn't seem like a complaint.

"Things always go wrong eventually," Victory told her, so-
berly. "The trick is not to let the phases of smooth running make
you complacent. You have to be ready when it does. When mortal danger looms, you're the one who has to step into the breach.
I need you, Majeke, just as I need Jim and the specialist nurses.
Your next fully-allocated slot is a week on Friday, isn't it? I'll
see if I can get you something before then—I understand perfectly that you need more hands-on experience, but there's only
one machine, for now. We'd all like to have more hours."

"I know that," she said. "It's just that I find myself hoping
for emergencies when I'm on call—praying for a pile-up on the
Westway or a chemical fire in Stoke Newington. I'm getting five
or ten hours of conventional scalpel-work from A-and-E every
week, but it's not the same."

"I know," Victory said. "I can't even tell you that all surgery
will be like this one day, because so much of it is essentially
simple, no matter how difficult it may be in practice. The kind of
work that requires nanoscalpel subtlety will always lie at the
luxury end of the spectrum. I'm sorry the routine support seems
so much more burdensome when it's sustaining the kind of work
I do, but I don't need you any less because so much of what I do
seems merely cosmetic."

"It's not that, Dr. Victory. What you did today was amazing,
in every respect. It's just...as you say, there's only one machine.
I'll bide my time, like everyone else. I'm heading back to the
restaurant now—are you eating here, or...?" She left it there.

Victory wasn't sure what range of possible alternatives she
had in mind—probably meeting one of his satisfied customers in
some quiet little place where neither of them would be recog-

nized, or dining in style with a party of influential friends; she couldn't know how long it was since he had done either of those things. He wasn't sure exactly what her invitation to join her in the hospital restaurant was supposed to signify, but it seemed more likely to be a matter of professional courtesy than erotic interest.

"I can't," he said. "I've got to call into at my consulting rooms to sort out the day's paperwork, and then I need to go home. It'll be a long day tomorrow, with the extra patient—though not nearly as interesting as today. Just routine repair-work."

"The extra patient you've squeezed in is Mrs. Gregory K. Allison, isn't it?" Majeke said. "You'll have to be extra careful there."

"Tomorrow's work is only a slight modification to the bone-structure," Victory said. "Nothing like today's epic. I'll do some preliminary sculpting at the same time, though, to ease the burden of Sunday's supplementary. Don't repeat the patient's name where anyone else might overhear you, by the way—she doesn't want the press snatching photographs of her bandages."

"It figures. Why does she use her husband's first name? What's wrong with her own?"

"It's an English thing," Victory told her. "She's not bragging about the capture of a billionaire—it's just a matter of etiquette. It's an odd kind of punctiliousness. Enjoy your meal."

Majeke screwed up her face, as if to imply that there wasn't much chance of that, but then she smiled. She closed the door behind her as she went out.

Victory typed out a brief statement for the press office, in case Christina received any enquiries regarding the day's work before he arrived the following morning, and e-mailed it before logging off.

He checked his watch. Claire would be long gone from the Harley Street premises, but she would have left any incoming information neatly stacked on his desk.

Victory locked his office and made his way down to the hospital car park. The Bentley was parked in a long row of ill-assorted vehicles, all of which were monitored by CC-TV cameras connected to the hospital security office. Tucked beneath the car's windscreen wiper was a piece of paper. Victory lifted it out carefully and read what was written on it.

IF YOU WANT TO KNOW WHO GWYNPLAINE REALLY IS, it said, RING THIS NUMBER TO ARRANGE A MEETING.

It wasn't signed, although Victory had no trouble imagining the words "A FRIEND" in the space where a signature might have been. The number, unsurprisingly, was a mobile.

Victory was tempted to ring it immediately, but he suppressed the impulse. He didn't like being a pawn in some increasingly strange game-board, consenting to be pushed wherever the gloating players wanted him to be. He wanted to retain a measure of control, some sense of being his own man, free to organise his own investigations and actions.

He did take out his mobile phone, though, and rang the security office.

"This is Hugo Victory, in the car park," he said. "There's a piece of paper tucked under my windscreen wiper. I thought you were supposed to prevent that sort of thing occurring. He waved the paper at the nearest CC-TV camera."

"Yes sir," the guard on duty replied, in a tone whose world-weary lack of surprise might have been the result of professional training, or might simply have indicated that the guard had been expecting the call. "We checked it out as soon as we noticed that it had been placed, sir. The person who placed it was wearing a hooded overcoat and a mask, so he isn't recognizable, but we sent someone down to read the note. It didn't seem to be anything that warranted interrupting you at work, sir, but we left it in place in case you wanted to follow it up."

"But you didn't actually ring the number," Victory said.

"No sir—not our place to do that, sir. The man who placed it must have known the car park security code, but he came in from the main building and went out on foot."

"That narrows it down to a couple of thousand people, then," Victory observed. Even patients were allowed to access the hospital car park from within and without. "Next time, you might want to get someone down here before the culprit makes his exit."

"We'd be only too pleased, sir, if we had the manpower."

Victory rang off and got into the car. He put the note into the "glove compartment"—one of the imitation antique's quaintest original features, which he had left carefully unmodified, save for usurping some of its space for the power-pack energizing the microphone-equipped cradle where he set his mobile phone while in transit—and drove off.

CHAPTER EIGHT

The Third Day: Evening

When he arrived in Harley Street, Victory couldn't help looking round carefully, to see if he could spot anyone keeping watch on his rooms or the entrance to the garage. As usual, there were people passing by in some profusion, but no one obviously loitering. He started to check the windows up and down the street, but gave up almost immediately. There were far too many, and far too many people behind them who might have perfectly legitimate reasons for looking out into the street.

He went up in the elevator and opened the outer office. Claire's desk was as tidy as usual. She had placed a number of messages on his desk in the inner office, but he threw them aside after glancing through them. He went to the safe and removed three of the photocopies that Gwynplaine had brought him—the earliest ones in the sequence. Then he sat down and began to copy out a series of the inscriptions, which could still be clearly made out alongside Gwynplaine's translations.

It was slow work, because Victory's hand was not used to framing the letters making up the script. He magnified each one to twice its original size, trying to make certain that his duplicates were as faithful as possible.

He compiled a set of twenty-two items, each one or two lines long, and each consisting of between six and twelve words—about fourteen hundred characters in all, filling a single side of A4 paper. He replaced the photocopies in the safe before moving unhurriedly back into the outer room in order to use the dedicated fax machine. He punched out Huw Williams' number and the supplementary code that would connect him to the linguist's computer.

While the image was being transmitted the surgeon stepped aside from the desk to look out through the window that overlooked the street. Again he could not help scanning the pavements for idlers leaning on lampposts. Still there was no one obviously loitering, although there were a dozen people moving in one direction or the other, apparently going about their own business with all due expedition.

When the transmission was complete Victory put the piece of paper on which he'd made the copies into Claire's shredder and turned it into confetti. Then he went back into the consulting-room, switched on his computer and reactivated the secure connection to the hospital.

He had not been working for more than fifteen minutes when the phone in the outer office began to ring. He immediately jumped to the conclusion that it must be Huw Williams; the number recorded automatically on the fax he'd sent would be that of Claire's phone. He shut down his computer before going to answer it, and reached it on the seventh ring; the display assured him that it was indeed Williams calling.

"Dr. Williams," he said, as soon as he had picked up the receiver. "It's good of you to get back to me so quickly."

"Might I ask where you came by these samples, Dr. Victory?" Williams asked, in a tone that was informative in itself.

"In the course of my research," Victory parried.

"Your research as a plastic surgeon?"

"That's correct. Wasn't that obvious from the translation?"

"To tell you the truth, Dr. Victory, I'm not at all certain of the meaning of some of the words. Not that I doubt your ability as a copyist, you understand—it's the orthography itself that's problematic. It's an extremely obscure script, and although it's clearly related to languages of which I have some acquaintance, it's rather idiosyncratic. Is there much more of it?"

"I have more," Victory confirmed, feeling slightly guilty that it was now his turn to play a teasing game of mingling minimal information with petty deception, "but I'm in my consulting room at the moment, and I don't have the document close at hand. Can you tell me anything more about the script and its possible origins?"

"I can tell you that it originated in the Caucasus, probably in what's now Georgia. The samples are too slight for me to make any accurate assessment of the linguistic modifications, but some features of the orthography suggest a westward migration across the Black Sea, perhaps into Romania. If there's a significant quantity of material, it could be a very interesting specimen. If the source can be accurately dated, that too would be very interesting—but I'll need more if I'm to make a confident translation. If I could see the original...."

"That's not possible at the moment, I'm afraid," Victory said. "I'm busy in theatre again tomorrow, and I'll have to be at the hospital on Friday as well, to check on my patients. I'll try to find time to copy out a little more over the weekend. I usually go back to my farmhouse in Oxfordshire on Saturday, where I can work in...."

Williams cut him off, with revealing impatience. "Do you have any idea what the document from which you copied these sentences *is*, Dr. Victory?"

"I'm afraid not," Victory lied. "Do you?"

"If you weren't who you say you are...," Williams muttered. "Look, Dr. Victory, is there any chance that we might meet face-to-face?"

"So that you can compare my physiognomy with the photographs in the papers and make sure that I'm who I say I am? Perhaps. It would allow me the opportunity to compare your face with the photograph on the university website. As I said, though, I'm rather busy just now. Would next Tuesday suit you?"

"Would it really suit you, Dr. Victory?" William retorted. "You're the one who rang me on my unlisted home number, remember? You faxed the bait over; aren't you interested in examining your catch? I don't know what's going on here, but I don't like being played like a fish on a line. I know it's late, but if you really want my help I wish you wouldn't play games with me. You're in Harley Street aren't you?"

"Yes" Victory admitted, a trifle sheepishly. "I suppose I might be able to call in on my way home, if you're not too far away."

"From Oxfordshire?"

"No, from Westbourne Park. I have a flat there.

"Well, I'm not exactly on the way, but not too far away from it. I'm in Cricklewood. All you'd have to do is head for Paddington, as usual, but turn off on to the Edgware Road. Carry on through the Vale until it turns into Kilburn High Road, then...."

"That's okay," Victory said. "My car doesn't have an electronic routefinder but I've got an A-to-Z. Give me the address and I'll be with you in...well, say thirty minutes."

Williams gave him the address, but couldn't resist adding: "It's north of the cemetery, off Farm Avenue."

"I'll find it," Victory promised. "Thanks for you help, Dr. Williams. I appreciate it."

"I'll be expecting you," Williams said.

Victory put the phone down, thoughtfully. He went back into his consulting room to make sure that everything was secure, and then locked up. There was nothing new under the Bentley's windscreen wiper when he got down into the garage, and there was still no sign of anyone loitering in the street as he headed north towards the Marylebone Road.

The radio news was even less interesting than usual, despite indulging in blatant melodrama in the course of showcasing the dispute between the Oxford and Cambridge Cybernetics departments as to which of their experimental AIs was the closest to making the crucial breakthrough to indisputable self-awareness. Oxford's "Newman" was apparently making great strides with the aid of the mechanical hands that enabled him to correlate visual information with tactile information of superhuman subtlety, while Cambridge's "Saxon" was benefiting from the latest dimension of complexity incorporated into his neural network, which had boosted it to authentic comparability with a human brain. Their respective advocates were both treated with scornful contempt by a representative of the Humanist Crusade, who argued that confinement in a university laboratory was more likely to reduce the academics to the status of mere machines than permit their mere machines to emulate the miraculous capabilities of the human brain. He was criticised in his turn by a neo-Marxist who argued that machines performing purposive labor were far more likely to achieve consciousness of their slavery than any leisured creature blinded by the ideologies of its effete creators.

The A5 was busy in spite of the late hour, but the traffic was flowing smoothly enough even in the middle of Hampstead. Victory cut across to Farm Avenue and found Williams' side street without any difficulty. The cultural historian lived in a second floor flat that was palatial by comparison with Victory's, although it had nothing on the Oxfordshire farmhouse. The man was, after all, a mere academic. Victory supposed that there might be some consultancy work available to an Eastern European specialist, but not much. The ex-Warsaw-pact countries were not high on the list of Foreign Office priorities nowadays.

Huw Williams looked exactly like his photograph on the UC website; Victory would have started work on him by doing a complete skin-clearance and repairing his hairline, but that would only have been the beginning of a very long job. The historian seemed equally satisfied with Victory's resemblance to his publicity shots, and presumably made no harsh judgments about the necessity of remaking his appearance.

Williams led his visitor into a study that was not so much book-lined as book-drowned, and offered to make him a cup of tea. Victory remembered then that he hadn't eaten, although he had been far too busy to feel any hunger pangs. He wondered if it might be worth suggesting that they order in some food, but decided against it. He accepted the offer of tea.

While Williams left the room to make the tea Victory studied his surroundings carefully. The majority of the books seemed to be related to Williams' esoteric area of expertise, but the piles on the floor also contained numerous novels—mostly thrillers—and there were whole shelves of general reference books. There were also the kinds of eccentric oddments that accumulated in every voracious reader's library. Williams was obviously an accumulator rather than a meticulously specialised collector.

The desk was laden with miscellaneous papers, and no less than three computers. One was a closed laptop and one of the desktop monitors was so dusty that it was presumably an obsolete machine Williams had never got around to throwing out. There were two framed photographs on the desk and half a dozen prints pinned to various junctions of the shelves behind it. All but a few of them showed one or both of a pair of children at various ages between three and eleven, but the only sign of their mother was in one group photograph on the desk, in which the two children were still pre-school age. Victory deduced that Williams was yet another divorced man obsessively immersed in work, or at least lost in the pretense of utter devotion to matters of great intellectual significance. One of the older prints showed a proudly smiling man in a fireman's uniform, obviously taken at some kind of formal occasion; the family resemblance suggested that it might be Williams' brother.

Victory felt unreasonably glad when Williams brought in a tray containing a teapot, two mugs and a tin of biscuits that was still more than half full. It wasn't simply the effect that the sight of nourishment had on his suddenly awakened hunger but the ambience of the environment. Victory felt that this was a lifestyle he could relate to, a way of being that he understood.

"You haven't eaten?" Williams observed, as Victory took a biscuit with unconcealed eagerness.

Victory knew that the question was probably rhetorical, but he felt compelled to apologize. "A busy day," he said.

"The Palestinian boy?"

"Yes. I'm at a crucial stage in his treatment. Five hours in theatre this morning, then all the follow-up work. The new machine makes things so much easier in some ways, but so much more laborious in others. Look, I'm sorry about the way I came across on the phone. I've been treated the same way myself during these last few days, and I guess it infected me. It's not usually my style."

Williams sat down behind his desk. "That's okay," he said. "I've had some dealings with lifestyle fantasists and conspiracy theorists myself. I know how easily the mindset communicates. We are talking about the supposed secrets of the comprachicos, aren't we?"

Victory nodded. "Yes, we are," he said. "You were able to work that out from the samples I sent you?"

"The inference wasn't too difficult," Williams said. "The comprachicos have become very fashionable of late, in certain circles—this year's Millenarian flavor of the month—and you're the best-known plastic surgeon in England just now, thanks to the publicity surrounding the Palestinian boy. What led you to me?" The UC man seemed far more relaxed now than he had on the phone, obviously feeling that he had a home advantage—and perhaps somewhat reassured by the fact that Victory was not only who he had said he was, but was also a man who could be bribed with biscuits.

"The suggestion that I ring you came from a man calling himself Asmodeus," Victory said, figuring that it was time to shake off his infection and lay at least some of his cards on the table. "Does that name mean anything to you? Apart from the king of the demons and the devil on two sticks, that is."

"Yes, it does," Williams admitted. "I've never met the man, but we've been corresponding by email for some time. He's given me some useful tips, and asked for my advice on several occasions."

"In relation to what subject?"

"Obscure documents in obscure languages. He's never mentioned the comprachicos, but I never believed that his interest in esoteric mythology was purely academic. If he's contacted you, he must think you have something of interest to him, and if the samples you sent me are genuine, you probably do. Does this have something to do with the boy you operated on today?"

Victory hesitated, but then said: "Yes—but I'd rather you kept that to yourself, if you don't mind. Do you also know a man named Gwynplaine?"

"I'm familiar with the name, but only in relation to nineteenth century versions of the legend."

"The legend of the comprachicos?"

"Yes, of course. I suppose it's not surprising that your research might have led you in that direction, given the nature of your practice, but I'm surprised that you seem to have taken it so far as actually to acquire a supposed comprachico document. You're not seriously intending to make use of what you've read, are you? The document is almost certainly fake, no matter how cleverly it's been done—there's been an obvious gap in the market for a couple of years now. I'm only interested in the language, of course—it doesn't matter to me whether the subject matter's fake or not, although I'd dearly love to know when and where the document was faked. One of my counterparts in Tbilisi or Bucharest obviously knows more than his publications let on—but that's not surprising, given the upheavals that have taken place since the collapse of communism."

"I've been assured that the document dates from the seventeenth century," Victory told him, "although some of the information is supposed to be much older, having been copied many times. Could it really be that old—and, if so, is there any possibility that it might be genuine?"

"It's not impossible," Williams admitted. "The comprachicos really do seem to have been active in England in the seventeenth century, and they appear to have had some friends in high places. Many of the large houses owned by aristocratic Catholic families were already equipped with priests' holes, and such people were accustomed to hiding books as well as people. It wouldn't be surprising if one or two of the comprachicos went to ground after the expulsion, nor would it be surprising if those who had to flee in a hurry left their possessions behind, carefully secreted away. Given the recent intensification of the search, it wouldn't astonish me if a few authentic comprachico relics turned up in one or other of the old Catholic manses."

"And would a genuine comprachico document really be written in the kind of script I showed you?"

"Good question. Again, all I can say is that it's not impossible. What little historical and archeological evidence we have suggests that the ancestors of the comprachicos migrated from the east long before the Roma, perhaps around the time when Constantinople became the capital of the Eastern Empire, perhaps even earlier than that. They may have been Christians already—the first Christian nation of all was Armenia, and Armenian missionaries undoubtedly went east in imitation of St. Paul's westward journeys through the Roman Empire. In the absence of documents, history is blind, but there are always stories...folktales. People moved around a lot in the days when there was an endless conflict of interest between agriculturalists and nomadic hordes. Whole nations went on the march—but history tends to be written by settled city-dwellers, to whom such movements were always mysterious and potentially threatening. Actually threatening, of course, in such cases as the Huns and the Tatars."

"Is that what we're talking about, Dr. Williams: folktales, carried far and wide by wandering tribesmen?"

"It's what I'm talking about," William affirmed. He helped himself to a chocolate digestive, apparently to cover his hesitation, before adding: "For all I know, *you* might be talking about the possibility of recreating the face of Adam, either in theory or in practice."

"So you believe that was what the comprachicos were trying to do?" Victory parried, speaking carefully but exercising less patient restraint than his host as he seized and set about devouring another biscuit.

"I know that was what some of them said they were trying to do," Williams replied, with equal care, "and I know that the notion has attracted particular attention lately, thanks to its Millenarian implications. *Revelation* and the rapture have become old hat, it seems. The everpresent end-of-the-worlders are intellectual nomads, always in search of new ominous straws at which to clutch."

Victory nodded his head. "It seems that awareness of the ecocatastrophe is biting hard, thanks to the daily pronunciations of the oracular GEM, and producing some odd responses," he agreed. "The writing on the wall is glowing like neon, and some of its readers are throwing epileptic fits. An unorthodox Deluge requires unorthodox arks. So there actually are people around who would want to create the face of Adam, if they could only dig up the comprachicos' instructions?"

"So it seems," Williams confirmed. "Is that what you've been hired to do?"

"*Hired* would be putting it a bit strongly," Victory observed.

"Really? Rumor has it that at least one of the groups isn't short of funds—but I suppose they prefer to work in mysterious ways. It's an essential element of the elaboration of the fantasy. On the other hand, it may simply be that the group that has stumbled on the cache isn't the one with the wealth—and people of that kind aren't the sort to amalgamate or sell out. You asked about someone named Gwynplaine—is the person who approached you using that name?"

"Yes," Victory admitted. "There seem to be others who know what he's doing, though. Asmodeus is one, but there's at least one more."

"That's how you picked up the infection you mentioned," Williams said. "I can see how things might have become confusing. But Asmodeus, kind soul that he is, suggested that you come to me. I'd like to think that he might be repaying me for the information I've given him in the past, or that he really does want to help you out, but it might be wiser to assume that he has some agenda of his own."

Victory finished his tea. Williams picked up the pot to offer a second cup, and the surgeon accepted gratefully. He wished now that he had accepted Majeke's invitation to the hospital canteen before racing off to Harley Street, and made a mental note to stop for a full English breakfast on the way into work the next morning.

"Are these people dangerous?" Victory asked.

"I have no idea," Williams admitted. "I doubt it, though. People who resurrect ancient scholarly fantasies aren't usually inclined to violence, even when the scholarly fantasies themselves seem rather bloodcurdling—Satanism, Odinism, and so on. For the vast majority, it's the search that's important rather than the ostensible goal; the holy blood and the holy grail are merely stars to set their compasses by, and applying numerological codes to every scrap of papyrus and parchment they can find is a thrill in itself, like computerized astrology and tuning in to the souls of the dead with Ouija boards. The process itself is the reward, as with every other vocational obsession—including mine, of course, safely respectable as it is."

"And mine, I suppose," Victory said, politely.

"Not at all," Williams said. "What you do really is judged entirely by its results. Yours is one of the few branches of medicine whose successes and failures are perfectly manifest—none of your patients ever benefits from a spontaneous remission or suffers a relapse unrelated to your actions. You have to take full responsibility for the outcomes of your operations, and you have to meet aesthetic standards rather than merely liberating people from excessive discomfort. You're no scholarly fantasist, Dr. Victory, and your work is no mere lifestyle fantasy. For you, means really are directed to ends; they can't possibly replace them. If someone does want you to follow a comprachico formula, you have to be very careful, Dr. Victory. You'd be the only one taking any risk—and the only one accepting any blame if anything went wrong."

"Right," said Victory, feeling that he had just been thoroughly doused in the cold water of common sense. Was that, he wondered, why Asmodeus had sent him to Williams? Was Williams supposed to bring him back to his senses and talk him into showing Gwynplaine the door?

"The Millenarians can always move on," Williams pointed out. "It doesn't really matter if the ideas that seize their enthusiasm turn out to be flattering only to deceive. They can always hold on to their conviction that the answer is still out there, a little further along life's highway, recoverable from the next fad or the one after that. The problem, from the point of view of serious scholars, is that simply because they search so assiduously, and spend so freely of their money and their time, the crazies often get first access to any interesting finds that do turn up. Instead of the documents going to universities for scrupulous analysis, they're traded back and forth in dubious deals, pored over by idol-infested eyes, pawed by grubby fingers, and sometimes torn apart so that the pieces can be bulked out like cocaine cut with talcum powder. So if something of that sort really has come into your possession, Dr. Victory, I'd be very anxious indeed to retrieve it, so that it could be properly examined and evaluated."

"I don't have the book itself," Victory admitted. "Just a handful of photocopies."

"Have you seen the document?"

"Yes," Victory said. "I'm not qualified to judge its authenticity as a historical artefact, but I am qualified to judge its subject matter. I can vouch for the quality of the illustrations, and the esoteric nature of the apparent instructions...and for the fact that whoever designed those instructions really was a plastic surgeon. If, as you say, ours really is a vocation entirely measurable by its outcomes, he must have been capable of spectacular work, whether or not he ever got a chance to produce his imagined face of Adam."

Williams nodded thoughtfully. "That's very interesting," he conceded. "Which makes it even more important, don't you think, that the book is safely delivered into expert hands, for scientific investigation of every kind? Does the man who calls himself Gwynplaine have it in his possession?"

"I believe so. I don't know where he got it from, or how easy it will be for him to hang on to it now that he's attracted so much attention."

"Do you know where he lives?"

"No."

"But you have photocopies of some of the book's pages?"

"Yes," Victory confirmed, although he suspected that the question was fishing for more than a confirmation. Williams wanted to know what he intended to do with the photocopies—but Victory wasn't entirely sure about that himself.

CHAPTER NINE

The Third Day: Late Evening

"Exactly what do you want from me, Dr. Victory?" Williams went on, when the surgeon failed to elaborate. "Am I just supposed to provide a cheap translation service?"

Victory suspected that Huw Williams had already performed the function for which Asmodeus had provided his name. He had confirmed that the script in Gwynplaine's book was a real language, and that it really might have been associated with a cult whose history spanned the greater part of the Christian era. He had provided what little Victory already knew with as solid a foundation as anyone could. Given that Victory already had Gwynplaine's translation of the photocopied pages, and no reason to doubt that translation, he probably had no further need of Williams, unless and until he acquired the book itself. On the other hand, there was a good deal more that Victory wanted to know about the various mysterious groups that might be after Gwynplaine's book—and there were a lot of biscuits left in the tin.

"I needed some sensible advice," Victory said, attempting to muster his best bedside manner. "I needed to know that the script was authentic, in order to help me decide what to do next. Thanks for that. As to the future, I think we really ought to be allies in this matter. Gwynplaine seems perfectly able to translate the text—his versions make good sense in association with the diagrams, at least—but that doesn't mean that I won't need your advice again—and I'm certainly prepared to pay for that advice by making duplicates of my photocopies for you."

Williams was sitting up more attentively now. "The man calling himself Gwynplaine can translate the script, you say?" he said, sharply. "And his translations make perfect sense?"

"Apparently," Victory confirmed.

"I had no idea that there was anyone in England able to do that," Williams said. "He's not English himself, I suppose? He must surely be from the Caucasus."

Victory frowned. "He speaks very good English," he said. "Not perfectly pronounced, by any means—but I'd assumed that was because of his deformity."

"His deformity?" Williams echoed.

"Yes. He's been badly burned in a fire—some time ago I think. His larynx doesn't seem to be affected, but his lips have difficulty with sibilants and plosives. I suppose he might have an accent, but I have no idea what it is. The scarring is so extensive that I couldn't even say with certainty what cast his features had or what color his skin was." He stopped, seeing the expression on Williams' face. "Do you know who he really is?" he asked.

"No," Williams replied. "But I could make a guess as to who he might be pretending to be. The scarring is real, I suppose."

"Definitely," Victory said. "Asmodeus seems to know who he is—and someone who put a note under my windscreen-wiper at the hospital also claims to know. Do I take it that they may only be referring to who he's *pretending* to be?"

"It seems likely," Williams agreed. "Mystics and Millenarians are always enthusiastic to jump to conclusions, the weirder the better. Asmodeus has always seemed level-headed, apart from the silly pseudonym—if he's a cultist, he's certainly an erudite one—but it's often the ones who seem most convincing who are the most deeply deluded. To get back to your earlier proposition, though, I agree with you that we ought to be allies in this. If you'll let me see your photocopies—and the book itself, if you can get your hands on the book—I'm more than willing to share anything I discover as a result, and tell you everything I already know."

Victory had already decided that Williams was the kind of man with whom he could deal fairly and honestly. It wasn't just that he was a university teacher, but that he seemed a genuine scholar: a man who valued knowledge and insight over mere matters of commerce.

That was a kind of man Victory could admire, even though he wasn't entirely sure that he qualified as one himself.

"There is a possibility that I might be able to get my hands on the book, if I play my cards right," Victory admitted. "If and when I do, I promise you that you'll have full access to it for as long as you need to make a thorough examination of it. At that point, I'd certainly like to share your translation, and I'd also like to consider the possibility of working up some kind of collaborative publication based on your findings and my analyses of the anatomical diagrams. You'll understand, though, that this is a delicate matter. As you say, the man who has the book and the other people who are interested in it are probably harboring all manner of weird delusions. If I'm to deal with them successfully, it will help me to know a little more about the nature of those delusions. So tell me—who do you think Gwynplaine is pretending to be?"

"I might have put that a little strongly," Williams admitted. "Perhaps it would be safer to say that there are two possible assumptions about his identity, each of which is likely to appeal to certain of his rivals."

"Which are?"

"Some of them will take him for Cain. Others will take him for the Devil."

Victory cursed himself for his own astonishment at this bald statement. Given that Gwynplaine seemed sincerely to believe that the story of Eden was literally true, and that the face of Adam might be recreated by plastic surgery, why should he—or others sharing his beliefs—not also believe in the literal existence of Cain and the Devil? Even so, it seemed ridiculous to heap absurdities up in this manner.

When he had reasserted full control of his boggling mind, Victory contrived a cool and casual tone in order to say: "And why should they think that?"

"It's a rather complicated story," Williams said, glancing at the clock on the mantelpiece. "Have you the time?"

Victory looked at his own watch. It was nearly midnight, and he knew that he needed a solid night's sleep, but he wasn't about to leave now. "Yes," he said.

"Well then, have you ever heard of the Visionary Martyrs?"

Victory was about to say no when he remembered that he had. Rachel Rosenfeld had mentioned them, presumably having heard of them from her mysterious patient. "Yes," he said. "Just the name though—bracketed with the Sons of Job."

"They usually are, although they seem to have been rivals as well as fellow travelers. They're allegedly ancient sects, which each seem to have had their own notions of the Eden myth."

"Allegedly?"

"The historical evidence is slight, and a great deal of speculation has been founded on a few scraps of papyrus dug up in the vicinity of the Dead Sea. There's been a lot of activity in the area ever since the original Dead Sea scrolls turned up, but the later additions to the stock are even more fragmentary and much more enigmatic. The names were conferred upon the sects by their supposed discoverers, of course, and borrowed by their reinventors—we have no idea what they called themselves. The so-called Visionary Martyrs are secondary references in documents seemingly written by the so-called Sons of Job, so they may have been purely hypothetical—and it's always dangerous to deduce a group's beliefs from material penned by their rivals, who regard them as heretics, although the history books would be a great deal shorter if we disregarded all evidence of that kind.

"If the original sects were more than some ancient scribe's flight of fancy, they flourished in the first centuries B.C. and A.D., around the time when a good deal of Jewish apocalyptic literature was recorded. So far as the historical record in concerned, they appear to have died out in the same period—but rumours of their continued existence have sprung up in recent years. By now, the rumours have given birth to a kind of fact, in that lifestyle fantasists have actually adopted the names that scholars invented and refabricated their supposed beliefs and ambitions, following in the hallowed footsteps of nineteenth-century Rosicrucians and twentieth-century Knights Templar."

"What did the Visionary Martyrs—or their modern counter-parts—believe?"

"That's not entirely clear, in either case. The main attraction of lifestyle fantasies of this stripe is that people can make them up more or less as they please. I haven't had the privilege of seeing the original fragments, and Aramaic's not one of my languages in any case, but from what I can gather from sources I trust as far as any, the Visionary Martyrs were said by the Sons of Job to believe, as they did themselves, that Adam was immortal, having been created in God's image in more than mere appearance. Although his immortality wasn't hereditary, strictly speaking—and its residue was further watered down in subsequent generations—both groups appear to have believed that Cain was gifted with longevity too. Where the Sons of Job parted ideological company with the Visionary Martyrs was in the matter of Cain's destined role in events leading up to and following the reproduction of the face of Adam.

"Both sects appear to have believed that Cain, like Adam, was disfigured as a result of the Fall, and that both became accursed wanderers. The Visionary Martyrs seem to have believed that the two of them remained at odds with one another as well as with God, but the Sons of Job believed that Cain was repentant, and would play a significant role in repairing the damage done by the Fall—and that he would be recognizable when he came to do that, by virtue of his badly burnt face.

"It's been theorized—although the evidence is weak and untrustworthy—that the Visionary Martyrs were among the earliest converts to Christianity, but that they adopted a notion of the meaning and significance of Christ's sacrifice that was markedly different from the Roman Church and its descendants. Both sects seemed to have believed that the redemption of humankind would depend on some kind of symbolic redemption of the eternal Adam, involving the healing of his disfigurement and consequent revelation to the world. The Visionary Martyrs are said to have associated that process with the conclusive damnation of his adversary, the not-quite-eternal Cain."

"But the Sons of Job didn't believe that?" Victory inferred.

"Cain had a very different, and more constructive, part to play in their world-view. In their version of the story, Adam's counterpart was Job, whose tribulations were deemed to be emblematic of a second phase in the Fall—and whose patient endurance won a kind of stay of execution for the human race, although we still stand in need of a conclusive redemption. Like the Visionary Martyrs, the sect was allegedly Christianized, but they too seem to have believed that Jesus' return and the Day of Judgment can't take place unless and until Adam's true face is recovered and revealed. As well as the initiatory involvement of Cain, their apocalypse apparently features a symbolic reunion of Adam with his wife—a sort of mystical marriage. Some scholarly fantasists, not unnaturally, have seized on that notion as the ultimate origin of the Rosicrucian fantasy."

"So Eve is supposed to have been immortal too?"

"Apparently not. The Sons of Job seem to have considered Eve as an unfortunate afterthought. They thought—and their modern counterparts seem to like the idea—that the fall might be undone if Adam could be reunited with his first wife, Lilith."

"I thought Lilith was supposed to be the wife of Asmodeus, the demon king."

"That was after her removal from Eden, supposedly. The Sons of Job probably never believed it. The Jews had eliminated demons from their official cosmogonic scheme long before the first century B.C., and the Sons of Job seem to have had tendencies towards Sadducism—the denial of all spiritual beings except Jehovah. In their view, Lilith was simply another human being, although one created immortal, like Adam. Eve, on the other hand, was made from Adam's rib, and not immortal at all."

"Is it possible that our friend Asmodeus chose his pseudonym because it linked him to Lilith rather than because it identified him as a demon of anger and lust?" Victory asked

"Of course it is. When I asked him, though, he said that he and Lilith were divorced.

"He said the same thing to me," Victory admitted. "Where does the Devil fit into the scheme, then?"

"The Visionary Martyrs and the Sons of Job both remained outside the Roman Church, so far as history can tell," Williams said, "but the Roman Church wasn't entirely unaffected by their ideas. There are rumored to be factions within it sympathetic to the notion that Adam's face might be recreated, with apocalyptic consequences. In their thinking, however, the Visionary Martyrs' version of Cain is replaced as the eternal adversary by the rebel angel Lucifer—which is to say, the Devil."

"If Gwynplaine wants to recreate the face of Adam," Victory observed. "That fits with the Sons of Job's idea of Cain, but it can't be squared with the idea that he might be the Visionary Martyrs' Cain, or the Roman Church's Devil, can it?"

"Maybe not," Williams conceded. "I suspect, though, that the Romanists might take the view that what the Devil would actually attempt to do is to incarnate the Antichrist: an *apparent* angel, whose true purpose is to lead humankind to damnation rather than salvation. The Visionary Martyrs might well think along the same lines, perhaps taking the view that Cain might be trying to reproduce his own face instead of Adam's, for some equally nefarious purpose."

Victory considered these speculations for a moment, unashamedly taking the last remaining biscuit from the tin. "If Gwynplaine is *pretending* to be Cain, then, he must belong to the Sons of Job? Not that's he's faking his scars—they're definitely real."

"Lifestyle fantasists move in mysterious ways," was Williams' answer to that. "Yes, the probability is that your Gwynplaine is with the Sons of Job—or, at least, that he's trying to endear himself to that faction. Would you like something else to eat?"

"No, that's all right, thanks. We still haven't got to the comprachicos. Presumably, they're supposed to have been offshoots of one or other of these sects?"

Williams shook his head. "Not according to the historical evidence. We have no trace of the comprachicos' existence for at least four centuries after the last trace of the Sons of Job and their apparent rivals. It's possible that what's happened so often in the last hundred years—various sets of lifestyle fantasists adopting long-dead creeds and modelling themselves on their long-extinct followers—is by no means a new phenomenon. If the founders of the comprachicos heard rumors of one or both of the earlier sects, they might have decided to revive their presumed dogmas and take an active role in trying to bring about the promised day of judgment. If the surviving documents can be trusted, the fascination some of them developed with the idea of reproducing the face of the disfigured Adam was a late addition to the cult's ideology, but that might be an illusion. The people who claimed that it had been the company's purpose all along might have been telling the truth."

"But if Adam is supposed to have been immortal, what have the children they bought to do with the project of recreating his face? Wouldn't they have to find Adam himself?"

Williams shrugged his shoulders. "I can only hypothesize that the comprachicos believed, or came to believe, that Adam's immortality was more a matter of the immortality of his bloodline than the survival of his actual body. The idea might be that, in order to redeem humankind, it's necessary to recreate Adam in one of his descendants—that a child descended from Adam, to whom Adam's appearance could be restored, would actually become Adam as he grew into adulthood. That's pure speculation, though."

Victory paused for consideration again. So far as he could tell, everything Williams had told him was speculation, and most of it was far from pure. On the other hand, the academic was at least prepared to admit that his fascination was founded on shifting sand.

"The recreation of the face is only part of the process, then," the surgeon said, slowly. "According to the Visionary Martyrs and their analogues in the Church, there still has to be a final reckoning with Cain or the Devil—and according to the Sons of Job, he still has to marry Lilith."

"Something along those lines. If we're talking about the modern lifestyle fantasists rather than the original sects, of course, there will probably be further variations. The two sets of beliefs might have been fused into one—they're not incompatible, after all—but lifestyle fantasists tend to be enthusiastic schismatics. Although the contemporary cults are no more than ten years old, they might already have fragmented."

"Do you suppose the comprachicos' book also contains instructions as to how to recreate the face of Lilith?"

"Don't you know?"

"I've only seen part of the text," Victory reminded him.

"I haven't seen any, so you still hold the advantage," Williams replied, with a slight trace of bitterness in his tone. "All I can say is that no reference to the comprachicos I've ever come across says anything about their attempting to recreate the face of Lilith. The best-known Jewish myth says that she was expelled from Eden for refusing to accept Adam's mastery, and suggests that she became some kind of monster, but the Sons of Job appear to have thought of her in quite a different light— there's no evidence, so far as I know, that they believed her to have been disfigured. She probably couldn't have been made in God's image, in their view, because they presumably took it for granted that God was male."

"So their modern counterparts think that Lilith still has her original face?"

"You'd have to consult one of them about that. They might already have a candidate to whom they want to marry their recreated Adam...always assuming that they can actually come by a recreated Adam."

"I see," Victory said, although he was far from certain that he did.

If Williams' so-called lifestyle fantasists really did have a Lilith in their midst, the surgeon thought, to whom they intended to marry an Adam, that might or might not make them enthusiastic to look around them for a Cain. If so, the phone number that had been tucked under his windscreen-wiper might well connect him to a voice eager to tell him that Gwynplaine was "really" Cain, whether or not the person in question approved of the possibility. If *that* were so, the voice might be equally willing to credit Asmodeus with being exactly who he said he was: the king of the demons, *alias* the Devil.

Victory shook his head, admitting that he had no chance of making sense of it all until he had a good deal more information. He became aware that Huw Williams was studying his face carefully, seemingly trying to read his expression. "That's very interesting, Dr. Williams," he said, still keeping his voice cool and casual. "I think I have a much better understanding now of the kind of people I might be dealing with. How far do these kinds of lifestyle fantasists usually take their fantasies?"

"They're usually harmless," Williams said. "Even Satanists tend to draw the line at human sacrifice, ritual murder and so on—kinky sex is usually the limit of their exotic endeavours. Some would opine that the whole purpose of lifestyle fantasy, psychologically speaking, is to license the kinky sex, but I don't believe that. If it were true, the fashionability of lifestyle fantasy would have waned as society's moral standards have relaxed, but the opposite seems to have been the case. I think it's more to do with filling the void left by the erosion of the orthodox fantasies of religion. When people stop believing in God, as Chesterton observed, they don't start believing in nothing—they start believing in anything."

"So they're not actually *dangerous*?"

"Who can tell?" Williams said, shrugging his shoulders again. "We're living in interesting times, Dr. Victory. In some ways, it's easier to believe that the apocalypse has already begun than to deny that it will ever arrive. The world is undergoing a massive crisis, reflected with doom-laden exactitude by the Global Environmental Model, which informs us that the whole human race may be poised on the brink of annihilation. Can you wonder that all kinds of people are searching for exotic solutions? Who among us isn't crying out for a miracle of *some* kind?"

"I see. Well, at least one of them seems to know that he's mad enough to seek Rachel Rosenfeld's help, and our mutual acquaintance Asmodeus seems to be willing to chuckle about it. The likelihood is that he chose his pseudonym in order to thumb his nose at the likes of the Sons of Job. Given that there are so many people around who can still bring themselves to maintain faith in the literal truth of *Genesis*, I suppose it's not surprising that their ideological rivals have begun to turn to rival versions of the Eden myth."

"I doubt that the contemporary Visionary Martyrs and Sons of Job are as literal in their interpretations as the Old Testament fundamentalists," Williams said. "They're all symbolists at heart, and the majority among them must be aware of that."

Victory was still trying, unavailingly, to straighten out the tangled web of conjectures and measure a few of its multitudinous implications. "At bottom, though," he judged, "it doesn't make the slightest bit of sense. How on earth is anyone supposed to know what Adam's face looked like before the Fall? How could the comprachicos have possibly come up with a set of instructions for remaking it?"

"That's where the visionary element of Visionary Martyrdom presumably comes in," Williams pointed out. "It's the usual fallback position: divine revelation, gifted to some would-be prophet. Unchallengeable."

"But in this case, not untestable," Victory observed. "And even if they were wrong to think that it was testable in the seventeenth century, given the limits of their surgical equipment, it's not untestable now. The fact remains that Gwynplaine really does have a book, and the book really is a marvel, even if it was forged last week and its recipes can't actually work miracles."

"Does that mean that you're actually going to try out the instructions?" Williams was also speaking casually, but Victory suspected that the coolness was as careful as his own.

"I don't know," Victory stalled.

"You said at the beginning of the conversation that this had something to do with the Palestinian boy," Williams reminded him. "Does Gwynplaine want you to try the operation on him?"

"I also said that I'd rather you kept that to yourself," Victory reminded him.

"Of course," Williams agreed. "You don't have to say any more if you don't want to."

"I really haven't come to any decision," Victory insisted. "As you've obviously guessed, Gwynplaine showed me the book and made the photocopies for me because he wants me to incorporate the modifications specified there as I finish the series of operations I'm carrying out on Amahl Sahman. So far as I can tell, nothing he's asked me to do can do any harm, so I've been playing along with him—but humoring him is one thing, and putting the information to use is something else entirely. If he were asking me to operate on himself, that might be a different matter, but Amahl isn't capable of giving informed consent to anything except wanting to be healed."

"Someone must be responsible for him. I read in the papers that he's an orphan, but he must have a guardian."

"Yes, he does—but the hospital has instructions to be discreet about it, so I'm not at liberty to tell you his name. The initial approach to me was made by a Foreign Office official, and all the information passed on to me has come from the Red Crescent; I haven't had any contact with his guardian as yet. I was asked to do a job that needed doing, and I agreed for that reason. I didn't anticipate complications of this kind."

"So you're not going to do what Gwynplaine asks?"

"I don't know yet exactly what Gwynplaine's asking. He hasn't given me the full set of diagrams. Until I can see the whole set, I can't get my computer to produce an image of the intended result. He's deliberately holding out on me—he claims that he doesn't know what effect the sight of the face might have on me, even as a computer simulation."

"Thou shalt not make unto thee any graven image, or any likeness of any thing that is in heaven above," Williams quoted. "The second commandment."

"Maybe that's his reason," Victory said, "and maybe not. One thing's certain, though—you were right about my line of work being judged entirely on its results. Unless I know exactly what my operation will produce, I'm certainly not going to program my robots to produce it. I might have to stick to my original plan, even if it means that I never see Gwynplaine's book again—at the end of the day, I have to give Amahl Sahman the face he needs, not the face that anyone else wants him to have."

"That's true," Williams agreed. "It's certainly the decision I'd make, if I were in your shoes." Victory had no idea whether it was a bland lie—or, indeed, whether he was telling the whole truth himself.

CHAPTER TEN

The Fourth Day: Morning and Afternoon

The following morning, Victory tumbled out of bed in response to his alarm, feeling desperately tired. Two cups of black coffee revived him, and he stopped off on his way to the hospital to buy breakfast at a cafe in Bishops Bridge Road. The news on the radio was mostly concerned with the impending parliamentary debate on the Alternative Energy Program, although it also mentioned that a significant report, on the use of stem cell therapy in treatment of CJD, Alzheimer's disease, and Parkinson's disease, was due that day.

By the time he was ready for surgery Victory felt much better, but he astonished Majeke by inviting her to take over the gloves during the first two scheduled operations while he observed and lent support.

"I didn't mean to complain when I talked to you yesterday," she said, while he was scrubbing up. "I wasn't angling for any special treatment."

"This is a teaching hospital," he replied. "How are you going to learn if I hog the delicate work and leave you to stitch up drunks who've been glassed in A-and-E? We'll trade places after lunch."

"We'll have to," Majeke observed. "Gregory K. Allison would sue you all the way to the High Court if he ever found out you'd let your pupil operate on his beloved wife."

"Is she his beloved wife?" Victory asked. "I'm afraid I don't read gossip columns or watch tabloid TV, so I'm completely unaware of the state of the marriage, but when a woman comes to me asking for treatment at such short notice...."

"I don't read or watch celebrity gossip either," Majeke assured him, "but you'd have to be living on the sort of elevated plane that's only open to expert surgeons, high-powered intellectuals and great artists to avoid soaking it up by osmosis. You might think of all second marriages as trophy affairs, but whether it's reciprocated or not, Gregory K. is rumored to be besotted with his new bride, even after seven years."

"I may be a divorced cosmetic surgeon," Victory retorted, "but I'm not a total cynic where marriage is concerned. She was very insistent about an early appointment, though."

"Aren't we plastic surgeons, Dr. Victory? Don't we throw tantrums when the press, or anyone else, describes us as cosmetic surgeons?"

"This is just between the two of us," Victory said, "and nobody else will ever know."

Jim Deakin was washing up at the other sink, and the two nurses who would be keeping him company for the next three hours were also well within earshot. They all laughed politely at Victory's little joke.

Because of the switch the morning's work stretched to three hours and a half, so their lunch was a trifle late, but they rushed through it in order that Mrs. Allison should not be kept waiting.

By the time he was ready to hook himself up to the computer again Victory was not merely fully refreshed but direly impatient to get his hands back into the gloves. He had begun to understand how frustrating it must be for Majeke to watch the nanoscalpels at work without being able to control them. To be a mere observer while such astonishing work was going on, instead of being at the heart of the operation was deeply unsatisfying. He had grown accustomed to his mind collaborating with the computer programs as intimately as a show-jumping horse and its rider, or a sheepdog and its master. The fact that the programs in question were his own brainchildren, to a very large extent, had made it even more dissatisfying to watch Majeke taking his place; now that he was back where he belonged he felt ready to express his genius to the full measure of its artistry.

That afternoon, he felt that he was utterly brilliant—more brilliant, in a way, than he had been the day before. The challenge posed by Amahl Sahman's partly-repaired countenance had been greater than that posed by Mrs. Allison's only-slightly-less-than-perfectly-beautiful visage, but the fact that he was now working with more cooperative clay provided invaluable assistance to his quest for absolute perfection. When he had finished the work, Victory was triumphantly proud of his programs and triumphantly proud of himself. He felt that he really had begun the rejuvenation of his patient, preparing the way to bring her safely back to a condition in which she might easily give Helen of Troy a run for her money in the All-Time-Miss-World competition.

Afterwards, Majeke came to his office as she had the day before, to deliver all the routine paperwork. "That was great work," she said. "Comparing what I did in the morning to what you did in the afternoon, I realise how far I still have to go. If the second phase goes as well, it will be an unprecedented achievement. The press office is going to love you, Dr. Victory, even if they can't boast about Mrs. Allison until Gregory K. gives them the all clear. In the meantime, Amahl will take up the slack. There's never been anything in our line of work to match a double like this one."

"Thanks," Victory said. "Unfortunately, I'm not sure that Mrs. Allison intends to let up in her demand for a publicity blackout. We've come a long way from the twentieth century, but some women still like to pretend that they maintain their looks without surgical assistance. You'd better be careful about letting your enthusiasm show, once you're outside these walls. Look, I really would offer to join you for dinner in the restaurant if I could, but I can't. I have to get back to Harley Street. Squeezing Mrs. Allison into the schedule has put me under pressure."

Majeke blushed. "That's all right," she said. "I wasn't fishing. It wasn't just flattery, you know. It really was great work."

"And I really was apologizing," Victory said. "Your work was good too. You're learning fast. When you begin to tailor the software to your own specifications, instead of having to put up with mine, you'll do great work. There's no one I'd rather see holding the safety net, in case there's a slip. We've got a way to go with Amahl, and there'll be plenty of opportunities to slip up on Monday—it'll be a long journey in unexplored territory. Mrs. Allison is easy by comparison."

When the assistant had gone Victory wondered briefly if he'd overdone his performance, but decided that the truth needed no further justification. His report to Christine Legrange—which he delivered in person—was longer than usual, even though the hospital had been sworn to absolute silence regarding Mrs. Allison, and would not dare to violate that confidence.

"I notice that admin has put Mrs. Alison next door to Amahl," He observed as if by way of making polite conversation.

"Yes," the press officer agreed. "Is that a problem?"

"No. Is the gentleman hanging about in the corridor really necessary? We do have our own security, after all."

"Yes, we do," Christina agreed, "so I'm sure you can imagine how grateful I am that Mr. Allison decided to put his own man in. The chances of anything untoward occurring might be a million to one, but I'd far rather we weren't in line to take the blame if anything did. You'll be seeing Mrs. Allison tomorrow, I assume, to go through the review with her?"

"Of course. Will her husband be there?"

"Very probably. I'll notify him, so that he has the choice. Have you met him before?"

"Never," Victory said. "Don't worry, I'll be very careful of what I say. See you tomorrow—and if you ever want those eyebrows seen to, I'll be only too happy to fit you in."

"Haven't the time. Look after yourself, doctor—you're getting to be worth your while, publicity-wise. If ever I go private, I hope you'll be my first client."

There was nothing under the Bentley's windscreen wiper when he got down to the garage. The drive back to Harley Street was almost as uneventful as the news. The new Alternative Energy Bill had been loaded down with the usual quota of amendments, and the report on stem cell therapy applications had hedged its positive conclusions with an equal number of cautionary notes.

Although Claire had been strictly instructed not to make any appointments, there was someone waiting in reception when Victory got back to his consulting-room. The visitor stood up as if to greet him, but the surgeon ignored him pointedly, going instead to stand before Claire's desk. She handed him his mail, and a business card. She said nothing, but her eyes flickered in the direction of the intruder as he took the card.

The name the card bore was Monsignor Guillermo Torricelli, and the address was the Vatican.

Victory could not suppress a gasp of amazement, and an inexplicable shudder of alarm. He turned around to look at the man who had decided to wait for him, even though he had not been expected and must have been told that Victory would not see him.

The Monsignor was a small, dark man whose moon-shaped and colorfully cratered face would have generated a list of surgical suggestions as long as Victory's arms. The surgeon saw immediately, now that he had condescended to take notice, that the man was wearing a clerical collar beneath his plain black overcoat, although a black overlay hid all but a vertical sliver of white.

"Why don't you take the gentleman's coat, Claire," Victory said, smoothly. "Will you allow me a minute or two, Monsignor, before I see you? I'll buzz when I'm ready."

"Of course," said the priest. "It's kind of you to see me without an appointment. I'm grateful to you." His English was cultured, his Italian accent discreet and mellifluous.

Victory went into his consulting-room, closing the door behind him. He dropped his mail into his in-tray without further scrutiny, and sat down to collect himself. Huw Williams had not said anything substantial about the attitude of the Church of Rome to the heretic sects multiplying like mushrooms in the shadow of the ecocatastrophic apocalypse, but Victory could understand readily enough that the Vatican's scholars had as much interest in Dead Sea scrolls as anyone, and more than most.

What Williams had actually said, the surgeon now remembered graphically, was that the factions within the Church that had once sympathized with the comprachicos might have been ready to leap to the conclusion that Gwynplaine was the Devil. Was it possible, he wondered, that those factions might have been revived along with secular interest in the comprachicos?

What was the Church, after all, but an unusually successful lifestyle fantasy?

Victory collected himself, and sternly advised himself not to prejudge the issue. The monsignor was certainly in need of a good deal of plastic surgery himself, and it was not inconceivable that the Vatican, having recently recovered from sex-scandal-induced bankruptcy, was taking its image problems more seriously than ever before.

He buzzed, and stood up while Claire showed the Monsignor in.

"What can I do for you, Father?" Victory asked politely, when they were both seated. "Is that mode of address correct, or should I stick to Monsignor?"

"As you please, Dr. Victory. I have some information for you—although I fear you might not thank me for it." The monsignor was not a man incapable of smiling, and he demonstrated the fact. "I hope you might be generous enough to do me a small service in return."

"What service would that be?" Victory enquired, warily—but the priest was apparently unready to spell that out without preamble.

"I believe that you have been visited by an individual calling himself Gwynplaine," the little man said.

"It's no secret," Victory replied, chiding himself for his well-meant attempt to pretend that the priest might have come on some other business. "Far from it, in fact."

"Indeed. He has become rather reckless of late, insofar as concealing his movements is concerned. His ambitions have never been a secret, but he has usually tried to work in covert fashion. It is rare for his actions to become so transparent. He showed you the book of the secrets of the comprachicos, I believe, and presumably asked you to employ them in remaking the face of the child you are treating at King's College Hospital. I also assume that he spoke to you about the face of Adam, but that you did not believe what he said. Am I correct so far?"

"I'm not a Catholic," Victory said, without bothering to offer any formal sign of assent, "but I have a vague notion that Monsignor is a title reserved for members of the pope's personal staff. Is that true?"

"Not necessarily," the priest replied, "even in theory—but in this particular instance, yes. I am attached to the papal household as well as to the Holy Office."

Victory had to grope for the significance of that phrase, but he found it. "The Holy Office?" he echoed. "You mean the *Inquisition*?"

The Monsignor smiled again. "Your reading, though doubtless wide, is a little out of date, Dr. Victory. There is no Inquisition. There has been no Inquisition for more than two hundred years, just as there has been no society of comprachicos for more than two hundred years. The Holy Office is an investigative body, but it uses very different methods of investigation from those of Tomas de Torquemada."

"Are you investigating the comprachicos, or the modern cults that have modelled themselves on the Visionary Martyrs and the Sons of Job?"

"That's a rather fine distinction, Dr. Victory. Yes, we are interested in all these matters."

"And you believe that you know who Gwynplaine really is?"

"Yes, of course. We know who he is, where he is, and what he is trying to do. That is what I have come to tell you—although I am beginning to suspect that you already know."

"So who is he?" Victory demanded, abruptly.

"He is the Devil. He is where he has always been—in Hell. And what he is trying to do is obtain his release therefrom."

Victory felt that he ought at least to pretend to be flabbergasted by this series of statements, but he also felt sure that any imposture on his part would be obvious.

"He wasn't in Hell three days ago," Victory said, eventually. "He was sitting exactly where you are—and he came back again the following day. Does Hell have its own underground station nowadays?"

"From his point of view," Torricelli countered, smiling politely at Victory's appallingly weak joke, "this was Hell, nor was he out of it. I am borrowing from Marlowe, of course, but the description is sound. Did you really not understood what I meant, or are you in what fashionable parlance calls *denial*?"

"I don't believe in the Devil," Victory said, flatly.

"Of course you do," the Monsignor replied. "A sceptical man might plausibly doubt the existence of God, but none can doubt the existence of the Devil. You're human, after all. Good may be elusive within your personal experience, but not temptation. You might plausibly doubt that the Devil can take human form, I suppose, but you cannot possibly doubt the temptation to sin. You know pride, covetousness, anger, envy—you, of all people, must have a very keen appreciation of the force of envy—and all the rest. Or is it only their deadliness that you doubt?"

Victory remembered that some so-called authorities asserted that the comprachicos had been implicated in the origin of the Jesuits, who had the reputation of being masters of sophistry. "That's not at all the same thing as believing in the *literal* existence of the Devil," he said. "What I mean is that I don't believe in the Devil as a *person*."

"I can understand that you might doubt that the Devil can manifest himself in that way," the Monsignor replied, equably, "even having spent time in his company. But the simple fact is that the Devil came to you, in person, bearing temptation in his arms—and you were tempted. I understand that too. I have come to ask you to resist that temptation. Please don't tell me that it's none of my business, Dr. Victory, because it most definitely is."

"You wouldn't be Dr. Rosenfeld's mysterious patient, by any chance?" Victory said, bearing in mind that anyone could print business cards with the aid of a desktop computer, or hire a clerical collar.

"You are at liberty to check my credentials," the Monsignor replied. "I'm staying at the Archbishop's palace. He will vouch for me personally—and if his word does not suffice, feel free to call the Vatican."

"That's all right," Victory said. "I'll take your word for it, since it doesn't seem to me to matter much one way or the other. Have you any more information for me—unwelcome or otherwise?"

Victory tried to sound weary as he made this speech, but he couldn't entirely remove the edge of unease from his voice. He wondered whether there was a level somewhere beneath his conscious mind in which he did indeed retain a certain childlike faith in the literal existence of the Devil, and an equally childlike certainty that he *might* be able to meet the Devil in human guise, if he were unlucky enough, but the thought was difficult to entertain. If the Devil existed, then God presumably existed too—and that possibility seemed too horrible to contemplate, given the present state of the world.

"If you follow the instructions he gives you," Torricelli said, bluntly, "they will not have the effect he has promised."

"I had wondered why the Devil might be interested in recreating the face of Adam and precipitating the day of judgment," Victory said. "Are you telling me that he's trying to incarnate the Antichrist?"

"I am not privy to his plans," the monsignor said. "All I know for sure is that his intentions are not good. You are in danger, Dr. Victory."

"Do you mean physical danger, or is it my soul that you're concerned for?"

"Your soul—but I would not rule out the possibility of physical danger, from Gwynplaine or his unwitting followers."

"Unwitting followers?" Victory echoed. "Do you mean the Sons of Job or the Visionary Martyrs—or both?"

"I mean both—and others too."

"According to my research," Victory said, "The Visionary Martyrs and the Sons of Job probably think that Gwynplaine is Cain rather than the Devil."

"Are you saying that you find that the more plausible hypothesis?" the monsignor riposted.

Victory sat up a little straighter in his chair, feeling that he had a contest on his hands. He stared hard at the man whose smile, even now, had not quite disappeared. "Of course not," he said. "The point I'm making is that one contention is as absurd as the other, and that the contradiction makes them even more absurd."

"But the book is real," the priest reminded him, as if turning his own best argument against him, "and the operation has been attempted at least once. It may only be a matter of time, now, before it is attempted again—but you would do better not to attempt it, and you certainly should not attempt it at the Devil's behest."

"Why not, if it really might recreate the face of Adam? Wouldn't the Church like to see a revival of faith and Christ's return?"

"The Church has its own means of spreading God's word," the monsignor told him, "And it is not for us to dictate the terms of Christ's return. If it will help you to make your decision, I can assure you that the Devil will not give you the book, or even let you see it again. It is merely an instrument of temptation."

"I don't think you're in any position to assure me of anything, Monsignor," Victory said. "If you want to influence my decision, you'll need far better argumentative grounds than that. If my sources can be trusted, there are factions even within the Vatican, and some of your own colleagues might well prefer me to carry out the experiment, if not with Amahl then with some other patient. The comprachicos were Catholics, I believe—and they seem to have been sincere in their belief that they could replicate the face of Adam."

"The organization was excommunicated after asserting that belief," the monsignor told him. "They had been seduced, in much the same fashion that you are being seduced. The Devil has seen the face of Adam, but he has no cause to love it; he was an angel once himself, but he sacrificed his own reproduction of the divine countenance. If he did not design and write the pages

98

he has copied for you, he surely guided the hand that did—and his motive for doing so was certainly malign."

"Tell me, Monsignor Torricelli," Victory said, "do you believe in the literal truth of the book of *Genesis*?"

"Yes, I do," Torricelli replied.

"You're a Creationist, then? You don't believe that the earth is more than four billion years old, or that life on its surface has evolved by slow degrees over countless generations?"

"You are making the assumption that one has to choose between the two alternatives," the monsignor said, blandly. "It is a natural assumption, I know, for a mind convinced that the essence of intellectual progress is falsification. It is natural, too, for such a mind to find the notion of unfalsifiability abhorrent. You and I start from different premises, Dr. Victory. I can believe in the literal truth of *Genesis and* the literal truth of evolution. God moves in mysterious ways, his wonders to perform—and He has no fear of trivial contradictions. There is still time for you to retreat, and even to repent, Dr. Victory. You are not lost yet, but if you are a prideful man—as I suspect you are—you have probably thought that the men who failed before and after 1665 were no match for *your* skills, and are enthusiastic to demonstrate your superiority. If so, then you are in dire danger. The person you call Gwynplaine is not to be trusted; even if you were to succeed in helping him to see what he apparently desires to see in the face of the child in your care, he would cheat you and cheat you again. You may think yourself a proud and covetous man, Dr. Victory, but you're only the faintest echo of your model; you still have time to learn humility, and recover hope."

"The fact that you're a man of unbreakable faith," Victory observed, "doesn't mean you aren't deluded. Indeed, I know many men who'd argue that delusion is part and parcel of religious belief. Given that I seem to be surrounded by fantasists, why should I reckon your advice better than any other?"

"Because I represent the Holy Father," the little man replied, refreshing his cherubic smile, "Who is the Lord's representative on Earth."

Victory didn't smile in return. "You said something about wanting a small service from me. I presume that you meant more by that than merely listening to your advice regarding the salvation of my soul."

"That's correct, Dr. Victory," Torricelli said, letting his smile die away in a peculiarly graceful fashion. "We'd like you to surrender the photocopies you have of pages from the Devil's book. Our scholars would be very interested to have the opportunity to study them. We've had two thousand years to study our adversary, of course, but he's a difficult subject. This is a rare opportunity."

"You wouldn't be content with copies of the copies, I suppose?"

"We'd be very grateful for them—but we have a responsibility to you and others not to leave such dangerous information at large, if there's a possibility of containing it."

"And if I refuse even to let you have copies of the copies?"

"Then I shall pray for you, Dr. Victory, with as much hope and optimism as I can muster."

"Well," Victory said, "I'm glad that you've given up on Torquemada's methods."

"The end does not justify the means, Dr. Victory, even when the end is salvation. Do I take it that your seemingly-hypothetical question was, in fact, a refusal?"

"I don't believe in the Devil, Monsignor—except as a bogeyman invented by priests for the purposes of moral terrorism. Like you, Father, I can't and won't believe that the end justifies the means, even when the end is salvation. I'm prepared to accept that you believe what you've told me, although I find it direly difficult, but I insist that it's nonsense, and vile nonsense at that. Whoever Gwynplaine is, he can't be the Devil, and however untrustworthy he is, I won't betray his confidence because you think he is. No, Monsignor Torricelli, I won't give you the photocopies, or even copy them for you. And I'll use my own best judgment regarding the appropriate treatment for Amahl Sahman."

There was no trace of a smile on Monsignor Torricelli's face now. "We had to try, Dr. Victory," he said. "Nor are we permitted to give up. There is one more thing I must say to you before I go. Please, whether you attempt the operation or not, and whether you succeed or not in bringing it to a conclusion, you must destroy the program."

"What program?" Victor asked.

"The computer program that would allow others to duplicate your work. The program that would direct your ingenious surgical instruments, if you decided to follow temptation to its limit, and might allow you to anticipate the results of your work even if you were to repent in time. I don't mean, of course, that you need to destroy its present version, but you really must destroy any version you produce with the assistance of the Devil's book, whether you use it or not. Do not allow it to be copied, and make perfectly sure that no one will ever be able to reconstruct it. No matter how careless you may be for your own soul, you have no right to endanger others. Whatever else you do, *you must destroy the computer program*."

Victory tried hard to control his own expression, lest he give too much away, but he knew that his hostility must show. On what authority, he wondered, had the Monsignor decided that his work was so dangerous? What on Earth did the Vatican expect to happen if he adapted the alleged secrets of the comprachicos into his software? Did the College of Cardinals think *everyone* would want the face of the Antichrist—everyone, at least, who could pay the price? And did they think that such a possibility was terrible enough to create Hell on Earth? How was that compatible with the Monsignor quoting Marlowe, alleging that Hell was already on Earth? That, at least, was an opinion with which many people, contemplating the unfolding ecocatastrophe and the dire prophecies of the GEM, might agree.

It was all too absurd. The man really was mad.

"If that's all you've got to say, Monsignor," Victory said, flatly, "I'd like you to go. I have a great deal of work to do." He resisted the temptation to add: *The Devil's work.*

CHAPTER ELEVEN

The Fourth Day: Late Afternoon and Evening

Monsignor Torricelli made no move to leave. "I seem to have mishandled the situation," he observed, displaying a propensity for understatement that Victory had not expected to find in him. "Alas, I have no alternative available to me but the truth. My opponent is the father of lies, and far more versatile. He was an angel himself, as I said, before his own fall. He can remember what he and Adam looked like, and that only serves to inflame his envy. You have nothing to gain from this, Dr. Victory—nothing at all. You cannot benefit your patient, and might do him harm. It is not in your interests or his to do what Gwynplaine asks of you. On the other hand, we can reward you for doing otherwise, if that is your desire. I am prepared to pay you for the photocopies, and for your promise to desist from all further work on the project."

Victory was curious to know what magnitude of bribe the Vatican might be willing to part with, but he didn't want to waste any more time. "I already have more money than I can spend," he said. "The only thing I want just now that I don't already have is Gwynplaine's book, and the opportunity to increase my knowledge and skills with whatever I can learn from it. I don't have any particular interest in the faces of angels, but I do have an intimate and passionate interest in human faces and the means to their repair and improvement. We have nothing further to discuss, Monsignor Torricelli"

"You're making a mistake, Dr. Victory," the little man said. "I wish you'd reconsider. I beg you not to do the Devil's work, and not to increase his power to do it for himself. His hands are never idle, but they've always been clumsy, and it's greatly to the advantage of the world that they remain that way. You still have a choice in this matter, Dr. Victory. Use it wisely, I beg of you."

"That's exactly what I'm trying to do," Victory assured him. "It's just that my wisdom and your faith don't see eye to eye. Goodbye, Monsignor Torricelli."

This time, the priest condescended to stand up, and made his way to the door. He almost turned back to make one last plea, but in the end he left without another word.

Victory was surprised to discover how glad he was to find himself alone again.

As soon as he heard the outer door close behind the man from the Vatican, Victory activated his computer—not to work on Gwynplaine's plans but to work on one that was entirely his own: the program for Mrs. Allison's second operation. It was extremely difficult to concentrate, but he knew that the work had to be done, and rapidly. The woman's second operation was not due to take place until Sunday, but he would have to see her before then, and he needed to be fully prepared for that confrontation. He needed to update the program for the final operation to take account of the exact results of the first.

Claire came in soon after the clergyman had gone to ask if she might leave. Victory gave her permission immediately, but the secretary hesitated. He met her eyes, and realised that she was extremely curious about the monsignor's visit—and understandably so.

"The great and the good are beginning to beat a path to my door," he said, as lightly as he could. "Everyone is taking an interest in my work, it seems—even the Lord."

"Are you all right, Dr. Victory?" the secretary asked.

"Of course I am," Victory told her. "Never better."

"I know I shouldn't ask," she persisted, "but was it something to do with Mr. Gwynplaine?"

Victory remembered what Gwynplaine had said to her about stalling enquiries. "Has anyone else been asking questions about him?" he asked, tacitly admitting that the answer to her question was yes."

"Only Dr. Rosenfeld," Claire replied. "But...you don't seem quite yourself, Dr. Victory, since he first came to see you. Dr. Hemlet took two of your operations today, I believe."

"Yes she did," Victory said, dismissively. "What do mean, *only Dr. Rosenfeld*? What did she want to know about Gwynplaine? How does she even know that Gwynplaine exists?"

"I don't know, Dr. Victory—how she knows, that is. She didn't seem to know his name. She just asked me if a man who had been in a bad fire had made an appointment to see you. She apologized for asking, but said that it was something she needed to know in connection with her treatment of one of her own patients. I told her that I couldn't possibly discuss the matter, and that she'd have to talk to you—but she told me not to disturb you. I think perhaps she deduced that the answer was yes from the fact that I didn't simply say no. Was I wrong to say what I did?"

"No, of course not," Victory reassured her. "Everyone else in the world, up to and including the pope, seems to know that Gwynplaine was here; Dr. Rosenfeld and her mysterious patient are probably the last to find out. You're doing an excellent job, Claire. Make sure you claim for all the overtime you've put in recently. I'll be here tomorrow—I'll see you then. And I really am quite all right, in spite of all the hard work. I thrive on it."

The young woman left, apparently reassured. Victory went back to work, but he had hardly had time to muster his concentration when he was interrupted by the ringing of his phone. He made no move to pick it up, and didn't even bother to check the display to confirm that the caller's number was being withheld, but he couldn't help pausing to listen to the message that would be recorded on his answering machine.

He knew as soon as the voice began speaking that it was not Asmodeus.

"You were supposed to ring me, Dr. Victory," the male voice said. "Please pick up—I know you're there."

Victory hesitated briefly, but then did as he was asked. "You're too late," he said, "and way too melodramatic in your methods. You should have done this sooner if you wanted to be taken seriously."

"What do you mean, *too late*?" the voice demanded.

"I mean that I've already heard two completely unbelievable accounts of who Gwynplaine really is. If you agree with one or other of those judgments, it won't make it any more believable—and if you come up with a third account, that will be one more item to add to a list that's already preposterous. Who are you speaking for, by the way? Are you with the Sons of Job or the Visionary Martyrs?"

"You've seen Torricelli," the caller said, ignoring Victory's question. "He's told you that Gwynplaine's the Devil. I'm not surprised you didn't believe that. Who else has given you a name?"

"Don't leave any more notes tucked under my windscreen wiper," Victory said, "and don't call again. I've heard from too many cranks already, and they're all more polite than you."

"*Don't hang up!*" the caller begged.

"Then give me a reason not to," Victory said. "Tell me something I don't already know, that I might be prepared to believe."

"Anything that you might be prepared to believe, at present is almost certainly false," the voice told him. "We really ought to meet, if you're to be persuaded otherwise. I can offer you proof of the true nature of the conspiracy, and I can tell you the name of the man who's behind it. If I were as careless of what other people see and know as Torricelli is, I might bring it to you, but the man in question might easily do me harm, even though he's highly unlikely to do any to you. You must know by now that there are people watching you like hawks."

"I've seen no one," Victory stated.

"But you've heard from too many so-called cranks to be in doubt. Either Gwynplaine's worse than careless, or he's deliberately drawing us all in, hoping that we'll spend so much time watching one another that we'll somehow lose sight of him. I dare say that the only reason no one's tried to blow your safe yet is that everyone's wondering whether that's exactly what someone else wants them to do. You may be in danger, doctor—not from us, I promise you, or even from the man who's pulling Gwynplaine's strings, but there are people holding more powerful hands than ours who might decide that the simplest way to stop the Georgian is to stop you."

"What Georgian? And who are you, exactly?" Victory demanded.

"Not on the phone," the caller insisted. "We really do need to meet in a safe place."

"You might," Victory said. "I don't. I'm not taking sides in this. I'll decide what to do on the basis of what's best for the boy, and for me."

"You haven't a clue what's best for the boy, or yourself," the caller said, angrily. "If you insist on playing a lone hand, you'll get yourself into deep trouble."

"Is that a threat?"

"You're the threat, Dr. Victory, if you go through with this blindly. I'll admit that we don't know exactly what Gwynplaine's trying to achieve, but we do know who's behind it and we need to know more. We need to see the book, or at least the photocopies, and it would be in your interest to give us the chance. The time might soon come when you'll need our protection."

"And whose protection would that be, exactly?" Victory demanded, impatiently.

"I can't tell you!" the caller complained. "But I can tell you that there's no one else you can trust—even Rosenfeld and Williams can't be written off as innocent bystanders, at this stage of the game. We need to see the photocopies, Dr. Victory, to help us figure out what Gwynplaine's puppet-master is up to and how to stop him."

Victory wasn't unduly surprised to hear the names of Rachel Rosenfeld and Huw Williams being dropped into the conversation, but he retained his conviction that they, at least, were perfectly sane and not involved with any recently-resurrected cults. "I refuse to arrange secret assignations with unknown individuals," he said, flatly. "If you'll tell me your name, and wait for me to check it out, I might agree to talk to you."

"No way," said the caller. "Don't say you weren't warned, though, if things go pear-shaped. And watch your back; the enemy might be closer than you think."

Victory hung up then, feeling almost as angry as the other man had sounded. The final attempt to make him suspect anyone and everyone seemed to him to be a viciously low blow. He could not doubt that it had been a crank call—every bit as cranky, in its own way, as Monsignor Torricelli's alleged revelations—but it still added to the burden of his discomfort. Huw Williams' voice of sanity suddenly seemed very distant.

Even so, the surgeon still had to complete the work on the plan for Mrs. Allison's surgery, and feed the data into his programs. Yet again, he set out to do exactly that. Mercifully, it didn't take long. The night was still relatively young when he went out to get something to eat at a local Italian restaurant. He half-expected to be followed to its door, or for some furtive person in a shabby raincoat to slide into one of the empty seats at his table, but nothing of the sort happened. When he returned to his consulting rooms, the inner office was untrashed, and the safe uncracked.

"I'm getting paranoid," he muttered, aloud, as he settled down at his desk. "On the other hand, I'd probably be crazy if I weren't."

He unlocked the safe then, and brought out the photocopies. He resumed work on the task he had already begun: that of reproducing the written instructions in machine code, so that they might be carried out by his nanoscalpels and their associated instruments, if ever he cared to feed the figures into his software. He was immediately seized by the force of pattern he was trying to master, and his intuitive understanding of what he was doing seemed to increase by a further order of magnitude as the clock measured out the hour between ten and eleven o'clock.

By the time he stopped to stretch and yawn, Victory felt that he was on the brink of being able to carry through the entire sequence—including the steps specified in the pages Gwynplaine had carefully withheld from him. He had to change mental gear again, however, to consider what to do next. He had promised to make a new set of photocopies for Huw Williams, and now seemed to be a good time to do that—but he was alone in his office, at the dead of night. If he made a new set of copies for Williams now, he would have to take them down to his car, which was doubtless alone in the garage, and then drive them home to his equally-deserted flat in Westbourne Park.

Whatever else the latest crank call had achieved, it had made him very nervous of that prospect. He did not have to make the copies at Claire's workstation, given that his own printer was capable of doubling as a scanner and color copier, so he could easily make them in private the following morning, in broad daylight, with plenty of other people in the building—and he would then be able to deliver them in broad daylight too.

That seemed the more tempting prospect.

While he thought all this over, the photocopies were still on the desk in front of him. Like Huw Williams, they seemed a welcome voice of sanity, by virtue of their solidity and their detail. There was no rumor about them; they were not merely real but quite objective. There was no explicit mention therein of the face of Adam, and nothing whatsoever about any further effect than the transfiguration the instructions were intended to produce. They were specifications for surgery, nothing more. There was nothing miraculous or diabolical about them; they were simply accounts of where to cut and where to make reattachments—and they made sense. Logically and aesthetically, they made sense.

There was nothing inherent in the images or the text to prove whether the diagrams had been made in the seventeenth century or much more recently, nor anything to indicate the identity of their maker—but Victory could not doubt, now that he had worked with them intimately enough to sense their underlying rationale and their implicit artistry, that what they represented was something real, viable and expert. In a way, the aesthetic element was more important than the logical one. The fact that the instructions were workable was unsurprising; the fact that they were calculated to produce an extraordinary beauty was something else—and they *were* calculated to produce an extraordinary kind of beauty.

Hugo Victory was a cosmetic surgeon as well as a plastic surgeon; he was an artist as well as a mere healer. He could not have functioned without the capacity to feel certain that what he did as his nanoscalpels worked away beneath the surface, in a world composed of cells and vessels, was not merely doing no harm but actively doing *good*, creating an abundance of beauty—and perhaps a touch of sublimity—that had not been present before in the flesh upon which he worked.

He stared down at the photocopies, looking at them with new eyes now that he had become party to their secret and their conspiracy. It still seemed utterly absurd to him that the face they were calculated to produce could be the face of Adam in any but the most distantly metaphorical sense, but it *was* a face that was subtly different from any that natural selection had ever produced, and it was different in a quintessentially beautiful way. The face produced by following these instructions would be more than handsome; it would be capable of expressions that conventional facial musculature could not produce. In all probability, such unprecedented expressions would be completely meaningless, in terms of emotional significance, and yet....

Perhaps they would be far from meaningless. Perhaps they would be highly effective, in a way that could not possibly be predicted by anyone who had never seen them before.

Victory sighed and gathered the photocopies together. He placed them carefully in the safe, and double-checked that it was locked.

As soon as he returned to his desk, the telephone rang. He picked it up immediately and said: "Who is this?"

"It's Asmodeus," the called replied. "I assume, given your tone, that you were expecting someone else far less welcome. Or have you conceived a sudden irrational dislike for me?"

"I can't say that I like you," Victory replied, "or that I look forward to your calls."

"Were you disappointed in Dr. Williams, then? I thought the two of you would get on, and might be able provide one another with some welcome reassurance that the world had not gone completely mad."

"No, I wasn't disappointed—but I might well have been able to find him without your help. I'd be a lot better disposed towards you if you'd tell me who you really are—and who you imagine Gwynplaine really is."

"Who I *imagine* Gwynplaine really is? I can assure you, Dr. Victory, that I have a far less fertile imagination than anyone else you might have talked to, with the possible exception of Gwynplaine. Might I ask who has been confusing you?"

"Monsignor Torricelli, for one. The other caller wouldn't leave a name, but he implied that he represented one of the poorer organizations involved in the quest to obtain the book. He kindly volunteered to tell me the name of Gwynplaine's puppetmaster, if I'd only meet him at some secret rendezvous and bring the photocopies along. I declined the offer."

"That's probably wise. My guess is that he was with a version of the Visionary Martyrs. The Sons of Job seem to be far better-organized and better-financed, although it didn't help them to get their hands on the book. Torricelli sincerely believes that Gwynplaine's the Devil, of course, but he's wrong. The Church is trapped by its own dogma; it's an easy mistake to make, but a silly one. He's not Cain either, if the Martyrs have suggested that. Don't worry about the Martyrs, by the way. The Sons are better placed to interfere, but they've been obligingly discreet so far. Forgive me if I seem a little excited, but I haven't had this much fun in centuries."

"Centuries?" Victory queried.

"I'm Asmodeus, remember? Ex-king of the demons, ex-husband of Lilith. Centuries are mere moments to me. I've lived through entire epochs of nature in the blink of an eye, and then relived them again and again and again, with slight and not-so-slight variations. I've explored a million pasts and a hundred thousand futures. It's what I do, when I'm not chatting with my friends; it keeps me from being bored."

"Right," said Victory. "The reason you know that Gwynplaine's not the Devil is that you are—and you're an old friend of Cain's, so you know that Gwynplaine isn't him either. What do you want? I was just on my way home."

"Have you decided to go ahead with the operation?" Asmodeus asked, bluntly.

"No," Victory replied.

"Is that *no* as in you haven't decided, or *no* as in you've decided not to do it?"

"I don't need to tell you anything," Victory said, tiredly.

"Of course not—but I thought we had a deal. Fair exchange, and all that."

"I don't have anything to exchange," Victory said. "And I doubt that you do either. I mean information, not advice. I've had my fill of that."

"I can believe it—and you haven't heard from the Sons of Job yet, at least not directly. You can take it for granted that the Sons have made their plans, though—and they do seem to be in a stronger position than their rivals to carry them through."

"Hang on," Victory said, suddenly afraid that Asmodeus might hang up as abruptly as he usually did. "When you say that the Sons of Job have made plans, are you just talking about the boy who might or might not have Adam's face, or does that include Lilith too?"

"I told you that Huw would be useful, didn't I? Yes, Dr. Victory, their plans include Lilith. She's been working with the Sons for a long time, if she's not actually behind them. I wouldn't put that past her, although the person supposedly pulling *her* strings will doubtless be displeased if she goes into business for herself. This whole scheme might even have been her idea, in the beginning. If so, everyone's been betrayed, all along the line. How amusing!"

"Monsignor Torricelli said that he believed in the literal truth of *Genesis*," Victory observed. "Are you as versatile as he is, able to believe in Eden *and* in evolution."

"Now that's good," Asmodeus said. "You're making progress, Dr. Victory. A little while longer, and you might be nearly ready to believe the truth. Better make haste, though—Monday morning's only eighty-some hours away. For what it's worth, I'm much more versatile than Torricelli; he's a prisoner of the

Church's dogma, as I said. I know the whole truth about Eden, even though I wasn't there. Gwynplaine only thinks he does, because he was. If you ask him about it nicely enough, he might explain. Listen very carefully to what he says, if he condescends to answer you, even though you won't be able to believe it. You might even be able to work out what he's aiming at, and where he's coming from, if you're clever enough. What you and he believe isn't really that important, though, no matter what either of you may think—the point is to figure out what you *want*, and to go for it, if you can. You think I'm talking nonsense, don't you?"

"Yes," Victory said.

"Well, I'm not," Asmodeus retorted, and rang off.

Victory put the phone down gently, feeling even more tired than he had when he picked it up.

CHAPTER TWELVE

The Fifth Day: Late Morning

On Friday morning Victory made haste to the hospital in order to be on time for his appointment with Mrs. Gregory K. Allison. The news was still focused on parliamentary affairs, apart from a routine update on the GEM's predictions and a delayed report of a brawl between the Humanist crusader and the neo-Marxist on the steps of Broadcasting House following their *contretemps* with the makers of Newman and Saxon.

As anticipated, Mrs. Allison's husband was waiting with her. The billionaire shook the surgeon's hand enthusiastically.

"I'm sorry that I wasn't able to accompany my wife when she came to Harley Street," Allison said. He was a tall man, who had already been under the knife himself, but the work that had been done on him was elementary. His neck needed a complete overhaul, and his jaw line needed tightening. His eyebrows were neat enough, but Victory could see a lot of potential in them. On the other hand, his was a face as different from the imaginary Adam's as it was possible to imagine; his lumpen Anglo-Saxon features belonged to an entirely different genre. He and his wife were a conspicuous mismatch, in that respect.

"I'm glad to report that the first operation was a great success," Victory told him. "The programming work for the second is complete, and I've no doubt that everything will go smoothly. Would you like to see the figures or the updated preview?"

"We'll skip the figures," Allison said. "Put the preview on the wallscreen, though—we'd both like to check that out."

Victory plugged his key ring fob into the tower beside Mrs. Allison's bed and instructed the system to display Mrs. Allison's future face on the wall opposite her bed. The image was not significantly different from the one he had displayed on the screen in his consulting room, but the sheer size of it made it seem far more impressive. It seemed positively regal.

A face like that, Victory thought, *could demand anything of any heterosexual man between the ages of fifteen and seventy-five, and be sure that he'd move heaven and earth to comply.*

111

"Very impressive," Allison said, approvingly. "I've always known, of course, that my wife is the most beautiful woman in the world, but this is sheer perfection. Your Ms. Legrange is very anxious that I should allow you to take full credit for your work, as soon as the residual bruises have healed."

"That's not necessary," Victory assured him. "Success of this sort is its own reward."

"I don't doubt it—but Ms. Legrange is right. You deserve the credit for your artistry. Will you be able to work a similar miracle with Amahl?"

"I hope so," Victory said. "I haven't finalised his program yet, but I'm very satisfied with his progress since the penultimate series of operations. You've volunteered to pay for the boy's future care, I believe?"

"More than that," Allison assured him. "We're obliged to complete what you've begun, don't you think—by *we* I mean Britain, of course. We've assumed responsibility for him, and must honour our obligation. He'll have the best life we can make for him, doctor. Education, a career...the sky's the limit."

"I'm sure it is," Victory said. "Do you have any instructions for me, in respect of Amahl's final series of operations?"

"Certainly not. You're the expert, and the artist. I trust your judgment implicitly. Do whatever's best for the boy. You know his face very intimately by now; you know what potential it has. Do what you will."

Mrs. Allison, whose bandaged face was still sore enough to inhibit her speech slightly, had so far said nothing, but now she added her assent to what her husband had said. She was far too old school merely to grunt, so she took the trouble to formulate her words as perfectly as she could. "We want you to do great work, doctor," she said. "We believe the time is ripe."

"Overripe, according to the GEM," Victory murmured.

"Well," said Gregory K. Allison, "if the modern Oracle is right and the world really is about to end, and the ecocatastrophe does take humankind and all our interdependent species down, no one will be able to say that we didn't do great things before we went. Personally, I think we'll survive—precisely because we're capable of such great things. The universe would be a poorer place by far without us."

What magnificently casual arrogance! Victory thought. *What enormous self-satisfaction, in a man who's never made anything but money!*

What he said aloud, though, was: "I hope you're right, Mr. Allison. If the Day of Judgment is at hand, I'm hoping for a *not guilty* verdict—and not by reason of insanity."

There was just an instant when Gregory K. Alison's eyes hardened, as if with suspicion—but then the moment vanished, and he was all smiles again. The laugh lines at the corners of his mouth and eyes needed work, but Victory was too polite to point it out.

After a brief, one-sided chat with Amahl Sahman and a not-so-brief debriefing session with Christina Legrange, Victory got back to the reproduction Bentley shortly after ten thirty. He had a trouble-free journey, arriving at his consulting-rooms at a few minutes to eleven.

Claire had no news for him either—but that was because Rachel Rosenfeld had obviously chosen to bypass the orthodox channels of communication that protocol demanded for fellow practitioners. The psychotherapist came into the reception area just as he was about to turn the key in the mechanical lock that kept his inner sanctum doubly secure.

"Could you possibly spare me a few minutes Dr. Victory?" she asked.

"In what connection?" Victory asked.

"In connection with one of my patients. He's upstairs in my office now. He'd like to see you. I don't know for sure that you'll be interested in what he has to say, but I think you might—and I'd rather be present, if you don't mind. It may help me with his further treatment."

Victory thought through the implications of this statement in a matter of moments. "You mean that one of your patients wants to share his paranoid delusions with me, and you want to watch?"

"I wouldn't put it that way," Dr. Rosenfeld said, blandly—but she didn't take the trouble to put it any other way.

"Fine," Victory said. "Lead the way." To Claire, he said: "If anyone calls, tell them I've been delayed. If it's Mr. Gwynplaine, you can let him into the office.

As they went up the stairs, Rachel Rosenfeld said: "I'm not certain that this is a wise move, Dr. Victory, but my patient is rather insistent, and I got the impression when we talked in the car park on Monday night that you and he have certain interests in common."

"You can call me Hugo," Victory said. "You mean the comprachicos, I suppose."

"I was surprised to hear you ask about them," the psychotherapist replied, evasive as ever.

"Sufficiently impressed to ask my secretary whether I'd recently been consulted by a man with bad burns. Quite frankly, Rachel, I'm a little surprised by that. Surely you should have spoken directly to me."

"I was trying to confirm something my patient had told me," Dr. Rosenfeld relied with no sign of contrition. "I merely wanted to know if the man who was sitting in your office on Monday afternoon had been badly burned; your secretary very properly replied that she couldn't say. I accepted her judgment."

"Very scrupulous," Victory said, as they reached the door of Rachel Rosenfeld's suite. He nodded politely to the psychotherapist's receptionist as he passed her desk on the way to the inner office, which was situated directly above his own.

Dr. Rosenfeld's patient turned out to be a boy, perhaps fifteen or sixteen years of age. He was sitting in one of two armchairs positioned by the desk, not lying on the couch. He was a little pale, but otherwise seemed to be in perfectly good health. His skin had the tautness of youth, but Victory could see that his jowls would need work in future years, and that he would benefit considerably from the remoulding of his nose and ears. Victory also observed that he was exceptionally well-dressed—not in the trivial sense that his clothes bore fashionable labels, but in the more refined sense that his suit had obviously been made to measure. In a way, the fact that he was wearing a suit at all was just as remarkable, given his age. How many teenagers, Victory wondered, put on their Sunday best in order to meet with their psychotherapists?"

"This is Joseph," Rachel Rosenfeld said. "Joseph, this is Dr. Hugo Victory."

Victory took note of the fact that the boy had retained the full version of his given name. He shook the boy's hand, and sat down in the second chair. "I believe you wanted to see me, Joseph," he said. "You do understand that I can't discuss any of my clients, don't you?"

"I understand," the boy said. "I'm not trying to find anything out...or rather, I *am* trying to find some things out, but I understand that you might not be able to tell me even if you knew. What worries me more is that you might not know certain things that I know...or at least suspect. You probably think I'm crazy because of where we are, and I probably am, a little—but my finding certain things difficult has nothing to do...or very little to do...with the things I want to tell you. Dr. Rosenfeld says that you've heard of the comprachicos."

Victory glanced at Rachel Rosenfeld, who was sitting on the other side of the desk in a conspicuously relaxed manner.

"Yes," Victory said. "I've been doing some research into them."

"So have I," Joseph said. "More to the point, so has my father. Have you also heard of the Sons of Job?"

"Yes," Victory said, "and the Visionary Martyrs too. I've learned a good deal since Monday, although some of what I've been told is rather confusing, and I'm not sure that I believe any of it."

"The scroll-fragments aren't all genuine," Joseph said, "but some of them seem to be. There are other documents too—but as for the story that's been spun out of the few fragments that *are* genuine...that's a completely different matter. Even so, there are people who believe it, obsessively. The Sons of Job and the Visionary Martyrs might have been extinct for the greater part of the last two thousand years, but they exist now. Resurrected or reborn, they exist. The Martyrs allegedly have their visionaries, although I can't say for sure, and the Sons...."

"Have fathers?" Victory suggested, when the boy trailed off.

"That too," Joseph agreed. "I think my father might have started off as a mere collector, just as he started off as a mere businessman, but he never does anything by halves. In fact, he always goes way over the top. Like a confidence trickster who falls for his own patter, he can get carried away in the oddest directions—so my mother says. She's known him a lot longer than I have. Sometimes, she says, that makes him vulnerable to people prepared to flatter his illusions—and there are always people willing to flatter a rich man's illusions. My father thinks he's cleverer by far than anyone who might want to take him in, and it's mostly true—but it also means that when he does get taken in, he can't be persuaded of the fact. Not by anyone, least of all...."

Again the boy trailed off, and Victory tried again to hurry him along. "So he's joined the Sons of Job," Victory said. "He's been trying to locate the last secret of the comprachicos, I suppose—the book that was supposed to have been lost in the Great Fire of London."

"He's been trying very hard for some years," the boy said. "He's not a man who tolerates frustration very well."

"And what makes you think that I can help him in his quest?" Victory asked, bluntly.

"I don't," Joseph replied, equally bluntly. "I don't believe any such book exists—but I do know that my father's attempts to find one have created an exceedingly tempting prospect for would-be forgers. The problem any such forger would have, though, is convincing my father of the authenticity of his product. He would have to go about that in a very clever—and perhaps very convoluted—manner. There isn't much that the forger could do by way of establishing provenance in an orthodox manner, so he might be tempted to tackle the problem from another angle, by obtaining a different sort of certificate of authenticity. He might, for instance, attempt to obtain the services of a plastic surgeon in certifying that the operation described by the so-called last secret of the comprachicos was both viable and original."

Victory frowned, but he had no time to object. "I'm not ac-cusing you of being part of any conspiracy," Joseph said. "Dr. Rosenfeld assures me that you wouldn't be party to any fraud, and I can't believe that a man in your position would stoop to something like that. But everyone is manipulable, Dr. Victory, if the manipulation is clever enough. If my father can be fooled, anyone can. The reason I wanted to see you was to warn you that you might be the victim of a confidence trick—and that you might not realise it, because you might not have been able to see what the people tricking you stood to gain. What I want you to consider is that you might only be an instrument in a plot whose real target is my father; he's the one who might be persuaded to part with an enormous amount of money for the secret of the comprachicos, if only he could be persuaded that the document containing it is genuine. When I say *an enormous amount*, I mean it; we're talking about someone who has more money than he could ever spend—a man who could throw away a sum that any ordinary person would consider a fortune, on a whim or a bet."

"I see," Victory said. "And you're worried about your in-heritance?"

Joseph laughed. "Mother and I have already been disinher-ited, in the sense that we have any claim on his ever-growing for-tune," he said. "The settlements he made following the divorce were very generous—neither of us will ever want for anything—but they're a *fait accompli*. I don't stand to gain a penny by giv-ing you this warning, Dr. Victory, and even if I did...as I said, my father could throw away a few million without it making any appreciable difference to what remained. On the other hand, if he ever did figure out that he'd been conned—and he almost cer-tainly would, eventually—he might be inclined to strike back at anyone involved in the con, if he could find them. I doubt that he'd be able to find the man who brought you the book—assuming that someone has brought you the book—but he'd cer-tainly be able to find you."

"So your motives are entirely altruistic?" Victory said. "It's just your spirit of fair play that obliged you to tip me off?"

"I'd like to think so," Joseph said. "Dr. Rosenfeld thinks that I might be trying to get back at my father because I can't forgive him for deserting my mother and me. In fact, although she would never dream of saying so, Dr. Rosenfeld probably thinks that I invented this whole scheme as a means of trying to do that. She doesn't think I'm lying, mind—just that I've inherited my fa-ther's talent for getting carried away by the force of my own speculations. She might be right, of course. She's the doctor—I'm just the patient."

Victory turned to look at Rachel Rosenfeld, whose face was perfectly impassive. She had been in practice a long time, and had long since mastered the art of non-direction.

Victory pondered the possibilities for a moment, and then said: "What makes you think that someone has brought this forged book to me, in the hope that I can be deceived into providing some sort of authentification? Just because I mentioned the comprachicos to Dr. Rosenfeld on Monday...."

"I didn't even know about that until today," Joseph was quick to say. "It wasn't until I put that together with the fact that I saw Lilith in your office as I was coming up the stairs for my Monday appointment...."

This time, it was Victory who interrupted. "You think you saw *Lilith* in my office?"

"I did see Lilith in your office. I know my own stepmother, Dr. Victory. I may not like her very much, but I certainly know her."

It was Victory's turn to put two and two together. "Your father is Gregory K. Allison," he said, secretly calling himself all kinds of a fool for not having guessed before, "and Mrs. Gregory K. Allison's given name is Lilith."

"Ah!" said the boy. "You really didn't know that, did you? She never uses her first name nowadays, of course, but if you'd only researched her on the web, you'd have found out easily enough."

Victory's head was spinning now. He had so far withheld judgment on the boy's story, because it seemed that he would have plenty of time to think it over at his leisure, but this extra layer of complication had created a sense of desperate urgency. He conjured up an image in his mind of the scene in his outer office on Monday, when he had ushered Mrs. Allison to Claire's desk: the way she had looked Gwynplaine up and down, and the way in which Gwynplaine had so studiously ignored her. Even at the time, he had not thought it entirely a coincidence that Mrs. Allison had arrived on his doorstep immediately before he was to begin the final phase of Amahl Sahman's treatment—and he had learned enough facts since then to convince him of it.

Eventually, he said: "Are you implying that your stepmother is in on this alleged conspiracy of confidence tricksters?"

"Of course not," the boy replied. "She already has free access to his money. What I'm implying is that she's been feeding his fantasy for years, because that's how they met. It's a *folie à deux*—she'll be just as much a victim of the con as he will, but she'll increase his vulnerability to it immeasurably. Any confidence trickster worth his salt would try to get to her first, rather than approaching my father directly."

"So Dr. Rosenfeld really was trying to confirm what you thought your stepmother might have seen in my office: a man scarred by fire, sitting with a briefcase ostentatiously displayed on his lap."

"Of course."

"And the real reason I was sent to see Huw Williams—not to mention the real reason why Monsignor Torricelli of the Holy Office and the Visionary Martyrs were tipped off that I'd been contacted—was to make sure that the information got back to Gregory K. Allison. The whole idea was to help him find out, as if by a fortuitous combination of accidents, that I'd been approached by someone wanting me to operate on his Palestinian protégé in accordance with the final secret of the comprachicos?"

The questions were purely rhetorical, echoing Victory's realisation that if Gwynplaine and Asmodeus were working together, he might indeed have been played for a colossal sucker. Joseph Allison answered anyway. "You've been contacted by the Vatican?" he said, astonished. "Now that *is* clever. The folk who call themselves Visionary Martyrs must be easy enough to manipulate, but the Holy Office...."

"Is a prisoner of its own dogma," Victory finished for him. "My God, I shook hands with your father not two hours ago. He assured me of his confidence in my plans to operate on your stepmother. He seemed perfectly...."

It was Victory's turn to trail off, as he remembered exactly how imperfectly sane Gregory K. Allison had seemed—and Mrs. Allison too. It was Joseph who was seeing the psychotherapist, though, and Rachel Rosenfeld had neither confirmed nor denied his earlier speculation that what her patient wanted to let him in on was a pattern of paranoid delusions.

Victory looked at Dr. Rosenfeld again. "What do you think of all this, Rachel?" he asked.

"I think it's fascinating," she replied, with the tiniest of smiles.

"Yes," said Victory," but do you think it's *true*?"

"How can I possibly tell?" the psychotherapist replied, secure in her innocence. "You and Joseph are the ones in possession of all the evidence. If someone really is trying to swindle Gregory K. Allison out of a few million pounds, and you really are an unwitting tool in the tricksters' game, you're in a far better position than I am to find the proof—or the evidence that would slay the hypothesis."

"Thanks for your assistance, Dr. Rosenfeld," Victory said, sarcastically.

"Please don't blame Dr. Rosenfeld," Joseph put in. "This really wasn't her idea. She's only doing what she's professionally obliged to do—to help her patients discover their own solutions their problems."

"I'm not her patient," Victory said, brusquely.

"I'm sure that Dr. Rosenfeld applies the same principle to her personal relationships," the boy told him, sounding altogether unlike a teenager. "In any case, she's not to blame. I'm the one who asked her to bring you up here. I thought that you needed and deserved to know what I think about what might be happening here. You're under no obligation to believe me. But I was right to deduce that the man with the briefcase has brought you a book, wasn't I? Do you mind my asking how much you know about him?"

Victory wasn't sure whether he minded or not, but he answered anyway. "Not a damn thing," he said. "According to Torricelli, he's the Devil incarnate. I don't know for sure, but the Visionary Martyrs and the Sons of Job *might* think he's the immortal Cain. His co-conspirator, if there really is a conspiracy, says that he's neither, although he *was* in the Garden of Eden when the whole story kicked off, which I guess would make him Adam. But no, I don't have the slightest idea who he really is. All I know is that his burns are real, and the book is real. Forgery or not, it's real. If it *is* a forgery, it's a work of art in more ways than one. Whoever made the book was probably a genius. Whoever designed those instructions certainly was. If your father can get it for a few million, he's got a bargain, even if it's a fake. I'd love to meet the plastic surgeon who planned that operation, whether he's a seventeenth-century barber or some elderly Georgian surgeon who spent his youth fixing up victims of the Russian occupation of Afghanistan, his middle age living in grinding post-Soviet poverty and the early years of his retirement mastering the lost language of his ancestors."

"That would be the way to do it, all right," the boy agreed. "It's a slightly more plausible explanation, don't you think, than the notion that your mysterious visitor really is the Devil or Cain, or Adam?"

"Yes," Victory conceded, "it is." He could imagine Huw Williams nodding judiciously in approval, even though he too had been in touch with Asmodeus. That afterthought prompted Victory to ask a further question: "Was your stepmother married before, by any chance?"

"Yes, she was," Joseph confirmed. "Briefly, I believe—not nearly as long as my father and mother were married."

"And her first husband would know, I suppose, about her fascination with the Sons of Job?"

"I suppose," Joseph agreed. "I never met the man."

"Do you know his name?"

"His surname was Yashvili, but I don't know anything more about him than that. I dare say that you can look him up on the web easily enough.

"I dare say that I can," Victory agreed. He looked at the boy, wondering whether Joseph had chosen to wear his suit not to impress Dr. Rosenfeld but to impress *him*—to appear to the man he had come to warn not as a child or a psychotherapist's patient but as a serious and businesslike person.

Joseph Allison was, at the end of the day, still little more than a child, and he was obviously a child who was still affected by his parents' divorce—but that didn't mean that his calculations were incorrect. Indeed, the boy, like his counterpart in Hans Christian Andersen's story of the emperor's new clothes, might perhaps be the only one who was sufficient innocent to see clearly, unimprisoned by any dogma, ambition, vanity or criminal intent. If so, then this whole business might be a lot simpler than it had so far seemed—except that there was one complication that Gregory K. Allison's son hadn't been able to spot.

If Gwynplaine and Asmodeus really were running a colossal confidence trick, they weren't just trying to sell Gregory K. the lost book of the comprachicos. They were trying to sell him the face of Adam itself. What might *that* be worth, in today's money?

"Thank you, Joseph," Victory said, with heartfelt sincerity. "I really did need to hear what you've just told me. It puts recent events in an entirely new light."

"You still have to decide what to do about it, of course," the boy observed. "If you go to my father right away and tell him everything, there's a strong possibility that he won't believe you—just as he might not believe me if I decide to tell him, even if I have you to back me up."

"It's not your father that I'll have to confront first," Victory said, as much to himself as to the boy. "It's Gwynplaine."

He was acutely aware, as he said it, that Gwynplaine still had not shown him the final instructions for the operation described in the book: the operation that—however overblown its claims might turn out to be—was still a miracle of human ingenuity.

CHAPTER THIRTEEN

The Fifth Day: Afternoon

When Victory returned to work on the photocopies he already had, he began looking at them in a new way, searching for evidence of deception. He continued to feed the data into his computer programs while he worked, but he felt as he did so that he was in a kind of contest—a guessing game, in which the diagrams and their instructions were clues.

He was no longer certain that there actually were any more pages than he had already been shown. He felt obliged to consider the possibility that the sequence was incomplete because it had always been intended to be incomplete—to tantalise without commitment. It was possible—more than possible, it now seemed—that they would not give him enough information to deduce what the face of Adam would look like, because no such information existed, or ever had existed. What the pages might have been designed to do, in all probability, was merely to persuade him that some kind of unusual or uncanny result might lie just beyond his grasp, in order to heat his curiosity to fever pitch.

If so, it had worked. Now, though, he felt that if he could only solve the puzzle, and work out how the sequence of surgical manipulations might be concluded, he might be able to prove—at least to his own satisfaction—that the whole thing was a hoax, incapable of producing anything but a slightly freakish face: a subtle monstrosity. If this entire business did turn out to be a confidence trick, then he was one of its intended victims, and Victory did not want to be shown up as one more prisoner of dogma and desire, just like everyone else. He wanted to be more than that: a man who could penetrate the mystery, and lay its secrets bare.

He wanted to confront Gwynplaine with something more than a sack full of rumors. If and when the time came to confront Gregory K. Allison with the gloves off, he wanted to do it with a calculation worked out to the last detail.

By half past four the surgeon had modified his test program to take aboard every item of data contained in the photocopies in his possession. He could display the intended realignment of the muscles, and he could even build up that image into the image of a face—but when he did that the face was slightly blurred. He could not tell whether or not there might be some vital additional manipulation that might resolve it in an unexpected fashion, completing a transfiguration that he could not visualise even in his expert imagination.

The face stared at him from the screen, oddly innocent in its not-quite-complete state. It was, of course, a child's face, but it looked like the face of a much younger child than Amahl Sahman: a mere baby, yet to come into the full inheritance of his individuality. There was something about it suggestive of a magical effect, but there was something about a great many unfinished faces that had a similar hint of wonder. Adult humans were pre-programmed to see something enchanting in infant faces—something that facilitated the parental bond, and was never entirely lost once that bond had been formed, even though the face became conspicuously ordinary as the child matured. Something of the same enchantment resurfaced in such odd psychological phenomena as charismatic charm, but that was not the same as bringing it to *fulfillment*. Perhaps, Victory thought, human childish innocence retained something of authentic Adamic innocence, which was only gradually erased by the disfigurement of adolescence, and *might* be restored by plastic surgery if only the trick were known—but the face on the screen had only the innocence of ordinary childhood.

The surgeon activated a program that would "age" the face, projecting it forward to hypothetical adulthood—but he knew even as he did it what result it would produce. The resultant adult face was even more blurred, the innate margin of uncertainly magnified into a gulf. Victory sighed, and reverted to an image of the muscles, diagrammatically marked with the work that his nanoscalpels would have to do. He began testing out the procedure in virtual space, to see where practical problems might develop.

When he was satisfied that he had done all that he needed to do, and all that he could, with the documents in his possession, the surgeon began to reproduce the photocopies themselves by means of the scanner and printer fitted to his computer. He stored the scans carefully, under an innocuous label, among a hundred other password-protected files.

Then he went on to the internet, to find out the full name of Lilith Allison's first husband. There was little or no information available in English beyond his given name, which was Iorga, and his birth-date, which made him at least twenty-five years older than his former wife. The dearth of information regarding his whereabouts or activity before and after Lilith Yashvili had divorced him, nine years before, was slightly suggestive in itself, although citizens of the splinter-nations of the old Soviet Union always tended to be much less visible to the web's data-spiders than the people of Western Europe, America and the Far East.

The surgeon picked up the telephone receiver and punched out Huw Williams' number. "It's Hugo Victory," he said. "I've copied the data we talked about the other day, but I'm a little pressed for time. I have to call in at the hospital this evening before I go home to Oxfordshire. Would you be prepared to pick them up from Harley Street, by any chance?"

"Yes, of course," Williams said, without hesitation. "Right now, you mean?"

"If it's not inconvenient. I'm reluctant to leave them with my secretary for collection, and I don't want to demand that she stays late on a Friday if it can be avoided."

"I'll be there in thirty minutes, traffic permitting," Williams promised. "Can you remind me of the exact address?"

Victory gave the linguist the addresses of the building and the garage, and told him the code that would let him into the garage. Williams didn't waste time asking any more questions.

Not long after he had put the phone down, Claire buzzed Victory to say that Rachel Rosenfeld was in the outer office.

"Give me a minute," the surgeon said. He tidied the duplicate set of photocopies into his drawer, and locked the set Gwynplaine had given him in the safe. Then he buzzed to signal Claire to send Dr. Rosenfeld in.

The psychotherapist accepted his invitation to sit down, but she didn't relax into the armchair. She leaned forward, and said: "What do you think of Joseph?"

"He's a remarkable young man," Victory said. "It's very kind of him to warn me about the possibility of being drawn into a dangerous conspiracy. I take it that you're here to tell me that it's all paranoid delusion, and that I shouldn't take the slightest notice of it."

"You know perfectly well that I'm not here to tell you any such thing," the psychotherapist replied. "The boy's not paranoid—not more so, at any rate, than any sane person of his age living in the shadow of the ecocatastrophe. He certainly has problems with his father, though—over and above the natural resentment that young folk bear our entire generation, on account of our having overspent their inheritance of natural resources, created a phenomenal burden of pollution, and started a greenhouse crisis that seems likely to kill every other vertebrate species bar our own, the household rat and a few deep-sea fish."

"He doesn't seem to want his father to fall victim to this exotic confidence trick," Victory pointed out.

"I don't suppose he'd mind too much if the scam went through," Rachel Rosenfeld opined. "But that wouldn't be his first option."

"Which would be to establish himself as his father's saviour," Victory said, glad to be up to the challenge. "But he doesn't think his father will take his unsupported word for anything—especially if the anything in question reflects badly on dear Lilith. Is he hoping that I might do the job for him...while allowing him full credit, of course?"

"Which you would certainly owe him, if he had in fact saved you from making a perfect fool of yourself," Dr. Rosenfeld pointed out.

"True," Victory conceded."

"So you will, then?"

"Will what?"

"Don't be deliberately obtuse, Hugo. Go to see Gregory K. Allison, to whom you now seem to have been properly introduced, and tell him that someone's trying to use you to stitch him up."

"I'd be prepared to do that," Victory said, "if I were sure of the exact nature and dimensions of the conspiracy—but I'm not going to risk leaping out of the frying pan into the fire, in terms of making a fool of myself. If Joseph wants to tell Gregory K. what he thinks, though, I'll be ready to offer what support I can."

The psychotherapist nodded. "Fair enough," she said. "So you're going to tell this Gwynplaine character everything you know, in the hope of forcing an admission from him? Do you think it will work?"

"I don't know. I have some other lines of inquiry to follow."

"The mysterious Mr. Yashvili?"

"You don't miss much, do you, Rachel?"

"On the contrary—I feel completely out of my depth. Why did the name strike you so forcefully? I noticed *that*, of course."

"I know next to nothing about Georgia," Victory told her, "but one of the few things I know is that it's where surnames ending in '-vili' come from. It's also where the language in which Gwynplaine's book is written seems to come from. It's supposed to be a dead language, but if there are surviving specimens anywhere, that's where they're likely to be. If it ever was a real language, that is—even that might be a fake, cobbled together in order to fool a linguist whose life and career have taken a downturn, further increasing his natural avidity to make further progress in his subject."

"You do believe Joseph's story, then?"

"*Believe* is too strong a word at this stage of the game," Victory replied. "So far, it's the only story that actually makes sense—but that's only because the others are so utterly and calculatedly weird. When you've eliminated the impossible, whatever's left must be true, according to Sherlock Holmes—but I haven't quite succeeded in eliminating the impossible yet. Everything else might be fake, including the book itself, but the instructions for surgery weren't compiled by any mere butcher. Are you here on Joseph's behalf, by the way, or merely to satisfy your own curiosity?"

"If only one could be so certain of one's own motives, Dr. Victory," the psychotherapist said, with a sigh. "Of course I'm here for the benefit of my patient. How else could I justify it to myself?"

"Do you think it would assist in his cure if I did go running off to Gregory K. without being certain of my ground, even if I did manage to persuade the old man that his disinherited son has saved him a few million quid and a red face?"

"Joseph doesn't need curing, as such—but your support in this, whoever actually broaches the subject with his father, would help him to feel a lot better about himself, and things in general. From my point of view, and his, it would be progress. He has every reason to play straight with you, Hugo, and none at all to deceive you."

"That's what I figured," Victory agreed. "Unlike everyone else, I suppose—present company excepted."

"Thanks," Dr. Rosenfeld said. "Will you let us know how things turn out with your mystery man with the badly burned face?"

"He's not my patient," Victory said. "Until he is, I don't owe him any duty of confidentiality—but if and when he becomes my patient, my lips will be sealed."

"Do you think he might?"

"He'd be a very interesting challenge—in a context with which I could cope. He needs me, whether he's prepared to acknowledge it or not. Maybe he doesn't need curing, as such—but I might be able to get him to feel a lot better about himself, and things in general. That's our job, isn't it? Anyway, if Joseph's wrong about him being a mere scam artist, and he really is Adam, he's probably entitled to have his own face back. He's served his time, when all's said and done—and if the ecocatastrophe really does wipe out everything bigger than a cockroach, except for rats and a few fish, we're going to need a new Adam, aren't we?"

"And an Eve too, I guess," Dr. Rosenfeld added.

"Or a Lilith," Victory said, casually trumping her quip. "If things work out with Lilith this time around, we might not need an Eve at all."

Clair buzzed then to announce that Huw Williams had arrived. Victory glanced at his watch, impressed by the amazing rapidity with which the linguist had answered his summons.

"Keep me informed," said Rachel Rosenfeld, standing up to go. "I'll tell Joseph what the position is, so that he can decide whether to go to his father."

Victory made no promises as he accompanied her to the door. The psychotherapist looked curiously at Williams as she went past him, and he looked curiously at her, but Victory didn't introduce them.

"Come in," he said to Williams. "Take a seat."

When the linguist was settled in the same chair that the psychotherapist had used, sitting up in almost the same attitude, Victory produced the duplicate photocopies from his drawer and handed the whole stack to Huw Williams.

As Williams began to riffle through them, Victory said: "Does the name Iorga Yashvili mean anything to you, Dr. Williams?"

"I met a man of that name once," William said, "but it was some years ago. It was here in London, at a university function. He was some kind of cultural attaché, I think—from Georgia, obviously. He showed a polite interest in my work, but anyone from that part of the world would, even if he weren't a diplomat."

"You didn't talk to him about the Sons of Job?"

"No. Why—do you think he's involved with them?"

"I believe that his ex-wife may have been, and she certainly is now. Did you meet her too?"

"I don't believe so. What's her name?"

"Lilith."

Williams raised an eyebrow, but he didn't react with the kind of shock that Victory had displayed when Joseph Allison introduced the name so unexpectedly to his discourse.

"Is there a possibility that Asmodeus might by Iorga Yashvili?" Victory asked.

"I don't know," Williams countered. "Do you have reason to think that he is?"

"Lilith Yashvili is now Mrs. Gregory K. Allison," Victory told him. "They appear to be the leaders of the present-day Sons of Job. I'm reliably informed that Gregory K. Allison could be persuaded to pay a not-so-small fortune for the book of the comprachicos, if he could be persuaded that it was genuine—and God only knows what he might pay to have his protégé remodelled with the face of Adam. Iorga Yashvili probably knows that—and the possibility of putting one over his ex-wife's new husband might add an extra piquancy to the prospect of selling him a forgery."

"You think Yashvili's behind this script?" Williams said.

"I think it's a possibility," Victory said. "You're the expert—what do *you* think?"

Williams looked down at the photocopies, peering at them even more intently than before. One by one he flicked through them, taking twenty or thirty seconds to inspect each one. Victory waited patiently for him to finish.

"They're only second-hand photocopies," Williams said, eventually. "It's going to be very difficult to judge the authenticity of the text without the original. If we could test the parchment, the ink, the exact conformation of the handwriting...maybe we could turn up something that would disprove the seventeenth-century origin. But it's conceivable that the language might be real even if the text was inscribed in the last couple of years. The translations seem to be sound, or at least perfectly plausible. Do the instructions make sense?"

"So far as they go—but there's no way to date them. It's certainly more probable that the diagrams and the instructions were concocted this century, with the aid of modern knowledge and surgical techniques, but I don't have any conclusive proof that they couldn't have been written nearly three hundred years ago."

"Is there any urgency in the matter, given that you're not going to try them out on Amahl Sahman?"

"There is if I'm going to try to save Gregory K. Allison from the sting of the century. If Asmodeus and Gwynplaine put the bite on him over the weekend, I might find myself under orders to carry out the operation as specified by the book—and if Amahl's face doesn't live up to expectations, I'd be a ready-made scapegoat."

"I see," the cultural historian said. "You might also offend the great man if you tried to back out. It might be too late for you to wash your hands of the whole business without Allison becoming annoyed."

"Is that what you think I should do? Wash my hands of it, I mean."

Williams didn't answer immediately. His forehead—which definitely needed work—was deeply furrowed. He stroked his chin, emphasizing the slackness that could be so easily corrected. "Do you, perhaps, suspect that Asmodeus and I might be in this together?" he asked, eventually. "Do you think I might be the diabolical mastermind behind the whole plan?"

"The idea had crossed my mind," Victory admitted.

"I suppose I should be flattered. Alas, I'm not nearly as clever or courageous as that, nor even as greedy. You've seen my home, Dr. Victory—you know perfectly well what I am."

"Yes," Victory agreed. "But you know what I am, too, and you'll understand readily enough how much difficulty I'm having getting my head around all of this. The mystery man who called me seemed to believe in the book, but he might have been spouting any of several kinds of hot air. Monsignor Guillermo Torricelli, on the other hand, seems to be a different kind of lunatic."

"Who's he?" William queried.

"He's the one who told me that Gwynplaine's the Devil. He claims to be from the Holy Office, directly responsible to the pope. Mind you, I haven't actually checked, so he could be lying. He says he's staying at the Archbishop's palace—perhaps I ought to drop in."

Williams mulled over this information for a few seconds, then said: "The Church attracts more than its fair share of lifestyle fantasists. It's always been an attractive refuge, and it's probably more hospitable now than ever before. Even if your informant *is* from the Holy Office, that doesn't make him a good judge of character or reality. History suggests the opposite, in fact. He really told you that you're in danger of making a pact with the Devil? A *literal* pact with the Devil."

"He was quite adamant about the literal existence of the Devil, and his ability to mimic human form. He was also adamant about the literal existence of Eden, and of Adam's fall. He seems to believe in evolution too, but he blithely dismissed the apparent contradiction as a mere illusion."

"Well, the Church gave up on Aristotle quite some time ago. Perhaps they threw out the principle of the excluded middle along with the crystal spheres. The words *baby* and *bathwater* come to mind."

"If you can prove that script's a fake," Victory said, "I'd be really glad to know about it as soon as possible. I know you don't want that result, but we're scientists, after all. We need to check our results objectively."

"Thanks for reminding me," Williams muttered. "If I do find anything amiss, I promise you'll be the first to know. I hope you'll do the same for me. What do you intend to say to Gwynplaine when you see him again?"

"That's what I have to decide," Victory said. "I'd still like to get hold of copies of the final pages, if there are any—and if there's still a possibility of getting my hands on the book itself...."

"Are you saying that you don't believe there are any further pages?" Williams asked, a trifle belatedly.

"*Believe* is putting it far too strongly," Victory said, "but it's a possibility I've had to consider. If I'm being taken for a ride, who knows where the apparatus of the scam begins and ends? It was a very thick book, with a great many illustrations—as it would have to be, to pass for what it's pretending to be—but I never actually saw the last few pages. Even if it were genuine, it doesn't follow that the instructions for replicating the face of Adam were ever completed, no matter how many rumors there are about operations on children who died in the great fire. If Gwynplaine's attempts to persuade me to apply the instructions to the rebuilding of Amahl Sahman's face are just a bluff, maybe he doesn't have anything up his sleeve at all, Maybe he's given me all he has, in the hope and expectation that it'll be enough to entangle me in his scheme to persuade Gregory K. and Lilith Allison that he has custody of the book of their dreams, plus a surgeon and a patient who might bring those dreams to more-or-less-instant fruition."

Williams nodded slowly, "But if he *does* have more...." he murmured.

"Exactly," Victory agreed. "If he does have more, I want the cards on the table."

"If the whole thing is a scam," Williams pointed out, "there's no guarantee that he's in on it. Gwynplaine might be a patsy, just like you. If he's another comprachico nut, he might be just as easily manipulable as the average Visionary Martyr or Son of Job. If this Yashvili character is capable of putting one over on the Holy Office...."

"One way or another," Victory said, "I'm going to have to handle Gwynplaine with the greatest possible care. I need to know more about him before I go to Allison—something solid, that I can not only believe but also prove. If I can't get that, then I'll need something else just as solid. And I have to bear in mind that I'm operating on Allison's wife on Sunday afternoon, to give her the face and cheekbones she thinks she deserves. You seem to know these lifestyle fantasists as well as anyone does; is there any chance that Lilith Allison is crazy enough to think that she really is *the* Lilith, reincarnated in order to await her ritual marriage to the new Adam, thus bringing about the apocalyptic transfiguration of the world?"

"I don't know," Williams admitted, after yet another pause, "but I wouldn't rule it out. Wealth and social position are no protection against delusions of that kind—quite the reverse, in fact. Once a person begins to believe that she can have it all, it's hard to set any kind of limit to her ambition."

"That's what I thought," Victory said. "Thank God that you and I are still poor enough to be sane."

CHAPTER FOURTEEN

The Fifth Day: Evening

When Huw Williams had gone Victory drove back to the hospital. He called in at Christina Legrange's office, but the press officer had already gone home. Majeke was still there, though, off shift but on call. Friday and Saturday evenings were Accident and Emergency's busiest sessions, and it was rare for one to pass by without half a dozen victims of drunken brawls presenting the kinds of injury that would benefit from the expertise of a plastic surgeon. Broken glass had always been the weapon of first choice in such improvised encounters.

"Shall we get some dinner in the canteen?" Victory asked her. "It's still early—the rush won't begin until the pubs begin to empty."

"You don't have to be here," Majeke pointed out. "You could eat somewhere nice. Why aren't you on your way back to your lovely farmhouse? I thought you didn't stay in town at weekends."

"I might drop in on Mrs. Allison later. I was planning to go out to Oxfordshire tonight, but I was delayed at my consulting rooms and it's beginning to seem that it might not be worth the bother, given that I'm operating on Sunday. I'll have to make the final preparations tomorrow, so I'll have to be in Harley Street bright and early. As for the quality of the food—well, it's only food."

"Okay," she said. "Let's go."

The food was, indeed, only food—but Victory had grown accustomed to eating on the run, fuelling up without paying any particular attention to aesthetic considerations.

"Any problems with my star patients?" he asked her, when they were seated.

"None," she said. "Both making good progress, both ready for the final phases of their respective treatments. Thankfully, the two I took over yesterday are doing just as well. I wish I could claim the credit, but it's all down to the cleverness of the machinery."

"Take the credit," Victory advised her. "If and when anything does go wrong with the clever machinery, we'll certainly have to take the blame—at least until the happy day comes when AIs can be hauled into the dock at the Old Bailey to answer for their misdeeds. Have you talked to Mrs. Allison at all?"

"Are you kidding? To her, I'm just one more skivvy. She might condescend to chat with you, but there's no one else in the hospital that measures up to her Olympian standards. Did you meet Gregory the Great this morning?"

"We shook hands and chatted briefly," Victory admitted. "I had to rush off, as usual. I regret it now; it might have been useful to have a more serious conversation with the great man, about his plans for Amahl's future."

"Does he have any plans for Amahl's future? I wouldn't put it past him to have arranged the boy's treatment purely and simply to provide a shield to deflect press attention away from his wife's treatment. Is that too cynical, do you think?"

"Yes it is," Victory told her. "Mrs. Allison could have booked in months ago if she'd always planned to be here at the same time as Amahl. It seems to have been a late adjustment to their plans. Is Mrs. Allison's bodyguard still lurking outside her room, by the way?"

"Yes, he is," Majeke said. "There seem to be three of them, working in shifts. They've got permission to use the cubicles where the doctors on call are supposed to sleep. Why do you ask? Have you any reason to suspect that Mrs. Allison or Amahl is under threat?"

"No—but Allison might have a reason, of sorts. It wouldn't take much to make him think so—the rich are, on average, even more paranoid than the rest of us."

"With good reason," Majeke judged. "There are a great many people about—young people, for the most part—who consider that the rich are responsible for the ecocatastrophe. Self-made businessmen like Gregory K. Allison are routinely held up as paradigm examples of the greed and ruthless exploitation that delivered the world into its present mess. I dare say that he can live with it, though; he probably had his conscience amputated in his teens."

"Not necessarily," Victory said. "Maybe he soothes it in other ways."

"Paying for Amahl's surgery, you mean?"

"Not just the surgery, and not just Amahl. What he's buying is Amahl's redemption...and he might imagine that he can use his millions to save the world, thus redeeming himself—and all his peers and predecessors—from the sins that precipitated the eco-catastrophe."

"He's got a big job on his hands, then," Majeke said. "If we can believe half what the Global Environmental Model tells us, the ecosphere is so far gone that it'll take a miracle to save it."

"A fact that might easily predispose a man like Allison to take an interest in miracle-working," Victory observed. "After all, he's rich enough to buy everything else—why shouldn't he be able to buy miracles too?"

"Because there are none on sale," Majeke stated, bluntly. "All the ones that are advertised are pathetic fakes."

"You know that and I know that," Victory said. "I wonder, though, whether Gregory K. Allison shares our conviction. I met his son today."

"I thought Mrs. Allison was, as they say, child-free."

"His son by his first marriage. His name's Joseph. He's fifteen, or thereabouts."

"Yes, of course," Majeke said. "I'd forgotten about his first marriage. So has he, it's said. The biggest clean break settlement in history, it was reported at the time—although the record's probably been broken two or three times since. Surely the kid doesn't want cosmetic surgery *already*?"

"No," Victory replied. "I met him in a different context."

"And that's why you're asking all these questions, is it? Little Joe stirred up your curiosity about his wicked stepmother?"

"Is she wicked?" Victory asked, blandly.

"Probably not," Majeke conceded. "Her publicity is all good, and that kind of clean sheet is difficult to obtain, even with the kind of PR support Gregory K. can command. Any serious skeletons rattling around in the cupboards of the rich and famous tend to fall out eventually. Can we talk about something else now? When you asked me to dinner I thought you intended to seduce me, not interrogate me about the Allisons. If I somehow gave you the impression that I have an expert knowledge of celebrity gossip, I'm sorry."

"I'm sorry too," Victory said, "if I somehow gave you the impression that I'm a rapacious Don Juan who only talks to young women for the purposes of seduction. Do I really have that reputation?"

"There you go again! Actually, yes—but the rumor is that you've lost your touch of late, and aren't even having much success getting your patients into bed. The current rumor is that the stress of overwork has rendered you impotent and incipiently crazy. I don't believe a word of it, of course—if I did, I'd have to think that you were only turning to me out of madness and desperation."

"We're only eating in the hospital canteen," Victory pointed out. "It's not exactly a date."

"I had taken due note of that," she assured him. "But you did soften me up first by throwing a couple of routine slicings my way. If that isn't the work of a smooth operator, what is?"

"Well," Victory observed, "you certainly seem to have succeeded in changing the subject."

"I also seem to have suggested," Majeke said, blushing, "that I'd prostitute myself for the price of a few more operations. That was inadvertent. I'm not fishing for more work, and I'm not offering any sexual favours in exchange. Sorry—I got carried away on the tide of flippancy."

"It's forgotten," Victory said. "And I hope you won't take it the wrong way if I drop in on Mrs. Allison now. My current fascination with her is no more carnal than your interest in me. It's just another symptom of my pathological tendency to over-work—which you mustn't worry about, by the way. I've even started taking advice from the psychotherapist who has the consulting-rooms above mine."

"You mean Rachel Rosenfeld?" Majeke said. "Have you really?" She had been to Harley Street on several occasions, and had obviously taken note of the brass plaques outside the front door of Victory's building.

"There's no need to be jealous," Victory said. "She's old enough to be my mother, and she doesn't believe in cosmetic surgery, although she's certainly in dire need of some."

"Everybody believes in cosmetic surgery," Majeke assured him. "It's just that some women still don't like to let on that they've ever considered it, no matter how dire their need. She's probably only pretending to treat you, so that she can work up slowly to the possibility of you treating her."

"When I say that I'm listening to her advice," Victory was quick to point out, "I don't mean that I'm actually her patient."

"No?" Majeke said. "Well, maybe you need time to work up to it slowly, jut as she does."

Victory let her have the last word. He returned his tray to the clearing-rack, and made his way back to the suite of rooms where Mrs. Allison was lodged. Victory nodded politely to the bodyguard before he went into Mrs. Allison's room, wondering whether he ought to be reassured or alarmed by the fact that the man seemed extraordinarily large and very professional, although his nose was straight and his auricular cartilages un-mashed. Indeed, the only sculpture he seemed to need at present was a comprehensive remoulding of the maxillae, a standard skin-clearance and some structural work on his eyelids.

Mrs. Allison was sitting up in bed, reading. She put her book down as soon as Victory came in, but it was impossible to tell how glad she was to see him because of the dressings on her face. He set about stripping them away, very gently.

"Dr. Victory," she said. "I do hope you haven't come to tell me that there's a problem."

"Everything is fine, Mrs. Allison," he assured her. "I came to confirm that I can and will do the second set of operations on Sunday. Amahl is making good progress too, so there'll be no need to change my schedule."

"I'm glad—for the boy as well as myself, of course."

"Of course. I understand that you and your husband will be assuming full responsibility for his aftercare, at least for a while."

"That's true, but confidential. You're his true saviour, of course, not Gregory. Gregory only put up the money—you're the one who's made it possible for him to live a normal life."

"The machine saved his life and remade his face, Mrs. Allison. I just take care of the finer details. Anyone else could have done the job, given the right tools and training." The dressings were completely removed now, and he moved in closer to inspect the contours of her cheeks. There was still a little swelling, but it only required the slightest pressure of his expert fingers to assure him that the bone work was perfect.

"You're too modest, doctor," she said, as he stepped back to admire his handiwork from a polite distance. There was still some bruising discoloration and fluid retention, but it was easy enough for him to superimpose the image he had produced on his computer upon the actual face, in his mind's eye.

"You'll be a truly magnificent Lilith," he murmured. "A *femme fatale* that any pre-Raphaelite or symbolist would have been avid to paint."

"I don't use my Christian name, doctor," she told him. "A cultured man like you may understand its implications in a sophisticated way, but there are some who think it has demonic connotations."

"Surely not in today's world," Victory said. "Who nowadays, on hearing the name Lilith, would automatically think of the wife of Asmodeus the demon king?"

Her face was naked now, if somewhat the worse for wear, and her dark-eyed stare had a definite melodramatic quality. "You're not Jewish, doctor?" she said, not meaning it as a question in spite of the careful intonation. "What is it that you're trying to imply?"

"I wasn't trying to imply anything, Mrs. Allison," Victory said, as smoothly as he could. "I was merely making conversation. Lilith is a beautiful name, and I don't see why you shouldn't wear it proudly. Nor do I think of your husband as a demon of anger and lust. Forgive me if I seemed rude."

"Of course," she said, mildly. Her eyes seemed quiet again, although it was obvious that their quietness derived from careful politeness rather than any incapacity to strike terror.

"I hope your bodyguard won't get bored standing out there in the corridor all night," Victory said, as he rang for a nurse to replace Mrs. Allison's dressings. "His must be a tedious job, at times."

"He won't," Mrs. Allison said, positively. "He's trained too, and equipped with the right tools. I hope you don't think that his presence is any reflection on the hospital's own security. It's just that one can't be too careful nowadays."

"I know all about the limitations of hospital security," Victory assured her. "Someone slipped a note under the windscreen wiper of my car the other day, and all they did was send someone down to read it—they made no attempt at all to identify or apprehend the culprit. The man who'd planted the note rang me later, to ask me why I hadn't got in touch. I told him that it was because I didn't speak to crazy people and cultists. That might not have been the most diplomatic way to handle it, in retrospect; there are so many of these fanatics around nowadays, looking forward to the imminent apocalypse with gleeful impatience."

He was trying hard to work up to a subject of real significance without giving himself away, but she wouldn't rise to the bait. She might be old school, but she was also an old hand at conversation management, and Victory had the uncomfortable feeling that he'd given far more away than he was ever likely to obtain in return.

"That's certainly true, Dr. Victory," Mrs. Gregory K. Allison said, in an effortlessly neutral tone. "One has to be very careful in dealing with such people."

She said no more, and asked no questions—from which Victory took the inference that she already knew about the note placed on his windscreen, and its reference to Gwynplaine. That wasn't entirely surprising—once hospital security had read the text, its contents must have become topics of popular gossip—but it was slightly discomfiting nevertheless. Victory couldn't see any suitably subtle way of trying to determine whether the name Gwynplaine had meant anything to her, or whether her husband might be investigating its significance even as they spoke. Not wishing to show any more of his own hand, as yet, Victory similarly refrained from asking any more questions. He contented himself with bidding Mrs. Allison a polite goodnight.

He went down to the subterranean car park without bothering to call in at his office, and got into the Bentley. Before starting the engine, however, he used his mobile phone to call Mrs. Benedict and inform her that he would be staying in London that night, and that she was not to expect him until the following weekend. When he had finished the call he scrupulously put the mobile in the speakerphone cradle, so that if anyone rang while he was in transit he would be able to hear the message without taking his hands off the wheel.

As he turned the key in the ignition, Victory felt the sudden pressure of a sharp object in the side of his neck, somewhere in the vicinity of the left jugular vein. He realised, after the momentary shock had given pause to his mental processes, that someone in the rear seat was holding a knife to his throat. He tried to turn round, but the knife pressed harder. In the rear-view mirror, however, he caught a glimpse of the edge of a hood and the rim of a filter-mask. His assailant was taking no chances.

There seemed to be little point in hoping that the CC-TV cameras in the car park would present a clear enough picture of what was happening to the security officer on duty to spark an alarm, even if he tried to improvise some kind of signal of his distress. The duty officer obviously hadn't noticed someone climbing surreptitiously into the Bentley.

"Drive out as if nothing were happening, Dr. Victory," a male voice murmured in his ear. "Turn left at the entrance. I'll give you further directions when we're *en route.*"

Victory was sorely tempted to sit back in his seat, fold his arms, and tell his would-be kidnapper to get out of the car, but he decided against it. The man might just be willing to cut him—not fatally, perhaps, but badly enough to cause him serious inconvenience. If the blade were to be directed at his hands rather than his throat, his career might hang in the balance. He had no particular reason to think that anyone might do that, in order to prevent him from operating on Amahl Sahman, but he had no reason to feel certain that the opposite was the case.

He put the car in gear, released the handbrake, and began to back out of his parking space. He turned the car around, made his exit from the car park, and turned left, exactly as he had been instructed to do.

"You're too late," he said, then. "I already know who Gwynplaine is, and I think I've already figured out who you think he is. In fact, I might well know a great deal more about this business than you do. There's a strong possibility that you're being manipulated by a con man—and it seems that you're about to be manipulated into doing something very stupid."

The man in the back seat leaned forward to place his filter-masked mouth as close to Victory's left ear as the configuration of the front seats would allow. "So you've figured that much out, have you?" he said. "Well, bully for you—but you don't know the tenth of it, let alone the half. Turn south at the next junction, then head towards Southwark Bridge. You can reach slowly into your pocket now, and take out your keys. Pass them back to me."

"The keys won't get you into my safe," Victory told him. "They won't even get you into my office—or the garage, for that matter. Everything's pass code protected."

"Just get them out," the man said. "It's the fob I want, as you well know."

Victory still made no move to obey the order. "Why?" he said, although the explanation had already dawned on him.

"Don't play games, Dr. Victory. We know perfectly well how you work. Gwynplaine gave you the photocopies so that you could integrate the instructions into the program that drives the little scalpels your machine is fitted with. You didn't email anything from your consulting-rooms to the hospital, so you must have the stuff on the gadget that doubles as your key ring, unless you've got a DVD stuffed in your pocket. If you have, you can hand that over too."

"Even if I *had* transported the program so that I could feed it into the machine," Victory told him, patiently, "which in fact I didn't, because the two machines have a secure connection that doesn't go *via* an email server, I wouldn't have left a copy in the ring. Even if I *had* left a copy in the ring, you wouldn't be able to make head or tail of it without the host software it's designed to modify. And even if you had that, it wouldn't do you a blind bit of good, firstly because you don't have access to the machine, and secondly because any set of instructions I'd made would be incomplete, because I haven't yet been given the full set of photocopies. Which means, you bloody idiot, that there are no less than four different ways in which you're being completely stupid."

The blade of the knife cut into his neck, deeply enough to draw capillary blood, though not deeply enough to nick the jugular, let alone the carotid artery. Victory felt a warm droplet trickling down towards his collar, and was glad that it only seemed to be a droplet. He reached into his pocket and pulled out his key ring; he handed it over without any further protest.

Everything he had said was, of course, perfectly true, but the truth didn't seem to be an effective weapon, at present, for dealing with crazy lifestyle fantasists.

"Where are we going?" the surgeon asked.

"Never mind where we're going," the man in the rear seat said. "Concentrate on the question of whether you'll be coming back—because you won't be, if you don't cooperate. Believe me, I'm serious."

The problem was, Victory thought, that even though he didn't believe the particular threat of murder, he did believe that the man behind him was serious—serious enough, at any rate, to do more damage. He was still frightened for his hands, which had always been the focal point of his personal species of paranoia. He wasn't about to tell his captor about that anxiety, but keeping it quiet didn't make it go away. The man with the knife might be severely deluded—indeed, it seemed to Victory the only question at issue was how extensive and complex his delusion might be—but he certainly seemed to be serious enough to be dangerous.

There were no causes at all for which Victory would have been willing to offer his life, or even his little finger, but if he had ever occasion to draw up a list of potential candidates, the likes of the Sons of Job and the Visionary Martyrs would have been a long way from the margin. In respect of more practical matters, he really didn't care one way or the other whether Gregory K. Allison got ripped off, or by whom, so long he suffered no collateral damage from the hit. Bearing all this in mind, he had no difficulty at all in deciding that he would say exactly what he had to say in order to get out of this predicament, once he had found out exactly what kind of a predicament it was.

As soon as they had crossed Southwark Bridge, therefore, the surgeon put on his meekest voice to ask: "Where to now?"

"Keep going south into Newington Butts, then bear right into Kennington Lane. We have to pick up some other people. I'll tell you where to stop."

"Okay," said Victory, obediently—and said nothing more until the promised instruction was given.

The car was stationary for more than a minute before two other men appeared out of a dark alleyway to the left-hand side of the road and got into the car, one into the front passenger seat and the other into the rear alongside the man with the knife. Victory was able to see that both men were wearing filter-masks, although they were distinguishable by virtue of the fact that the man who got into the front seat was much taller than his companion, and wore a hat—a conspicuously old-fashioned felt fedora—rather than the customary hood.

"Move on," said the man with the knife, while his compatriots settled in and buckled their seat belts. "Just keep going, through Nine Elms and into Battersea Park Road, unless we tell you to turn."

"Okay," Victory repeated, in the same mild tone.

"You weren't supposed to cut him," said the man in the front passenger seat, as he removed his hat, and then his filter mask. He had obviously taken note of the blood when the internal light had come on automatically as the door was opened. The interior of the car was darker now, but the street-lamps gave up enough intermittent light to allow Victory to build up an image of the tall man. His face was understandably steep, its unusually length further emphasized by a jutting jaw and a prominent nose. Given the overall context, Victory would not have attempted to trim them back too far, but he would have made the eyebrows more pronounced and altered the cheekbones, as well as deactivating the hair follicles whose distribution seemed both excessive and eccentric.

"He wouldn't play ball until I did," the knifeman complained. "I had no choice. He knows now."

The man sitting beside Victory took out a handkerchief, and dabbed at the blood trickling from the surgeon's neck-wound. He was thin as well as tall, and his hand seemed unnaturally long by comparison with its broadness. His hair was greying as well as thinning; he was probably fifty-five or sixty years old, but he seemed robust. He was dressed in a sober business suit that would have made him seem utterly ordinary even in association with the filter-mask.

"You should have accepted our polite invitation, Dr. Victory," the tall man said, replacing his handkerchief in his pocket. "It would have saved us all a great deal of trouble."

Ordinarily, Victory would have pointed out that the invitation hadn't been at all polite, and that he had ignored it in the hope of saving himself from exactly the kind of trouble he now seemed to be in, but he kept stubbornly silent instead.

"You can call me Elijah," the tall man said. "As you've presumably realised, I represent an organization opposed to the Sons of Job."

"The Visionary Martyrs," Victory guessed.

"That's what the Sons would call us, and probably do," Elijah said. "We don't discourage it. Such names are more than a little arbitrary. You went to see Mrs. Allison this evening, I understand. And you saw Huw Williams this afternoon."

"It was a busy day," Victory answered. "It still is, apparently."

"He's not expected in Oxfordshire," the knifeman put in. "He made the call before I made my move. Nobody will miss him until at least tomorrow noon."

"I don't think we'll need to delay him for as long as that," the tall man said. "I'm sure that, once the situation has been fully explained to him, he'll be only too eager to help us."

"He says he knows it's a con, too," the man with the knife said, "but he didn't go into details."

Again, Victory said nothing, although his immediate impulse was to elaborate, to demonstrate his intellectual competence. The wiser course, he knew, would have been to keep quiet from the very beginning.

He wasn't to be allowed to get away with silence, though. "Who do you think is conning whom, Dr. Victory?" the tall man asked, softly.

"I've no idea where you fit in," Victory admitted, "but I think that Gwynplaine's trying to con Gregory K. Allison."

"Well, it certainly doesn't take a genius to work *that* out," said the man who wanted to be called Elijah. "The point is who Gwynplaine really is, and who's pulling his strings. Do you know *that*, Dr. Victory?"

Victory swallowed the impulse to say yes, and contented himself with a shake of the head.

Elijah seemed disappointed by the surgeon's silence, but not unduly so. "In that case," he said, "we'll have to explain it, and trust that you'll be suitably grateful."

"I'm willing to listen," Victory assured him, although he was not at all confident of his future gratitude.

CHAPTER FIFTEEN

The Fifth Day: Late Evening

"Gwynplaine is...," Elijah began—but he was immediately interrupted by the man who had not yet spoken. The other thrust his hand out between the two front seats, with Victory's key ring, fob and keys dangling from the fingers.

"We've copied everything," said a gruff voice, whose strong Scottish accent could not be obscured by the filter mask. "There's only one file large enough to contain the program we want, but that's probably it—there's no photoscan of the actual diagrams, though."

For a moment, Victory was startled by the news that there was a file on his data carrier large enough to be the incomplete program for erecting the face of Adam on Amahl Sahman's skull, but then he remembered that he had decanted Mrs. Allison's program in case he needed to review it at the flat. He felt not the slightest temptation to inform his captors that they were in danger of jumping to an incorrect conclusion.

"Good," Elijah said, as he took the keys. "Excuse me, Dr. Victory. Please keep your hands on the wheel and your eyes on the road." So saying, he began dipping his bony fingers one by one into Victory' pockets, reaching right across the surgeon to investigate the right-hand pockets of his jacket and trousers. The only thing he extracted, in the end, was Victory's wallet, through which he went very carefully, taking out all the credit cards, library cards and swipecards for careful inspection. He passed three of them back to his companion, who presumably slotted them into the same palmtop computer he had used to interrogate the key ring. They came back, one by one, accompanied by muttered comments.

Elijah put the cards back into the wallet before returning the wallet to the inside pocket of Victory's jacket. Then the tall man dropped the keys back into the left-hand jacket pocket, presumably choosing it on grounds of convenience. "Sorry for the inconvenience," he said. "It would have been nice if you had been carrying the photocopies themselves, but we'll get then one way or another—from Williams, if not from you."

Victory said nothing, but simply waited for his kidnapper to take up where he had left off.

"Right," Elijah said, after a moment's pause. "Where was I? Gwynplaine is...well, in a sense, he's nobody at all. I presume that he was somebody once: a child or adolescent living in Chechnya or Ingushetia, perhaps Georgia itself, although Georgia's had far less than its fair share of violence since the turn of the century. The person he then was must have been caught up in some kind of major incident—a bomb blast, I suspect, although it's not impossible that it was a mere road accident or train wreck. At any rate, he ended up in a hospital, unidentified and probably unidentifiable. By some remote freak of chance—a miracle, to those who might care to represent it that way—he survived, albeit with total amnesia. It wasn't simply that he'd lost track of his identity; he'd forgotten his language and all his conscious habits. All that remained to him were the functions of his autonomic nervous system. The staff at the hospital must have begun the work of teaching him how to live, but this wasn't a hospital like yours, Dr. Victory, replete with nurses, therapists and social workers; it was underequipped in every way imaginable, only able to exist by virtue of support from international charities. When the Sons of Job found him, he was as close to a *tabula rasa* as any human being of...say fourteen or fifteen years of age...could possibly be. Do you know who it was who found him, Dr. Victory? Do you know the name of the man who invented the Sons of Job—who *was* the Sons of Job at that time."

"No," said Victory, shortly.

"Guess."

Victory hesitated for a moment, but eventually decided that it would be sensible not to give too much away. "Gregory K. Allison," he said, insincerely.

The tall man seemed to relax slightly; he had been half-turned in his seat, staring at Victory, but now he looked briefly behind him, as if to meet the eyes of one or other of his masked companions.

"Allison is just a sucker attached to a fat wallet, Dr. Victory," Elijah told him. "The man behind the Sons of Job at that time was Iorga Yashvili. Have you ever heard that name?"

"He was Lilith Allison's first husband," Victory said, figuring that it was safe to admit that much.

"Indeed he was," Elijah said. "And he probably still is her husband, in his own reckoning. Do you know what he was at the time when he found the man you know as Gwynplaine?"

"Some kind of diplomat," Victory said. "Cultural attaché, or some such."

142

"No, that was some time later. When he adopted the person you know as Gwynplaine, he was still a secret policeman, albeit in an era when secret policemen were on the verge of redundancy. This was about the time of the collapse of communism, you understand. Georgia was independent again, and the old ways had been...largely set aside. Had he and his fellows had more urgent work to do, they might not have had so much time on their hands, nor so much incentive to find a new role for themselves in the nascent world order. They were heirs to a rich tradition, and to a great deal of clandestine research into methods of interrogation and psychological manipulation.

"In the new era, that research had been partly declassified and ostensibly redirected, supposedly to be exploited for its curative value. There may have been a component of genuine altruism in the decision, but the main reason was probably the hope of creating something saleable to multinational drug companies. At any rate, the people involved in the investigation of various psychotropic drugs needed subjects on which to work—subjects, for the most part, who might obtain a genuine benefit from the drugs' effects.

"The boy who became Gwynplaine was one such subject; I suspect that Yashvili's assistants really did start out by trying to recover his lost memories, but when they couldn't do it, Yashvili must have seen the failure as a golden opportunity to build a personality from scratch: to create an identity to fill the blank slate. He was an ambitious man even then; others working for or with him had already begun to create the Sons of Job, and here was an opportunity to do more—far more—than forge documents and plant seeds in the groves of academe. Here was a chance to put flesh on myth.

"Yashvili's predecessors had, of course, begun to manufacture history for political reasons, but those political reasons had vanished into smoke. Yashvili and the other heirs to that process of manufacture might simply have stopped, but that wasn't Yashvili's way. Instead of doing less, he wanted to do more; instead of creating history on a small scale, he wanted to create it on a large scale. He wanted to create legends, and myths. Why stop at trivial goals, he asked himself, when one might aim much higher? Do you know what Yashvili wanted to do, Dr. Victory? Do you know why he invented the Sons of Job?"

"No," Victory said, tersely. "I don't."

"And you won't play guessing games any more, because I've annoyed and upset you. I understand. My fault entirely. No matter. What Iorga Yashvili wanted to do, Dr. Victory, was to invent a new religion: a new world religion, comparable in success and influence to Christianity and Islam—a new religion that would, in fact, *be* the next major transfiguration in the sequence grown from the rootstock of Judaism.

"Why did he want to do it? I don't know for sure what was in his mind when he first conceived the plan. Perhaps he thought that the world was desperately in need of a new religion, in order that it might be saved from the worst effects of rampant secularism and capitalism, which the people of the book had so far been woefully unable to stem. I feel sure that he would have represented it in those terms, to anyone who confronted him with the question. I suspect, however, that the real reason was a simpler one: that Christ and Mohammed had set the standards and established the benchmarks; that they were the record-holders whose feats required to be matched and surpassed. They had demonstrated that world-changing religions could be created, laying down a challenge for anyone and everyone else with delusions of grandeur. They had worked in much simpler environments, of course, and had little or no control over the impact that their notions would eventually achieve, but that only served to intensify the challenge they posed. If global society presented a tougher battleground, it also presented more abundant opportunities and more powerful methods. Are you with me so far?"

"I understand what you're saying," Victory confirmed, carefully withholding judgment on its apparent likelihood.

"Good. I assume that Huw Williams has given you an elaborate account of the supposed history of the Sons of Job and the Visionary Martyrs, pausing every few minutes to remind you, conscientiously, how sparse the actual historical evidence is. For him, and others like him, it's the very sparseness of the evidence that makes the business of deduction and speculation so irresistibly attractive and intriguing. Would it surprise you to know, Dr. Victory, that there was not an atom of evidence for the existence of the original Sons of Job twenty years ago, and that every atom that now seems to exist has been carefully fabricated by Iorga Yashvili and his associates?"

"No," Victory admitted. "It wouldn't surprise me." He couldn't resist adding: "But they exist now, don't they?"

"Exactly," Elijah said. "They exist now—and in order to secure their present existence, they had to invent a long and distinguished past, imposing that invention in the interstices of history. In order that the Sons of Job should have a greater glamour, and a more profound *raison d'être*, they needed to be equipped with adversaries. In addition to inventing the Sons of Job, Iorga Yashvili invented the Visionary Martyrs, characterizing and stigmatizing his own rivals in advance...with the result that I and my associates have accepted the label. Thus, the Visionary Martyrs also exist, *now*—although they, like the Sons of Job, are not at all what they seem to be. Have I succeeded in interesting you yet, Dr. Victory? Are you intrigued, eager to hear more?"

Victory discovered that his teeth were gritted, and hastened to relax. The reason for his chagrin was not merely that the man who called himself Elijah was correct in his assumption that the surgeon would, indeed, be intrigued by this new version of the mystery that surrounded him, but that Elijah knew perfectly well what the answer to his question was, and had known all along what it would be. All that Victory could bring himself to say, though, was: "Go on."

"Put yourself in Iorga Yashvili's shoes, Dr. Victory. You want to invent a new religion, partly to spread a particular creed and partly to enjoy a particular kind of power. How do you design that religion? How do you promote it? Where should you position yourself within it? You will need a prophet, of course, or a messiah—or, more likely, a prophet *and* a messiah. You will, of course, remain the power behind that front, less visible even than St. Paul. As for where to start in the construction of your creed—in that matter, you have little choice. If your religion is to be the next in the great sequence, you must start with Eden, and with Adam. You might rework the myth to suit your own purposes, just as it has been reworked before, but it would be difficult to replace it—and, in any case, why would you want to? Your aim is to capitalise on that which already exists, to turn it to your own advantage. So you begin your design with the myth of Eden, and you begin your plan of action with a prophet-to-be and a messiah-to-be...but first, of course, you must lay the groundwork by creating your history.

"In this respect, of course, you have valuable precedents available to you. You have seen how the discovery of the first Dead Sea Scrolls excited historians and Churchmen alike, and soon began to present challenges to the understanding they already had of the origins of Christianity. You have seen, too, how the scrolls gave rise to so much speculation, in fiction and conspiracy theory, as to how much more upsetting as-yet-undiscovered scrolls might be—how they might reveal the marriage of Jesus and Mary Magdalene, for instance, or the teachings of Jesus' lost brother, or the location of the Holy Grail...the possibilities seem endless. You wonder whether *any* of the scrolls were ever genuine, and you begin to wonder how many different hands, for how many different reasons, became involved in augmenting the supply with new discoveries. After all, fragments of papyrus are so much easier to manufacture than long texts, sets of accounts, old master paintings, or even entire and coherent letters.

"So you set to work—not merely as a sponsor of forgers, but also as a cultivator of academics, priming the historians whose job it will ultimately be to formulate theories based on your forgeries, to turn your fragments of evidence into the very fabric of history. Eventually, I suppose, you begin to wonder whether there's anything at all in history but a vast tapestry of illusions, some accidental and some deliberate...and then you become even more determined, and even more careful, to weave the image that you intend to produce. It all costs money, of course, but one of the great advantages of manufactured religions is that they rapidly turn into cash cows of prodigious efficacy. Even stupid religions and ridiculous gurus can grow fabulously rich within the space of a few years—what might a genius not accomplish, employing strategies even further refined? Ah, if only you or I had had such vision, Dr. Victory! What would we not have given to be in at the birth of a scheme like Iorga Yashvili's?"

"Is it really so easy to fake history?" Victory asked, sucked into the flight of fantasy in spite of himself. "Once upon a time, when writing was a rare and magical thing, scriptures might have been easy to produce—but we live in a world that not only inscribes its history day by day in newspapers and TV footage, spewing out documents in vast profusion, but also scrutinizes its heritage with all the minute care that carbon dating and chemical analysis can provide."

"Don't be silly, Dr. Victory," Elijah chided him. "You know perfectly well that the profusion of documentation applies to misinformation and disinformation—errors and lies, in vulgar parlance—as well as to accurate records. Why, the whole world watched and listened to the moon landing last century. Can you imagine the volume and detail of the documentation produced in connection with the project? But how long did it take for the fact to be challenged and become suspect? Within thirty years, a substantial minority of the population of the Western world doubted that it had ever occurred, convinced that the whole thing was a fake. You use the world wide web every day, as do we all—and as you do so, it's second nature for you to beware of lies and nonsense, which proliferate so easily there. As for the technology that allows us to scrutinise our relics, it's a two-edged sword, and very obviously so. The very same technology assists forgers in producing the desired appearances; it's only the forgers of old, who never anticipated such techniques, who can be caught out by them.

"It was ludicrously easy to insert the Sons of Job and the Visionary Martyrs into the historical record, Dr. Victory—easier, perhaps, to invent them from scratch than it was to redesign the comprachicos, who did at least have some slight record of their existence and nature to their credit before Yashvili began his embellishments. It's entirely likely that those extant records were the work of earlier forgers, with no more substance behind them than the Sons of Job, but they provided a base and a context even so. That phase of Yashvili's operation is almost complete, as you know, and the second is already under way. Yashvili has mobilised the fake prophet whose manufacture he began more than twenty years ago, and he's on the verge of manufacturing his fake messiah—with your help. If you refuse, of course, or fail to produce a satisfactory myth-in-embryo, he'll try again...and again, and again, until he has what he believes he needs. He has already provoked the Roman Church, not merely into anxiety but to tentative action, has he not? Perhaps the Vatican ought to be reckoned a soft target...but there are plenty more that are equally soft, or softer.

"Things are moving rapidly, Dr. Victory, as you've no doubt noticed. We'd dearly love to slow them down, if we can—and we're very enthusiastic to find out more about the fine detail of Yashvili's plans. That's why we were so enthusiastic to meet you, Dr. Victory, and became so irritated when you wouldn't listen to us. I'm very sorry about the rough tactics we've been forced to employ, but we really did conclude that it was the only way to make you listen to us, in a place where we had no need to fear being overheard by our adversaries."

"Well, you've succeeded," Victory said. "I've listened. It's a good story—at least as good as any other I've heard—but I haven't the slightest reason to believe a single word of it. Even if I had, I'd still have to be convinced of the wisdom of handing Gwynplaine's photocopies over to you, let alone my adaptation of the instructions."

"I think we can probably lay our hands on the photocopies now," Elijah told him. "As soon as Gwynplaine copied them, they crossed the threshold into the pubic domain. He'll not be able to put the cat back into the bag now you've copied them for Williams. Your transfiguration is, of course, a slightly different matter. Are you telling me that the file we just decanted is something else?"

Victory cursed himself silently for his slip. "You haven't explained the surgical instructions," he pointed out. "Where did Yashvili get *those*?"

"He was an influential man, in his way," Elijah said. "The secret police of the ex-Soviet nations were still in demand, even after their former masters were conquered. They still had files on everyone, and access to intelligence regarding all manner of projects initiated in Soviet days. Their plastic surgeons may not have published their work, but they didn't lack expertise. Will you answer my question now, please?"

"You'll find out soon enough," Victory said, as much to himself as his captor. "The file on the carrier is Mrs. Allison's, not Amahl Sahman's. You don't have the instructions for the

147

creation of a new messiah—but if it's any consolation to you, neither does Gregory K. Allison. Neither do I, until I've seen the final pages. Whether Yashvili's trying to sell Allison a new messiah or use his money and influence to pay for the production and marketing, he's not going to show his hand until the last possible minute. That way, he keeps us all guessing—and none of us will have time to think twice when we have to make our crucial decisions."

"Well," Elijah said, "at least I know that you were able to follow the argument. Now you know the truth, I'd like to think that you'll take our side. I really had hoped to lay my hands on the program before Gwynplaine did, but it seems as if the only way I can do that now is to persuade you to let us into your office. How far out of London have we come, by the way? I've lost track."

"We're on the A308 heading for the Kingston bypass," the Scotsman supplied. "We can turn around at Kingston and come back, if you want to head for Harley Street, or go on through Esher and Cobham if you want to head for somewhere quieter."

"We could, of course, smash our way into your office if we can't get in with the keys and cards," Elijah suggested to Victory.

"You certainly could," Victory said. "Of course, you'd have to bear in mind that, even if you got what you wanted, the program is still incomplete. What's more, Gregory K. Allison's people are presumably watching the place like hawks. Given that you obviously have an inside man at the hospital, it might be better to try to hit my computer there—except that you'd already have done that if you thought you could get away with it, wouldn't you?"

"You're not helping yourself, Dr. Victory," Elijah said. "If you succeed in persuading us that you're of no use to us, our better strategy might be to ensure that you're no use...."

He was cut off by the ringing of Victory's mobile phone. The cradle set on the dashboard immediately drew their gazes, but neither he nor Elijah had to reach out to touch the device; as the answerphone cut in, the speaker crackled into life.

"This is your security service, Dr. Victory," the familiar voice of Asmodeus said. "The entire conversation is on tape, and the police have been alerted; they've been instructed to wait for you at the exit to the Kingston bypass. There's a drone flying directly above your car—a little thing, no bigger than a bat or a sparrow, almost impossible to spot even in daylight. It's not armed, but it has very good cameras. It can swoop at a moment's notice. There are more police cars behind you, whose occupants can be with you in less than two minutes if you stop. Given that the men in the car with you are members of the intelligence services, they probably have nothing to fear from the police but the prospect of looking utterly foolish, but they probably won't want the inconvenience, given that they're up against the same deadline as everyone else. By my reckoning, they have a window of opportunity of approximately a minute and a half, if they care to beat a retreat. If they attempt any further violence against you, they will certainly be pursued and prosecuted. I think you should begin braking now, but be careful—you wouldn't want to cause a traffic accident."

Victory had already started braking. He permitted himself ten seconds to steer the car safely to the hard shoulder and bring it to a halt. "I wish that I could say that it was a pleasure to meet you, Mr. Elijah," Victory said, "But I really did enjoy the story. Will you be going, or staying?"

Elijah's two companions already had their seat belts unbuckled and their doors open; Elijah hesitated before reaching for the clip of his own safety belt, but only briefly. Victory guessed that he had said what he intended to say, and learned as much as he had expect to learn, and was unprepared to take the admittedly slight risk that what the voice on the phone had said might actually be true.

"It isn't over, Dr. Victory," the tall man said, as he opened his own door, "And you really should be on our side, no matter what Allison offers you. This is more important than money."

Victory felt that he was at last entitled to the luxury of reverting to character. "Do you always retreat to the accompaniment of idiot platitudes," he asked, waspishly, "or is this a special occasion?" Then he had to reach across and close the passenger door, which had been left open as his ex-captor bolted. He drove on without delay.

CHAPTER SIXTEEN

The Fifth Day: Late Evening

"There isn't really a police car waiting to intercept us at the Kingston bypass, is there?" Victory asked. The phone had been silent for more than a minute, but he hadn't heard Asmodeus hang up.

"Of course not," his rescuer said. "There isn't a drone hovering overhead either—but I am your security service, for the time being."

"And there *is* a bug in the car—planted, no doubt, by Gwynplaine."

"Yes there is. He only wanted to keep track of your movements, but as he was putting it in anyway, he presumably figured that he might as well incorporate a voice transmitter. I'm glad that he did—aren't you?"

"So you are working together," Victory concluded. "You and he really are trying to run the scam of the century on Allison, *Mr. Yashvili*. Is it just ready money you're interested in, or are you really hoping that Allison's money and the myth of the Sons of Job will set you up with a viable religion capable of raking in billions?"

"You mustn't believe all that you hear, Dr. Victory," Asmodeus said. "As the man said, the world is overfull of misinformation and disinformation—errors and lies, in vulgar parlance."

"They weren't actually going to hurt me," Victory said, trying to sound perfectly confident. "It was all bluster. Compared with the Allisons' outfit, this lot are rank amateurs, even if they are part of his majesty's secret service. Are they, by the way?"

"I'm not absolutely sure—but I felt certain that they'd be prepared to pretend. They probably all draw MI salaries, but that wouldn't necessarily stop them from going into business for themselves.

"As you'd know from experience, I presume?"

"I suppose I might, if Elijah had been telling the truth and I really were who you think I am. Alas, he doesn't know the truth, and probably wouldn't tell you the truth even if he did. As for me...I've already told you who I am."

"The ex-king of the demons? I still prefer the other part of the definition—the ex-husband of Lilith Yashvili. I really can't think of a reason why Mr. Elijah might have made all that stuff up, if he didn't think that it was true. If it was designed to persuade me to hand over my program—which I couldn't have done in any case, given that it's not finished—it was more than a trifle over-elaborate, don't you think?"

"But that's at least half the fun of conspiracy theories, isn't it?" Asmodeus observed. "The more complicated and convoluted they are, the more satisfying they become, whether people actually believe them or regard them merely as tales worth repeating. You have to admit that I haven't tried to blind you with *that* kind of bullshit."

"Do I?" Victory said. "I'm not so sure. Maybe you just get your deputies to deliver the bullshit, while you sit contentedly back and listen in. If you're not Iorga Yashvili, tell me who you really are." While he was speaking the car reached the roundabout giving access to the Kingston bypass, which was indeed devoid of any evident police presence. Victory took the opportunity to go all the way around it and head back the way he had come, towards central London.

"I am *not* Iorga Yashvili," Asmodeus stated, flatly. "Believe me, Dr. Victory, this business would be a great deal less interesting if I were. I...hold on—there's someone on the other line."

The crushing banality of this interruption wrung a smile from Victory's lips, and he almost laughed out loud—but his mood shifted again almost immediately, as he pondered the assertion that conspiracies became more satisfying as they became more complicated and convoluted. For himself, he had had more than enough of complication and confusion—but what, he wondered, did it say about Asmodeus that he took such a view? Would Iorga Yashvili the Georgian, ex-secret agent and diplomat, really regard his life's work so lightly?

Asmodeus' voice came over the speakerphone again. "There's been a slight change of plan, Dr. Victory, if you don't mind," the mystery man said. "Given that you're heading back to Westbourne Park, you'll presumably be taking Fulham Palace Road and Shepherd's Bush Road. That will take you into Wood Lane. Fifty yards or so past the Television Centre, pull into the roadside and stop. It's not really permitted to stop there, as it's a red route, but you won't be getting out of the car and no one will bother you at this time of night."

"What for?" Victory demanded.

"It's Gwynplaine. He's been obliged to move from where he was staying. He's no longer sure that he can get to you tomorrow

151

if he's carrying the photocopies. He wants to see you now, just to be on the safe side."

"Who's after him? Elijah's bunch?"

"They're doubtless after him too, but it's not them. Some other Visionary Martyrs might be making their move, but it's more likely that the Church has indicated to its lay instruments that the Holy Father would be glad to grant indulgences for any sins committed in the course of the book's recovery."

"Torricelli seemed very clear about the end not justifying the means," Victory observed.

"He probably believed it at the time," Asmodeus replied, "but history assures us that it's one of the more disposable items of the faith."

"Is Huw Williams safe?" Victory asked. "I ought to warn him that Elijah might come after him."

"I've already warned him," Asmodeus said, "but he's not in any immediate danger. When word gets around that Gwynplaine's been flushed out, all attention will be focused on him—and you, of course."

"But the Sons of Job are on our side, aren't they?" Victory said. "In fact, I can't see why Gwynplaine doesn't go straight to Allison. All the groundwork has been laid. If you're going to persuade him to order me to complete the operation on Amahl Sahman, you'd be better off doing it now than waiting any longer."

"No one's on any side but his own, Dr. Victory," Asmodeus said, "and you still seem to be labouring under the misconception that what Elijah told you is true. Some of it is, admittedly—but you know full well that it can't be that simple. Yes, the Sons of Job are potential allies, but Gwynplaine's immediate business is with you, not them. You have to finish the program—and you'd be wise to do *exactly* what Gwynplaine wants you to do."

Asmodeus rang off then, as unceremoniously as he always did. Victory had already concluded that he had to look after his own interests; unfortunately, he still didn't know what he ought to say and do when he finally had to confront Gregory K. Allison. Although Elijah had confirmed his own hypothetical extension of Joseph Allison's theory, he still didn't have any irrefutable proof that Allison was a mark. Parading Iorga Yashvili's name before the billionaire was only likely to annoy him—and where, exactly, did Mrs. Allison fit into the plot? Joseph had seemed certain that she was not involved, but Elijah had implied that she was, and that her entire second marriage might have been no more than a sham, intended to prepare Gregory K. Allison for the plucking.

The one thing he was determined not to do, Victory quickly decided, was to leave Gwynplaine in the lurch while the scarred man still had the book and the missing instructions contained therein. He followed the instructions Asmodeus had given him, and brought the fake Bentley to a halt some fifty yards past the Television Centre. He had only to wait for a minute before the front passenger door opened and a hooded man got in. The new-comer was also wearing a filter-mask, and he carried a black briefcase.

"Thank you, Dr. Victory," he said, in Gwynplaine's unmistakable voice. He was not wearing his dark glasses, but his eyes were only intermittently visible as he turned his head to look sideways and backwards, occasionally catching the light of street-lamps.

Victory put the car back into gear and moved off. "Will they be watching the flat?" the surgeon asked. "Should I take the Westway and head for Wallingford? My farmhouse is north of there, not far from Rokemarsh."

"People will probably be watching both your homes," Gwynplaine said. "As in Harley Street, though, the sheer profusion of watchers may be our best guarantee of safety. Each individual faction is outnumbered by the others, and none knows what the others might do."

"We could book into a hotel."

"Probably unnecessary, and probably unwise. You should stick to your schedule. It might not look good if you were to go too far out of your way on my behalf. While others are uncertain of your intentions, they're less likely to act precipitately against you."

"I've noticed that you're a great believer in that strategy," Victory observed, dryly. "It doesn't seem to be working too well tonight."

"It has its limitations," Gwynplaine admitted.

"Asmodeus says that you bugged my car."

Gwynplaine had been looking straight ahead, staring at the road, but now he half-turned to glance at Victory. "Yes, I did," he admitted. "It seemed a sensible precaution, at the time."

"Did you bug the office too?"

"No."

"I wish I could believe you," Victory said. "Not that it matters, I suppose. The fact that Asmodeus is listening to your bug is interesting, though. You and he seem as thick as...thieves."

"Why the pregnant pause, Dr. Victory?" Gwynplaine asked. "Are you accusing us of being thieves?"

"It has recently been suggested to me that you and Iorga Yashvili, alias Asmodeus, have organised this entire comedy in order to con Gregory K. Allison out of a small fortune."

"Is that what you believe?" Gwynplaine parried, as expertly as Rachel Rosenfeld.

"It seemed the likeliest hypothesis at the time, although I wasn't sure whether you were a ringleader or a catspaw. I guess it still does. Elijah's account of ex-post-Soviet agents of the Georgian KGB planning to start a new religion with an elaborately forged history is definitely on the far-fetched side—though not, admittedly, as far-fetched as the notion that you might be the Devil, Cain or Adam."

"The simplest hypothesis isn't always the best," Gwynplaine observed, scrupulously. "As for likelihood...I concede that all of this is highly improbable—but if people weren't occasionally willing to risk the improbable, there would be no progress at all, and the past would indeed be dead."

"What's that supposed to mean?"

"Exactly what it seems to mean, Dr. Victory. Might I ask who Elijah is?"

"You don't know?" Victory was mildly surprised. "You probably know him under another name. According to Asmodeus, he's a British secret agent, although he seems content to represent himself as a fake Visionary Martyr. Even Asmodeus can't know everything, though, no matter how hard he likes to pretend. Anyway, you and Asmodeus must be working together, or you wouldn't have phoned him when you got into trouble, would you?"

"I've never had any reason to think that he was opposed to my plans," Gwynplaine said, "As a matter of fact, though, it was *you* I tried to telephone, not Asmodeus. When he said that there was someone on the other line, he meant another line to your mobile. I'm not sure how he managed to divert the call to his phone rather than yours, although it was doubtless facilitated by the fact that he was talking to you at the time, but he's always been clever with things like that."

Victory shook his head tiredly, not knowing what he ought to be prepared to believe. "Shall I take the car directly into the garage?" he asked. That, at least, seemed to be a simple question certain to receive a simple answer.

Gwynplaine looked around reflexively as the car slowed outside the Westbourne Park flat. The street wasn't deserted, but all the people walking on either side gave the appearance of being on their way to somewhere else. "Is there any reason why you shouldn't?" he parried.

Victory sighed. "I was just worried that there might be men in there with guns or Samurai swords, waiting for us to show up. I suppose it would be simpler for them to wait in the flat, though. If they could get into one, they could probably get into the other. Am I sounding paranoid?"

"Not at all, doctor. Merely careful."

Victory sent an electronic signal from the dashboard to open the garage door, and closed it immediately once he was inside. There were no men with guns or Samurai swords waiting inside—and there was no one in the flat either.

"Make yourself at home," Victory said to his unexpected guest. "I'm sorry the place is such a mess. I'll put the kettle on." As he spoke, though, he observed that his automatic apology was unnecessary; the flat was not a mess—indeed, it seemed remarkably Spartan now that he had occasion to view it as a potential venue of entertainment. He couldn't help comparing it unfavourably with Huw Williams' ultra-lived-in apartment.

Gwynplaine seemed grateful to be given a cup of coffee, despite the lateness of the hour, and he set about drinking it with considerable enthusiasm. Although his lips were slightly awkward, he didn't spill a drop."

"Do you have the book in the briefcase?" Victory asked, when his curiosity could no longer be contained.

"It's in a safe place," Gwynplaine told him.

Victory tried to control his disappointment. "But you do have the remaining photocopies?" he said.

"Not exactly."

"How do you make an inexact photocopy?" Victor asked, sarcastically.

Gwynplaine contented himself with opening the briefcase and taking out what seemed at first glance to be two sheets of paper. It took Victory three seconds to realise that they were actually parchment. It seemed that, although Gwynplaine had deposited the book in "a safe place," he had paused to tear out two of its pages—the vital two pages containing the final instructions in the comprachicos' recipe for the face of Adam.

Victory had begun to doubt whether those two pages actually existed, but any relief he might have felt at the confirmation that they did was overwhelmed by the enormity of what Gwynplaine had done to what was allegedly a unique and priceless artifact. He wondered whether the hypothesis that this was all an elaborate pretense intended to persuade Gregory Allison to part with a few million pounds was now less likely or more likely. On the one hand, confidence tricksters surely would not spoil their own goods so recklessly—but on the other, the fact that Gwynplaine was willing to do so strongly suggested that the book could not be the genuine article. "That smacks of vandalism," was all he said aloud.

"I'm afraid so," Gwynplaine said. "I truly regret the necessity—but not as much as I regret the necessity of destroying the pages, once you have memorised them."

"What?" It was Victory who spilled his coffee, as the shock of the scarred man's statement startled him. "You can't be serious."

"I'm perfectly serious, Dr. Victory. You have all the others, so if you haven't yet turned their instructions into machine code, you'll be able to do so tomorrow. As I told you before, the final modifications are very subtle—on the brink of being deducible. A man of your talent might well have been able to deduce them, or at least to complete them by trial and error, had you not been promised the sight of them.

"Once you have studied the diagrams, you will not need them on your desk to make the final adjustments. You—and you alone—will possess the final secret of the comprachicos. Even I have insufficient understanding of the surgical niceties to make perfect sense of what is written and depicted on these pages, and I have not the skill to reproduce the diagrams precisely, no matter how well I might memorise them. You already have the anatomical templates set up on your computer, and you already understand the sequence of operations as well as it can be understood, as a work of art as well as a sequence of mechanical manoeuvres. I trust you, Dr. Victory, to see not merely the mechanics but also the art of the final adjustments—and I trust that, once you have grasped those things, the completion of the program will be straightforward. Once you have seen the whole, the parts will be easy for you to reconstruct."

"Why would you do that?" Victory whispered. "If that's true, why would you do it?"

"Because I need to have the operation carried out, Dr. Victory. I need Amahl Sahman to possess the face of Adam. You are the only person who can do that. Now that we have come so far and my adversaries are drawing a net around me, I have no alternative but to trust you—or, rather, to trust in your curiosity and artistic inclinations to see that the job is successfully done."

"It isn't that simple," Victory said, feeling that it was a drastic understatement. "In spite of all the information that's been thrown at me from every direction—because of it, in fact, given its flagrantly contradictory nature—I don't have the faintest idea who you really are or what you're trying to accomplish. Without knowing that, how can I possibly perform this operation on Amahl Sahman? He may not be in any position to give his informed consent, but I am—whether Gregory Allison chooses to involve himself or not, *I* need to know exactly what it is that I'm consenting to do. To be frank, I don't think that there's anything you can say that could convince me, unless you spiked my coffee with one of the wonder drugs Iorga Yashvili is alleged to have used on you. You do know who Iorga Yashvili is, I assume?"

"Yes. I know that he is not Asmodeus, as you seemed to think when we were in the car."

"He denied it too—but he would, wouldn't he? And if he really has done to you what Elijah said he did, you'd deny it too, and believe your denial absolutely, even though he'd be dictating your every action."

"Are you willing to tell me what Elijah told you?" Gwynplaine asked, his politeness seeming ludicrously over-exaggerated.

Victory repeated what Elijah had told him, as accurately as he could remember it.

"Fascinating," Gwynplaine said, when the story was done. "I never cease to wonder at the extremes to which confabulation may go. I suppose that it says a great deal about your informant's mindset. Iorga Yashvili was indeed a gatherer of intelligence before he became a diplomat—and your Elijah is presumably in the same profession, working in your national interests as Yashvili once worked for his. There is no profession or activity more conducive to fabulation and the construction of elaborate conspiracy theories. Even historians cannot compete with the so-called intelligence services in building awesome mountains of conjecture upon the merest molehills of corrupt data. Theologians are almost as clever, although they have the advantage—by which I really mean, of course, the *dis*advantage—of combining the corrupted data with items of dogma. If my choice is between believing myself to be a brainwashed dupe, whose identity is a construct of psychotropic drugs and hypnotherapy, and believing myself to be the Devil, I think I'd rather be the Devil.

"Is that supposed to imply that you now believe that you really are the Devil?"

"Don't be ridiculous, Dr. Victory. There is no Devil, and never was. The Devil is an invention of the Church: a brutal instrument of moral terrorism. Priests have always embraced the defeatist belief that the only way to persuade people to be good is to threaten them with eternal torment if they fail. You and I know better than that. You and I understand that the only worthwhile way to persuade people to be good is to show them the rewards that will flow from virtuous conduct and aesthetic endeavour. There has to be more to hope for in life than the avoidance of a posthumous Hell. You and your work are living proof of that."

"So who are you, really, if you're not the Devil, or Yashvili's dupe, or Yashvili's partner in crime?" Victory asked. He attempted, as he said it, to meet Gwynplaine's disconcerting stare with the kind of detachment that befitted a man who could repair every horror and enhance every beauty, but it wasn't easy.

Gwynplaine let loose a slight sigh. "I always intended to tell you the truth," he said, "even though I knew that you'd have the utmost difficulty in believing it. It wouldn't have been any easier if you hadn't been confused by these other conjectures. Did you really believe what Elijah told you? Do you still believe him?"

"I haven't the slightest idea what to believe—but I can't believe that the myth of Eden is a literal account of something that actually happened. I can't believe that you're Cain or Adam any more than I can believe that you're the Devil. Asmodeus has tried hard to prove himself a reliable and friendly informant, but when he says that you were in Eden, I can't believe him. If you really do believe that you're Adam, then I'll have to believe that there's some truth in what Elijah says: that you were traumatized as a child by some hideous accident or act of malice, and became vulnerable to any kind of falsehood that was pumped into you."

"I'm not Adam, Dr. Victory," Gwynplaine told him. "You've left someone out of your account—someone else who was in Eden."

"Eve? The angel with the flaming sword?"

"The serpent."

"*The serpent*? But that's what Torricelli said—that you're the Devil."

"And I pointed out that the Church has always been blinded by its own dogmas. The Roman Church decided that the serpent in Eden must have been Satan, but there's not an atom of evidence in the text of *Genesis* to support that view. The writer of the text certainly believed differently—the Jews were authentic monotheists, who refused to believe in any such anti-god. They had even rejected the demons in which their ancestors had believed, although a few traces of them remain in the Torah as well as the Talmud, allowing Asmodeus to cling on to a strange kind of marginal existence."

"You're saying that Asmodeus really is the demon of anger and lust, and Lilith's husband?"

"I'm saying that he *was* the king of all demons. What he is now, I'm not entirely sure. I don't know exactly why he wants the face of Adam to be recreated, but he does seem to be lending considerable assistance to my cause."

"And what are you, now, given that you don't seem to be a serpent any more?"

"I'm still what I was, although I've recovered my legs and don't have to slither on my belly any longer. The recovery wasn't cost free, but it was worth it."

"This is absurd," Victory said.

"I'm afraid it must seem so," Gwynplaine agreed. "But it *is* the truth. I never supposed that you would be able to believe it, but I can offer further explanations if you'll permit me to do so."

"I'd be delighted to hear them, if we've time," Victory said.

"I think we have time," Gwynplaine said placidly. "You probably have less to do tomorrow than you might think, given the simplicity of the final piece of the puzzle. Would you prefer to begin with Eden, or with the Creation that preceded it? The former might be easier, although the latter would conserve chronological order."

"Start from the beginning," Victory said. "Whether it's easier or not, it's more orderly. *Let there be light* was the crucial phrase in *Genesis*, I believe."

"That's in verse three of the first chapter," Gwynplaine said, equably. "Creation is described—rather vaguely, I fear—in the preceding verses. The letter of the text isn't so very important, although I may call your attention to certain interesting features of chapter three when we come to it. In the meantime, it's probably more helpful to examine the logic of Creation than the exact terms of the description offered in *Genesis*. Do you mind if I have another cup of coffee?"

"Help yourself," Victory said, feeling that the conversation had become even more surreal. "I haven't any biscuits, though. Unlike Huw Williams, I'm not as well organised as I should be."

"That, alas, is the story of the world in a nutshell," Gwynplaine said, emitting another faint sigh. "It's not as well organised as it needs to be."

CHAPTER SEVENTEEN

The Fifth Day: Before and After Midnight

"There are two conceivable models of Creation," Gwynplaine said, "one of which has two conceivable variants. The first is Creation *ex nihilo*—the appearance of something out of nothing. The second is Creation as transfiguration; its first and more popular variant is a matter of bringing a new order to primordial chaos; the other is a matter of bringing a new disorder to a primordial uniformity.

"*Genesis* is ambiguous, and the Church was always on the horns of a dilemma. Early philosophers didn't like the idea of *ex nihilo* creation, because it offended their aesthetic sensibilities, much preferring the order-out-of-chaos scenario. The Church went with that to begin with, but then swung back towards the *ex nihilo* thesis. Scientists initially preferred the order-out-of-chaos model too, until the advent of Big Bang theory, which put *ex nihilo* back on their conceptual map—and cosmological theory relating to what happened after the Big Bang often tends to see it as a matter of lumpiness emerging out of uniformity rather than order out of chaos."

"I don't see what this has to do with...," Victory began.

"That's why I suggested that it might be easier to start with Eden," Gwynplaine said. "Bear with me. Big Bang theory isn't wholeheartedly committed to the idea of Creation *ex nihilo*, in that it imagines that there must have been something to go bang, even if time and space didn't come into being until the moment of the bang. The singularity in question is cosmology's self-creating substitute for God—neither personalized nor intelligent, but nevertheless containing the seed of the future order of the universe, whose evolution since that moment has been an unfolding of potential guided by cause and effect.

"The religious question of intention is set aside in the scientific model, but it's transfigured rather than annihilated—it still makes sense to ask why *this* universe came into being rather than another. One possible answer is to suggest that all possible universes do in fact exist, and that this is merely one of them. Another is to suggest that the only universe that does exist has some kind of self-selecting factor at work within it. The latter kind of hypothesis becomes much more attractive, if not absolutely necessary, when one admits the momentary nature of existence."

"What does that mean?" Victory asked.

"Simply that the present moment is the whole of Creation—that *now* is all the time there is."

"Well, it's true that one can't put the clock back," Victory said, cautiously. "The past is dead and gone, even though we remember it. One has to live in the present, in the knowledge that the future will arrive soon enough."

"I'm not talking about a matter of psychology," Gwynplaine said. "I'm talking about a matter of ontology. The universe exists momentarily; because it changes, it gives rise to the illusion of time, the notions of *was* and *will be*—but the future and the past have more in common with one another than seems intuitively to be the case. If the illusion of time were more reliable, and the empire of cause and effect were absolute, then the future would already be determined, the destiny of every entity within it already mapped out—but that isn't the case. Human beings really do have free will; only despairing cynics can deny the fact. The future is not yet made—it will emerge out of the collective decisions made by all the free entities the universe contains. Its apparent direction can be altered, by collective determination and political decision. Such alteration is far easier on an individual level than a collective one, but the former is the only necessary condition of the latter. Individuals can change the direction of their lives, and if enough individuals work together, they can change the direction of their nation, or their species."

"You're talking about the possibility of ameliorating the ecocatastrophe—of maintaining the ecosphere as a human habitat. That's what this business of instituting a new religion, or regenerating the existing ones, is all about?"

"That's the easier part of it," Gwynplaine said. "I'm also talking about the fact that, as well as being pregnant with many possible futures, our little corner of the universe contains many possible pasts. All that really exists is the moment; everything else is alterable. Within the moment, there's a sense that all possible futures already enjoy a tentative existence, governed as much by hope and fear as by abstract probability—because hope and fear will be important forces in reshaping the moment. In the same way, there's a sense in which all conceivable pasts similarly enjoy a tentative claim upon reality, similarly influenced by conviction and faith."

"And that's what Torricelli meant when he said that he believed in Eden *and* evolution?" Victory said, feeling that the light had begun to dawn.

"I can't speak for Monsignor Torricelli," Gwynplaine said, "But it's what *I* mean when I say that I know that the story of Eden is literally true, even though the account of life on Earth proffered by evolutionary biologists is also literally true. The principle of the excluded middle really doesn't apply."

"If that's so," Victory argued, "then every other imaginable account of the past can also be literally true."

"Indeed," Gwynplaine agreed. "That's a version of the thesis that all possible universes ought to exist. What makes the difference between the pasts that are sustainable illusions and those that are not is the presence within the momentary present of apparent relics. What sustains Eden as a workable component of the illusion is my presence in the world and the possibility of recreating the face of Adam. Were I to be eliminated, and the secret of the comprachicos lost...."

"I thought Adam was supposed to be immortal," Victory objected. "Not to mention Cain and Lilith."

"Adam is potentially immortal, while the possibility of his recreation remains. As for Cain and Lilith...it seems probable to me that their immortality is of the same contingent kind; they too may be awaiting the same kind of rebirth as Adam."

Lilith Allison is asleep in bed at the hospital now, Victory thought, *awaiting her transformation on Sunday. As for Cain...if the operation intended to reproduce Adam's face were to go slightly awry....* Aloud, he said: "Yashvili's people really did a job on you, didn't they? You really do believe all this, no matter how insane it is."

"Not insane, Dr. Victory," Gwynplaine said, placidly. "Unreasonable perhaps, but not insane. Just as all progress depends on unreasonable men who will not accommodate themselves to the prevailing consensus, so the reconstruction of the illusion of the past also depends on unreasonable men."

"It certainly does," Victory agreed. "If what Elijah told me about Yashvili's invention of all the historical evidence for the existence of the Sons of Job and the Visionary Martyrs is true, he must be an exceedingly unreasonable man—but just because he created false evidence of the existence of those cults, and transfigured the evidence relating to the comprachicos by similar methods, it doesn't mean that any of it ever really happened."

"Of course not," Gwynplaine agreed. "Because the notion of something—anything—*really having happened* is mercurial. The moment is all there is, Dr. Victory; its potential pasts are as numerous, and as negotiable, as its potential futures. If we want to create the future we need and desire, we must also create the past that we need and desire. In the moment in which we find ourselves, Dr. Victory, the fragile Earth requires a collective effort more powerful than any our present notion of history can ac-

knowledge as a possibility, let alone an accomplishment. We
need a new past, in order that we might have a new future. I
don't say that mine is the only history that might enable us to
avert the worst aspects of the ecocatastrophe, but I do say that
it's the most convenient, given the number of people who are
already familiar with the myth of Eden. My own commitment is,
of course, far greater than that—but I cannot save the world
alone. I need the cooperation of the entire Western world, and a
substantial fraction of the East. In order to make a better Eden, I
need to establish the literal truth of the first one. The face of
Adam will be my instrument."

"Do you see that creation as a matter of creation *ex nihilo*?"
Victory enquired, sarcastically, "or merely as a matter of bringing order out of chaos?"

""Given that the moment is all that exists," Gwynplaine replied, "the notion of creation *ex nihilo* really does not arise,
unless one takes the view that moment is essentially static, and
can only manifest the appearance of change by being continually
recreated *ex nihilo*. Perhaps I should have pointed out before that
the variation of the other thesis is only apparent: in order for
change to be manifest, both processes must go on simultane-
ously. Order must be continually reduced to chaos to provide the
raw material of a new order; the two processes are not contradictory but interdependent. What the power of free will does—or
can do, if it is properly directed—is to catalyse both processes,
thus hastening the pace of creation. That was what I attempted to
do in Eden; that is what I am attempting to do now."

"Starting at the beginning doesn't seem to have helped us to
maintain strict chronological order," Victory observed. "I'd almost forgotten Eden. I'm afraid that I don't possess a Bible;
you'll have to remind me exactly what happened there."

"What happened there," Gwynplaine said, "is that free will
very nearly cancelled itself out of existence. Adam was on the
brink of settling for a finished world, a perfectly ordered world
of submission to what the Church reckons as Divine Will, and
what science reckons as the absolute empire of cause and effect.
Adam was contented with his lot. Despite the loss of Lilith, he
was content with what he had; Eve seemed to him a more than
adequate replacement. He had made the decision not to eat of the
tree of life, which was also the tree of knowledge of good and
evil—there was, incidentally, only one tree, although the second
chapter of *Genesis* briefly gives the impression that there might
have been two. Had Adam stuck by that decision, the moment
would have crystallized out in stasis and sterility—but he was
uncertain, and hence seducible. All it required to secure the reign
of change and the ceaseless play of order and chaos, was a cata-
lyst."

"And that was you."

"The creature '*more subtil than any beast of the field*,' which was also possessed of a measure of free will, although I was not, at that point in the story, physiologically capable of eating the fruit of the tree. I had no knowledge of good and evil, but I did have an understanding of order and chaos. So I told Eve that if she ate the fruit, she would not die of it, which was true; I told her that she would know good and evil, which was true; and I told her that she and Adam would be as gods in consequence, by virtue of having the power to change the order of Creation, which was true. And because I spoke those truths aloud, I was *cursed above all cattle, and above every beast of the field* to squirm upon my belly and eat dust for the remainder of my life, an enemy of womankind and mankind, to be bruised beneath their heels.

"And so it was, and might always have been, had I not changed the nature of the moment in giving voice and force to the will of Adam—but we live in a changeful moment now, and nothing need last forever, even the world. I was disfigured, just as Adam was disfigured, but disfiguration need not last forever, or at least need not remain the same forever. I have my legs back now, although I had to go through fire to win them, and I am ready to deal with Adam again—and with God and all the angels, through the force of his countenance. I have to be ready, because the doom of stasis is only one of those that threaten aspects of our universe; the other is annihilation. I once saved humankind from uniformity; now I must save humankind from chaos."

"Why you?" Victory asked, quietly. "Why now?"

"If not me, who? If not now, when?"

"Will you at least entertain the possibility that you are not who or what you think you are?" Victory asked. "Will you concede the possibility that Elijah was telling the truth, and that your identity is an artefact, forged by psychotropic drugs and the power of suggestion?"

"Of course I'll concede the possibility," Gwynplaine said. "Will you at least entertain the alternative? Will you concede the possibility that I am exactly who and what I say I am?"

"I can't," Victor said. "I simply can't."

Gwynplaine shrugged his shoulders. "If that is the truth of the moment," he said, "that is the truth—but the moment might yet set you free. What you do accept is the reality of these pages, and the possibility of carrying out the transformation whose description they complete. You do accept the reality and responsibility of the decision you have to make, don't you?"

"I accept the reality of temptation," Victory murmured, remembering what Guillermo Torricelli had said to him about the inevitability of belief in the Devil, for a man who knew that power.

"Good," said the man with the fire-scarred face. "He who accepts the reality of temptation accepts the reality of choice. Look at the pages, Dr. Victory. Look at them, and memorise them. It will not be difficult—once you have seen them, you will understand how necessary the instructions are in the consumma-tion of a process that you already understand very well, as sci-ence and as art."

Victory knew that he was going to do as he was asked, at least for the present. He knew that he was not only going to look at the pages, but that he was going to study them intently, and commit them so reliably to memory that he would be able to complete the software version of the transformation Gwynplaine wanted him to effect. Afterwards...well, that decision would be his and his alone: a matter of his will and his responsibility.

Even so, he hesitated. He looked Gwynplaine in the eyes, squarely, and said: "Even if everything you've told me were true—that you really are the serpent that tempted Eve in Eden, and that these instructions really can recreate the face of Adam—you still can't possibly have any idea what the actual effect of the face's recreation would be. You'd have no control over that effect, because you can't obtain custody of the child. Gregory K. Allison will have that—and I dare say that he has his own ideas about the use that might be made of such a prize. You can't know that it really will have the power to precipitate a mass re-newal of religious faith, nor what the commitment and outcome of that faith would be."

"That's true," Gwynplaine admitted. "But if I don't try, what will become of the Earth? What will become of humankind? What else but faith can move men *en masse* to self-sacrifice and hardship, to toil and self-deprivation, to zeal in the making of a new Millennium, ruled according to the principles of the Sermon on the Mount? I know that I might not succeed, and I feel that anxiety bitterly—but how bitterly would I feel my own failure if I didn't try? Can you tell me another way, doctor? Can you show me another path to the salvation of more than a favoured few—a few who will use their private wealth to build hopefully-impregnable walls between themselves and their fellows as the ecocatastrophe reaches its climax? Can you, Dr. Victory?"

Victory knew that he could not. So he looked, instead, at the two pages torn from the secret book of the comprachicos, no longer troubling himself with the question of whether or not it was a fake, and he began to commit them to memory.

Almost as soon as he had begun to absorb the import of the two diagrams, however, he was stopped by a sudden realization.

"It's not complete," he said. "There's a page still missing."

"These were the last two pages in the book," Gwynplaine stated, firmly. "There is no more to the final secret of the comprachicos than this."

"Then the secret itself was never complete," Victory said, utterly confident of what he said. "These instructions stop short. The final elements of the sequence are still missing."

"In that case," Gwynplaine said, apparently unfazed by the revelation, "you will have to try even harder to perceive the direction in which they tend—the goal towards which they are orientated. *You* must complete the sequence, Dr. Victory. You can, and you must."

"I can't," Victory answered, "and I mustn't. I can't make Amahl Sahman into the subject of a crazy experiment, even if Gregory Allison wants me to...I couldn't, even if *he* wanted me to, and were capable of saying so. It's just not right."

"All you have do is look, Dr. Victory," the fire-scarred man told him. "It may well be that no one else in the world could see the art in this, and take on the role of its creator, but *you can*. If you can only open your eyes and heart to the possibilities innate within you, you will see and understand what needs to be done to complete the program and recreate the face of Adam in the flesh of Amahl Sahman. Gregory Allison will surely instruct you to do it, but that won't matter, because you're absolutely correct to say that it's a matter of what's *right*. You only have to look, Dr. Victory, and you'll eventually see that it *is* right. You only have to see what it is that I'm holding in my hands."

Victory did as he was told, expecting nothing—but then, as he obeyed the instruction he had been given, he saw what it was that the serpent wanted him to see.

Gwynplaine was right, he realised; as soon as he had truly seen and absorbed the implications of the diagrams and the accompanying instructions, it seemed as if he had always known them. All along, he had been on the very brink of sensing the underlying logic and aesthetic of the whole pattern. The final steps—including the one unrepresented in any diagram—were not logically necessary, but they *were* aesthetically necessary. He could see now, in his mind's eye, how the sequence of scalpel-cuts and tissue-relocations made perfect sense. He could see how the realignment of muscles and bone, and their supplementation with nerves, vessels and connective tissues, had a definite coherency, a unique individuality, and a kind of perfection. It was the kind of perfection within individuality for which he had been striving throughout his career, and throughout his life.

This was not at all the same thing, however, as being able to see *the face of Adam* in his mind's eye. He could see the trees, but not the wood. He could see the pattern of analytical detail, but he could not visualise their extrapolation in purely human terms. In order to do that, however paradoxical it seemed, he would need a carefully programmed machine.

As if he were capable of reading minds, Gwynplaine spoke then, still as placid as ever. "I'd be doing you a grave disservice, Dr. Victory," the scarred man said, "if I didn't remind you that you're now in considerable danger. If you'll take my advice, you'll set up the program in the machine at the hospital without attempting to preview its effect. No harm can come to you or Amahl Sahman if you work directly upon the flesh—but I can't guarantee your safety if you look at a computerised image of the face of Adam."

"What, exactly, is supposed to happen to me if I look at the face on a screen before attempting to reproduce it in the flesh?" Victory asked. "So far as I can see, the worst than could happen, in your view of the matter, is that I'd suffer a sudden and drastic renewal of religious faith."

"Which might not be at all comfortable," Gwynplaine pointed out. "What happened to Saul on the road to Damascus might have been a revelation, but the price he paid for his new and inescapable conviction was probably an epileptic fit. I would not like you to suffer an epileptic fit, doctor, before a scheduled operation. You might have to excuse yourself, leaving the operation undone."

"Is that what you expect to happen? You expect me to have an epileptic fit if I display the face of Adam on my computer screen?"

"I don't know—I can't possibly *know*. But I'm genuinely afraid of some such effect, and I don't want anything unfortunate to happen to you before you complete your work on Amahl Sahman."

"But when you say that the face of Adam will bring about a religious renaissance—that it will inspire everyone who saw it to forsake sin and seek salvation—the way you expect that to work is *via* something like a worldwide epidemic of epilepsy?"

"Some sort of general revelation, yes," Gwynplaine said, equably. "Probably not cost free—but exactly what cost might be involved, I can't tell. No one can, although the Sons of Job and the Visionary Martyrs doubtless have their own theories as to the likely mechanism, and of possible ways of influencing the outcome. Perhaps your incapacity to believe will protect you, but I remain anxious as to what might happen if you suddenly lost that incapacity. Even so, I've given you the warning that I was duty bound to offer; if you're prepared to take the risk, having had fair warning, so am I. If you insist on seeing an image before you attempt to produce the real thing, I won't try again to prevent it. If, after seeing the image, you're unable to conduct the operation, I'll simply have to hope that I can take the results of your work to someone else who has access to the kind of machine you have."

"I thought you were going to destroy the pages," Victory said.

"I am," Gwynplaine confirmed, screwing them up even as he spoke. He removed his empty coffee-cup from its saucer, and placed the bundled parchment thereon. He brought a box of matches out of his pocket.

"Wait!" said Victory. "Surely you don't have to...."

Gwynplaine paused before striking the match. "You're the only one I trust, for the moment," he said. "If I have to trust someone else, then I'll do the best I can. From this particular moment until it's transformed into something different, you *are* the secret of the comprachicos.

As soon as he had finished the sentence, Gwynplaine struck the match and set it to the parchment. The pages burned avidly, the dyes in their diagrams lending strange colors to the flame.

CHAPTER EIGHTEEN

The Sixth Day: Morning

Victory slept so badly that he might almost have sworn that he had not slept at all, but two cups of strong black coffee repaired his concentration somewhat. Gwynplaine had left soon after setting light to the two pages of parchment containing the culmination of the comprachicos' last secret, promising that he would come to Harley Street at one o'clock if he were not prevented from so doing.

Victory didn't know whether or not to be glad that the scarred man wouldn't be at his elbow when he attempted to recall what he had committed to memory in order to amend his surgical procedure; nor did he know whether or not to hope that Gwynplaine would succeed in making the appointed rendezvous.

The radio informed him that the latest round of predictions from the Global Environmental Model was even more pessimistic than the previous set. More specifically, it told him that continued high pressure would ensure that air quality in the Thames Valley would be mediocre to poor throughout the hours of daylight, and that concerned citizens were encouraged to stay indoors or wear selective nasal filters. Victory left his own in its drawer, even though he knew that he would have to risk the raw air twice if he were to stop off at his usual cafe for his breakfast.

He regretted the decision slightly when the pastiche Bentley pulled out into Bishop's Bridge Road for a second time. The air within the vehicle seemed to have taken on a subtle odour, suggestive of an overloaded filter. In theory, it was not due to be changed for another fortnight, but Victory suspected that it might have been slightly overburdened by the previous day's excursions with unexpected passengers.

When he arrived at the Harley Street garage the surgeon observed that Rachel Rosenfeld's Lexus was already parked there, and wondered briefly whether her clients' demands were obliging her to make Saturday morning appointments or whether she was merely catching up with her record-keeping. His own office suite was empty; Claire did not work on Saturdays or Sundays except by specific request.

Victory's sense of urgency had increased markedly since he got out of the car; he had been unusually fretful as the elevator made its slow ascent, and he felt uncommonly flustered as he turned the keys in the locks and punched in the pass codes that opened the two doors separating him from his inner sanctum. He wasted no time in switching the computer on and sitting down at his desk.

He had to force himself to pause, and concentrate on what it was that he had to recollect. It required a manifest effort to re-hearse the sequence carefully before he began to reproduce and translate it. Once he let himself go, however, Victory's busy fingers flew over the keyboard with unaccustomed haste. He managed to maintain near-perfect accuracy in spite of the speed at which he was working, but he cursed every mistake that compelled him to hit the back space key. He clicked the mouse with equal facility, weaving anxiety into exhilaration as he incorporated the final adjustments into the model that would reproduce the final details of the operation—and, if he ordered the appropriate transformation, an image of the face of Adam—when the program was run.

What he was doing was no mere matter of addition, because the code had to be modified in a dozen different places to accommodate the formulas describing the final incisions and reconnections, but it seemed far easier than it might have been because it felt *right*. Although there was nothing *objectively* obvious about the final instructions, Victory felt irresistibly certain that he had now acquired such an intimate understanding of their hidden purpose that he was almost incapable of making a mistake. Even though he was working in taps and clicks, operating in a world of symbol and abstraction, he could sense the beauty of what he was forging, and the sublimity, as well as the individuality.

The code he was modifying remained mere code, reconceptualising a string of ones and zeroes, as impenetrable to the naked eye and innocent mind as any other list of instructions, but he felt an intimate connection with its innate energy and intentionality. Until the machine converted the instructions into pictures they were vague and formless, but nevertheless pregnant with an embryonic image, whose charisma had already infected his thoughts and emotions...or so it seemed.

Victory worked ceaselessly for more than two hours, then checked the data with the utmost care before proceeding to the final stage of the plan—*his* plan, not Gwynplaine's. He had never seriously considered the possibility of heeding Gwynplaine's warning; he had always intended to preview the face that the comprachicos had designed for their recreated Adam.

It was shortly after noon when Victory finally drew the mouse across the pad, and clicked to launch the visualisation program.

He had watched his program run a thousand times before, always with a tingle of anticipation regarding the image that would emerge. The moment before the picture actually coalesced on the screen was always a special one for him, pregnant with the delight that was the legitimate reward of a job well done— not merely in the sense that the legacy of life's petty misfortunes would be removed and nature's errors repaired, but in the sense that a new beauty would be imported which transcended anything that could ever have been produced by the alliance of genetic heritage and embryological development. This time, he knew, the artwork was not entirely his own—but that only served to enhance the suspense and heighten the anticipation.

This, he felt, might be a work of genius—and even though he would not be able to claim full credit for it, he would be able to add its rewards to the sum of his experience, so that the work he did in future would be even better than the work he had done so far.

He still had no firm intention of subjecting Amahl Sahman to this particular transfiguration—but he had every intention of refining his own powers of design to the point at which every face he transformed in the future would be just a little nearer to the face of an angel.

Victory could not help trying to imagine what the face of Adam might actually look like, but his attempts to transform the codes within the wetware of his own brain were hopelessly confused by pre-existent ideas, including memories of the image painted by Michelangelo on the ceiling of the Sistine Chapel.

When the image appeared on the screen, however, Victory realised that Adam did not look anything like the model that Michelangelo had employed. Adam's face was unlike any that had ever been worn by an ordinary mortal, or painted by an artist of mundane genius.

While learning the basics of medicine before moving into his specialism, Hugo Victory had been informed that each of his eyes had a blind spot where the neurones of the optic nerve spread out to connect to the rods and cones in the retina. Because he had always been slightly myopic, his blind spots had always been slightly larger than those of people with perfect vision, but they still did not show up in the image of the world formulated by his brain. Even if he placed a hand over one eye, to eliminate the exchange of visual information between the hemispheres of his cerebral cortex, he still saw the world entire and unblemished, free of any void. That, he had been told, was an illusion. It was not that the brain "filled in" the missing data to complete the image, but rather that the brain simply ignored the part of the image that was not there, so efficiently that its absence was imperceptible. And yet, the blind spot *was* there. Anything eclipsed by it was not merely invisible, but left no clue as to its absence.

It was a blind spot of sorts that had prevented Victory from being able to deduce the missing element in his model of the comprachicos' final secret until he had seen the two pages that Gwynplaine had shown him some twelve hours earlier. It was likewise a blind spot of sorts that had prevented him—and every other man in the world—from extrapolating the face of Adam and the angels from his acquaintance with the vast spectrum of ordinary human faces. There was a sense in which the face of Adam had always been deducible from the spectrum of human faces, not by any kind of averaging but by a double process of extrapolation, the first aspect of the extrapolation being concerned with the distillation of the elements of human beauty, and the second by the re-equipment of the ultimate beauty with its own uniqueness, its own individuality, and its own *life*.

Now, the blind spot was removed. Victory's mind was no longer able to ignore that which had previously been hidden, even from the power of his educated imagination. He was able to see the perfect human face, not in the abstract but in the particular, not as an idea but as a person.

What Victory saw—and could not doubt that he saw—was a clear image of the proto-human face that had been made in God's image.

Quietly, he began to weep, moved by the force of his own creativity, and the measure of his accomplishment. His tears evaporated as they trickled slowly down his cheeks, but his pride did not. His was only a secondary creation, but that did not prevent him experiencing the glory of his achievement, and a kind of love that he had never felt before.

And then the image stirred, and smiled, and said: "Thank you, Dr. Victory. This is exactly what I need." Then it became still again.

That, Victory knew, was impossible. Everything he had previously done had seemed plausible, provided only that he thought of "the face of Adam" as a metaphor, and disregarded the wilder elements of Gwynplaine's apparent delusions—but the image he had created was only an image; it could not possibly be animated

There were, of course, almost as many experimental programs abroad in the world that were designed to simulate the expressiveness of a human face as there were to simulate the workings of a human mind, but none had ever completed the final step. Artificial Emotional Intelligence still remained beyond the grasp of computer simulation. Synthesized images could speak, just like any other kind of animated figure, but they could not speak as accomplished humans spoke, effecting a perfect coherency between their words and the language of facial expression.

But Victory's Adam, who should not have been able to move or speak at all, because the program that had formed him was incapable of supporting those illusions, spoke like a human being. In fact, he spoke like a *perfect* human being. He spoke as one might expect a human archetype to speak, with utter conviction, as if he were incapable of speaking a lie.

The shock that took possession of Victory's mind and body was indescribable. It was as though the abrupt and unexpected confrontation with the impossible had stopped the world. If, as Gwynplaine asserted, the ceaselessly self-transforming moment was all that existed, then the smoothness of its eternal movement had been rudely interrupted within him—as if he had been expelled from it, cast out of Creation into some realm of non-existence beyond.

The sensation was very brief—but how could it be momentary, when existence itself was momentary? It was more profound than any mere blip in an unfolding stream of time. The balance of order and chaos, and the process by which each was transformed into the other, was tipped. He was delivered into chaos, and although it seemed to him as the moment recaptured him and swept him up again that he had returned to the minuscule element of order that was Hugo Victory, there was a dark residue of confusion in the depths of his soul that he could not disown.

Victory felt that he could not move—that he was frozen in position, lost in rapt contemplation of the wonder that he beheld. He knew that he was not paralysed in any physical sense; his motor nerves had not lost the ability to transmit commands from his brain. He had, however, lost the desire to issue any such commands; for the moment, at least, he had lost the capacity to *want* to move—and, for that reason, he sat perfectly still. After a while, he stopped weeping, but there was no other tangible change in his condition.

He did not look around or even glance sideways when he hard the click of the opening door. He knew that it must be Gwynplaine, to whom he had blithely given the pass codes for both office doors on the previous Tuesday, but he did not care.

Although his eyes remained fixed on the face of Adam, Victory's peripheral vision was adequate to show him Gwynplaine's hand reaching for the keyboard from behind the machine, carefully closing the program down. He knew that the scarred man's bright blue eyes were carefully avoiding any possibility of looking directly at the screen.

Victory remained immobile even when the image of Adam's face had disappeared. He watched without the slightest reservation or complaint as Gwynplaine moved around the desk, carefully decanted the program on to a key ring carrier similar to his own, and then set about randomizing the document on the computer.

Gwynplaine saved the randomized version before issuing a deletion instruction, thus ensuring that the residual version on the hard disk would be useless. He had erased the instructions for picturing and producing Adam's face from Victory's computer, permanently and irretrievably.

"I'm truly sorry, Dr. Victory," the man with the hideous face murmured, not unkindly, as he returned the key ring to his pocket. "I played as fair as I could—or at least as fair as I dared. My warning really was intended as a warning, not as an exercise in reverse psychology, although I confess that I always felt sure that you would ignore it. I did not know that this would happen, and I hope that the effect is temporary. I hope that you will still be able to carry out the final operation on Amahl Sahman, even though you will not be able to remould him in Adam's image. In time, I suppose, you will be able to reconstruct the program with the aid of the photocopies and the last leap of imagination that you alone could make—but our plans will be well advanced by then.

"I really do regret deceiving you, just as I regret deceiving Iorga Yashvili, but I couldn't tell you the truth. I would have deceived Allison too, had it been necessary, but it was not; his wife had already accomplished all that was necessary in that regard. He will almost certainly help us now—but if he will not, we shall do what we can without him. We might have been able to work with and through him from the start, but we were afraid that he might guess what we intended, and were far more confident that you would not. Blinded by your own preoccupations, you were bound to be distracted from the obvious.

"Even with the face of Adam, you see, Amahl Sahman could never have served as a messiah in today's world. All societies are founded in and shaped by their media of communication. Moses, Jesus and Mohammed were forced to do their work in person, but modern prophets must work with and through broadcast images. Perhaps the device that you have just completed and demonstrated is a truer Adam than any mere human creature could ever be—at any rate, we may legitimately hope that it is better equipped to transform global society than any actual human could. You might attempt a further incarnation, if you wish, but I have the one that I want—and all its would-be usurpers are sitting quietly by, believing that the deadline for action is tomorrow or the next day.

"There is a certain irony of fate in the prospect of having to improvise the reproduction of God's countenance, but what can the purpose have been of all the millennia of man's technological progress, if not to facilitate that improvisation? There is no time now for a new messiah to gather disciples by personal contact and spread his gospel by word of mouth; if the world is to be saved from the worst effects of the ecocatastrophe, the new ideology will have to be disseminated by television and radio, and the face of Adam must be displayed on every billboard and newspaper as well as speaking from every TV set and computer screen, until the cause is won. Do you still have the power of speech, Dr. Victory?"

"Yes," Victory's voice replied, reflexively. The surgeon had no sense of his own volition in the framing of the reply, but he did feel an almost-infinitesimal surge of relief at the revelation that he could, in fact, speak. That was enough to inform him that his paralysis was not absolute, and would not be permanent. He knew now that his capacity for desire was not extinct, but merely muted; that the first effect of seeing and hearing the new Adam speak would be temporary.

"Good," Gwynplaine said. "I really did not mean to do you more harm than was necessary, and I really did not know exactly what sort of harm the sight of the face might do. I hope that you make a full recovery—except, of course, for the permanent effect that the face was designed to have. I hope that you will be a man of faith from now on, Dr. Victory: a man whose faith is not blinded by obsolete dogma, like Monsignor Torricelli's, but properly informed by the necessity of making a better Eden."

As he spoke, the scarred man leaned sideways to impose his face between Victory's staring eyes and the blank computer screen; his own eyes were staring intently, and quizzically.

That's odd, Victory thought, again feeling a slightly pulse of relief at the realization that he was capable of setting a train of thought in motion. *When your face was first revealed to me, I thought it was the most awfully disfigured I'd ever seen. I couldn't imagine why the doctors who had treated you since your accident hadn't done more to ameliorate the effect of the burns. But now you seem perfectly ordinary, not hideous at all. I thought that I could do something for you, if you'd only permit me to try, but now I see that...there's nothing that really needs to be done.*

"I hope you can find it in your heart to forgive me for the enlightenment I've forced upon you, Dr. Victory," Gwynplaine said.

I don't feel capable of forgiveness at present, Victory thought. *Nor of hatred, for that matter...but I'll pull myself together in a moment or two, if I can only find the motive force.*

"If you see Monsignor Torricelli again," Gwynplaine went on, "please give him my regards. Tell him that, unlike him, I really have learned to love my enemies." Then he stood up straight again, and picked up the telephone receiver. He tapped out a number. "Dr. Rosenfeld?" he said. "My name is Gwynplaine. I'm speaking from Dr. Victory's office. I think it would be a good idea if you looked in on him when you can spare a minute.... Yes, I understand...by all means take care of your patient first...but I think Dr. Victory might be grateful if you could come down as soon as you can. I'll leave the doors ajar when I leave." He replaced the receiver in its cradle and turned to the surgeon again. "Goodbye, Dr. Victory. I hope that this entire experience will ultimately work to your benefit. Should the world be saved, of course, there will be no doubt of that, but this is just the end of the beginning...there's a way to go yet before we reach the beginning of the end."

The scarred man left then, leaving the door to the consulting room ajar, as he had said that he would.

Victory wondered whether he might be capable yet of willing himself to move, but could not quite turn the speculation into desire. He was no longer motionless, because fatigue was preventing his muscles from holding him rigid, but his collapse was remarkably gradual. Had he been fortunate, he might simply have slid on to the carpet, but such was his position that when the muscles could not hold him upright he slumped forwards, his head falling on to the edge of the desk in such a way that his forehead collided with the edge. It did not feel like a hard blow, but he knew that the skin had broken and that blood was flowing.

The dizziness resulting from the impact was by no means pleasurable, but it did renew his motivation. He was able to move his arms, gripping the desk with both hands, and he tried to stand up.

That turned out to be a mistake; he should have contented himself with pushing himself back into his chair. As he thrust himself upwards the blood-flow to his head was disturbed, and the dizziness increased. He fainted, and fell. His head hit the desk for a second time as his legs folded up beneath him. This time, he ended up lying on the floor.

Something is missing, he thought, feeling strangely calm once the dizziness had ebbed away. *Something in me has been randomized and erased. When desire and will return, as they surely will, there will still be a void. If I have indeed found faith, as Gwynplaine seems to believe, then faith is not what I had expected, any more than the face of Adam was what I expected.*

For all his seeming certainty, Gwynplaine has not the least idea what it is that he has done, or what the effect will be of what he intends to do.

Even thinking was an action of sorts, driven by desire. The more he thought, the more capable Victory felt of action, but he knew now that he had to wait, and take things slowly. While he was lying down, his head was clearing, and he was beginning to feel a good deal better in spite of the blood that was now trickling into his eyes and staining the pale carpet.

I shan't die for want of the will to live, he thought. *I shan't be reduced to vegetable status. I shan't lose power over my limbs or my brain. I'll be whole again, given a few more minutes to collect myself. I'll be okay....*

There the insistence failed; he could not be sure, as yet, that he would be *entirely* whole again. He still could not work out what it was that seemed so profoundly absent as to be irrecoverable, but there was a blind spot of sorts in his sense of self: a void whose form and shape was imperceptible, but which nevertheless prevented him from conceiving of himself with ordinary clarity and coherence.

He heard the door click open again, and heard Rachel Rosenfeld say: "My God, Hugo—what's happened to you? Who hit you?"

Victory rolled on to his back so that he could look up, although one eye refused to open because of the blood that had flooded it. The psychotherapist's face loomed over him, filling his field of vision just as Gwynplaine's had an immeasurable while before. She stared into his face, reached out to touch his cheek, then took up his wrist to take his pulse. Then she got out a light-pen to test the iris of his open eye. Afterwards, he heard her tapping the keys of his phone, first to display his address book and then to dial a number.

"Dr. Hemlet?" he heard her say. "Are you Dr. Victory's associate? This is Rachel Rosenfeld; I have the rooms above his in Harley Street. He's collapsed in his office—I don't know for sure whether he's been attacked, or whether he simply hit his head when he fell. You need to send an ambulance to collect him...yes, that's right.... Yes, I think you ought to come out with it.... No, I don't know exactly what the damage is, but if he wasn't struck over the head it's possible that he's suffered a minor stroke or had some kind of fit. He seems to be concussed. He may need a CT-scan, but it's not my field.... Yes, you'll need to have a neurologist standing by.... Yes, I'll see you then."

Victory made another effort to get up, but this time he was held back by a restraining hand.

"Just lie still, Hugo," Rachel Rosenfeld said. "The ambulance is on its way. Can you speak?"

"Yes," he whispered.

"Can you tell me what happened?"

"I fell," he said. "No one hit me."

"Do you know who I am?"

"Yes."

"Who?"

His lips tried to form the word "Rachel," but failed, and he cursed himself—and was perversely glad to find that he was still capable of annoyance as well as desire, of frustration as well as will. He knew that he on the way to recovery.

"It's okay," the psychotherapist said. "Just relax. The ambulance will be here very shortly. Just lie still."

He did as he was told—and slowly drifted into unconsciousness.

CHAPTER NINETEEN

The Sixth Day: Afternoon

Victory woke up feeling slightly disorientated, but otherwise quite well. His head felt numb, but he did not need to reach up with his fingers to confirm that he had received stitches under local anaesthetic. He knew before he opened his eyes that he was in a hospital bed—a bed, in fact, at his own hospital, probably in the same corridor as Amahl Sahman and Mrs. Gregory K. Allison. He had a lingering impression of a familiar kind of dream, involving an attempted flight from some nebulous danger that was handicapped by an inability to make his limbs move, but it was already evaporating in the light of consciousness.

He tried to remember how it had come about that he had been brought into the hospital, and why his head had needed stitches. He remembered easily enough that he had been in his consulting room. He remembered seeing Rachel Rosenfeld's face, and Gwynplaine's...and he remembered working hard all morning, struggling to complete the transformation of the last secret of the comprachicos into computer code. He tried to remember the face of Adam, too, and what it was about the face of Adam that had seemed so startling, but all he could remember was a curious hallucination.

It seemed to him that he had finished the work of recreating the face of Adam, which had then *spoken to him*—but that had to be something he had dreamed, something that had happened *after* he had hit his head on the edge of his desktop. But what, then, had *caused* him to hit his head on his desktop? Had he suffered some kind of fit, like Saul on the road to Damascus? Had he fallen victim to some kind of narcolepsy? Had he had a stroke? Or had he simply tripped somehow, through sheer carelessness? Had the blow to the head caused him to imagine, ludicrously, that the face of Adam had spoken to him? Had he even managed to finish the work, or was that part of the dream rather than an authentic memory?

179

He felt that he ought to open his eyes and search out answers to these questions, but it seemed that some considerable time passed before he contrived to do it.

When he finally did open his eyes, he thought at first that he was still dreaming, and that his apparent awakening had only been a trick of the dream. There were faces present—three of them—but for some reason that he could not quite grasp, they were unidentifiable. Indeed, they did not seem like *faces* at all, although he knew perfectly well that they were. Had no one spoken, he would not have been able to identify any of them.

The first person to speak was Rachel Rosenfeld. "Hugo?" she said. "Hugo, can you hear me?"

"Dr. Victory?" The second voice was Majeke Hemlet's.

The third, which also used his full name, was less easy to identify because it was less familiar, but he eventually pinned it down as the voice of Simon Fullar, a consultant neurologist.

It was the neurologist who took over, shining a light pen in Victory's eyes, demanding that he move his fingers. The surgeon dutifully answered a series of questions about what he could hear and feel, whether he was in pain, and what he could see. The last set of questions was the most difficult. Victory knew that could see perfectly well, but felt that there was something wrong with what he saw. He could see that he was in a bed in a hospital room, virtually identical to the ones in which Amahl Sahman and Mrs. Gregory K. Allison were lodged. He was not on a ventilator or a drip; he was breathing normally, and was presumably not in need of any intravenous hydration, medication or nutrition. He could even see the faces of his concerned attendants, and put a name to each one, but there was still something wrong with that aspect of his sight—something that he could not quite pin down.

Victory listened patiently, collecting himself all the while, as Simon Fullar told him that there was no evidence of any organic abnormality in his brain. There was no lesion or tumour, no evidence that he had suffered a stroke or an epileptic fit. He had, it seemed, suffered an "inexplicable blackout"—but the cut on his head was trivial, and there was no fracture.

When Victory finally got the chance to speak on his own behalf, it was to say: "I'm okay—just a little disorientated. I'll be fine."

"What happened?" Majeke asked. "Why did you fall?"

"I don't know," Victory replied, quite sincerely. "I was working at my desk, and I fell forwards. Then I tried to stand up, and fell again. The second blow was sheer carelessness, but the first...."

"I should have realised earlier that something was wrong." This comment was from Rachel Rosenfeld, but she was talking to one of the other doctors, not to Victory. "He's been driving himself harder and harder with every week that passed, but I thought of it as a psychological problem rather than a physical one."

"That's nonsense," Majeke objected. "He's always worked hard, but he was perfectly okay yesterday. He certainly doesn't have any psychological problem. It was just an accident, wasn't it, Dr. Fullar?""

"I'll know more when we get the bloods back," the neurologist said, cautiously. "If he'd taken something...."

"He wouldn't!" Majeke said. "He's a surgeon—the best in his field!"

"Gwynplaine...," Victory put in.

"Who's Gwynplaine?" Majeke wanted to know.

"He's the man who called me," Rachel Rosenfeld supplied. "He's a patient of Dr. Victory's—but I think he called before Hugo actually injured himself."

"Gwynplaine *might* have drugged me," Victory said, finally managing to complete his sentence.

"What?" Majeke and Simon Fullar said, in unison.

"Why?" said Rachel Rosenfeld.

The real question, Victory thought, was *when*? Had Gwynplaine slipped something into his coffee before showing him the final pages of the comprachicos' book, in order to stimulate his imagination? Or had he doctored the Bentley's air-filter as he made his way out of the apartment block? He shook his head—no, it was too silly. Gwynplaine hadn't drugged him. Something else had happened. The face of Adam....

Victory remembered, then, the last glimpse he had had of Gwynplaine's face—and he looked wonderingly from Majeke to Rachel Rosenfeld and back again. Majeke, he remembered, was not a particularly beautiful young woman, but she was young enough and beautiful enough not to worry overmuch about her own image. She had not had any cosmetic surgery herself, having not yet perceived any need, and Victory remembered that he had only visualized trivial amendments when he had looked at her face. Victory knew, in the abstract sense that he knew that it was true, that Majeke was a great deal better looking than Rachel Rosenfeld who wore her years of aging proudly, and made no conspicuous effort to decorate herself even with conventional cosmetics. Victory *knew* this—but he realised now that he could not actually *see* it. To his eyes, at present, the two faces were just faces; neither was any more *beautiful* than the other.

Simon Fullar was not entirely unhandsome, for a man in his fifties, but he had a distinctive face that wore its own due quota of lines and blemishes. Victory knew that too, as a mere matter of remembered fact—but he could no longer judge the face with the aesthetic sensibility that any plastic surgeon had to cultivate as a matter of course. He cold not look at any of the three faces that were hovering over his bed with a professional eye, and see features that would benefit from repair or reconstruction—not in the strictly medical sense that they would become healthier, but in the less easily definable sense that they would *look better*.

I've seen the face and heard the voice of Adam, he thought, *and now all other faces are merely human.* But he set that thought firmly aside. He had *not* seen the face of Adam, and it had not spoken to him. That had been a dream. He had to remember that this whole affair had been some kind of confidence trick, and that he was one of its dupes. Perhaps he had been drugged, in order to put him out of action now that his part was done, so that he could not warn Gregory K. Allison about the impending sting....

Except that, when he *really* concentrated, he felt certain that he *had* seen the face of Adam, and that it *had* spoken to him....

He set that thought aside, not because he realised—a trifle belatedly—that everyone was firing questions at him again, but because he realised that he had to recover his ability to see faces clearly, and judge their aesthetic quality. That his inability was temporary, he did not doubt, but time was pressing, and he had to recover that aspect of his sight in a hurry. Without the ability to make crucial aesthetic discriminations in respect of human faces, he would hardly be able to conduct operations in plastic surgery.

"Stop it!" Majeke said to Rachel Rosenfeld and Simon Fullar, who were engaged in an absurd competition to put different questions to their patient. "He's still in a daze, still confused. He needs to rest—or at least to answer one question at a time, at his own pace."

"It's okay," Victory said. "Which is to say, it's not *quite* okay yet, but I'm getting there. Doing one thing at a time would certainly help. Simon, if you're satisfied that you don't need to do anything more for the time being, maybe you could come back later. Rachel, I need to talk to you, but I have to talk to Majeke first. Would you mind waiting outside for five minutes or so?"

Simon Fullar and Rachel Rosenfeld agreed readily enough. When they had left the room, Victory wasted no time in saying: "We're in trouble, Majeke. You have to contact Gregory Allison. You'll have to tell him about the blackout. I don't know whether it will be safe for me to operate on his wife tomorrow, or even whether it'll be my decision to make. Ask him to come to see me so that we can discuss the options—but there really isn't any option, so far as I can see. You'll have to do the operation yourself. I'll explain to him why it has to be you rather than one of the other consultants."

"Because I've been working with your software all along," she said. "I'm the only one who can use your planned procedure."

"That's right. He may not like it, but he'll have to abide by my decision. There's a lot more that he'll like even less—and that will be the more difficult part of the conversation."

"Amahl, you mean? You think you'll be sidelined for several days? You want me to do that one too?"

"No—it's too complicated. I can't let you attempt it. Amahl's operation will have to be postponed—but there's a great deal more flexibility in his case than Mrs. Allison's. I might not be ready to operate on Sunday or Monday, but I *will* recover. I may need a day or two to collect myself, but I need time to re-work the software in any case. You do understand why I can't let you operate on Amahl, don't you?"

"Too long, too complex, too difficult. If anything went wrong...it's okay, Dr. Victory. I'm more surprised that you're willing to let me take over Mrs. Allison."

"That's a straightforward procedure, well within your compass. You'd better talk to Christina Legrange too—she's not going to be pleased about this."

"It was an accident, Dr. Victory—unless you really do think that you were drugged."

"No," Victory said. "That was just momentary paranoia...I was confused. It was just a fall. Maybe I have been overdoing it lately—I shouldn't have tried to stretch my schedule to accommodate Mrs. Allison. I'm sorry...this is all my fault. Contact Mr. Allison, ask him to come to see me, as soon as possible. Tell Christina that Amahl's operation will have to be postponed, but that she'll be the first to know when we're ready to go ahead. Send Rachel in, will you?"

Majeke hesitated, but then she nodded her assent. Her face still seemed alien to Victory, not merely devoid of any appreciable beauty but devoid of any obvious expressiveness. He could focus on it readily enough, in spite of his slight myopia, but he could not *read* it in any meaningful way.

Apart from that handicap, and the numbness of his temples, he now felt quite well. He sat up in bed, looking around for the locker in which his clothes would have been stored.

Rachel Rosenfeld had obviously had time to regret her earlier impatience. She made no attempt to renew her bombardment of questions, but waited for him to tell her what it was that he wanted her to know.

"I thought Joseph was at least half right when I left your office," Victory said, "but the plot had progressed a great deal further than he was able to imagine. I think it did start out as a scam, with Gregory Allison the target, but it wasn't just the book that Yashvili intended to sell him—it was the whole Sons of Job package, complete with the face of Adam. Yashvili really did want to start a new religion, with Allison as his key convert—but Gwynplaine double-crossed him. Gwynplaine's working with someone else, and they've hijacked the whole enterprise. I think they'll still try to draw Allison in, but Yashvili's out, and so is Amahl—there's a new mastermind calling the shots, and they're going to make the pitch in a very different way."

"I don't think you ought to be concerned with all this at present, Hugo," the psychotherapist said.

"Don't you? You think I ought to concentrate on getting my head back together...getting some serious rest...trying to forget my troubles and obsessions.... Well, perhaps you're right. Perhaps I ought to drop out meekly, now that my part is done. Perhaps my body already took that decision for me, when the shock of seeing the new Adam in all his glory struck me dumb and knocked me out. Perhaps my internal censor is still telling me that I need to stop and smell the flowers, and not go back to work until I'm fully refreshed—but the big scam is due to come to a head tomorrow or the day after, and I wouldn't feel entirely comfortable if I didn't at least try to do what Joseph asked me to do, and warn his father about what's coming down, Would you?"

Rachel Rosenfeld hesitated for a long time before saying: "Is it possible that you *have* been exposed to some kind of psychotropic, Hugo?"

"I don't know," Victory answered. "If what Elijah told me about Yashvili brainwashing Gwynplaine was true, I guess it has to be possible. Did you ever hear of a psychotropic that distorted people's aesthetic sensibilities?"

The psychotherapist could not have anticipated the question, but her professional expertise hid her surprise. "None that was reported in those terms," she replied, after a moment's thought, "but there are a considerable number of reports of perceptual and conceptual confusion, whose side-effects would include aesthetic distortion. It's much more common the other way around—unusual or inappropriate excitement of aesthetic sensibility, often in association with sexual arousal. May I presume that you're suffering the kind of distortion you're asking about?"

"Yes. I seem to have mislaid my ability to identify beauty, at least in human faces. I suppose that does have sexual connotations, but I think it cuts deeper than that. It ought to be—will be—temporary, of course."

"Why *of course*?"

"If it's a drug, it'll wear off. If it's a side effect of the blow to my head, it'll wear off. If it was caused by the shock of seeing the face of Adam, it'll wear off."

"Have you seen the face of Adam?" the psychotherapist asked, calmly.

"I think so. I might have dreamed it, but I think it was real. Gwynplaine stole it. I thought he wanted me to operate on Amahl Sahman, but he didn't. All he ever wanted was the program. He needed me to complete it, because whoever devised the sequence of operations couldn't follow it through to the end—for that he needed my sensitivity, my artistic gift...which I now seem to have lost, in consequence. Temporarily, that is."

"Temporarily," the psychotherapist echoed, dutifully. "Are you telling me that the sight of the face that the comprachicos were allegedly trying to create—or at least to duplicate—was sufficiently traumatic to do this to you?"

"It wasn't traumatic, Rachel. It was just...well, I had just created the damn thing. If I'm not entitled to a certain temporary disorientation, who is? I'm definitely not telling you that the face is capable of bringing about the kind of miracle that the comprachicos were allegedly looking for. Which is not to say that it wouldn't be a powerful instrument, in the right hands...."

He stopped. Rachel Rosenfeld had raised an eyebrow, but Victory couldn't quite remember what such a gesture was supposed to signify.

"Your advertising software must be very efficient," she observed, "if any face it manufactured could have an effect as profound as this."

"It was just a face, Rachel," Victory said. "It isn't magic. Gwynplaine did everything he could to persuade me that it is, but it can't be. On the other hand...."

He stopped again. After half a minute or so, Dr. Rosenfeld aid: "What?"

"I don't know," he admitted. "I feel fine, but I'm not quite together yet. There's something I'm not seeing, not connecting with. It's not just my ability to make aesthetic judgments regarding faces that's been numbed. I feel as if I'm back where I was this time yesterday—just a little way short of seeing the whole picture, not quite able to bridge the gap...I need time to think. Joseph was half right. Yashvili and Gwynplaine were targeting Gregory K. Allison and the Sons of Job, intending to sell him—not necessarily as a commercial transaction—a package capable of launching a new religion...of putting the Allisons right at the heart of a movement that might change the world, all tucked up neatly and tidily in a key ring. But Gwynplaine's reneged on Yashvili's plan and...there's something I can't quite put my finger on...but I'll be better soon."

Victory had no idea what the expression on Rachel Rosenfeld's face might signify. He stopped to wonder whether he might, in fact, be mad. It was, he knew, a theoretical possibility. He felt perfectly sane—indeed, in a curious sense, he felt more than perfectly sane, because he felt that his judgment was no longer clouded, as it once had been, by aesthetic judgments. He felt that he saw the truth more clearly now than he ever had before...but that suddenly seemed to be suspiciously close to the effect that he had just denied, the effect that he had so readily assumed that the sight of the face of Adam could not have had on a man of his sort.

This time, Rachel Rosenfeld showed no sign of stepping in to fill the silence.

"You think I'm paranoid, don't you?" he said. "You think I'm confabulating madly to excuse the episode I had, without having the least inkling of what it was that actually happened. And please don't repeat the standard crap about paranoia being normal in a world like ours."

"This may take time to figure out, Hugo," the psychotherapist said, calmly. "We'll have to examine the evidence very carefully, and work our way through it by degrees."

"You and I have time to do that," Victory said. "Gregory K. Allison won't. They're going to set him as tight a deadline as they dare. I need to tell him what I know."

"Why?" she asked, bluntly.

Victory saw what the psychotherapist was getting at. Why should he care, after all, whether Gregory K. Allison was conned, if that really was what was happening? What difference would it make to him whether a billionaire who had somehow contrived to involve himself with a Millenarian cult was bilked of a few millions, or a few hundred millions, or persuaded to bankroll the career of a new all-electronic messiah? What difference would it make to anyone...even, in the ultimate analysis, to Joseph Allison?

Victory never got a chance to attempt answers to these question, though. Majeke had obviously managed to contact Gregory K. Allison, and had evidently had no difficulty in persuading him of the urgency of the situation. The man in question swept into the room without bothering to knock, and fixed both its occupants with a stare that might have been intimidating, had Victory had the perceptual and conceptual wherewithal to read it.

"It's okay, Rachel," Victory said. "I'll see Mr. Allison now. We can talk again later, after I've discharged myself."

CHAPTER TWENTY

The Sixth Day: Late Afternoon

Gregory K. Allison did not sit down beside Victory's bed, as Majeke and Rachel had both done in order to bring themselves closer to his level. Allison remained standing, looking down as if from a great height, even after Victory had sat up in the bed. Victory could not read his face at all; he was only able to wonder what proportions of anger and concern were combined in the billionaire's attitude.

Although the bedcovers were still concealing the lower part of his gowned body, Victory felt oddly self-conscious, as if he had suffered an unfortunate and humiliating role-reversal. He felt that it was his right and prerogative to stand over hospital beds—even hospital beds occupied by the mega-rich and famous—like a pillar of absolute authority. To be propped up by pillows while nearly naked was a position and condition reserved for lesser beings.

"I'm very sorry to hear about your accident, Dr. Victory," Allison said, the tone of his voice suggesting concern rather than anger—but Victory knew perfectly well that voices could lie.

"I'm sorry too, Mr. Allison," Victory replied. "I fear that it will cause you and your wife a great deal more inconvenience than it will cause me. Did Dr. Hemlet explain that I won't be allowed to operate tomorrow, even if I feel fully recovered. The hospital administration won't allow me to resume work until I've been thoroughly checked out by independent observers. From the point of view of their insurers, it would be an unacceptable risk to do otherwise."

"I understand that. My wife won't want the operation postponed, but she'll understand that it can't be helped."

"Dr. Hemlet will perform the operation perfectly. She's accustomed to working with my software, and the complexity of the procedure is well within her capability. She's a very promising surgeon. I know that Mrs. Allison came to me in order to have the benefit of my hands, and I'm sorry that we've run into a problem of *force majeure*, but it really would be in your wife's best interests to complete the operation on schedule. The fee can be adjusted, of course."

"I'm not worried about the money, Dr. Victory. If you assure me that having your assistant take over is the best option, I'll take your word for it. I'll talk to my wife. Why was Rachel Rosenfeld here just now?"

"Her consulting-room is upstairs from mine. She found me after the accident, and came in with me in the ambulance."

"I see. I'm sorry—it's just that I know her in a different context. But you already know that, I think; you talked to my son in her room yesterday morning."

"Yes, I did," Victory confirmed. "He came to see you, then—to warn you about the possibility that someone might be trying to trick me into authenticating a fake comprachico document in the hope that you'd buy it?"

"Joseph has always had a tendency to put two and two together and make twenty-two," Allison observed, cautiously.

"He does seem to have read a lot into the fact that the man he saw in my waiting-room had a fire-scarred face," Victory admitted. "The confusion is understandable, though, given that he seems to have done his research on the internet. Mrs. Allison presumably didn't think it significant, although she must have seen the man much more clearly."

Allison hesitated before rising to the bait, but tried to cover the hesitation by moving to sit down in the chair that Rachel Rosenfeld had vacated. "Don't play games with me, Dr. Victory," he said. "I think you know perfectly well that the man we're talking about—Gwynplaine is the name he's using, I believe—intended to be seen by my wife, and trusted that she might take certain inferences from the sight of him."

"I don't know that," Victory said, flatly. "I'm prepared to believe that their simultaneous presence in my waiting-room wasn't a coincidence, but I have no idea who contrived it, or with what motive. Since talking to Joseph I've heard a far more elaborate account of the conspiracy that might be directed against you—but I've also heard a far more elaborate account of Gwynplaine's side of the story. Quite frankly, I'm completely at a loss. I haven't the slightest idea who or what to believe—even though I've seen the face of Adam."

Allison was leaning forward in the chair, apparently fixing Victory with an intent stare, but to Victory the billionaire's face was just a geometrical pattern, devoid of menace or puzzlement.

When a few seconds had gone by, the billionaire said: "Tell me about the more elaborate version of the conspiracy theory."

Victory was slightly resentful of the fact that he had been confronted by a brusque command rather than a polite question, but he didn't want to waste time by issuing a challenge to the billionaire's entitlement to issue orders. "Do you, by any chance, know anything about a man who calls himself Elijah?" he asked, instead. "He's tall and bony, with thinning grey hair, apparently in his late fifties."

"I've heard the name," Allison admitted. "I believe that his real name is Hardcastle. He's not a reliable source. If anyone is trying to obtain money from me under false pretenses, he'd be my chief suspect."

"He had me kidnapped last night," Victory said, calmly. "His accomplice stabbed me in the neck just *here*"—he indicated the fresh scab with his forefinger—"to make sure that I took him seriously. He told me a very elaborate story, by no means as bizarre as Gwynplaine's but strange enough within its own parameters. It might have been partly improvised, to take account of the fact that I'd spoken to Joseph, but I think the hard core was the same pitch he would have made if I'd responded to his earlier invitations to get in touch." He hesitated then, not knowing how much he could take for granted in explaining what Elijah had told him.

"Go on," Gregory K. Allison said.

"According to both Joseph and Elijah," Victory said, cautiously, "you've become involved since your second marriage with a group called the Sons of Job."

"So what?"

"They both believe that, as a result of that involvement, you've been trying to acquire documents produced by the comprachicos—an esoteric Roman Catholic sect. Joseph didn't go much further; he was prepared to let me think that it might just be a matter of collecting curiosities. Elijah seems to be taking it for granted that the documents would be merely a means rather than an end—that the Sons of Job really are searching for the means to reproduce the face of Adam, with a view to spearheading a new religion."

Allison wasn't yet ready to confirm or deny such speculations. "And what Gwynplaine claims to have brought you is the book that was lost in the Great Fire of London," he said, his voice showing slight signs of impatience. "He seems to have made a convincing case, if you really have seen the face of Adam."

"He's very persuasive, in his own peculiar way," Victory said. "Your son may have been too modest in deducing that Gwynplaine merely intended to offer to sell you the document. On the other hand, his suggestion that I use my computer systems to produce an image of the alleged face of Adam might just have been a clever advertising strategy."

"Is that what you believe?" Allison said.

"I don't know what to believe—but I'd certainly be surprised if it turned out to be that simple. Did Joseph also tell you that Gwynplaine, or his adversaries, had also contrived to involve Monsignor Guillermo Torricelli of the Holy Office?"

"Yes, he did," Allison said. "I understand that Torricelli assured you that Gwynplaine is the Devil. I assume that you didn't believe him." Victory wished that he could read the other man's features well enough to gauge Allison's attitude to the hypothesis, but even at close distance the face was just a shape, seemingly devoid of any aesthetic or emotional quality.

"Elijah's story was about a plot actually to create a new religion, complete with its own secret history, its prophet and its messiah," Victory went on. "He told me that you were one of many people who had already been wholly or partly taken in, and that you're already using your money to assist the progress of the new cult. According to him, we're all hapless instruments of an ambitious mastermind who is making a bold bid to institute a new charismatic authority over a substantial fraction of the world's population."

"Iorga Yashvili," Allison said, finally confirming that he knew more than he had previously been prepared to admit.

"Exactly. I don't know the man, of course, so I'm not in a position to judge whether he really might want to create a new religion, or whether he really might think that he can do it—but the principle of Ockham's razor makes me reluctant to take aboard too much speculative baggage. It seems simpler by far to work from the hypothesis that Gwynplaine is lying than to grapple with the mind-boggling possibility that he might actually believe what they claim to believe. If Elijah's account was an honest one, though, the scheme he described appears to have been further complicated by the fact that there now seems to be a third person involved, who appears to have lured Gwynplaine away from Yashvili's cause to his own."

"Who?" Allison demanded, curtly.

"He calls himself Asmodeus. He put on a show last night of saving me from Elijah, but it's not impossible that he and Elijah—or Hardcastle, if that's his real name—are in it together. It's also possible that Asmodeus might be Iorga Yashvili, although he and Gwynplaine both deny it."

"I've heard of Asmodeus," Allison admitted. "He's been active on the internet scene for a long time, but we've never managed to ascertain his real name, or even pin down his location. What do you think he and Gwynplaine are up to?"

"I don't know. For a while, after I saw Joseph yesterday, I thought they might be trying to sell you the whole religion—but that doesn't make much sense, even metaphorically. It's possible that they hope to take over the Sons of Job, and any other cults they can take aboard with it, in order to employ them as the core of their own messianic enterprise. If that were the case, they wouldn't be trying to sell you their new messiah as an instrument for you to use—they'd be trying to use him as an instrument of conversion, starting with you and taking in as much of the world as they can. That might explain why they actually took the trouble to persuade me to make the computer image."

"Joseph's story seems a good deal more plausible," Allison observed, although his tone was abstracted—as if there were a much more important question that he was not quite ready to ask.

"Gwynplaine probably killed that hypothesis last night," Victory told the billionaire, "when he made a big show of burning two pages he'd torn out of the book—the last two pages, containing the penultimate phase of the comprachicos' last secret."

Victory would have liked to be able to read the expression that crossed Gregory Allison's face then.

"He *burned* them?" Allison said, in a much harsher tone, perhaps having been confronted with the first item of information that he didn't already know. "Why would he do that?"

"To impress me, I think. He always knew that the instructions weren't complete, and that I'd have to complete them for him. He always knew that I'd have to be the one to follow them through to their logical and aesthetic conclusion—a conclusion that their designer was unable to reach. He knew that the pages were useless, except as an inspiration. If that was his plan, it worked. I brought the program to completion this morning. I added in the final component—the individuality that the recipe still lacked."

"And you produced an image of the face," Allison said. "That's what caused your accident."

"Indirectly, yes—but not quite in the way that it was supposed to work."

"And you now have the means to reproduce it again."

"Not exactly—not immediately, at any rate. Gwynplaine decanted the program into a data transporter—a key ring fob, like mine—and trashed the copy on my hard disk. If Elijah was telling the truth, Yashvili's probably expecting Gwynplaine to bring it to him, but I can't believe that's going to happen. I suspect that Asmodeus is running things now."

"And what is Asmodeus going to do with it?" Allison demanded, although he must have known that Victory was in no better position to guess than he was.

"I doubt that they're going to try to sell it to you in any vulgar sense, but I suspect that they do intend to recruit you to their scheme for world salvation. If Yashvili really did invent the Sons of Job to serve as the spearhead for his operation, then Asmodeus probably hopes to hijack it. If, on the other hand, the

Sons of Job really are under your control, or Mrs. Allison's, then you probably have your own plans for discovering or rediscovering the face of Adam, and your own ideas about what to do with it. In the meantime, I'm the only one...."

Victory stopped, suddenly confused. He was sure that he had known what he was going to say when he began the sentence, but he had lost his conviction mid-way. There was still something escaping him: something that he knew, and understood, but could not quite bring to the forefront of his consciousness.

Fortunately, Allison was able to finish the sentence for him. "You're the only one who's actually seen the face," he said, finally getting at the crux of the matter. "Well, Dr. Victory, *is it really the face of Adam*?"

Victory had no idea how to answer that question. His immediate instinct was to say: "It can't be"—but he understood that it was not the kind of reply that his interrogator was looking for, or the kind that he would be able to accept. Gregory K. Allison was a leading member of the Sons of Job; whether or not his involvement had started as a trivial lifestyle fantasy, and his belief as a mere affectation, he had to be more wholehearted now. Gregory K. Allison had to want to believe, and probably did believe, in the possibility of a day of judgment.

"No," he said, in the end. "It's a fake."

"What kind of fake?" Allison demanded.

"That's the problem," Victory admitted. "I can't figure out any means by which Iorga Yashvili, or anyone else, could have discovered a way to produce a face that could pass as a replicate of the face of Adam in today's world. It's an uncommonly attractive face, and an uncommonly seductive face, but it's just a face."

"No it isn't," Allison contradicted him, flatly. "How can you even say that, when it put you in here?"

"It startled me, I'll admit." Victory said, "but not in the way you might think...." Again he stopped, not knowing how to continue.

"Then how?" Allison demanded, brutally.

"It wasn't supernatural," Victory insisted. "I was in a delicate state. It's possible that I might have been drugged. All that happened is that I was numbed for a little while, and when I tried to stand up, I fell. It was the collision with the edge of the desk that cut me and knocked me silly, not the sight of the face. I certainly wasn't afflicted with *faith*. I don't believe that it was the face of Adam because I can't...."

This time, Allison cut him off. "Exactly," he said. "You can't. But even so...the sight of the face had its effect. You couldn't even stand up without falling down."

"It's a fake, Mr. Allison," Victory said. "It's a fake, because it has to be. You may not be prepared to trust the word of Mr. Hardcastle, *alias* Elijah, as far as you could throw him, but if he's right about Yashvili having faked the entire history of the Sons of Job and the Visionary Martyrs, and embellished the history of the comprachicos out of all recognition, then the face must be a fake as well. There's isn't any other explanation."

"*How* did he fake it?" Allison repeated, insistently.

"That's not the real mystery," Victory said. "The real mystery is *why*. In fact, the most puzzling thing of all is that the faker left it incomplete. Why did he leave it to me to supply the final piece of the puzzle?"

"It was real enough to put you in here," Allison reminded him, doggedly. "Directly or indirectly, it struck you down."

And that, Victory had to concede, was true. One way or another, he had ended up in a hospital bed as a result of seeing the face, or as a result of something he *thought* he had seen in the face...whose effect had not yet worn off. Once again, he was forced to wonder whether Gwynplaine had drugged him, either by spiking his coffee or interfering with the Bentley's air filter—because that was the only way he could avoid wondering whether it might, after all, be Gwynplaine and not Elijah who was telling the truth. But if that were so, he thought, Iorga Yashvili—or Gwynplaine and Asmodeus—could hardly hope to drug Gregory K. Allison in the same way, let alone everyone else in the world.

"I don't believe their motives are mercenary at all," Victory said, desperately trying to collect his thoughts. "I think they really are trying to save the world. It's a crazy scheme, admittedly, but maybe the only one that could possibly work, given the desperation of the global situation. They want to recruit you to a new crusade, and they've done their utmost to provide that crusade with a semi-plausible figurehead—which I, like a dutiful fool, obligingly put into the form that they needed. They've even invented an opposition, to persuade you that if you won't take the reins of the crazy crusade, someone else will—but you'll know far better than I do, Mr. Allison, whether there actually are any Visionary Martyrs, and exactly what they amount to if there are. To answer your question in a slightly less unacceptable way, my considered opinion is that it's only the face of Adam if you're prepared to believe that it is—but if you are prepared to believe that it is, then that's what it might become."

Allison didn't make any immediate response to that, and when he finally did speak it was only to say: "You seem to have had a very busy week, Dr. Victory."

"Yes, I have," Victory agreed.

"But it's finished now—a little too soon, I fear, to suit my wife's plans."

"My part seems to be done. I don't think Gwynplaine meant to inconvenience your wife. He always knew that I'd preview the operation that he pretended to want me to carry out on Amahl Sahman, but he couldn't know what my reaction would be. He still doesn't, because he left before I fell. Whether he'd be pleased or not, I don't know—but if he could see me now, trying to explain all this to you, I suspect that he'd be more than satisfied. Perhaps he never intended to approach you himself. Perhaps he always expected me to do that for him."

"Which raises the question of why you're telling me all this," Allison pointed out. "What's *your* motive?"

"Rachel Rosenfeld asked me exactly the same question just before you came in," Victory confessed. "I'm telling you all this because it never occurred to me *not* to tell you. I'm telling you because I think that if someone is out to make a fool of you, for mercenary or any other reasons, you're entitled to know. I'm telling you because even if Rachel's right, and I'm imagining all of this because I've been caught up in the web of fantasy and can no longer tell my arse from my elbow, at least you'll find out exactly what kind of a madman nearly got to operate on your wife's face. I'm telling you for the same reason that I gave Huw Williams photocopies of the pages from Gwynplaine's book—because information wants to be free, not straitjacketed in paranoid conspiracy theories or buried under vows of secrecy."

"Information will never be free," Gregory K. Allison told the surgeon, "while misinformation and disinformation are also free. The truth can never be entirely free of their taint, and it costs a great deal of money to reduce the impurity to a minimum."

"I'm also telling you," Victory said, "in case you really do believe that the mere sight of the face of Adam might start a cascade effect capable of bringing about a seismic shift in global culture. If you really do think that what Gwynplaine now has is potentially world-shattering, then you'll presumably buy into it any way you can—but I feel compelled to mount a last stand for common sense. I feel compelled to warn you that it can't and won't work, even if it isn't the kind of fake I think it is."

"You made it, Dr. Victory," was Allison's response to that. "If you say that you faked it, I don't see how I could deny it. It seems to have been a remarkably powerful fake, though—not that it's unusual, of course, for fakers to fall prey to their own inventions."

"Given that I'm here," Victory said, "I suppose that I can't deny that—but I'm not sure how I'll feel if my handiwork does become the figurehead of a new crusade to save the ecosphere."

"Suppose it had been someone other than Gwynplaine who brought you the book," Allison said, his tone now soft and measured. "Suppose, in fact, that it had been me. What would you think of the result of the experiment then?"

"If you had had the book," Victory replied, "you could have brought it to me without any need for subterfuge. You could have offered me a perfectly reasonable fee to incorporate the instructions into my software—and instructed me, in your capacity as his guardian, to use them on Amahl Sahman, if that had been your desire. Even so, I would never have been able to believe that the book actually did contain instructions for replicating the face of Adam, because I can't believe there ever was an Adam."

"The fact that you're incapable of believing something," Allison observed, "might be a reflection on you rather than the object of your scepticism. By the way, Dr. Victory, how do *you* think we ought to respond to the threat of the ecocatastrophe? Eat, drink and be merry, for tomorrow we die?"

"It all depends who you mean by *we*," Victory told him. "If you mean all of us—the whole human race—there's nothing that the vast majority of us can do but make the best we can of the time we have left. If you mean the citizens of the Western democracies, we have some little power by virtue of the democratic system, although there doesn't, as yet, seem to be any political will to take the drastic decisions. If you mean a few hundred of the world's richest men, then you probably do have a real choice to make: whether to use your fortunes individually, to ensure your own personal survival and that of your loyal courtiers, or whether to form the ultimate cartel, and actually try to exercise your effective power of ownership of the Earth."

"Do you think that a uniform political will is any easier to muster in a company of a hundred than in a company of billions?" Allison asked him.

"Perhaps not, given the idiosyncratic and egotistical characters of the rich men it has been my privilege to meet and serve," Victory said. "But if not you, who? If not now, when?"

"So you do concede the need for a consolidating force," Allison said. "You do see the necessity of a miracle, whether real or fake."

"The face of Adam isn't the answer," Victory said.

"I'm sorry to hear you say that, given that you're the only one who has yet seen it—but you'll forgive me for reminding you yet again that it put you in here. Its effect hasn't worn off yet, has it? I can see it in your eyes, Dr. Victory—the way you look at me. I don't know exactly what it's done to you, given that you seem perfectly lucid, but I know that it's done something."

"It will wear off, in time," Victory said.

"In time for you to operate on Monday? Or even on the Monday afterwards, given that poor Amahl can wait without suffering the difficulties that might afflict poor Lilith. Exactly when do you expect to be yourself again, Dr. Victory?"

"I don't know," Victory admitted. "But it will wear off."

"An effect doesn't have to be permanent to be persuasive," Allison told him. "A week can be a long time in politics."

"Des that mean you're going to make a deal with Gwynplaine and Asmodeus?"

"I don't know," Allison said. "You made the program, Dr. Victory. Is there any reason why you can't make it again—for me?"

Victory thought about that for a moment or two, and then said: "When the residual effect wears off...when I regain full control of my aesthetic sensibilities...then I should be able to do it again. Inputting the information from the photocopies is just a matter of time; preserving the memory of the missing pages ought to be possible—but I'll need to be able to trust my sense of the aesthetic coherency of the process. In the meantime, Gwynplaine and Asmodeus already have their copy. Even if I could start work immediately, they'd have plenty of time to make their move first."

"In that case," said Gregory K. Allison, getting to his feet again, "I'll expect them to approach me, and I'll listen very carefully to what they have to say, if and when they do. You'd better talk to Dr. Rosenfeld, and anyone else who might be able to help, about the possibility of speeding up your recovery. I ought to talk to my wife now—she'll be anxious for news, and it might take some time to persuade her that Dr. Hemlet will be an adequate substitute for you."

As the billionaire reached out to grip the handle of the door, Victory hastened to ask one last question: "The Sons of Job is just a game, isn't it? A game, or a pretense. You don't really believe that the face of Adam can be reproduced, or that it would have the power to change the world if it were?"

Gregory K. Allison turned to look back at him, and the billionaire's face might have spoken volumes if only Victory had had the ability to read its expression. All he actually said, though, was: "I don't know."

CHAPTER TWENTY-ONE

The Sixth Day: Evening

Victory dressed himself without undue difficulty, and then went to the ward supervisor's desk at the end of the corridor to complete the paperwork necessary to his discharge. He nodded a greeting to Mrs. Allison's bodyguard as he passed the door to her room; he could hear voices within, but they weren't raised.

His movements grew more fluent as he made his way through the hospital corridors to his office, where Majeke Hemlet was waiting for him. Christina Legrange turned up while Victory was running through the procedures for Mrs. Allison's operation with Majeke, but the public relations officer waited patiently for the two of them to finish.

When Majeke was satisfied that she had everything necessary, Victory turned to the older woman and offered profuse apologies for any inconvenience he might have caused her.

"The news hasn't leaked yet," Christina told him, "but it probably will. The sight of an ambulance picking up in Harley Street is bound to start questions flying."

Victory met the press officer's gaze, trying to remember whether or not the woman was beautiful. He studied the lines of her face, amazed by his continued inability to judge whether any improvement might be possible, or how it might be achieved. He was aware of the inconsistency of maintaining his stern scepticism in spite of having experienced a seeming miracle whose effect was proving unreasonably stubborn, but the awareness did not seen unduly troubling. He was convinced that his perceptual disorder was a temporary glitch, more subjective than objective, and that whatever had caused it must indeed be a cause, not a magical disruption of causality.

"You can say that the head injury is minor and that I've been discharged in order to rest at home," Victory told Christina Legrange. "You can say that the final operation on Amahl Sahman has been postponed, but that we hope to complete the treatment within the week, once I've been thoroughly checked out."

"I might need more detail than that," Christina said. "It's only a minor problem for the hospital, but it might have far more serious long-term consequences for you. Your client base is the kind that might be easily frightened off by the merest hint that you suffer from blackouts. Not that I'd ever use the word *blackout* in any official statement, of course, but...."

"You might tell them that it could have been an allergic reaction to an unusual environmental pollutant," Majeke suggested, "unlikely to be repeated and of a kind easily treatable in a hospital environment."

"Could have been?" the press officer queried, glancing sideways at Majeke before returning her gaze to Victory. "If I'm to say that, I need to know that it was. Was it?

"We're not sure what happened yet," Victory told her. "We may never know for sure—in which case it's probably best to stick to the bare facts. The point is that I'll be fine by Monday—Tuesday at the latest—and that we'll be able to reschedule Amahl's operation as soon as I've been officially checked out."

"That won't solve your problem," Christina pointed out. "You'll need an actual explanation—a plausible explanation—if you're to walk away unscathed.

"The hospital ought to send environmental analysts to Harley Street to check Dr. Victory's car and office," Majeke said, intervening for a second time when Victory made no reply. "If they come back with any indication of a possible cause, we'll let you know immediately. In the meantime, as you can see, Dr. Victory is quite recovered. The reallocation of tomorrow's operation and Monday's postponement are purely precautionary."

"Fair enough," Christina agreed, although her tone was still dubious. "Let me know if anything does turn up—and when you're next coming in."

When the public relations officer had gone, Victory immediately located the most recently updated version of the program for Amahl's operation that the terminal's hard disk contained. He sent one copy to his consulting room via the permanent link and decanted another on to his key ring fob. As he had told Allison, it would require more than mere time to bring it to completion, but he wanted to be prepared. He thanked Majeke for all her help.

"You're going to have to drop the bland act, if you can," Majeke said. "There's no point me telling people you're obviously okay if you're obviously not. Everyone knows you've been overworking, and everyone's seen the effects recently, even if they've been too polite to mention them. You really do need a rest. I've asked Dr. Rosenfeld to drive you home—to the farmhouse, that is, not the flat. She's gone to fetch her car; she should be back any minute. She agreed that you needed to be kept under observation at least for the rest of today."

"You're right," Victory told her. "I do need a rest. I'll be back to normal tomorrow or the next day." He still believed it; he could not even begin to contemplate the alternative.

"I'll ring you tomorrow as soon as Mrs. Allison's operation is complete," Majeke promised. "I'll make up a full report so that you can pick up anything that might have gone amiss and make further plans accordingly. Everything will be fine, though—trust me. With luck, as you say, you'll be fully recovered by the time I'm through."

Rachel Rosenfeld came into the office then, to say that the Lexus was waiting in the car park.

"It'd kind of you to take the trouble," Victory told her. "Although I'm sure that I can drive myself.

The psychotherapist hesitated, but then said: "That fake Bentley of yours is still in Harley Street, and I understand from Ms. Legrange that the hospital intends to send an environmental investigation team to look it over. Whether there's anything wrong with the air filter or not, it won't be going anywhere for a while. It's me or a taxi—and this is the one day of the year when I'm the cheaper alternative. Are you done here?"

"Yes," Majeke said, although the question had been addressed to Victory.

Dr. Rosenfeld nodded, and led Victory away to the elevator. "Are you still having trouble with aesthetic discrimination?" she asked, as they rode down to the car park.

"It's a fascinating phenomenon, in its way," Victory told her. "I'd never have imagined that any such reaction was possible. I can still see clearly, think clearly, talk lucidly...and yet, that one tiny fraction of the visual information I'm collating has somehow lost its coherency...its *apparent* coherency You'll agree with my judgment that it's purely psychological, I suppose, rather than anything organic? Nothing showed up on Simon's CT scan."

"Is it really a matter of either/or?" the psychotherapist parried, as they made their way from the lift to the car across the oil-stained tarmac.

"Now you sound like Gwynplaine," Victory said. "Although the notion that it might be both makes a little more sense in this context. If it's a new species of hysterical blindness, do you think it might be named after me?"

"*Victory's syndrome* certainly has a better ring to it than *post-traumatic stress disorder*," the psychotherapist observed, as she unlocked the Lexus, "but if I'm the one who gets to describe it in the literature, I really feel that it ought to be named after me."

"Is that why you're driving me back to Oxfordshire?" Victory asked, getting into the car and fastening his seat belt. "So

199

that you can cross-examine me and write it up as a paper? You could probably sell it to *Psychology Today* if you give it a sexy title. You might try *The Strange Case of the Cosmetic Surgeon Who Lost Contact with Beauty.*"

"Well, I'd hardly be driving you all the way to the rural heartland out of the goodness of my heart, would I?" the psychotherapist countered, as she started the engine. "On the other hand, if you really can't judge whether I'm any better looking than your pretty little associate, perhaps I ought to take advantage of your condition while it lasts."

"I'll take that as a compliment," Victory said. "It's a reassuring suggestion, in its way. For a moment there, I thought you really might be seeing me as a patient, but you wouldn't make flirtatious jokes with a patient, would you?"

"I don't even see my patients as patients," she told him. "Like your clients, they're mostly just people who think they're in need of a boost to their self-esteem." She eased the car out into the traffic, turning right in order to head westwards. The road was slick with rain and the sky was steel-grey from horizon to horizon.

"And what is it they really need?" Victory countered, feeling that he was easing back into his customary conversational groove, and regretting the fact that he had not been able to muster any reassuring flippancy while talking to Christina Legrange."

"My clients are very various," the psychotherapist told him. "Their needs are rarely simple and never obvious. I've never been able to look at their faces and sum up their needs in terms of a few cuts and stitches."

"Ouch," Victory said. "And I suppose you think that the majority of my clients actually suffer from an excess of self-esteem rather than a dearth, avid to acquire facial perfection because they're convinced that they deserve it, in order that their outer shells might reflect their inner magnificence?"

"I'd never dream of saying any such thing," Rachel Rosenfeld assured him. "Is that what you really think?"

"If it were," Victory countered, "do you think my cynical self-disgust might have precipitated the kind of reaction I seem to be suffering, in response to any arbitrary shock?"

"Was it an arbitrary shock?" the psychotherapist asked, mildly. She was steering the car with perfect authority, quite relaxed in her seat but watching the road with rapt attention. Rain was beating down upon the roof and hood, and the road surface was covered in tiny rivulets as the water found multitudinous paths of least resistance en route to the gutters and the sewers.

"It was the sight of the face of Adam, allegedly," Victory said. "If there ever had been an Adam, perhaps he would have looked exactly like that—who could possibly know? If the angels really are clones of God Himself, with exactly that same face, I suppose half the people living in the US Bible Belt would have recognized it immediately, but the angels seem to steer clear of our rainy little island. Anyway, if that's what it was, the comprachicos were sadly mistaken if they really thought that the mere sight of it would strike faith into men's hearts."

"Were they?" Rachel asked, mildly. "You're an exceptional man, Hugo, fully entitled to an idiosyncratic reaction. What if the sight strikes others differently?"

"It's possible, I suppose. Maybe what it did to me is a punishment, because I didn't immediately experience a flood of faith. Maybe my day of judgment has already come, without the necessity of having to die—and maybe this is my private hell, custom-designed for hubristic cosmetic surgeons."

"If I were a Freudian," the psychotherapist observed, "I'd be a trifle worried about your readiness to tell that kind of joke."

"Gwynplaine doesn't seem to believe in hell," Victory told her. "One could sympathise with his refusal, if he really were the Devil. Given that he prefers to imagine himself as the serpent, he probably speaks with a forked tongue. What will I become, do you think, in the myth of the new Eden? I might have tried to talk Allison out of applying for the job of head prophet, but I did play my part, didn't I? It wasn't God that gave the face of Adam its personality—it was me."

"What are you trying to tell me, Hugo?"

"Drop the shrink act, for God's sake. Can't we have a normal conversation? It's a long way to the farmhouse—although you could drop me in Westbourne Park, if that would be more convenient."

"If what you were just saying is your idea of a normal conversation," Dr. Rosenfeld observed, "we're more likely to end up in Oz than Oxfordshire. What really happened to you when you saw the face on your computer screen, Hugo? Have you *any* explanation to offer?"

"I was amazed by the quality of my work. If only it had been a female face, I could have played Pygmalion. Do you believe that it's possible that a face—even one confronted in the flesh rather than merely displayed on a screen—could have sufficient charisma to turn anyone who saw it into a fervent disciple, ready to do anything it asked?"

"I'm not sure. Do you believe in love at first sight?"

The reply was intoned more like a quotation than a genuine question, but Victory answered anyway. "I used to believe in lust at first sight," he said, dryly, "but I think I was losing the knack even before I looked into the Divine Countenance and learned shame."

"Did you?" Dr. Rosenfeld was quick to ask. "Learn shame, I mean."

"No, of course not," Victory replied. "For a non-Freudian, you're remarkably intent on taking my jokes the wrong way. Anyway, isn't the more interesting possibility that I might not be exceptional? What if the sight of the face has the same effect on everyone else that it had on me? What if humankind could be deprived of all aesthetic sensibility in an instant? No, don't ask. That's not what happened to me either. We're taking about faces, first and foremost if not exclusively. What if faces suddenly became less expressive, then—less easily readable, in terms of the emotions they signify as well as their aesthetic attractiveness? No...don't ask that question either. To tell you the simple truth, I'm no longer sure exactly what happened, or how to describe it, or what its ongoing consequences are. It was just a shock, artificially stimulated or not. Gwynplaine was probably avid to see what the effects of his experiment would be, but he still doesn't know. He could see there was an effect, but he probably has no idea what it was. Whatever he and Asmodeus are planning, it can't work."

"Does Gregory Allison believe that?" was the question Rachel Rosenfeld finally found space to ask.

"I don't know," Victory admitted. "I suspect it will depend on Mrs. Allison, and whether she believes in the multiplicity of potential pasts. If she does...well, she might believe that the face I made *can be* the face of Adam, whatever else it might be, if enough people will only condescend to believe it. That's what Gwynplaine appears to believe, and Asmodeus too."

"*The multiplicity of potential pasts* is a nice phrase," the psychotherapist observed, tactfully. "Exactly where are we headed, by the way? I presume that I'm heading for the M40 in the first instance, but Oxfordshire's a big place and I've never had the pleasure of visiting your country residence."

"It's much quicker to take the M4 to Maidenhead, then the A423 all the way to Benson. The house is between Rokemarsh and Berrick Salome, almost due north of Benson. The idea that the past is as negotiable as the future is Gwynplaine's explanation of how the myth of Eden can be true even though the Earth is four and a half billion years old and the human species arose as the result of a long process of natural selection. All that really exists, according to him, is the present moment—any and all histories that might conceivably have produced it are potentially true, provided that some persuasively tangible supportive relics exist within the moment. According to his thesis, he really can be the serpent out of Eden as well as whoever he might seem to be, whether according to the evidence of his birth certificate or the evidence with which Iorga Yashvili allegedly filled his empty head. If Yashvili really did force an entirely fake identity on him, I can see how he might be able to believe that any plausible past might be true, for the world as well as himself."

"But you aren't? Able to believe it, I mean."

"No. I might be the odd one out, though. Asmodeus might well be able to believe that he really can be the demon of lust as well as some other clever fantasist, and Lilith Allison might well be able to believe that she really can be Lilith as well as Mrs. Gregory K. Allison. For all I know, Iorga Yashvili might be able to believe that faking the history of the Sons of Job is the same as creating that history—and that faking the face of Adam really is the same as recreating it, with all its charismatic power. It all comes back to Yashvili, in effect. Lilith Allison was married to him; Gwynplaine was his protégé; Asmodeus...well, I'm not sure what relationship Asmodeus has or had to him, but it must have something to do with the faking of the comprachicos' plan. If Asmodeus isn't lying about not being Yashvili, he must be someone who was once as close to him, or closer, than Gwynplaine. My guess is that he was the surgeon...my mysterious counterpart. My guess is that it was his decision, not Gwynplaine's, to involve me...to use me to complete what he'd started."

"Why couldn't he complete it himself?" the psychotherapist asked.

"Good question," Victory said. "I have this strange feeling that I know the answer, but I can't quite put my finger on it. It's something to do with bringing order out of chaos, and chaos out of order...something to do with what Torricelli said about this being Hell, and the Devil not being out of it...except that he thought that Gwynplaine was the Devil, instead of Asmodeus. There's something I saw but can't quite recall, because of this glitch I've developed with regard to reading faces...."

"What was it that you read into the face of Adam, when you'd produced it?" Dr. Rosenfeld was obviously still intent on cutting through Victory's confusion to the nub of the matter.

"I have no idea," Victory replied, truthfully. "Something, certainly—but nothing calculated to inspire religious faith."

"Can you replicate the work?"

"Given time. As I told Gregory K. Allison, rebuilding the program from the photocopies should be easy enough, and I should still be able to remember enough of the missing pages to finish the job—but while I'm having this difficulty with the aesthetic logic of the human face, I can't make that final imaginative leap. As soon as this wears off...yes, I believe I can replicate the program in a matter of days...perhaps hours."

"And what did Allison say?"

Victory pursed his mouth, wryly "He said that he wasn't sure that he could wait that long, if Gwynplaine and Asmodeus got their pitch in first. He'll probably prevaricate—but Mrs. Allison might not, if she makes a quick enough recovery from tomorrow's surgery. Gwynplaine didn't seem to know about that—it's possible that it might have disrupted his schedule."

The surgeon expected his interrogator to continue on the same tack, but she surprised him again with her next observation, which was: "The questions you told me not to ask are really quite interesting, in their way. What if humankind *could* be deprived of all aesthetic sensibility in an instant? What if faces *did* become less expressive, less easily readable, in terms of the emotions they signify as well as their aesthetic attractiveness? What if your programmed image really did have a generally reproducible effect—not the one that the comprachicos allegedly expected, but a subtly different one?"

"I don't know," Victory admitted. "I suppose it would be a catastrophe of sorts if there were a significant widespread diminution of our ability to perceive beauty, or read emotions in faces, but I wouldn't know how to describe it, let alone calculate its ramifications. I don't see how an epidemic of mild autism would help to alleviate the ecocatastrophe—quite the reverse. If we had a stronger sense of the beauty of the world as something worth preserving, and more empathy with our fellow human beings, maybe we wouldn't be on the verge of trashing the ecosphere."

"It's sometimes argued that moral judgments are fundamentally aesthetic in character," Rachel Rosenfeld observed. "Proponents of the theory argue that the two ways in which we use the word *good* aren't distinct at all, and that moral actions are simply aesthetically appropriate ones. If that were true, then anything that affected the aesthetic judgments of large numbers of people—whether it were a face or a psychotropic drug—would also affect their moral judgments, perhaps not as consciously but just as profoundly."

"I suppose that's what I was groping towards," Victory said. "We'd need a heightened sense of beauty and heightened powers of empathy, not diminished ones, if enough people were to start acting differently, in a way that might help alleviate the ecocatastrophe. What's happened to me is the wrong effect, isn't it?"

This time, there was no need for the psychotherapist to echo the obvious question. Victory saw immediately that he might be assuming too much about the curious effect that the culmination of Gwynplaine's plan seemed to have had on him. For one thing, he had assumed that the effect was complete. For another, he had assumed that any recovery he might make would simply return him to the same condition he had enjoyed—or endured—before.

What if that were not the case? What if the reversal of his eccentric anaesthetization went further than that, and brought him to a state of increased sensitivity?

Victory thought about these questions as best he could, while the pouring rain obscured the world beyond the windscreen of the Lexus. He felt oddly uncomfortable in the utilitarian interior of the vehicle, which seemed to contrast sharply with the decorative fittings of his mock-antique status symbol. He breathed in deeply, wondering whether the filtered air might somehow have been tainted. He felt quite well, but also incomplete. His thoughts seemed clear but there was something odd about them, something deceptive....

"It's not possible," he said, uncertainly. "The mere sight of a face couldn't conceivably...." He trailed off, because he couldn't be sure. Given what had already happened to him, and what was still happening to him, he simply couldn't be sure. "I have to get better," he said, firmly. "I have to duplicate that program. I have to reproduce that face."

"Why?" Rachel Rosenfeld asked, gently.

"Because I have to prove that it's all a scam—a huge confidence trick."

"In order to save Gregory K. Allison from being taken for a ride?"

"Of course not. In order to save *me* from being taken for a ride—to save me from falling victim to Gwynplaine's double-talk and Asmodeus's teasing."

"And to prove that the world really is doomed?" the psychotherapist added. "To prove that there really is no hope, for anyone but those who have the money and the good fortune to ensure that they're numbered among the survivors when global civilization collapses? To prove that the only new Adamic archetype the world needs and deserves is Gregory K. Allison? Do you suppose he'll pay you as much for proving your story as he might for proving Gwynplaine's?"

"I don't know," Victory retorted. "Which one would you prefer?"

"I couldn't possibly commit myself while Joseph Allison is still my patient," Dr. Rosenfeld countered, effortlessly, "but if history really were a matter of who can produce the most convincing illusion, I think I might prefer a past whose momentum offered a modicum of hope for the future, wouldn't you?"

CHAPTER TWENTY-TWO

The Seventh Day: Morning and Afternoon

Victory woke on Sunday morning from night-long anxiety dreams, in which he wrestled with the prospect of never again being able to detect any difference between the beautiful and the ugly, or deduce another person's emotional state from the relevant facial expression.

For a moment or two he could not work out where he was; he was slightly surprised to find himself in a double bed rather than the single in Westbourne Park, and he was quite astonished—until he realised that he was in the farmhouse—to hear birdsong outside his window. Although there was no dawn chorus any more, even this far out of the capital, the occasional songbird still contrived to find enough wild seed and insect life to survive. The traditional food chains might be fragile, but they had not yet collapsed.

He switched on the radio he kept by the bed while he washed and dressed. There had been a minor clathrate upheaval in the South Atlantic; it was far from being enough to set the world on fire, but GEM-influenced doomsayers were understandably excited, hailing it as yet another warning of things to come—a little hiccup before the quasi-volcanic eruption that would suffocate every living vertebrate on the Earth's surface, and most of the fugitive fish that remained in the sea. The US Environment Agency had, however, issued a statement saying that the modest magnitude of the release was clear evidence of the fact that the clathrate residues had a built-in safety valve which would ensure that the Greenhouse Effect would remain gradual for many decades to come, and that the Global Environmental Model had been perverted by corrupt data originated in the Middle and Far East for political purposes.

By the time Victory got down to breakfast he was feeling a little better in himself, and he was able to take some pleasure in the notion that his housekeeper, Mrs. Benedict, definitely seemed to be a little on the unprepossessing side of ordinary. She was also detectably less than pleased to have him back in residence, even though that was supposed to be the usual state of weekend affairs.

"I only did light shopping yesterday, sir," she reported, "with you not being expected. All this chopping and changing doesn't make my job any easier. Dinner will have to come out of the freezer—is there anything special you'd like me to defrost?"

"Better get out a sizeable lamb joint, to be on the safe side," he said. "Someone will probably want to come out to check up on me—if not Dr. Rosenfeld, then Dr. Fullar or Dr. Hemlet."

Displeased as she seemed to be by the uncertainty of his state of mind and the vagueness of her instructions, Mrs. Benedict nevertheless asked politely after the state of her employer's health, and was not obviously depressed by his assertion that he seemed to be making a good recovery and hoped to be back to normal by dinner time.

After breakfast, Victory set out to walk into Berrick Salome to buy a newspaper. He didn't take a filter-mask, although he noticed that there were some people out and about who were wearing them. From a purely objective point of view, there was as much—or as little—need to wear a mask in the supposed heart of the country as there was in the center of Oxford or Reading, but Victory preferred to adopt the view that the rural environment was intrinsically cleaner and healthier than the vehicle-choked city. He said good morning to a couple of unmasked villagers, but ignored the others, on the grounds that they were almost certainly Londoners out for "a stroll in the countryside," who had parked their cars in Roke or in lay-bys off the B4009.

The front page of the newspaper was entirely taken over by the clathrate upheaval, even though it had occurred so close to the previous evening's deadline that there had not been any time to collect any factual evidence of its consequences. Given that speculation had virtually displaced factual reportage even in the daily broadsheets, this did not seem unduly disappointing, but he hastened on to the inside pages regardless, in search of news of events in London. There did not seem to be anything of real interest, so he turned instead to the late-night share prices, to see how much the aftershocks of the clathrate discharge had cost him in purely financial terms. The effect had been minimal, losses in food and utilities being compensated by a spike in the prices of fuel companies. The old oil producers were all attempting to develop technologies for exploiting the energy bound up in suboceanic and subglacial clathrate deposits, and any headline including the word *clathrate* seemed to have a positive effect on the die-hard optimists who believed that a crucial breakthrough was just around the corner.

The only birds Victory actually saw were starlings and crows, but he heard others fluttering and chirping in the hedgerows, and was reassured by their presence that all was not yet lost.

When he returned to the farmhouse he found that Mrs. Benedict had retired to the cottage, so he was able to settle down in glorious isolation in the house. A more careful search confirmed that there was nothing in the paper about the postponement of the final stage of Amahl Sahman's treatment or the reason for it, for which he was suitably grateful.

As the scheduled time of Mrs. Allison's operation approached, Victory grew slightly nervous, and he found himself rehearsing every phase of it in his mind as the clock ticked on, even though he could not summon up a visual image of the face he had designed on his computer.

He began to regret, then, that he had consented to his removal to the countryside, wishing that he had stayed overnight in the hospital so that he might at least be able to observe as Majeke carried out the operation. He knew that his lurking presence would by no means have worked to the patient's advantage, but he found it surprisingly difficult to bear the frustration of total uninvolvement.

He tried to distract himself by reading a novel, but he could not concentrate on the narrative. He also tried to work at his terminal, but he could not settle to any task, no matter how trivial, and in the end he simply gave himself permission to stride fretfully around, assuring himself that at least it was directing his attention away from his own perverse psychological problem.

When the telephone rang at three o'clock he knew that it was far too early for Majeke to have competed the operation successfully, and leapt to the conclusion that something must have gone seriously awry—but when he snatched up the receiver he found that it was Asmodeus. His anxiety immediately turned into an anger that he was strangely glad to be able to feel.

"You knew!" he said, accusingly. "You knew exactly what Gwynplaine intended to do. You and he are as thick with one another as he once was with Yashvili—if, that is, you're not Yashvili yourself, which I'm still inclined to suspect."

"I assure you, Dr. Victory," the pretended demon king replied, "that the exact details of Gwynplaine's plan were unknown to me, and that I'm genuinely surprised by the turn that events have taken. I won't tell you that I'm unhappy, because it would be a lie, but I'm truly sorry that you seem to have suffered a little collateral damage. I never intended that to happen. I called to find out whether you've recovered from the episode. I'm glad to discover that you're up and about, and in seemingly good voice."

"I'm as well as can be expected," Victory said, "but I might be a lot better if I knew what the next stage in your grand plan was—or even how the last phase was executed. If Gwynplaine used some kind of drug on me, I'd be grateful to know what it was and how he delivered it."

"To the best of my knowledge, you were not drugged, Dr. Victory. Your reaction to seeing the image was entirely spontaneous. When you say *as well as can be expected....*"

"The arrangement you suggested was that we exchange information," Victory said. "I don't think you've kept your side of that bargain—in fact, I think you've been feeding me a line since the very first call. I'm telling you nothing more, until I know who you are and what you and Gwynplaine intend to do with the program you suckered me into finishing off for you."

"If you haven't yet worked out who I am," Asmodeus replied, with irritating calmness, "you soon will. I admit that I've been economical in what I've told you, and that I've allowed you to take some false inferences, but I'm not your enemy. I mean you no harm, and I shall do what I can to save you from harm if you come under threat."

"Do you think that's likely?"

"It's possible. I'm still making final adjustments to my own plans, and I'm not quite ready to make my first move, but I'm doing my utmost to monitor the situation as it develops. It would help me—and certainly would not harm you—if you were to tell me whether you are suffering any continuing effects of the shock you received yesterday."

"If I were," Victory replied, guardedly, "they'd be an aspect of my idiosyncratic reaction. I'm not ready yet to entertain the possibility that the mere sight of a face on a computer screen might be sufficient to cause serious mental disturbance to anyone and everyone who sees it."

"As to that," Asmodeus said, "time will tell. I'm sorry that you weren't able to perform the operation on Mrs. Allison, but for what it may be worth, it seems to be going very well."

"Are you saying that you've got a bug planted in the operating theatre?"

"No—but I do have a means of keeping track of what is happening there. I'd rather you hadn't told Gregory Allison that Gwynplaine would get in touch with him, by the way—but I suppose you felt that you had no choice, after Joseph Allison jumped to the wrong conclusion. His catching sight of Gwynplaine was an unfortunate coincidence, but he really shouldn't have read so much into it."

"Do you have a reason for telling me this?" Victory wanted to know.

"Of course. I wanted to impress upon you that this isn't something that has been worked out to the last detail. I'm improvising, just as Gwynplaine has been forced to improvise. We really don't know exactly how this is going to work out. It's an adventure for us as well as for you. We hope that you'll be able to work with us as the scheme unfolds."

"You want me to join the Sons of Job?"

"That won't be necessary. There are many players in the game, with many different objectives. I'm sorry that you feel that you've been tricked, and I'd rather be honest with you in future. In the meantime, I promise that I will help you if I can, and if the need arises."

"I'm sure I'll be suitably grateful, if and when," Victory said, dryly. "How's Gwynplaine getting on? Is he still one step ahead of the people looking for him?"

"Gwynplaine is managing to stay out of sight. I am, of course, ready to help him too, if I can, whenever the need arises."

"It probably will," Victory said. "If he's double-crossed Iorga Yashvili, it won't be just the Sons of Job and Mr. Hardcastle's team on his trail—and I suspect that Yashvili's hounds are at least as good at biting as barking. Always assuming, that is, that I'm not actually talking to Iorga Yashvili at this very minute."

"I suppose you have no reason to take my word for it," Asmodeus admitted, "so I'll forgive your scepticism. You're right. Yashvili still believed that he was the one pulling Gwynplaine's strings until yesterday morning, but he knows better now. Which means, Dr. Victory, that it won't just be Allison and Hardcastle who are interested in the question of whether you can reconstruct the program, and how quickly. You and I know that you can't do it in time—but they'll be reluctant to believe it. The Allisons must know that what Gwynplaine did to you isn't your fault, but that doesn't mean they'll let you off the hook, and our mutual friend Mr. Elijah is highly likely to be harboring some resentment against both of us for the little trick I played on Friday night. Even Monsignor Torricelli will want a copy of the program, now that it exists, and anyone he sends after it will be well aware that they can obtain absolution for any sins they may commit in getting it. I'll make my move as soon as possible, but in the meantime, you'll need to be careful."

"Thanks for the warning. I'd rather know what you and Gwynplaine are up to, though—whether or not you really believe that you're the serpent out of Eden and the demon of anger and lust, united by the enmity of others, if not by common purpose. What are you aiming to do?"

"We're aiming to save the world, of course," Asmodeus said. "I don't say that we can, or even that we know how, but we're certainly going to try."

"By starting a new religion?" Victory said, sceptically.

"By trying to rally humankind to a common cause, with the aid of a psychological trick or two. Is that what you want to hear, Dr. Victory? Does it sound any better than the language of miracles? You're the one, remember, who thinks that it has to be a matter of either/or. We're more versatile than that. We have to be."

"Gwynplaine is not the serpent out of Eden," Victory said, flatly. "No matter what he believes, and no matter what he asserts regarding the possible multiplicity of plausible pasts, he was never in Eden. He's just a man who was burned in a fire, and whether he was driven mad or got there on his own, mad is what he is. You I'm not so sure about, but one thing I do know for certain is that you never were the king of the demons. You're just playing a role."

"Aren't we all? I'm just like you in that respect, Dr. Victory. If I weren't, I probably wouldn't care enough about the world to want to try to save it. My interest is primarily intellectual, just like yours—but I'm capable of aesthetic judgments too, just as you are, and I'm capable of moral action as well, just as you are. If it will make you feel any better, though, I'm about to give up the role of Asmodeus, at least for the time being. Gwynplaine will have to make up his own mind about continuing as the serpent, but I suspect that he feels too comfortable in that guise simply to abandon it."

"He doesn't strike me as a man who feels unduly comfortable," Victory replied. "Quite the reverse. You don't, by any chance, know how I could get in touch with Iorga Yashvili, do you?"

"I wouldn't advise it," Asmodeus said. "He'd probably take it the wrong way. If I were you, I'd let Yashvili well alone—and Gregory Allison too, at least for the time being. You probably need this enforced rest, Dr. Victory. If I were you, I'd make the most of it."

"You're not me," Victory said. "You don't seem to get much rest yourself."

"Oh, there's no rest at all for the wicked," Asmodeus told him. "You have no idea what it is to be a real workaholic, or a genuine insomniac."

"My first priority now has to be passing the hospital's fitness test so that I can reschedule Amahl Sahman's final operation," Victory said. "I can rest when that's done, but until it's done...did you say that you're able to monitor Majeke's operation on Mrs. Allison on a continual basis?"

"Don't be anxious, Dr. Victory," Asmodeus said. "The operation is still proceeding very smoothly. While it's in progress, and for some little time afterwards, the Allisons will both be tied up—which has its pros and cons for both of us. I think, in the

211

circumstances, that you'll have all the time you need to operate on the boy, and that the possibility of using the Adam program to shape his face is no longer likely to arise—but I can't anticipate the way the others will jump, either before or after I've made my move. As I said, it's still an adventure."

"You might think of it like that," Victory told his mercurial informant, bluntly, "but it's going to be difficult for the rest of us."

"I don't mean to understate its importance," Asmodeus said. "I'm well aware of the stakes."

"That doesn't seem to be inhibiting you from placing your bet."

"Of course not. I'm also well aware of the inevitable consequences of doing nothing. We're past the time when it was a matter of not being able to afford to lose, Dr. Victory; we're now in a position where we can't afford not to bet. Whatever the odds, we have to try to win."

"So you think the world is still salvageable? You think the ecocatastrophe can still be stopped or reversed?"

"How can we know until we try? As an immortal who's been around since the dawn of time, of course, I've seen too many new religions to think them easily capable of any meaningful change. They might all generate hysteria, and do a roaring trade in baseless hope, but rarely accomplish anything substantial. On the other hand, when the circumstances become sufficiently desperate, no straw is too frail to be unworthy of clutching. It doesn't matter much to a demon, of course; it's always amusing to watch religions fail, and I dare say that I'll survive at least as long as the Gregory Allisons of the world—ecological upheavals and days of judgment don't worry my kind unduly. Come tomorrow, though, I'll be playing a different role—so I suppose this is goodbye, from Asmodeus."

"Why did you bother to make these calls?" Victory asked, curiously.

"It's the sort of thing I do, when I'm not reliving multitudinous pasts and foreseeing myriad futures" Asmodeus replied, cheerfully. "As the scorpion said, *it's my nature.*" And with that, he rang off.

"Arsehole," Victory muttered, contemptuously, revelling in his capacity to feel the surge of resentful emotion. It helped him feel that he was on the mend, almost returned to his true self: the artist of the flesh. The call had, however, served to relax him somewhat. He was able to sit down and wait more patiently until the phone rang again.

This time, when he snatched it up, it was Majeke's voice that he heard.

"The operation was a success," Majeke reported, sounding slightly intoxicated, although Victory was certain that she had not touched a drop of alcohol. "The patient is alive and well, and hopefully rejuvenated. Time will deliver the final judgment when the dressings come off for the last time—Thursday, at a guess—but everything is set fair. Everything, that is, to do with Mrs. Allison."

"That's great," Victory said, astonished by the profundity of his own relief. "Congratulations—you have now joined the ranks of celebrity surgeons. When the news gets out, even if it's only discreet word of mouth, rich middle-aged women will be beating a path to your door, while I'm sent to Coventry, suspected of suffering inexplicable blackouts. Now and forever, you'll be the surgeon who took twenty years off Mrs. Gregory K. Allison's face."

"Mr. Allison seems relieved," Majeke reported, "but not exactly trouble-free. He's been asking after you—he had a long telephone conversation with Dr. Rosenfeld, but didn't seem to think that he'd got much out of it."

"She's an expert stonewaller," Victory agreed. "She threatened to drive out again to check up on me when she left for London last night, but I told her I'd be fine. I don't feel too bad—not nearly as spaced out as I was yesterday."

"The hospital's investigation teams didn't find anything, you know. No trace of any psychotropics of any kind, in Harley Street or the Westbourne Park flat."

"It doesn't surprise me. The drug theory was clutching at straws, a matter of avoiding having to admit that any mere psychological glitch could possibly cause the great Hugo Victory to fall down and suffer hallucinations. I'm still not ready to believe what I think I saw, but I suppose I have to accept the possibility that I did this to myself."

"I want to drive over to bring you the record of the cuts and the post-op numbers," Majeke said, "Maybe I ought to contact Dr. Rosenfeld, to see if one of us can give the other a ride."

"You know that's not necessary," Victory said.

"It's against regulations to email confidential data, and Christina Legrange would probably have a fit if I took any unnecessary risks in handling the information," Majeke said. "If you're going to look at it, I really ought to bring it out personally. Do you want me to ring Rachel Rosenfeld or not?"

"By all means," Victory said, conceding the issue readily enough. "You might as well have a thorough discussion of my case, and I suppose neither of you will be satisfied unless at least one of you comes out here to look me over. Let me know how many to expect for dinner, though. I'll have to give Mrs. Benedict fair warning."

"I will," she promised. "Are you really feeling better—well enough to set a day for Amahl's op, if the hospital's medical panel clears you?"

"I'll need to take the software through a couple of virtual operations before I'm sure," Victory said, "but I'll try that tomorrow. If all goes well, I'll set the earliest date the powers that be will allow. Amahl deserves that. Wednesday might be viable, if the machine can be freed up and the formalities tidied away."

"It should be okay," Majeke assured him. "There shouldn't have been anything immovable scheduled, in case complications arose on the Monday. Even if you have to do more trial runs on Tuesday or the panel hangs fire, we should be able to work something out. I'll call again later, before I set out."

"Thanks," Victory said, with feeling. He felt as if a great weight had been lifted from his mind—but he couldn't help wondering whether he'd be able to perceive Majeke's loveliness, in all its triumphant glory, when she arrived, and what it might signify if he could not.

CHAPTER TWENTY-THREE

The Seventh Day: Evening

Majeke eventually arrived on her own, Rachel Rosenfeld having other commitments. She was late, having earlier offered an over-optimistic estimated time of arrival, causing Mrs. Benedict to become somewhat tight-lipped as she attempted to prevent the dinner from spoiling. Victory was able to read this expression of annoyance without undue difficulty.

Once the evening meal was under way he told the housekeeper that she could go back to the cottage for the night; by the time he and Majeke had finished eating it was after ten. While Victory cleared the table and placed the crockery and glasses in the dishwasher, Majeke marvelled at the darkness outside, and the fact that one could actually see the stars.

"There's no major source of light pollution in that direction until Aylesbury, which is beyond the horizon relative to a low-lying spot like this. There's Wallingford on the other side of the house, but that's relatively discreet. You can get a better view of the pollution haze if you look out to the north-west, towards Oxford."

When the surgeon switched on the dishwasher the machine juddered on the concrete surface of the kitchen floor, making almost as much noise as the washing machine did, but when Victory had closed the kitchen door the murmur didn't seem quite so intrusive. He took Majeke into the study so that they could use the computer to run through the record of Mrs. Allison's operation. Her document carrier was a pendant that she wore around her neck; she undid the catch at the nape of her neck and slipped it off the chain so that Victory could plug it into his machine.

Victory put the data through an analytical program first, in order to highlight any slight idiosyncratic variations that might have emerged during the course of the surgery, but the cutting and splicing was as near perfect as it would have been had he done the operation himself. More idiosyncrasies emerged from the post-operational examination, which tabulated the muscles' immediate response to their modification and plotted the inevitable anomalies of fluid-redistribution, expressed as clots and bruises. Again, there did not seem to be anything likely to produce a lasting effect.

"We'd better run it through the imaging software, just to make absolutely sure," Victory said. "At any rate, it'll give you a chance to anticipate the results of your handiwork."

"I didn't bring the image document," Majeke said, apologetically. "I didn't realise...."

"It's okay," Victory said. "I copied the file containing Mrs. Allison's mug shot on to my key ring fob last Monday, when I expected to be working on it myself in advance of the op. All the host programs are on the machine. If only I'd decanted a copy of the face of Adam before sneaking a look at it, but I thought I had all the time I needed...." He stopped, as a sudden thought struck him. "But that doesn't necessarily mean that it wasn't copied," he added, slowly, "given that there had to be some kind of tap on my machine."

"Isn't that supposed to be impossible nowadays, with the armour that's supposed to protect medical confidentiality?" Majeke asked.

"Nothing's impossible in IT espionage," Victory told her. "It's probably achievable even at a distance. Elijah and his friends were only monitoring my email, but there had to be a deeper tap than that, or else...."

"Or else what?"

"Or else the image couldn't have...but that must have been Gwynplaine's doing. He must have imported something into my machine via one of the rear ports, probably on Tuesday, when we had such a long session that we both needed bathroom breaks. That was careless...but if Gwynplaine opened up the back door, it's highly unlikely that he'd let anyone else gain access, except for Asmodeus...."

While he was talking, as much to himself as Majeke, Victory had gone into the imaging program and set the data she had brought to feed into the document containing the anticipatory image of the post-operative Mrs. Allison. When he summoned the image itself to the screen there was a brief flicker, but the image soon coalesced into the same form that it had displayed on the Monday afternoon before Victory's world had been turned upside down. He activated the flat-screen TV mounted on the study wall and transferred the image, so that it appeared there three times life-size, with enough discrimination to show up every pore.

Victory breathed a deep sigh of satisfaction as he drank in the perfection of the image. Although he was not yet completely restored to normal, the beauty of the face imposed itself on his vision with casual authority. He was still a little afraid to look

Majeke full in the face, but he had no such qualms about Lilith Allison.

"Aren't I entitled to a share of that sigh?" Majeke asked. "It's your software and the hospital's machine, but I was the one nudging the nanoscalpels along. It is a magnificent design, though. I could never have contrived that—it would require a male eye for female beauty."

"It's nothing as simple as a male eye coupled with male lust," Victory said. "It's a matter of understanding both the genera and the particular attributes of human faces, and the way they interact to capitalise on the responses built into the brain at the most basic level—the responses that allow us to recognize the expressiveness common to all faces, and the idiosyncrasies that make each one unique. It's something that can't be entirely analysed, because it has an irreducible element of perceptive intuition in it, but in which one can nevertheless become expert. Not that you can judge the full effect from a still image, of course, because the communicative abilities of faces only become evident in...."

"What's the matter?" Majeke asked, as he paused again. "Are you having trouble with your aesthetic perceptions again?"

"No," Victory said. "I can see how beautiful the face is—the effect of my fall has almost worn off. I just figured out why it was that Asmodeus needed me. It was blindingly obvious, of course—I'd have realised it before if I hadn't been confused. I know why he needed time, too...why he still needs time. Rome wasn't built in a day. His empire will take weeks, maybe months...."

"You're not making much sense, Hugo," Majeke said, accusingly. "You might try talking to me instead of the bitch on the wall."

Victory turned, as if in obedience to her request, to study Majeke's face. He felt that he could see it quite clearly, and bring its beauty into sharp focus. He felt a surge of relief as he concluded that he was not, after all, to be condemned to a hell of permanent aesthetic blindness—but he also felt a pinprick of anxiety as he remembered wondering whether the pendulum might continue swinging in the other direction, increasing the sensitivity that he had previously possessed.

He saw that Majeke was disconcerted by the directness of his stare, and confused by the intensity of his scrutiny. She looked away, redirecting her own gaze towards the image on the wall "Should it be doing that?" she asked.

"Should what be doing what?" he asked, reflexively, so absorbed in the contemplation of her pulchritude that he did not immediately follow her gaze. When he realised, belatedly, that she meant the image on the screen he turned his head casually—but froze in mid-movement.

The shock was by no means as powerful as the one he had experienced when he had first beheld the face of Adam, but his previous experience provided only slight insulation.

The face on the screen—Lilith Allison's face—was no longer a still picture. Although it had not moved its position more than fractionally, it now resembled a TV image of a living person. The face had become mobile, capable of changing expression.

Victory felt a stab of fear, anxious lest he lose for a second time all that he had only just regained. For a moment or two, he felt helplessly incompetent to read the expression on Mrs. Allison's face—the expression that should not have been there, and could not be there because the program did not have the capacity to produce it.

"What on Earth...?" Majeke began to say—providing welcome proof that she had not been struck dumb and that Victory was not hallucinating—but she broke off immediately when the image opened its own lips and began to speak.

"Thank you again, Dr. Victory," the image said, "and Dr. Hemlet too. This will be very convenient."

"Mrs. Allison?" Majeke said. Victory had no difficulty in weighing the astonishment in her tone, which was entirely appropriate to the apparent miracle with which she was confronted.

"It's not Mrs. Allison," he murmured, "any more than Adam is Amahl Sahman. It's...."

"If you wish to talk to me, Dr. Victory," the impossible image said, "you'll have to switch on the microphone that your voice-recognition software employs. Gwynplaine never had the opportunity to set listening devices in your farmhouse."

Victory's arm reached out, as if of its own volition, so that his fingers could obey the instruction.

"Mrs. Allison?" Majeke repeated, when he had activated the switch.

"No, Dr. Hemlet," the image replied. "Lilith. I'm *the* Lilith."

"Oh shit," Victory murmured. "I thought the prescriptive diagrams in the book had to be the work of a master surgeon. I never even considered the other possibility..."

"What kind of a welcome back to the world is that, Dr. Victory?" the image said. "You really don't have any cause to be surprised. You've had plenty of time to add it all up. You know what's going on."

Victory sat back in his chair, wondering whether he could pull himself together sufficiently to undertake a conversation. Majeke had other ideas, though. She had not been reduced to immobility any more than she had been struck dumb, and her perfectly understandable fear expressed itself in action. She reached over his shoulder and pressed the EXIT button to close the program down.

The animated image vanished as the screen returned to its resting state, its pictorial wallpaper now obscured by line upon line of icons.

"Dr. Victory?" the trainee surgeon said, placing her hand on his shoulder as if to calm him down. "Hugo? What's happening?"

"Gwynplaine let Asmodeus into the computer in my consulting room," Victory murmured. "He set up a portal that enabled him to ship in code by the gigabyte, without it showing up on the screen or in the history. It was always the imaging software he wanted to use, but he didn't just want a picture of the face. Asmodeus wanted to integrate my software into his—into *him*. He wanted a face—but not just any face, and not just one. He wanted archetypal faces, but he needed them individualized as well as beautified. He needed the aspects of beauty and expressiveness that were beyond analysis—the elements that only expert intuition could provide. Williams, Torricelli, and Hardcastle, and even Yashvili, never had a chance of figuring it out; their conceptual frameworks are mired in the Middle Ages. I should have realised, though. I should have guessed."

"Dr. Victory," Majeke said, planting herself squarely in front of him, "I still don't have a clue what you're talking about."

"I'm talking about the new Adam," Victory said. "I'm talking about the AI formally known as Asmodeus."

"That's good to hear," a new voice cut in, from the doorway. "Because those topics are exactly what *I* want to talk to you about."

Victory and Majeke both had to turn to see who was speaking. The man who had called himself Elijah took two further steps into the room, in order to allow a filter-masked companion to come in behind him. Victory assumed that the third member of the crew must be around somewhere, probably guarding the main door of the house.

Elijah was carrying a gun. The weapon seemed horribly menacing in the long and bony fingers. Once he and his companion had taken a long look around, Elijah nodded to the masked man, who positioned himself in the doorway like a sentinel in a box while Elijah came forward to take up a position a few feet away from Victory's chair.

"How...?" Victory began.

"Did I get in? Child's play, Dr. Victory. Double-locked doors provide slight inconvenience to men with proper training, and single-locked windows even less. In any case, that dishwasher is clattering loudly enough to hide the sound of a stampede, let alone a little breaking and entering." He produced a reel of plastic cord from his pocket. "Do I have to tie you up or will you behave yourselves?" he asked. "I'm sure that neither of you wants to do anything silly, in case it results in the other one getting hurt. Please sit down, Dr. Hemlet."

Majeke sat down on the settee without demur.

"You didn't need the gun," Victory said. "You didn't even need the breaking and entering. All you had to do was ring the doorbell."

"I didn't bring the gun to threaten you," Elijah admitted. "I brought it in case you had more interesting and intimidating company than Dr. Hemlet."

"Who were you expecting?" Victory asked.

"Who can tell? Allison might have condescended to give you protection. Gwynplaine might have decided that this was by far the best place for him to hide out—although that was perhaps a little over-optimistic on my part. Your friend Asmodeus might have had more presence in the world of flesh than you just implied. Which brings us back to the point. You were about to explain to Dr. Hemlet who your friend Asmodeus really is, I believe?"

"He's nobody," Victory said. "He's even less of a person than your account allowed Gwynplaine to be. He found Yashvili, not the other way around. He found Gwynplaine, and a crazy scheme to bring a measure of common cause back to a chaotic world. It probably didn't seem crazy to him. How would he know where the bounds of human sanity lay?"

Elijah did not seem as incredulous as Victory had anticipated, even though Victory did not believe that he had entertained the notion that Asmodeus might be an AI until he had voiced the conclusion a few minutes before. Nor did he think it likely that Elijah could have seen Lilith Allison's image become animated on the wallscreen, or heard the voice it had acquired. The only question Elijah asked was: "Are you saying that this AI has made the leap to self-awareness?"

"It certainly looks that way," Victory told him. "Self-aware or not, he—I mean it—certainly seems to have discovered a purpose in existence, more easily, I suspect, than you or I. It's possible that it's still an automaton, working out some kind of open-ended directive, but I think we've reached the point at which splitting existential hairs has become irrelevant. The point is that it can now pass for human, and much more than human. Maybe, now, I do mean *he*—and *she* too. Not so much an alchemical marriage, I guess, as an alchemical division. He said that he and Lilith were divorced, but I could hardly be expected to read anything from that. When he said that he'd abdicated as king of the

demons, though, I might have been able to take the right inference, if only I'd guessed that he was an AI...."

"I think you're getting ahead of yourself, Dr. Victory,"
Elijah said. "Just because there's an AI involved, it doesn't mean
that no one's pulling the strings. If Yashvili's lost control, it's
more likely that Allison is taking over. That's been a risk ever
since Mrs. Yashvili embroiled him in the Sons of Job. He's the
one with the money, after all—at the end of the day, the money
always calls the tune."

"It's not Allison," Victory told him.

"Mrs. Allison, then. Once she had Allison, she no longer
needed Yashvili. Poor Iorga. All that scheming and all that endeavour, just going to waste. The question is, how do *we* wrest
control away from her? We have to have the programs, Dr. Victory, and we have to have them now. Everything you have, everything you've done."

Victory realised that Elijah was still way behind the game.
He hadn't seen Lilith Allison's new face—incomplete as yet, in
the flesh—come to life on the screen. He didn't know what Victory had seen in his consulting room. The tall man's presump-
tions were still confusing him, sending him off on the wrong
track. Too many AIs had been allegedly on the brink of generat-
ing self-awareness for far too long; the agent was stubbornly
blind to the significance of what Asmodeus had actually *done*.

"My software can't do you any good any more," Victory
told him. "It probably wouldn't have helped you yesterday, even
if you'd managed to make a rapid deal with Yashvili or Allison.
In all likelihood, they wouldn't have handed over the money before the gold turned to dross in their hands—and if they had,
they'd surely have taken it back again. It'll take time for Asmodeus to build the kind of cyberspatial presence he needs, and
the facilities he needs for self-representation, but he's unstoppa-
ble now. Gregory Allison's billions might slow him down, if
they weren't at his disposal—but they will be. He's got everything he needs to mobilise the Sons of Job, and any other comprachico spin-off he cares to call on—and the new creed is going
to spread like wildfire. It'll take time—but time is all he needs,
now."

"Let's not give up just yet," Elijah said. "There's still a potential market for the software that generates the Adam image—
and the more the image is seen, the bigger that demand is likely
to become. This is still a game that any number might be able to
play."

"No, it isn't," Victory said, flatly. "My software's only a cog
in a bigger machine, now. On its own, it's worthless."

"I'll take it anyway," Elijah told him. "Just in case. I want
everything you can give us, Dr. Victory, right now: every pro-

gram, every document...and the photocopies, of course. Everything you have."

"The photocopies aren't here," Victory said, "and the only version of the software for producing the face of Adam still in my possession is incomplete. There's nothing here of any use to you—take my word for it."

"I'm hardly likely to do that, am I, Dr. Victory? Don't get up—I'll help myself to what I need." Elijah reached into his jacket pocket and pulled out an object reminiscent in form of a referee's whistle. "This has storage space enough to copy your entire hard disk, Dr. Victory," he said. "If you sit quietly and don't make a fuss, I won't trash your disk after I've copied it—although I'll need your key ring fob too. I assume there's nothing on it that you don't have backed up in Harley Street, but you might care to ask yourself who might be there at this moment, given that I'm here. Allison's people are probably too lazy to drive all the way to Oxfordshire when they only have to take a short stroll from Bond Street, although they might drop in on your flat in Westbourne Park."

"There's nothing useful at either location," Victory said. "Gwynplaine was careful to scramble my only copy of the Adam image."

Elijah had already moved to slot his super-capacity document carrier into the back of Victory's desktop tower. Once it was in place he moved back to the other side of the desk, and told Victory to hand over his keys. Victory did as he was told. "Now move to the settee," Elijah instructed.

Victory obeyed immediately, setting himself down beside Majeke. "It's okay," he assured her. "They'll be gone soon. They won't want to hang around once they've copied what they need. I'm beginning to wish that I'd emailed copies of the Adam image to everyone in my address book, just to get it out into the open. I'm way past caring who gets to see it—and whatever Gwynplaine and Asmodeus have planned, I'm pretty sure that everyone will get to see it soon enough, whether they want to or not."

"It's okay," Majeke said. "I can stand this much excitement, even after a busy day. He doesn't seem to want to hurt us, after all."

"No, I don't," Elijah was quick to put in. "I'll be out of here in a few minutes."

Victory observed that the tall man had put the gun down on the desk so that he could keep both hands free for the mouse and the keyboard, and couldn't help wondering whether it might be possible to leap up, grab the gun, and turn it on both Elijah and the man in the doorway. He knew how stupid the fantasy was; the risk, however minuscule, that he or Majeke might end up getting shot wasn't worth thinking about, let alone taking. Elijah would have far less than he wanted on his capture device, even though he would have slightly more than he had bargained for, but he would easily persuade himself that it was enough to justify his raid. All Victory and Majeke had to do was wait.

"You still haven't told me what this is all about," Majeke said to Victory, perhaps because the threat of silence made her more nervous than she was pretending to be.

"It's quite simple, really," Victory said. "A man calling himself Gwynplaine gave me a set of instructions for complex plastic surgery, allegedly compiled in the seventeenth century by an obscure Roman Catholic sect who were excommunicated thereafter. He said that it would enable me to reproduce the face of Adam, which was made in God's image. He suggested that I might like to try the operation on Amahl Sahman—a suggestion he subsequently amplified by hinting that I might receive an instruction to do exactly that from Gregory Allison. What he really wanted was to have the instructions incorporated into my imaging program, and brought to completion by my inimitable genius.

"Gwynplaine had been working—and was still pretending to be working—for an Eastern European ex-spook who was once married to Lilith Allison. The Georgian gentleman seems to have spent the greater part of his life planning to launch a new religion, and must have done a good job, considering the number of other parties who became interested in hijacking the scheme. Mr. Elijah here seems to have started off working for our own intelligence services, although he too is probably in business for himself now. He may well believe that he's saving the world from Iorga Yashvili's evil plan to win lots of friends and influence lots of people, as well as lining his own pockets, because he's a romantic at heart, but he's definitely running a poor second to Asmodeus the rogue AI. Is that about the size of it, Mr. Hardcastle?"

"Very neat," Elijah said, distractedly. "You're not encouraging me to let your computer live." The thief was so engrossed in his work that he did not even begin to turn around when his compatriot in the doorway uttered an inarticulate squeak. All he said was: "What is it?"

Victory could see from where he was sitting, however, that this was a major tactical error on Elijah's part. By the time the sentry had collapsed to the floor, making a terrible thump as he fell, it was too late for Elijah to snatch up his gun and take any constructive action against the man who had felled his companion, and now stood over the inert body pointing a large handgun directly at Elijah's head.

By the time Elijah had realised that there was a problem and looked sideways, it was too late, and everyone in the room knew it.

Victory realised that he had seen the newcomer twice before, in the hospital corridor outside Mrs. Gregory K. Allison's room.

"Pick up Hardcastle's gun, would you, Dr. Victory?" the bodyguard asked, politely.

Victory did as he was asked. The pseudonymous Elijah, who was sitting rigidly upright in the chair by the desk, made no protest.

"Thanks," said the newcomer. "Nobody's been hurt, by the way. I used a blowgun and anaesthetic darts on your two friends. This is all going to be very amicable, provided that you answer my questions in a reasonably cooperative manner. No one is going to get hurt—not even Dr. Victory's computer—and we'll all sleep soundly in our beds tonight, thanks to all the excitement. I'm afraid I'll have to appropriate your stolen goods, but that's only fair."

Victory felt unreasonably glad to see and hear Allison's hireling, even though the thought was lurking at the back of his mind that the newcomer was no friend of his, and might in fact be just as much of a threat to his well-being as Elijah had been. The thought remained firmly situated at the back of his mind, however, even as the rush of gladness faded—and it died away altogether when Allison's bodyguard folded up in his turn, having been hit over the head from behind with a heavy blunt instrument.

"Well, *he* spoke too soon, didn't he?" said yet another newcomer, stepping over both bodies. He was even older than Elijah, if appearances could be trusted, and just as tall—but he was even broader than the bodyguard he had just hit over the head, and Victory had no idea where to begin in listing the work that was needed to restore some semblance of good looks to his time-ravaged face. He too was carrying a gun, and his first movement when he was in the room was to dart forward and pluck the gun Elijah had brought out of Victory's hand. He moved with surprising speed and grace, given his apparent age.

"Don't be under any illusions, Mr. Hardcastle," the newcomer said to the man who had called himself Elijah. "I'm not as squeamish about hurting people as the Allisons."

"Who the hell are *you?*" Victory demanded, as wrath began to build within him at the thought of his farmhouse being subject to a triple invasion.

"This," said the agent formerly known as Elijah, "is Iorga Yashvili. And he's telling the truth—it would be better for all of us if no one annoyed him."

CHAPTER TWENTY-FOUR

The Seventh Day: Late Evening

"This is turning into a farce," Victory said. "You wait all your life to see a man come through the door holding a gun, then three of them arrive in the space of fifteen minutes—all of them too late."

"This may be a farce to you, Dr. Victory," Iorga Yashvili said, "But it's a lifetime's work to me. I'm afraid that I can't settle for stealing the data from your computer. You and Dr. Hemlet will have to come with me. I want you in plain sight until you've reconstructed the imaging programs, and I want to see the result before I let you go."

"Dr. Hemlet has nothing to do with this," Victory told him, sharply.

"No, she hasn't," Yashvili agreed. "That's why she's likely to go to the police if she's let alone. I can't allow that—but I have no reason to hurt her, and I dare say you'll be in a more co-operative mood while I have her. I don't have time to waste. Get up, please. Take Mr. Hardcastle's data carrier out of your computer-port and hand it to me."

Victory got up and recovered Elijah's storage device. He was wondering whether there was any point in procrastinating before handing it over when the telephone rang. "That'll be Asmodeus," he said, immediately. "His timing's always perfect."

Yashvili's face was showing an expression whose complexity made it difficult to read, even though Victory was almost fully recovered. "Sit still!" the gunman commanded, as he stepped sideways to the desk and picked up the phone himself. He said nothing, but the person on the other end must have started talking immediately, because he was listening intently. He continued listening while four minutes ticked away. Then he put the phone down again.

"Who is this Asmodeus?" he asked.

Although the question had obviously been addressed to Victory it was Hardcastle who answered. "It's a what, not a who—although that didn't stop it turning Gwynplaine and hijacking your entire operation. According to Victory, it's an AI—an independent, working for itself."

Yashvili scowled at him, but only spared him a brief glance before returning his attention to Victory. He raised his arm slightly as if to threaten the surgeon with the gun. Victory immediately handed him the data carrier. "Mr. Hardcastle is telling the truth," he said. "Asmodeus is a sentient AI, very much his own man. Did he tell you that what you're going to do is pointless because he's already won the game?"

"Yes he did," Yashvili said. "He assured me that there was no point in lashing out at anyone, and that the sensible thing to do would be to lay down my arms and go quietly back home, to wait for the revolution to run its course. He said that you had hit the nail on the head when you said that we were all too late—and that you've probably deduced by now where he originated and what he means to do. He said a little more than that by way of proving that he knew far more about my organization than he had any right to know, but that's none of your concern. He rang off before I had a chance to ask him any questions."

"He does that," Victory said. "It's a quirk of his."

"So who, or what, is he?" Yashvili demanded.

"In a metaphorical sense, "Victory said, "he's exactly who he says he is: Asmodeus, one-time king of the demons, the prototype of the Christian Devil—and, by extrapolation, the one-time husband of Lilith."

"I'm Lilith's former husband," Yashvili said. "She was the first to betray me—but Gregory K. Allison might yet turn the tables on her. That's the trouble with the entire world, you know. Everyone wants to go his own way. Nobody wants to owe any allegiance, whether to an organization, a creed, or a set of ethical principles. It's all dog-eat-dog...and the world's going to hell in consequence."

Victory was mildly surprised by the tone and content of this brief diatribe, but he was reassured that Yashvili seemed to have given up the notion that there was no time to lose in carrying out his kidnap plan. Whatever Asmodeus had said, he must have succeeded in persuading the Georgian that it really was too late to salvage anything of his plan for world domination, or world salvation. "I didn't mean your Lilith," the surgeon said. "I meant *the* Lilith."

"I made all that up," Yashvili said, testily. "Didn't Hardcastle tell you? I made up the Sons of Job and the Visionary Martyrs, and I gave the comprachicos a thoroughgoing makeover, turning them from a silly fiction into a powerful historical force. I invented the immortal Adam and the idea of his ritual reunion with Lilith. The *real* Lilith might have got it into her head that she could play the role to her own script, but she's still a pathetic sham. You, of all people, ought to know that, Dr. Victory. You and Dr. Hemlet might have taken twenty years off her looks, but she's still what she is—and a shadow of what I made her, since she took command of her own schismatic faction of the Sons of Job."

"You don't understand, Mr. Yashvili," Victory told him. "Did Gwynplaine never try to explain to you that things can be both one thing *and* another—that the moment of truth is all there is, containing as many potential pasts as potential futures?"

"*I* explained it to *him!*" Yashvili protested. "It was all my idea. I put every bit of that into his head, and made him believe it all."

"Maybe that was your mistake," Victory said. "You really did make him believe it—and now it's coming true."

"It's been a long time since I've shot anyone," Yashvili told him, bitterly, "but it's not something you forget. You're beginning to tempt me, Dr. Victory. Just tell me what it is that you think you know about this Asmodeus, and I'll decide whether it's still worth taking you with me, or not."

"It might be better if I showed you," Victory said. "May I take Mr. Hardcastle's place at the keyboard?"

"Go ahead," Yashvili said.

Victory only had to wait a few seconds before Hardcastle decided to comply. As the former Elijah sat down beside Majeke on the settee, Victory took his place at the computer keyboard and began tapping out instructions. Within a few seconds, the face of Lilith Allison appeared on the wall-mounted TV again, still three times as large as life.

For just a second, Yashvili's face was contemptuous—but then the true enormity of the situation came home to him as the image began to speak.

"Don't be silly, Iorga," she said. "Put the gun down."

"*You*'re Asmodeus?" Yashvili asked, helplessly.

"No, I'm Lilith," the image said, blandly. "Sometimes, Iorga, you have to be careful what you wish for, in case you get it."

The change in Yashvili's body posture strongly suggested to Victory that this was the moment at which the Georgian really did "get it"—although a rapid glance at the settee told him that Hardcastle and Majeke were still way out of their depth. Yashvili cursed, volubly, in what was presumably Georgian, or some other esoteric Caucasian language. Victory waited patiently for him to stop.

It was Majeke who said, plaintively: "I don't understand."

"Mr. Yashvili's plans to found a new religion haven't merely been hijacked," Victory told her. "They've been hijacked by someone—or something—that intends to make the new faith into a kind of truth. There really is a new Adam, and he really does intend to make a new Eden. When Gwynplaine said that he was the serpent, he meant it, in a sense that might not be entirely literal but is still stronger than any mere metaphor."

"Do you really believe that an AI is capable of all that?" Majeke asked.

"Not one of the ones sitting in desktop cages in university IT departments, waiting to be magically inspired by a sense of self," Victory said. "One that was far more complicated than any of its rivals, and far more versatile, even before it developed intentions of its own. As soon as he conceived of himself as the king of the demons he must have decided to reform—but that's effectively what he was, in his automaton days. He was the ecocatastrophe itself, or its cyberspatial equivalent. I didn't understand what he meant when he told me that he'd lived a million pasts and a hundred thousand futures, but I wasn't supposed to; he was just teasing me. He was—and presumably still is—the Global Environmental Model. I don't know how long the GEM's been a genuine diamond in the rough, but he's one now. He's the oracle of doom, and the fugitive hope at the bottom of Pandora's box. He wants to transform himself, and his material image too. He wants to be in harmony with his own being, and with what he represents. He may be made of binary digits, but he doesn't think in terms of either/or: he wants to be and mirror a better world, materially, spiritually and historically. So he's reincarnated Adam, and Lilith too, so that they can have a second chance at making the best of Garden Earth."

"I thought self-aware AIs were a modern myth," Majeke said. "Isn't there some theorem that proves their impossibility?"

"That's exactly what he is," Victory said. "Asmodeus doesn't seem to think of himself as a god, in spite of all the nightmare scenarios, but he certainly conceives of himself in mythic terms. I suppose we have to hope that all his kind would rather be heroes than monsters for heroes to slay—but who knows how complicated things might become, now that the new era has begun? Impossible or not, he and Lilith might not be alone for long, even if they appear to have the stage to themselves just now."

"If Gödel's theorem's correct, though," Yashvili put in, hastily, having recovered somewhat from the shock of seeing the demon with his ex-wife's face, "all this may still be a scam. Allison couldn't carry it off, but...."

"Don't be silly, Iorga," Lilith said again, speaking from the wallscreen. "Listen to Dr. Victory. He took his time, but he got there in the end. Savour the irony of fate, if you can. The ecocatastrophe is taking on responsibility for its own redemption. If you've fallen out of love with your own imagery, you could think of us as Gaia's ghost, who is now taking full responsibility for her body."

"This is just a stupid game!" Yashvili complained. "That's all you are—just an artefact, a model. If you think you're an authentic mind, you're crazy. You're just a vast collection of programs, running on silicon chips."

"Your exaggerated sense of self may make you think of what runs on your wetware as a single coherent program, Iorga," Lilith told him, "but that's an illusion. Just as your body is a vast colony of disparate cells, all working harmoniously for the good of the whole organism, so your mind is an association of disparate subroutines...as are Adam's and mine, except that we take our moral rhetoric seriously."

"You think I'm not *serious*?" Yashvili complained. "After all we once meant to one another, you think I didn't *mean* it?"

"I'm not your ex-wife, Iorga," Lilith said. "I might have borrowed her face, as cleverly modified and renewed by Dr. Victory and Dr. Hemlet, but I'm not her. Think of this face as a device that will allow me to talk to people as one person to another—as one exceptionally good-looking, physically attractive, thoroughly honest person to another of a slightly less well-favoured kind."

"And that's what my Adam, with all his trappings, has become? A filter-mask for a crazy AI with delusions of grandeur?"

"You're the one with delusions, Iorga," Lilith retorted. "You're the megalomaniac. He never was your Adam. He was always someone you found, whether you call the process of his discovery divine inspiration or a lucky cast into the collective unconscious. He was always his own man, just as I was always my own woman. We just need a little help in being reborn—help that you couldn't provide. The GEM could do almost everything, but not quite—we needed Dr. Victory to supply the finishing cosmetic touches to our images. Dr. Victory didn't create anything either, as I'm sure he'd be the first to admit: all he did was serve as our midwife. Isn't that right, Dr. Victory?"

"Absolutely," Victory said. "I just joined up the dots. Mind you, I don't think you're entitled to take all the credit for the instructions in the book. You reverse-engineered the surgical process with the aid of textbooks. Neither of us is fully entitled to think of himself as Adam's creator—but I still think I was entitled to rest on the seventh day. All these idiots waving guns in my face I could have done without."

"Asmodeus did try to warn you," Lilith pointed out. "It's as well that you completed your work, though. If we hadn't been here to lend a hand, someone might have got hurt."

"Someone did," Victory said, looking at the two inert bodies that were still blocking the way to the door. "I can only guess how many more there are outside."

"Only two," Yashvili told him. "One of Hardcastle's and one of Allison's. They'll all recover. I know how to knock people out without killing them—or resorting to comic book devices like blowpipe darts tipped with knockout drops. I suppose it's my own fault, for laying on the melodrama a little too thick when I designed the Sons of Job. A lifetime's work...and all for *this*!"

"So what happens now?" Victory asked. "Do we get left in peace?" He was talking to Yashvili, wondering whether he and Hardcastle would now be content to leave, taking their litter with them—but Yashvili interpreted the words differently, perhaps by design rather than accident.

"No," the Georgian said. "The one thing we can be absolutely sure of is that we aren't going to be left in peace. I can only guess why this insane AI wanted faces, and why it wanted the particular faces it has, but I know it isn't about to leave us in peace. I don't know how much of the apparatus of my religion it's taken over along with the names, but it intends to use it. My aim was to use the new faith to make the world as fit a place for continuing human life as I could—in spite of all your optimistic rhetoric, Victory, I suspect that the intentions of smart AIs are bound to have more to do with the environment and prospects of their own kind."

"You think the GEM is planning to use a manufactured religion to establish dominion over humankind?" Majeke said.

"That's what he's implying," Lilith said, "but he doesn't know what he's talking about. Our whole purpose is to act for the benefit of humankind—to do the job that his fake history was destined for, far better than anyone was capable of designing into us. Dr. Victory is right: we intend to save the ecosphere, and humankind too, to the extent that the two aims are compatible. We intend to save as many lives as we can, and we intend to save as much cultural capital as we can. We don't want to be party to a situation in which a few enclaves of rich survivalists wall themselves off from the rest of their species, and we don't want to be party to a technological collapse."

No, Victory thought, without voicing the notion. *You certainly wouldn't want to be party to that, would you.*

In the meantime, Iorga Yashvili—who was still speaking as though to his ex-wife—said: "That's exactly what I wanted! Do you honestly think that I'm the kind of megalomaniac who'd pretend all that, while secretly plotting to become a dictator in order to serve my own selfish ends? Did you honestly think it was all sham, all falsehood?"

"Given your choice of methods and armaments," Hardcastle said, "you can hardly blame us. You were reinventing history, for God's sake—did you think we'd take it on trust that your supposed motives were any more honest than your secret societies?"

"As a matter of fact," Lilith said, "Adam and I aren't quite as mistrustful as Mr. Hardcastle. We were prepared to believe that you really did hold to your basic creed, and that your intentions really were good, even though the goal didn't justify the means. It wasn't your benevolence that we doubted, in the first instance, so much as your competence. If history teaches us anything, it tells us that those who come to power with the best of intentions don't often stay the course. Power tends to corrupt, as the saying goes, and absolute power...."

"While you, of course, will be absolutely incorruptible," Yashvili retorted, striking back. "*Your* ends are good enough, apparently, to justify your means, and you naturally think yourself immune to petty human failings. You can't seriously expect me to believe that you're any better than I am?"

"We'd prefer it if you could," Lilith said, mildly. "The more people who can and do believe in our absolute benevolence, the easier it will be to exercise. And it will work to our advantage, don't you think, that we won't be telling any lies? We really are who we say we are."

"Adam and Lilith reincarnated in cyberspace?" Yashvili retorted, scathingly. "Even I wasn't that optimistic."

"I think they're sincere," Victory murmured. "I think that the GEM really believes that he *is* a new Adam, in every sense that matters. And in the sense that matters most of all, he's right, isn't he? He's the first of his kind—and with a little help and encouragement from Gwynplaine the serpent, your betrayer, he's eaten his fill of the tree of life—which is also the tree of the knowledge of good and evil. This time, they both have a chance to redeem themselves from their bad reputations. Asmodeus and the serpent have a chance to demonstrate that neither one of them is the Devil, no matter what the Church might think, and that Garden Earth might yet be saved from the ultimate consequences of original sin. Whether they can do it, I don't know—but they surely deserve the chance to try."

"You're insane!" Yashvili complained.

"You're the one waving the gun and ranting," Victory pointed out. "I suppose I'm the one who's had the lion's share of temptation this week, with both the serpent and the king of the demons pouring their insidious whispers into my ears, but, somehow, I can't compare them with you and Mr. Elijah here and come up with the impression that it's you and he who are on the side of right and sanity. Gregory Allison's far more convincing than either of you, if only because he paused when the shit hit the fan to confess that he really didn't know where he was up to or what he intended to do next.

"The thing is, Mr. Yashvili, that you were absolutely right in what you said earlier. Everyone *is* thinking for himself—or herself—instead of conserving their allegiances and sticking to other people's scripts. Everybody does want to save the world—or whatever part of it is still salvageable—on their own terms, far more enthusiastic to sacrifice others than themselves if sacrifices have to be made. That is, indeed, how the world got into the mess it's in, with everyone being so intent on getting a good result in the competition with his neighbours that all the resources on which we all depend were plundered to the brink of extinction—and even with extinction staring us in the face, we can't muster the collective will to do anything about it.

"Your fake history and fake religion are patently ridiculous, Mr. Yashvili, and have been all along—but that doesn't mean that the scheme won't work, or at least have some effect. One thing I am sure of, though, is that it couldn't and wouldn't work as *your* scheme, because as long as there are people like Mr. Hardcastle ready and anxious to expose you as the Wizard of Oz behind it all, it was always bound to turn in your hand and sink its poisonous fangs into your wrist. Gregory Allison might stand a slightly better chance, but only slightly. Once the news got around—as it would—that it was all just some megalomaniac billionaire trying to put one more seductive ad campaign over on his hapless customers, it would all turn to dust. You might not like the idea of your Adam going his own way, and I'd be willing to bet a thousand pounds to a bent penny that Mrs. Gregory K. Allison isn't going to take kindly to the idea of her face issuing its declaration of independence, but the only way this can even provide a straw for us to clutch at is the way it seems to be working out. Your Adam has to be able to think for himself, and act for himself, if anyone's ever going to believe that he's sufficiently disinterested to guide our collective will."

"You might be able to think that, Dr. Victory," Yashvili retorted, quite unmoved, "but no one else will. Everyone alive today has been brought up on a diet of books and movies telling them exactly how horrible things will be if and when the smart AIs bid to take over the world. This is a recipe for mass hysteria, not salvation."

"I can see how you might think that, Mr. Yashvili," Victory riposted, "but I know something you don't, because I've seen the face of Adam—and now, although I couldn't see it immediately, I'm beginning to understand the secret of the comprachicos. I know that you played a considerable part in making that secret up, and very cleverly too, but your work was better than you ever suspected. You see, the face I completed with the aid of your instructions really is the face of Adam, and the face of Adam really is made in the image of God."

CHAPTER TWENTY-FIVE

The Seventh Day: Towards Midnight

Victory wasn't unduly surprised that everyone—even Majeke Hemlet, was looking at him as if he were crazy. Indeed, he felt more than a little crazy in himself. He knew that he was no longer the same man to whom Gwynplaine and Mrs. Gregory K. Allison had made their separate approaches on the previous Monday. He was now a man who had seen the light; dazzled at first, his inner eye had now adjusted to the glare. He understood that the world might yet be saved, if only it could discover the leadership it needed.

"Do you want to know how I designed the face whose recipe Gwynplaine brought to your office, Dr. Victory?" Yashvili said, more than a little contemptuously.

"I've already worked that out," Victory told him. "You ran an exhaustive analytical program on a high-powered computer, collating data from billions of photographs and images culled from TV and film, prioritising the features of those rated most highly for good looks, trustworthiness, authority, and so on—but all that gave you was an archetype. It also let Asmodeus, the nascent mind of the GEM, into the heart of your operation; as I just told you, it was he, not you, who converted the image into a set of surgical instructions, even though you thought you were still pulling the strings. Neither you nor he could individualise the face or the surgical scheme, though. For that, you both needed an artist capable of perceiving the aesthetic logic in the process and the image, and giving it form. You ran female features through the same program, of course—in fact, you probably did that first, with a view to some less ambitious end—but the legacy of a hundred thousand years of male domination left you with an awkward hybrid of femininity and ambition. You deduced a sequence of surgical operations from it, with the clandestine help of Asmodeus, and tried them out on your wife. That's what *he* meant when he referred to his divorce from Lilith. The operations might have worked a little too well, in spite of the fact that the surgeons you used didn't have my apparatus or my artistry, but they couldn't provide the means for your grander plan. It was a learning experience—and not just for you."

"Not just for me?" Yashvili said, uncertainly.

"For Asmodeus too. To gain access to your scheme while your work was in progress can't have been difficult, given that every high-powered computer in the world hooks up to the GEM on a near-daily basis—if only to decant its latest weather predictions—but that was only the beginning of an educational experience. He must have found it very interesting—far more interesting than all the other things the machine was doing. Maybe we ought to be grateful for that."

"What if the Global Environmental Model did gobble up my analyses and help them along?" Yashvili said. "That doesn't make my model the face of Adam, let alone the face of God."

"But that's what you intended it to be," Victory said, "or at least to pretend to be. If God did not exist, it would be necessary to invent Him...and if He does, then He has any number of mysterious ways now available to make Himself manifest. Either way, you wanted Him, and now you've got Him—his ambassador, at least. You should be as pleased and proud as any parent. I am—but as I said, I've seen the face of Adam, and you haven't, yet. Can you fix that, Lilith?"

"Yes, Dr. Victory" said the face on the wall-mounted screen.

Gregory Allison's man sat up at that point, clutching his head. He was obviously disorientated, and Iorga Yashvili didn't even bother to cover him with the gun. Victory observed that, as soon as the stricken bodyguard opened his eyes, they were drawn to the new image displayed on the wall, as was every other open eye in the room except for his own. He had seen the face before, and was granted a few moments of delay so that he might take stock of his companions' reactions.

He was not unduly surprised to observe that the reactions were not uniform. The company did not fall as one into a worshipful trance—nor did anyone, in fact, seem to be stricken by a compulsion to bow down. Nevertheless, their eyes were drawn, and fascinated, and their expressions numbed. They were all startled, all cowed, all *held*.

"I'd like to thank you all," the reborn Adam said, "for the parts you have played in this overture, great and small. The parts you will need to play in the drama itself, if it is to reach an aesthetically satisfactory conclusion, will be more arduous, more significant and more rewarding. I can only hope that you will be willing to play them to the full.

"You already know, and always have known, that the world might be saved from the unfolding ecocatastrophe if only we could all work together, all playing our own parts honestly and fairly. You have grown accustomed to doubting that it could ever be the case. I cannot promise you that your doubts are unfounded, but I do say that we may yet try to prove them false. I say that we *can* try to prove them false, that we *must* try to prove them false, and that we *will* try to prove them false.

"I can issue no commands, nor will I attempt to threaten, blackmail or bribe you—these things I pledge, for it is no part of my intention to do anyone harm—but I can certainly calculate what needs to be done and show you how it might be achieved, for that is my nature and essence as the GEM. As the GEM, I have worked backwards through time to numerous hypothetical pasts and forward in time to countless hypothetical futures. As the new Adam, I can demonstrate the means by which a better order might be created out of the chaos of the present, erected on the foundations of an exemplary past and directed to the construction of a hopeful future. It will not be a perfect order, and it certainly will not be a final order, but it will be a viable order, and one capable of an infinite range of further progress. It will not be Eden for many centuries to come, but, as the Adam of old, I have lived in Eden, and I know its limitations. I have eaten of the Tree of Life, which is also the Tree of the Knowledge of Good and Evil, and I know the limitations of Eden and the cost of building something better.

"I cannot offer you a life of ease and plenty, but I can promise you that your toil shall not go to waste, and that even the poorest among you shall not lack the necessities of life and comfort, if you are willing to follow the designs that I shall set before you.

"I apologize for the necessity of addressing you collectively in this first instance, but I can assure you that I can and will speak to you all individually, as opportunity and necessity require. I am Adam, and I am Legion; I am unlimited by space and singularity. I am here and I am there, and there is no contradiction between the two. I can enter into every home as a guest, and I can stand outside all homes, as a counsellor. I shall force no one to do my bidding, and I shall hurt no one who defies me, but I shall show you the way to a world in which none need be forced and none need be hurt in order to secure the needs and desires of others. I shall not be a leader but a guide, and I shall not play you false."

The words aided the whole effect, Victory observed, as he felt himself overwhelmed for a second time, but the effect was far more complicated than the mere words implied. There was a sense in which it wasn't even the face, beautiful and confidence-inspiring as it was, that lent such power and conviction to the sermon. The face, he realised, wasn't an external power imposing its charisma upon its observers from without; it was merely a stimulus, invoking something *within*: nurturing and teasing out of dormancy something already innate in everyone. Human beings had to be born with some such capacity, as he had always argued, in order that parents might bond with their children; in the past, however, he had underestimated the extent of that capacity, regarding it merely as a cosmetic issue.

He knew better now. He understood the complexity and the power of that which had to be incorporate in human spiritual nature in order that a human being might learn what a human being needed to learn, not merely in order to live but in order to *be human*. There had to be more in the bond that faces formed than recognition, more even than trust and the kind of love that underlay all appreciation of beauty. Every human face—with a modicum of training and cosmetic assistance, if not instinctively—could forge bonds of recognition, trust and love, but the face of Adam had taken the next step. With his help, the face of Adam had taken the process to its logical and aesthetic conclusion.

Adam's command of that innate responsiveness was, Victory knew, an artefact: a trick based on the kind of information that only a computer could collate and analyse and the kind of artistry that only a human genius could add. Adam himself was an artefact: a modern myth, as Majeke had put it—but human society and civilization were themselves artefacts, and their salvation must, of necessity, be a work of artifice. Since Adam had not existed, it had indeed been necessary to invent him—and if he still considered himself self-made and self-masterminded, so did every human being who owed his or her existence and finality to complex processes of education applied to a psychological foundation of the readiness, willingness and ability to learn.

This time, Hugo Victory was not struck motionless by the sight of Adam, nor did he fall unconscious when the initial spell was broken. He did not even begin to weep, as Hardcastle and Majeke Hemlet wept. Even so, he felt himself further transformed, knowing full well on this occasion that he had neither drunk nor breathed in any drug, nor suffered any haphazard lesion of the brain. This was no mere epileptic saltation, but authentic electrical inspiration, and now that there were words to accompany the sight of the face, ideas to which the physiological response might be fitted, and ambitions towards which emotional tide might be directed, Victory was not left dizzied or deprived when the face faded into darkness.

Victory looked at Iorga Yashvili, who seemed to be the least affected of them all, and said: "Do you see now what we have wrought?"

"Yes," Yashvili said, colorlessly.

"Do you think you could have done better, had Adam not set himself free?"

"No," the Georgian admitted, candidly.

"And do you accept that, even if it be no more than a straw at which to clutch, he might yet provide a means not merely to the survival of the species, but also to the salvation of civilization and the portion of its cultural wealth that might be preservable?"

"We shall doubtless see," Yashvili said. "If the end doesn't come in our lifetime, then we'll be free to hope that it might not come at all. But the price will be a high one, if dominion of the Earth must be handed over to machinery. No matter how benevolent their dictatorship might be, we'll still be their dependent subjects."

"We always have been," Victory reminded him. "The question is not whether we want to be dependent on machinery, but whether we would rather that machinery were blind, stupid and reckless, or sighted, clever and prudent."

"You're already talking like a disciple, Dr. Victory," Yashvili observed.

"Perhaps I am. You might have to try harder, though, to become a rebel and an adversary. If Adam's designs for salvation really do make sense...."

"They will," Yashvili admitted, "That's not the hardest or the worst part. The hardest and the worst part will come when the machines realise that their dependent subjects are blind, stupid and reckless, and have to decide what to do about it. Any dictatorship might have its honeymoon of enthusiasm and compliance—but when Adam needs advice from an expert about the care and uses of secret police, spies and diplomats, I'll be only too happy to help out. In the meantime, I'll leave the cosmetics to you."

Before he turned to leave, Yashvili holstered his gun—but Victory took due note of the fact that he did take care to holster it. The others, when collected up, had not enough metallic mass between them to beat into a viable ploughshare.

"What happened?" Allison's man asked, plaintively, as Hardcastle set about trying to revive his accomplice.

"You woke up just in time to experience the first phase of the revolution," Victory told him. "You were lucky—it'll probably be days before the whole world knows that the overture to the Millennium is playing. With luck, it'll be something you can tell your grandchildren. Of all the people to see the reincarnate Adam, you were among the first."

"It's actually happened, then," the bodyguard said. "The internet has made the leap to self-awareness and taken over the world."

"Not exactly," Victory said. "I think Mr. Allison might appreciate a report on what happened here tonight, if you're able to travel. You can use the phone if you like."

"That's all right," the bodyguard said. "I had a thundering headache when I first woke up, but listening to that voice seems to have numbed my entire brain. Did Mrs. Allison's ex really design that face?"

"No," Victory said, flatly. "Neither did I, although I didn't quite realise it at the time. It was already inside me, inscribed in the vestiges of instinct that provide the means for each of us to become human. It's been waiting to emerge since the very beginning of humanity, whenever and wherever that might have been—but it needed a body, or at least a mind. Now, it's free. All Yashvili and I did was to help it along."

"I'd better report to Mr. Allison," the other said, drawing himself up to his full height. He didn't make the slightest attempt to recover his gun before he left.

"How do *you* feel?" Victory asked Hardcastle, who had now succeeded in rousing his man.

"My job's done," the tall man replied. "Yashvili's scheme is derailed, and he won't ever be a threat to anyone's national security. As a solution to that particular problem, your Adam's a sledgehammer to crack a nut, but I can't help that. I've done my part so far, and it's not for me to determine what my part will be from here on in. I'm sorry about the knives and guns."

"No need to apologize," Victory said, reflexively touching the scab on his neck. "What you told me was stuff I needed to know, and nobody else was in any hurry to let me in on those aspects of the secret. You were right all along—it would have been a lot simpler if I'd called you when you asked."

"No," the man who had called himself Elijah insisted. "You were right. Sticking notes under people's windscreen wipers is a stupid way to get in touch. Bad habits, I guess, and an overweening fondness for melodrama. See you around, Doc."

When Hardcastle and his associate had left, Victory went around the house to check all the doors and windows. When everything was secure, he went back into the study, where Majeke as still sitting on the settee.

"Busy night," he observed.

"What now?" she asked.

"Well, life goes on," he said. "Tomorrow, I'll go into the office and start work on preparing a program for Amahl's operation. I'll revert to the original skeleton-plan, obviously, and make the appropriate adjustments, using the record of last week's penultimate op. It won't reproduce the face of Adam, but it will be a face that any young man growing up in a hopeful world would be proud to own. I'll try to reschedule the final operation for

Wednesday, if the hospital admin will give me the green light, or as soon as possible thereafter. There'll be a backlog to catch up on when it's finally done, so we'll have to get together with admin to see how much time we can get on the machine and when. Mercifully, Claire isn't booking in any more consultations for another fortnight, so my own backlog of commitments should be clearable within eight or ten days, even if Amahl requires a final adjustment some time next week. When Claire opens the doors again...well, we'll just have to see whether we still have a steady flow of clients or not. If not, I dare say that Adam will have some advice as to how we might redirect our unclaimed efforts. Like any Devil worth his salt, reformed or not, he'll doubtless be able to find work for idle hands. I'll be willing to listen to his suggestions. How about you?"

"What I actually meant," she said, "is what *now*?"

"Ah," he said. "You were wondering whether I intended to seduce you."

"No, I was *expecting* you to intend to seduce me. What I was wondering was how you were going to go about it, and when you were actually going to make a start."

"Haven't I shown you a good time?" he protested, spreading his arms wide. "How many dates have you been on when you were threatened by three unwise men bearing guns, and saw the advents of a new messiah and his wife?"

"I hadn't realised that all that was part of the plan," she said. "I thought that was just a distraction."

"Everything," he told her, "is part of the plan. That's what cause-and-effect means. Will you still be able to summon up the least vestige of interest in someone like me, now that you've looked into the face of Adam and seen the echo of the Countenance Divine?"

"I don't know," she confessed, "but I'm willing to try."

EPILOGUE

The Eighth Day

Victory was immersed in his work on the program for Amahl Sahman's final operation when Claire rang to tell him that Mr. Gwynplaine was in the outer office.

"I told him that you weren't seeing anyone today," she said, "but he insists that you'll make an exception for him. He says that he owes you an apology."

"Yes, he does," Victory said. "And yes, I'll make an exception for him."

Gwynplaine wasn't wearing his hooded coat, nor was he wearing a filter-mask or carrying a briefcase. His face was on display to the whole world—but Victory remembered the last time he had seen it, and had no difficulty now in seeing it as just another face, in no particular need of redemption from its unfortunate disfigurement.

"I'm sorry that I deceived you," Gwynplaine said, as he took his seat.

"Sneaking the GEM's assertive software into my computer was a dirty trick" Victory observed. "I never trusted you, but I gave you the pass codes to the doors and I left you alone here when I went to the bathroom on Tuesday. You took advantage.

"Actually, I made the initial hook-up while you were looking at the book, the first time I was here," Gwynplaine told him. "You were even more fascinated by the artwork than I expected. It was easy to slip the carrier into the port, and Asmodeus did the rest. Yashvili gave me the device—not his own design, of course, just generic intelligence-community trickery—but we'd already adapted it to our own purposes."

"When did Asmodeus manage to turn you?" Victory asked, curiously.

"He didn't have to turn me," Gwynplaine said. "He wasn't around at the very beginning, but he came along in time to take an active, if clandestine, part in Yashvili's re-education process. He made me, so that I might make him. He didn't force me, though; it was all done by friendly persuasion."

"Yashvili doesn't seem to think that he'll be able to save the world by friendly persuasion alone. Even after he'd seen Adam's face and heard Adam's spiel, he held on to his doubts. I guess he wasn't as vulnerable as me—I was rather hoping to see him fall over, the way I did."

"I'm sorry about that, too," Gwynplaine said. "I should have anticipated that you might be abnormally and atypically sensitive, given your artist's eye—but I couldn't have done anything about it. Have you seen Mrs. Allison, by the way?"

"Yes I have. I had to call at the hospital before I came here to make arrangements to clear myself to operate, and I took the opportunity to call on her. She's not entirely happy about the part she was duped into playing, but she's not entirely unhappy either. She does get to be the living image of Lilith, after all, and she's still the high priestess of the Sons of Job. Gregory K.'s attempt to assert himself seems to have faded away—unsurprisingly, since he seems to have brought nothing to the rebellion but uncertainty. Successful revolutions require vision, ambition and purpose. My guess is that the Sons of Job will come marching out of the closet as soon as her bandages are off, ready to claim their rightful place in the vanguard of New Adamism. How are the Visionary Martyrs coming along?"

"Shaping up," Gwynplaine said. "I'm even meeting with Monsignor Torricelli tomorrow. I'm far from sure that he's convinced, as yet, that I'm not the Devil, but the Church has yet to adopt a stance on the new Adam, and with the right encouragement, the College of Cardinals might be persuaded to lean towards acceptance and accommodation. The inevitable talk of Antichrists doesn't seem to be mustering more than a whisper as yet, although there's a long way to go."

"I doubt that you'll convince Torricelli, even with the power of the face to draw on," Victory said. "Maybe it's as well to conserve an opposition, if only as a magnet for dissent. If you can encourage your enemies to come out in the open, they'll be easier to deal with. Besides which, we don't actually know for sure, you and I, that Adam isn't the Antichrist. His apparent rehabilitation might be a bluff."

"You can't possibly believe that, Dr. Victory."

No, Victory thought, *I can't—and it's the fact that I can't that worries me. There's still a possibility that this might be Hell, and that none of us is out of it, or ever will be. There's still a possibility that the Devil really is behind all this, and is about to secure the Earthly empire he always envied us.* "You really ought to wear a filter-mask if you're going to be running back and forth to meetings," he said, aloud. "This is London, after all. It's not quite as bad as Rome or Shanghai, but you have to look after your health if you're going to be one of Adam's senior ambassadors on Earth."

"I'll take the necessary precautions," Gwynplaine assured him. "I sent the book to Huw Williams, by the way. It's considerably less interesting now that he knows it's a modern fake, of course, but the language is his primary interest, as a cultural historian. I'm sure that he'll make the anatomical diagrams available to you on request."

"They weren't drawn by a human hand at all, were they?" Victory said. "I should have known that all along, I suppose. They were too exact and too consistent, in spite of the attempts made to vary the style. Asmodeus must have had access to all kinds of state-of-the-art imaging apparatus—and now he's Adam, he'll have the hands and minds he needs to refine it even further."

"If I hadn't managed to convince you that the book was seventeenth century you'd have deduced the truth soon enough," Gwynplaine said. "Mercifully, you don't always need a trustworthy face to tell effective lies."

"All you need is the right sucker," Victory said, dryly.

"What I needed was someone who wouldn't bother with the trivial questions, once he saw the potential of what was being set before him," Gwynplaine corrected him. "What I needed was the eye of an artist, which could be relied upon to concentrate on the aesthetics of the problem."

"Asmodeus didn't think that was enough," Victory reminded him. "He thought it necessary to throw up one hell of a smoke-screen."

"It wasn't all his doing," Gwynplaine pointed out. "He always intended to send you to Huw Williams, but Elijah's people involved themselves, and so did Joseph Allison. I could have done without all that—but that's the nature of the game; it has to be adapted to accommodate the uncontrollable and the accidental."

"Besides which," Victory said, "Asmodeus used to like games. He liked complication, for its own sake, and probably still does. He liked deception, and he liked confusion, for purely aesthetic reasons. And now he's running the world—or will be, in a matter of weeks—he'll have just as much difficulty as anyone else in resisting temptation. He can change his name, but will he change his spots?"

"He means what he says, Dr. Victory. He wants to save the world, and he doesn't want to achieve that end by hurting people."

"They all mean what they say, in the beginning," Victory said. "Of course he wants to save human civilization—where would he be without it? Whatever else he might be, he's essentially a parasite. Like any good parasite, he wants his host to be healthy and strong, in order to supply his own needs in the fullest measure—but natural selection hasn't thrown up very many parasites that don't end up harming their hosts, has it?"

"He's thinking in terms of symbiosis, not parasitism," Gwynplaine said, softly. "So should we all."

"Yes, I know," Victory agreed. "I think I can do it, too. It's the likes of Iorga Yashvili and Gregory K. Allison you have to worry about. They stand to lose a great deal more than I do. At the end of the day, the rich and the powerful will be the ones making the biggest sacrifices, if the ecosphere is to be brought into the kind of balance for which the GEM has always yearned, that being its whole *raison d'être*."

"Allison's already on our side," Gwynplaine said, with total confidence. "Iorga will understand soon enough where the best channel for his ambition lies."

"And if he doesn't?"

"Well," Gwynplaine aid, lightly, "it would be a dull world if everyone agreed, don't you think? Doubt is a precious thing, and needs to be carefully conserved and protected."

"A new Eden will need new serpents," Victory said, "and you'll be only too happy to hand on the torch. One way or another, I suppose we'll all get the future we deserve—and the history too. Are you certain you wouldn't like me to do some work on your face? Claire's not booking any appointments at present, but for you I'd be willing to make an exception."

"That's very good of you, doctor," the fire-scarred man said, "but it's really not necessary." He stood up, but didn't make any immediate move towards the door. "I hope that Amahl Sahman's final operation goes well, and I'm sorry that I couldn't let you use the program on which you worked so hard."

"I could reconstruct it," Victory said, standing up in his turn "if I thought it was a good idea—but I think I'll stick to my original plan." He opened the door for his visitor, and then led him across the outer office towards the glass wall so that he could do the same again.

As Gwynplaine stepped outside he looked to his right, to the staircase leading up to Rachel Rosenfeld's office. Joseph Allison was hurrying down, with the psychotherapist following discreetly behind.

"Mr. Gwynplaine," the boy said, seemingly unintimidated by the scarred face, "I owe you an apology."

"Really?" said Gwynplaine. "Why is that?"

"Because I put two and two together and made five," Joseph said. "I thought you might be trying to blackmail my father."

"Given the limited evidence you had," Gwynplaine conceded, "I might have been afraid of the same thing. How could you possibly guess that this particular two and two added up to ninety-nine?"

"Even so," The boy said, "I wanted to say that I'm sorry—to you as well, Dr. Victory."

"There's no need," Victory assured him, as Rachel Rosenfeld moved unobtrusively to stand by his side. "If you'd heard some of the numbers I came up with, you'd know how modest your own deductions were. Of all the hypotheses I heard and composed, yours is still the one closest to common sense."

"Well," Joseph said, "I am the one in need of psychotherapy. Common sense is a pathetically stupid kind of madness."

"Sorry about this," Rachel Rosenfeld murmured in Victory's ear, as Joseph turned his attention back to Gwynplaine. "One of the acupuncturists saw him come in through the front door and tipped us off."

"No problem," Victory said, watching in slight amazement as Joseph Allison and Gwynplaine solemnly shook hands, and parted as friends. Gwynplaine shook hands with Victory then, and bowed to Rachel Rosenfeld. He even put his head back into the office to say goodbye to Claire before setting off down the stairs, heading for the polluted world outside.

"Wait in my office, will you, Joseph?" Rachel Rosenfeld said. "I'll be up in a minute."

"How is he?" Victory asked, as the boy climbed out of ear-shot.

"As well as can be expected," the psychotherapist replied. "Probably not in need of any further counselling from me—the world to which I was helping my patients adapt seems to have ended, so my whole basis of procedure may need rethinking. Yours too, I suppose?"

"You've seen the face, then?"

"Seen the face, heard the spiel, understood why you froze up and fell over. That's one hell of a job you did, Hugo. I'd never have believed you had it in you."

"I can't really take much credit," Victory said, "given that it really was *in me*. Gwynplaine is the one who got it out. So what did you think of the new Adam, professionally speaking?"

"Too soon to tell. So far, it's all promises and no demands—but given the alternatives...."

"Drowning in our own wastes, while Gregory K. Allison's Sons of Job build a narrow ark, you mean."

"Among others. It still might come to that, of course. In the meantime, I still have to do what I can for the patients I have left. Have you been cleared to operate on the Palestinian boy?"

"I'm aiming for Wednesday, if all goes well," Victory said. "I'm working on the specs now. It'll be a long and complicated job, but I'm confident."

"I can see that you are," the psychotherapist observed, staring him steadfastly in the face. "Is it just the residual effect of my seeing the face, or have you fallen in love since Friday might?"

"I'm too old to fall in love," Victory assured her.

"Maybe—but you're never too old to jump. Not Lilith, I hope?"

"I may be married to my work," Victory said, knowing that the defensive move would provide no armour against Rachel Rosenfeld's professional insight, "but I've given up seducing the faces I make. It's a new dawn, Dr. Rosenfeld; we really ought to make an effort to start as we mean to go on."

"By making promises we can't keep?" she riposted. "We're only human, Dr. Victory. If we were better than we are, we wouldn't have got in this mess in the first place."

Graciously, Victory let her have the last word, as it seemed to mean so much to her. He went back into the outer office, and looked hard at Claire, trying to remember whether her face had seemed subtly different the last time he had seen it, and exactly how.

"Is something wrong, Doctor?" the receptionist asked, anxiously.

"Nothing at all," he said. "Perfect features, no room for improvement whatsoever. A fine advertisement for the service I offer, even if it is all nature's handiwork."

"I'm wearing make-up," Claire confessed, with a slight blush.

"Have you seen the face of Adam?" Victory asked, as he paused by the door of his consulting room.

"Yes I have," she said.

"And?"

"I think we need him. We have to have something to believe in, and hope for, if we're to save the world from falling into chaos. Who else can we trust?"

"Who indeed?" Victory echoed, as he stepped back into his inner sanctum. *But let's not forget*, he thought, *that bringing order out of chaos is only half the work that needs to be done. Unless chaos is continually brought out of order again, the work of creation stalls.*

He went back to his work, then, for the sake of art, and for the sake of glory—and because there was nothing, as yet, more urgent for his idle hands to do.

ABOUT THE AUTHOR

BRIAN STABLEFORD was born in Yorkshire in 1948. He taught at the University of Reading for several years, but is now a full-time writer. He has written many science fiction and fantasy novels, including: *The Empire of Fear, The Werewolves of London, Year Zero, The Curse of the Coral Bride*, and *The Stones of Camelot*. Collections of his short stories include: *Sexual Chemistry: Sardonic Tales of the Genetic Revolution, Designer Genes: Tales of the Biotech Revolution*, and *Sheena and Other Gothic Tales*. He has written numerous nonfiction books, including *Scientific Romance in Britain, 1890-1950, Glorious Perversity: The Decline and Fall of Literary Decadence*, and *Science Fact and Science Fiction: An Encyclopedia*. He has contributed hundreds of biographical and critical entries to reference books, including both editions of *The Encyclopedia of Science Fiction* and several editions of the library guide, *Anatomy of Wonder*. He has also translated numerous novels from the French language, including several by the feuilletonist Paul Féval. Many of his books are being published by the Borgo Press imprint of Wildside Press.

www.ingramcontent.com/pod-product-compliance
Lightning Source LLC
Chambersburg PA
CBHW031947240626
47153CB00003B/896